"*Anvil* is a charming book, chock full of interesting characters, and set in an even more interesting fantasy world. . . . Done with a fine balance of sarcastic humor, imaginative world-building, and heroic action, *Anvil* is a truly enjoyable book. . . . A surprisingly fun—yet thoughtful—read which can be highly recommended." —*Cinescape* (Mania.com)

"Baker brings her offbeat characters and lively style to her first fantasy novel about an ex-assassin currently known as Smith. . . . A fun mix of medieval style and almost contemporary elements." —*Locus*

"*The Anvil of the World* by Kage Baker is an eccentric and often very funny fantasy. . . . A deadly and absurd magical duel of Fatally Verbal Abuse is reason enough to read the book. Baker piles on such delights." —*The Denver Post*

"The combination of adventure, tongue-in-cheek humor, and captivating characters makes Baker's *The Anvil of the World* an impressive fantasy debut." —*Rocky Mountain News*

"Kage Baker's engaging fantasy *The Anvil of the World* [is] filled with bizarre characters, magic, demons, assassins, fried eel, and a duel using Fatally Verbal Abuse. *The Anvil of the World* can be favorably compared to Terry Pratchett's Discworld series; there is even a European flavor to it. Every page adds a complication in a never-ending series of adventures. . . . *Anvil* is original and funny."
—*The Cincinnati Enquirer*

"The author of the rollicking yards about the Company, which controls time-travel, drops the SF veneer for a just-as-rollicking fantasy of three-dimensional travel. . . . Whoopee! Imagine an Errol Flynn classic ebulliently reimagined by Monty Python director Terry Gilliam; that's this wacky romp whose pace never flags." —*Booklist*

"Wild, witty, and often pointed . . . Baker's many admirers will find this one well worth a visit." —*Kirkus Reviews*

"Baker has always displayed a sly sense of humor in her work and in her new novel, she gives it full rein. . . . It's a lively, highly enjoyable change of pace for her and for her growing audience." —*San Francisco Chronicle*

"There's never been a fantasy novel quite like this. Dark humor, broad slapstick, sharp dialogue, breathtaking action, bittersweet romance—it's all here, with unexpected and gratifying emotional impact. Baker echoes the best of fantasy tradition, integrating history, adventure, and thoughtful social commentary while creating a wholly original and extraordinary work."

—*RT Book Reviews* (4 ½ stars, a Top Pick)

Books by Kage Baker

The Anvil of the World
Dark Mondays
Mother Aegypt and Other Stories
The House of the Stag
The Empress of Mars
Not Less Than Gods

THE COMPANY SERIES

In the Garden of Iden
Sky Coyote
Mendoza in Hollywood
The Graveyard Game
Black Project, White Knights: The Company Dossiers
The Life of the World to Come
The Children of the Company
The Machine's Child
Gods and Pawns
The Sons of Heaven

THE
ANVIL
OF THE
WORLD

Kage Baker

A TOM DOHERTY ASSOCIATES BOOK
NEW YORK

This is a work of fiction. All of the characters,
organizations, and events portrayed in this novel
are either products of the author's imagination
or are used fictitiously.

THE ANVIL OF THE WORLD

Copyright © 2003 by Kage Baker

All rights reserved.

Edited by David G. Hartwell

A Tor Book
Published by Tom Doherty Associates, LLC
175 Fifth Avenue
New York, NY 10010

www.tor-forge.com

Tor® is a registered trademark of
Tom Doherty Associates, LLC.

The Library of Congress has catalogued
the hardcover edition as follows:

Baker, Kage.
    The anvil of the world / Kage Baker.—1st ed.
        p. cm.
    "A Tom Doherty Associates book."
    ISBN 978-0-7653-0818-4
    I. Title.

PS3552.A4313A85 2003
813'.54—dc21

                                        2003042649

ISBN 978-0-7653-0819-1

First Hardcover Edition: August 2003
First Trade Paperback Edition: June 2010

Printed in the United States of America

0   9   8   7   6   5   4   3   2   1

To LINN PRENTIS

Without whom my first novel would have been thrown off the front porch into Pismo Creek, to the edification of none but a transient population of mallards.

TROON, the golden city, sat within high walls on a plain a thousand miles wide. The plain was golden with barley.

The granaries of Troon were immense, towering over the city like giants, taller even than its endlessly revolving windmills. Dust sifted down into its streets and filled its air in the Month of the Red Moon and in every other month, for that matter, but most especially in that month, when the harvest was brought in from the plain in long lines of creaking carts, raising more dust, which lay like a fine powder of gold on every dome and spire and harvester's hut.

All the people of Troon suffered from chronic emphysema.

Priding itself as it did, however, on being the world's breadbasket, Troon put up with the emphysema. Wheezing was considered refined, and the social event of the year was the Festival of Respiratory Masks.

⌇

On the fifth day of the Month of Chaff Storms, as a cold wind scoured the walls of Troon with stubble and husks, a man in a fish mask sat at a table in the Civic Ballroom and wished he were anywhere else.

He belonged to that race called the Children of the Sun, and, like others of his kind, he had skin and hair the color of a sunrise. They were an energetic, sanguine, and mechanically minded people, tracing their lineage back to a liaison between a smith god and a fire goddess somewhere in the deeps of time. They were consequently given to sins of an ecological nature (the slag heaps from their smelters were mountainous), and they were also quarrelsome (their blood feuds were legendary).

It was a particularly nasty blood feud that had sent the man in the fish mask fleeing to distant Troon, and he now sat alone at a table, watching the masked dancers as he glumly sipped beer through a long straw. It wasn't his kind of party, but his cousin (to whom he had fled) insisted he attend. The masked ball was held on the final night of a week of breathless celebration, and everyone of distinction in Troon society was there.

"Er—Smith?"

The man in the mask turned his head, peering through the domed lenses of his fish eyes. The name *Smith* was an alias, only the latest of many the man had used. He got awkwardly to his feet as he saw his cousin approaching. His cousin's costume was fine and elaborate, robes of red-gold brocade and a fire efrit mask. No less elaborate was the costume of the lady his cousin had in tow: butterfly wings of green and purple foil and a butterfly mask of the same material.

"This, madam, is Smith. My caravan master," explained his cousin. "A most experienced veteran of transport. A man in whose expert hands you may trust the rarest of commodities."

This was not exactly true. Smith had never led a caravan in his life, but his cousin's freight and passenger service had lost its former master to a vendetta on the day of Smith's sudden arrival in Troon, so Smith was learning the business.

"How nice to meet you," said the woman in the mask, and shot out a black and curling tongue. Smith started, but the tongue was merely a feature of the mask, for it was hollow, and she poked it now into a tall glass of punch.

"Honor on your house, lady," Smith murmured.

His cousin coughed, and said, "Smith, this is Lady Seven Butterflies of Seven Butterflies Studio. You will be privileged to transport her celebrated creations!"

"I'm delighted," said Smith, bowing. "Rely on me, lady."

But Lady Seven Butterflies had lost interest in him and fluttered off to the punch bowl. His cousin leaned close and grabbed him by the shoulder. They bumped papier-mâché faces as he hissed, "Very important client! Almost ready to sign a contract granting us exclusive transport rights! Used to go with Stone and Son until they broke goods in transit. Vital we catch the ball, cousin!"

Smith nodded sagely. "Right. What are we shipping for her?"

"One gross of glass butterflies, what else?" said his cousin impatiently, and turned to pursue the lady. Smith sat down again. It was a good thing his new job would require him to be on the open road a lot. He didn't think people in Troon got enough oxygen.

He watched the dancers awhile in their stately pavanes, watched the symmetrical patterns their trailing brocades left in the rich layer of floor dust, and brooded on the sequence of events that had brought him here, beginning with an innocent walk to the corner for an order of fried eel.

That he had reached that time in life when really good fried eel was at least as interesting as romance made his subsequent misadventure all the more unexpected. Nor was he especially attractive. Even the girl's brothers had to admit there must have been a mistake on somebody's part, though they weren't about to retract their vow to see Smith's head on a pike, since without benefit of hot-blooded youth or personal beauty, he had nevertheless sent three of their kinsmen to the morgue.

He sighed now, swirling his beer and noting in disgust the fine sediment of dirt at the bottom of the glass. He thought of waving for a waiter, but his cousin came bustling up again with somebody new in tow.

". . . with complete confidence, my lord. The man is a seasoned veteran of the roads. Er—Smith! I have the *great* honor of commending to your care the very noble Lord Ermenwyr of the House Kingfisher."

"Honor to your house, lord," said Smith, rising to his feet though he'd never heard of the House Kingfisher.

Lord Ermenwyr was doubled over in a coughing fit. When he straightened up, dabbing at his lips with an embroidered handkerchief, Smith beheld a slender young man. A pomaded and spangled beard was visible below his half mask, which was that of a unicorn's head. He had extended the unicorn theme to an elaborate codpiece, from which a silver horn spiraled up suggestively. The eyes behind the mask had the glitter of fever.

"Hello," he croaked. "So you're the fellow taking me to Salesh-by-the-Sea? I hope you've had some training as a psychopomp too. I expect to die en route."

"His lordship is pleased to be humorous," said Smith's cousin, wringing his hands. "His lord father has paid a great deal for his passage to the health resort at Salesh, and I have written to assure him in the strongest terms that Lord Ermenwyr will arrive there safely."

"Really?" said Lord Ermenwyr. "Watch this, then." He reached out with the toe of his boot and drew a bull's-eye in the dust. Stepping back several paces, he hawked and spat in a neat arc, hitting the center of the target with a gob of blood.

"You see?" he said brightly, as Smith and his cousin stared. "Utterly moribund. Don't worry, though; I've got embalming spices in my luggage, and Daddy won't mind my early demise much, whatever he may have written."

Smith's cousin closed his mouth, then said hastily, "It's simply the inconvenience of our local weather, my lord. I myself coughed up a little blood not an hour ago. It passes with the first winter rains!"

"I'll be in Hell or Salesh by the time they start, I devoutly hope," snarled the young man. He turned a gimlet eye on Smith. "Well, caravan master, I suppose we're starting at some ungodly hour in the morning? If I'm still moaning on my painful couch at cockcrow, you'll leave without me, no doubt?"

"The caravan departs from the central staging area by the West Gate an hour before dawn, my lord," said Smith's cousin helpfully.

"Fine," said Lord Ermenwyr, and turned unsteadily on his heel. "I'm going to go get laid while I'm still among the living, then." He staggered off into the crowd, hitching up his spangled tights, and Smith looked at his cousin.

"Does he have anything catching?" he demanded.

"No! No! Delicate lungs, that's all," chattered his cousin. "I believe his lord father's apt phrase was—" From the depths of his brocade he drew out a heavy, folded parchment to which was affixed a ponderous seal of black wax. "Here we are. 'Hothouse lily.' In any case the young lord will be traveling with a private nurse and ample store of physic, so your sole concern will be conveying him in one piece to Salesh-by-the-Sea."

"And what if he dies?" asked Smith.

His cousin shivered and, looking quickly at the letter as though it might overhear him, folded it again and thrust it out of sight. "That would be very unfortunate indeed. His lord father is a powerful man, cousin. He's paid a great deal for this passage."

Smith sighed.

"The lad'll be in a palanquin the whole way," added his cousin, as though that answered everything. "You'll have him there in no time. A routine trip. Your first of many, I'm certain, to the continued honor and glory of our house. Ah! You'll excuse me—I must go speak to . . ." He turned and fled into the crowd, in pursuit of some other bedizened customer.

Smith sat down, and took another sip of his beer before he remembered the mud at the bottom of the glass.

⌒

The gonging of the cistern clock in Smith's apartment warren woke him, and he was up and pulling on his coat in very little time. He paused before arming himself, considering his stock of hand weapons. He settled for a pair of boot knives and a machete; nothing more would be needed, surely, for a routine trip to the coast.

He was, accordingly, surprised when his cousin met him at the West Gate in the predawn gloom with a pair of pistol-bows and a bolt bandoleer.

"You've used these before?" his cousin asked, draping the bandoleer over Smith's shoulder and buckling it in place.

"Yes, but—you said—"

"Yes, I know, it's all routine, easiest road there is, but just consider this as insurance. Eh? And it makes a man look dangerous and competent, and that's what the passengers want to see in a caravan master," explained his cousin. "There you are! The picture of menace. Now, here's the cargo and passenger manifest." He thrust an open scroll at Smith. Smith took it and read, as his cousin ran off to shriek orders at the porters, who were loading what looked like immense violet eggs into one of the transport carts.

There was, indeed, a gross of glass butterflies, being shipped from Seven Butterflies studio to the Lady Katmile of

Silver Anvil House in Port Ward'b. To Be Handled With Exquisite Care.

There were twenty sacks of superfine cake flour from Old Troon Mills, destined for a bakery in Lesser Salesh. There were thirty boxes of mineral pigments from the strip mines in Outer Troon, to be delivered to Starfire Studio in Salesh Hills. No eggs, though, violet or otherwise.

The passengers were listed as Lytan and Demara Smith and Family, custom jewelry designers, of Salesh Hills; Parradan Smith, courier, of Mount Flame City; Lord Ermenwyr of the House Kingfisher, and Servant. All Children of the Sun.

Also listed was one Ronrishim Flowering Reed, herbalist, of Salesh-by-the-Sea. From his name he was probably a Yendri, one of the forest people who occasionally fought guerrilla wars with the Children of the Sun over what they felt was excessive logging.

Smith looked out at the boarding area and spotted the Yendri, taller than the other passengers, wearing fewer clothes, and standing a little apart with an aloof expression. The Yendri people had skin that ranged in color from a gently olive complexion to outright damn *green*, and were willowy and graceful and everything you'd expect in a forest-dwelling race. They were thought by the Children of the Sun to be arrogant, uncivilized, untrustworthy, and sexually insatiable (when not perversely effeminate). They said exactly the same things about the Children of the Sun.

The other passengers were equally easy to identify. The Smiths were clearly the young couple huddled with a screaming baby, waving a sugar stick and stuffed toy at him while their other little ones ran back and forth merrily and got in the way of the sweating porters. Parradan Smith must be the well-dressed man leaning against a news kiosk, reading a broadside sheet. Lord Ermenwyr, who had evidently not died in the night, sat a little apart from the others on one of many expensive-looking trunks piled beside a curtained palanquin.

He had changed his unicorn costume for a black tailcoat and top boots, and combed the spangles out of his beard and mustache. It failed to make him look less like the pasty-faced boy he was, though his features were even and handsome. His eyes were unnervingly sharp, fixed on the screaming infant with perfectly astonishing malevolence. He glanced up, spotted Smith, and leaped to his feet.

"You! Caravan Master. Is that damned brat going to squall the whole trip? Is it?" he demanded, folding his arms as Smith approached him.

"I don't think so," said Smith, staring down at Lord Ermenwyr's eyes. His pupils were like pinpoints, perhaps because of whatever drug the lordling was smoking in the long jade tube he presently had clenched between his teeth. It produced trailing purple clouds, vaguely sweet-scented. "Should you really be—"

"Smoking? It's my medication, damn you! If that child isn't silenced at once, I'll not be answerable for the consequences. I'm a sick man—"

"Master, you're raving again," said a silken voice from behind the curtains of the palanquin. "Stop that at once."

"—And if I'm harried to an early grave, or should I say an earlier grave, *well* then, Caravan Master, you'll pay for it in ways you can't even begin to—"

"Nursie warned you," said the voice, and an arm flashed between the curtains and caught Lord Ermenwyr around the knees. He vanished backward into the depths of the palanquin with a yelp, and there were sounds of a violent struggle as the palanquin rocked on its base. Smith stepped quickly away.

"Er—Smith!" cried his cousin. "I'd like you to meet your subordinates."

Smith turned to see a crowd of caravaneers who clearly disliked being described as his subordinates. They gave him a unanimous resentful stare as he approached.

"May I present the esteemed keymen? Keyman Crucible, Keyman Smith, Keyman Bellows, Keyman Pinion, Keyman Smith."

They were, as all keymen, compact fellows with tremendously developed arms and muscle-bulging legs, and so alike they might have been quintuplets.

"Nice meeting you," said Smith. They grunted at him.

"This is your runner." His cousin placed his hands on the shoulders of a very young, very skinny girl. She wore the red uniform and carried the brass trumpet of her profession, but she was far from the curvaceous gymnast Smith fantasized about when he fantasized about runners. She glowered up at Smith's cousin.

"Take your hands off me or you'll hear from my mother house," she said. Smith's cousin withdrew his hands as though she were a live coal.

"Young Burnbright hasn't earned her full certification, yet, but she's hoping to do so in our service," he said delicately. "If all goes well, that is. And here, Smith, is our culinary artist! May I present the two-time winner of the Troon Municipal Bakeoff? Mrs. Smith."

Mrs. Smith was large and not particularly young, though she had a certain majesty of bearing. She looked sourly on Smith.

"Do you do fried eel?" Smith asked hopefully.

"Perhaps," she said. "If I'm properly motivated. If I have the proper *pans*." She spat out the last word with bewildering venom, turning her glare on Smith's cousin.

He wrung his hands. "Now, dear Mrs. Smith—I'm sure you'll manage without the extra utensils, this one time. It was necessary."

"Leaving half my kitchen behind for those bloody things?" Mrs. Smith demanded, pointing at the carts laden with giant eggs. "They take up three times the room of an ordinary shipment! What was wrong with regular crates, I'd like to know?"

"In addition to her other talents, Lady Seven Butterflies is a genius at innovative packing and insulation," said Smith's cousin earnestly. "She had the inspiration from Nature itself, you see. What, after all, is the perfect protective shape devised by Nature? The egg, of course—"

"Balls," said Mrs. Smith.

"—with its ovoid shape, elegantly simple yet strong, a holistic solution providing plenty of insulating space for the most fragile creations—"

"How am I going to feed my boys, let alone serve up the gourmet experience for passengers so grandiloquently advertised on your handbills, you imbecile man?" shouted Mrs. Smith.

"We'll work something out," said Smith, stepping between them. "Look, I'm traveling pretty light. Maybe we can take some of your pans in the lead cart?"

Mrs. Smith considered him, one eyebrow raised. "An intelligent suggestion," she said, mollified, as Pinion and Crucible seized up a vast crate marked KITCHEN and hurried with it to Smith's cart. "We may get on, young Smith."

"Of course you will," said Smith's cousin, and fled.

It was nearly light. Those whose duty it was came yawning and shivering to the West Gate, bending to the spokes of the great windlass. The gate rose slowly in its grooves, and a cold wind swept in off the plain and sent spirals of dust into the pink air. A trumpeter mounted the turret by the gate and announced by his blast that another day of commerce had begun, for better or worse, and Burnbright answered with a fanfare to let the passengers know that it was time to board.

The keymen mounted to their posts and began cranking the mighty assemblage of gears and springs in each lead cart. The passengers took their seats, with the Smiths' baby still crying dismally, as the last of the luggage was loaded by the porters. There was a moment of dithering with Lord Ermenwyr's palanquin until it was lifted and lashed in place atop his trunks. Purple fumes escaped between the fluttering curtains, so it was evident he was still alive in there, if preserving a sullen silence.

Mrs. Smith mounted to a seat beside Crucible, pulled a pair of dust goggles over her eyes, and with unhurried majesty drew out a smoking tube and packed it with a particularly pungent blend of amberleaf. She held a clever little device of flicking flint and steel to its tip, shielding it from the wind as she attempted to ignite the amberleaf.

Burnbright sprinted to the front of the line, backing out through the gate and calling directions to the porters as they wrestled the wheels of the lead cart into the grooves in the red road, worn deep by time and utility. Smith's cousin clasped his hands and prayed, as he always did at this point; and Smith, realizing belatedly that he was supposed to be in the lead cart beside Pinion, ran for it and vaulted into his seat, or attempted to, because the crate marked KITCHEN occupied that space.

Pinion just looked at him, poised over the tight-wound coil. Smith, determined to show he was game, climbed up and perched awkwardly atop the crate. He looked forward at Burnbright and waved.

She lifted her trumpet and blew the staccato call for departure. Then she turned and ran forward, swift as flight; for behind her the keymen threw the release pins, and the caravan lurched rumbling out through the gate, late as usual, a dozen linked carts impelled by gear-and-spring engines, following the grooved stone, bearing their disparate cargo.

Mrs. Smith got her tube going at last and leaned back, holding it elegantly between the first two fingers of her left hand, blowing a plume of smoke like a banner. In the cart behind her, the Yendri coughed and waved fumes away, cursing. The rising sun struck flame on the flare of Burnbright's trumpet.

They were off.

⤷

"This is pretty easy," remarked Smith after the first hour of travel. Troon was a distant clutch of towers behind them. Before them and to all sides spread the wide yellow fields, unrelieved but for the occasional bump of a distant harvest village. The red road stretched ahead, two grooved lanes running west to the infinite horizon, two parallels running east, and Burnbright had slowed to an easy mile-devouring lope a few hundred yards in front.

"You think it's easy, do you?" said Pinion, giving the key a gentle pump to bring the next spring into play. Once the initial winding had got them going, the keymen maintained forward momentum by steadily cranking.

"Well, yes," said Smith. "Look at it! Flat as a board. No place for a bandit to hide as far as the eye can see. Nobody's at war, so we don't have to worry about any armies sweeping down on us. Nothing to do but chug along, eh?"

"Unless a dust storm comes up," Pinion told him. "Which they tend to do, now the harvest's in. I've seen some cyclones in my day, I can tell you. Even the regular prevailing wind'll fill the channels in the road with dust, and if the little girl up there doesn't spot it in time, we might all rattle off the road into a field, or hit a block at top speed and strip all our gears—that's lovely fun."

"Oh," said Smith. "Does that happen often?"

"Often enough," said Pinion, pumping the key again.

"At least it doesn't sound like I'll need these," said Smith, looking down at his pistolbows.

"Probably not," conceded Pinion. "Until we reach the Greenlands."

"What's in the Greenlands?"

Pinion was silent a moment.

"You're a city boy, aren't you?" he said at last.

"I have been," said Smith, shifting on top of the kitchen crate. "Come on, what's in the Greenlands? Besides a lot of Yendri," he added, glancing back at their sole Yendri passenger, who had wrapped a scarf about his nose and mouth and sat ignoring the others.

"To begin with, that's where you've got your real bandits," Pinion said. "And not your run-along-by-the-side-of-the-road-and-yip-threateningly bandits either, I'm talking about your bury-the-road-in-a-landslide-and-dig-out-the-loot bandits. See? And then there's greenies like that one," he went on, jerking a thumb in the direction of the Yendri. "They may *say* they're for nonviolence, but they're liable to pile rocks and branches and all kinds of crap on the road if they're miffed about us cutting down one of their damn groves to build a way station or something."

"Huh." Smith looked back at the Yendri uneasily.

"Of course, they're not the worst," added Pinion.

"I guess they wouldn't be."

"There's beasts, of course."

"They're everywhere, though."

"Not like in the Greenlands. And even they're nothing to the demons."

"All right," said Smith, "you're trying to scare me, aren't you? Is this some kind of initiation?"

"No," said Pinion in a surly voice, though in fact he had been trying to scare Smith. "Just setting you straight on a few things, Caravan Master. I'd hate to see you so full of self-confidence you get us all killed your first day on the job."

"Thanks a lot," said Smith. The caravan went rumbling on, the featureless fields flew by, and after a moment Smith looked down at Pinion again.

"I did hear a story about the Greenlands, now that I come to think about it," he said. "In a bar in Chadravac Beach, about six months ago. Something about a demon-lord. He's supposed to be called the Master of the Mountain?"

Pinion blanched, but did not change expression. He shook his head, pedaling away stolidly.

"Don't know anything about that," he said firmly, and fell silent.

~

All that day they traveled across the yellow land. With no companion but the sun, they came at evening to the way station, marked out by a ring of white stones.

It was a wide circular area by the side of the road, with grooves for carts running off and grooves for running back on. There was a tiny stone hut surmounted by a windwheel pump, enclosing a basin where a trickle of water flowed, drawn up from deep beneath the plain. The moment they had rolled off the road and into the circle, the Yendri was out of his cart and staggering for the pump house. He monopolized it for the next quarter hour, to the great annoyance of the other passengers, who lined up behind the hut and made ethnically insulting remarks as they waited.

At least the diversion kept most of them occupied as Smith oversaw making camp for the night. He didn't really have much to do; the keymen, long practiced in this art, had quickly trundled the carts in a snaked circle and set to erecting tent accommodations inside it. Burnbright and Mrs.

Smith were busily setting up the kitchen pavilion, and politely implied that he'd only get in their way if he lent a hand there.

Smith noticed that Lord Ermenwyr was not among the carpers at the water pump, and he wondered whether he ought not to see if the lordling had died after all. As he approached the palanquin, the curtains parted and a woman slid out with all the grace of a serpent and dropped lightly to the ground.

Smith caught his breath.

That she was beautiful was almost beside the point. She had a *presence*. Her body was lush, tall, perfect, powerful. Her mouth was full and red, and her sloe-black eyes ought to have been sullen but glinted instead with lazy good humor as she saw Smith gaping at her.

"Good evening, Caravan Master," she said, and the voice matched the body: sultry, yet with an indefinable accent of education and good breeding.

Smith just nodded, and collected himself enough to say, "I was coming to inquire after the lord's health."

"How nice. His lordship is still with us, I'm happy to say." She tilted her head to one side and occupied herself a moment with loosely braiding her hair, which was black and thick as a bolt of silk. Having pulled it up into an elegant chignon, she drew from her bosom what appeared to be a pair of stilettos of needlelike fineness and thrust them through the glossy coils.

"I . . . uh . . . I'm very happy to hear that. We're just setting up the tents now, if he'd like to rest," said Smith.

"That's very thoughtful of you, but my lord has his own pavilion," the woman replied, opening one of the trunks and drawing out a bundle of black cloth patterned all over with little silver skulls.

"I'd be happy to help you, miss—"

"Balnshik," said the woman, smiling. "Thank you so much, Caravan Master."

What an exotic name, Smith thought dizzily, accepting the load of tent material while Balnshik bent over the trunk to rummage for poles. Something about the name suggested flint knives and attar of roses, and perhaps black leather . . . though she was modestly attired in white linen, and he dragged his attention back to the fact that she was a nurse, after all. She drew out a tent pole now and gave it a quick twist. In her deft hands it shot up and expanded to twice its length, spring-loaded.

"I'm—Smith," he said.

"Of course you are, dear," she told him. "Just spread that out on the ground, won't you?"

He helped her assemble the pavilion, which was quite a large and sumptuous one, and then there was a lot of collapsible furniture to be set up, so it was a while before Smith remembered to inform her, "We'll be serving gourmet cuisine shortly, as advertised. We can offer his lordship—"

"Oh, don't worry about him; the little beast can't keep down anything solid," said Balnshik serenely, tossing a handful of incense onto a brazier.

"I can hear every word you're saying, you know." Lord Ermenwyr's voice floated from the palanquin. He sounded peevish.

"What about some clear broth, darling?"

"No. I'm still motion sick and, anyway, it'll probably be poisoned."

Balnshik's eyes flashed, and she turned to Smith with a charming smile in which there were a great many white and gleaming teeth. "Will you excuse us, please? I must attend to my lord."

So saying, she vaulted into the palanquin, vanishing

behind the curtains, and Smith heard the unmistakable sound of a ringing slap, and the palanquin began to rock and thump in place once more. It seemed like a good idea to leave.

He wandered over to the kitchen pavilion, where Mrs. Smith had lit a fire and set saucepans bubbling at magical speed, and was now busily dabbing caviar on little crackers.

"Can you prepare an order of clear broth?" he asked.

"What, for the greenie?" She glared across at Ronrishim Flowering Reed, who had finally relinquished the hut and was now seated in front of a tent, apparently meditating. "Bloody vegetarians. I hate cooking for those people. 'Oh, please, I'll just have a dish of rainwater at precisely air temperature with an ounce of mother's milk on the side, and if it's not too much trouble, could you float a couple of violets on it?' Faugh!"

"No, actually, it's for Lord Ermenwyr." Smith looked over his shoulder at the palanquin, which was motionless now.

"Oh. The invalid?" Mrs. Smith turned to peer at the pavilion. "Heavens, what a grand tent. He's a nasty-looking little piece of goods, I must say, but as he's dying I suppose we must make the effort. A good rich capon stock with wine, I think."

"Parradan Smith's a gangster," Burnbright informed them, coming close and appropriating a cracker.

"Get away from those, child. What do you mean?"

"I peeked when he was washing himself, and he's got secret society tattoos all over," said Burnbright, retreating beyond the reach of Mrs. Smith's carving knife. "And he's got an instrument case he never lets go of almost. And knives."

"How do you know they're secret society tattoos?" Smith was troubled.

"Because he's from Mount Flame City, and I'm from there

too, and I know what the Bloodfires' insignia look like," said Burnbright matter-of-factly. "Their deadly enemies are the House Copperhammer. When they've got a war on, you find body parts in the strangest places. All over town."

"Lovely," grunted Mrs. Smith.

"He's listed on the manifest as a courier," said Smith, looking out at the man in question, who sat just inside the door of a tent, polishing his boots. Burnbright nodded sagely.

"Couriering somebody's loot somewhere, see. I'll bet he's got a fortune in that instrument case. Unless it's a disguise, and he's accepted a contract on one of the other passengers and he's biding his time before he kills them!" she added, her little face alight.

"Wretched creatures. He'd better leave *me* alone; I never travel unarmed," said Mrs. Smith, handing her the tray of hors d'oeuvres. "Go set that on the buffet and inform the guests that the main course will be served in half an hour. Grilled quail glazed with acacia honey, stuffed with wild plums."

～

It was as good as it sounded. Even the Smith's infant stopped crying for a while, given a leg bone with sauce to suck on.

When twilight had fallen Balnshik emerged from the palanquin, carrying Lord Ermenwyr in her arms like a limp rag doll, and settled him in the splendid pavilion before coming out for a plate for herself and a bowl of broth for her lord. She made as profound an impression on the other males in the party as she'd made on Smith. Even the Smiths' two little boys stopped chewing, and with round eyes watched her progress across the camp.

She seemed not to notice the attention she drew, was courteous and formal. Smith thought he saw her glance sidelong at the Yendri, once, with a glitter of amused contempt in her eyes, before there came a querulous feeble cry from the pavilion, and she turned to hurry back to Lord Ermenwyr.

"Clearly she doesn't think much of Mr. Flowering Reed," pronounced Mrs. Smith, and had a drag at her smoking tube. She was sitting at her ease with a drink beside the fire, as the keymen cleared away the dinner things for her.

"Except I hear the Yendri are supposed to have really big, um, you know," said Burnbright. Mrs. Smith shrugged.

"It depends upon what you mean by big, dear."

"I think we made pretty good time today," said Smith. "No disasters or anything. Don't you think it went well?"

"Tolerably well," said Mrs. Smith. "At least there weren't any breakdowns this time. Can't count the hours I've wasted at the side of the road waiting for replacement gears."

"Have you been with the caravan long?" Smith asked her.

"Twenty years, next spring," she replied.

"Traveled much through the Greenlands?"

"Far too often. What about you? Have you a first name, Smith, by the way?"

Smith glanced over at Pinion, who was scouring out a pot with sand, and lowered his voice when he spoke. "I've been here and there. And yes, I have a first name. But . . ."

Mrs. Smith arched her eyebrows. "It's like that, is it? Lovely impersonal name, *Smith*. Rather fond of it, myself. So, where were all your questions leading?"

"Have you ever heard of somebody, a demon or something, called the Master of the Mountain?"

Mrs. Smith gave him a sharp look, and Burnbright cringed and made a gesture to ward off evil. "Clearly," said Mrs. Smith, "you're not from the interior. You're from the islands, I'd bet, or you'd know about him."

Smith wasn't anxious that anyone should know where

he'd been born, so he just said, "Is he in the Greenlands? Is he a demon?"

Mrs. Smith waved her drink at the Yendri, who was just retiring into his tent. "That one could probably tell you more, though I doubt he would, however nicely you asked. You haven't heard of the Master of the Mountain? Half demon and half something else, or so the story goes. Yendri, possibly, though you wouldn't know it from the way they hate him. Mind you, he's given them enough reasons."

"What reasons?" Smith drew closer, because she was lowering her voice. She hitched her folding chair a little nearer to him and pointed off into the night, toward the northwest.

"You'll be able to see it, in a week or so, poking up out of the horizon: a black mountain like a shark's tooth, perfectly immense. That's his stronghold, and he can look down from up there on every inch of the Greenlands, and you can bet he'll be watching us as we creep past on our tiny road. If we're very fortunate, he won't trouble himself to come down to say how d'ye do.

"I don't know how long he's been up there; a couple of generations, at least. There's talk he used to be a mercenary. Certainly he's some sort of powerful mage. Demon-armies at his beck and call, spies in every city, all that sort of thing. These days he contents himself with swooping down and raiding our caravans now and again. But there was a time when he singled out *them* for the worst of his plundering." Mrs. Smith pointed at the Yendri's tent.

"No idea why. You wouldn't think they'd have anything worth stealing, would you, in those funny little brushwood villages of theirs? Something personal, seemingly.

"In any case—you're aware they used to be slaves, the Yendri? No, not to us—that's one thing they can't blame us for, at least. It was somewhere else, and somebody else enslaved them, until they overthrew their masters and escaped. There was some kind of miracle child whose birth sparked the slave rebellion. One of their greenie prophets carried her before them like a figurehead, and they all emigrated here. When she grew up she became their Saint. Heals the sick, raises the dead, most beautiful woman in the world, et cetera. You haven't heard of the Green Saint either?

"Well. So the Yendri settled down as a free people then, with no troubles except the Master of the Mountain raiding their villages with dreadful glee, which I understand he did on very nearly a weekly basis. And then, oh horrors! He captured the Green Saint herself.

"Though I have heard she went and offered herself to him, if he'd stop being so terribly evil," Mrs. Smith added parenthetically, and drew on her smoke again. "However it happened—she moved in with him on his mountain, and while she didn't exactly convert him to a virtuous life, he did stop burning the poor greenies' wigwams about their ears. Not that they were grateful. They were furious, in fact, especially when he and she proceeded to have a vast brood of very mixed children. Said it was sacrilege."

"A demon and a saint having kids?" Smith pondered it. "Funny."

"Not to the Yendri, it isn't," said Mrs. Smith.

"Let's talk about something else," begged Burnbright.

So the subject was changed. Not long afterward the fire was banked, and everyone retired for the night, with the exception of the Smiths' baby, who cried for a good hour.

⌐

The next day, once camp was broken, proceeded in much the same way as the previous one had. Endless hours they rumbled across the empty fields, and though Smith watched the horizon, he saw no threatening darkness there, not that day nor on the next few to follow. The Smiths' infant cried, the Yendri kept himself aloof, Parradan Smith killed no one, and Lord Ermenwyr did not die, though he remained in his palanquin as they traveled and the purple fume of his irritation streamed backward in the wind.

⤻

"Mama!" shrieked the Smiths' younger boy, pointing behind them. "Dragons!"

It was the fifth day out, and the Smith children were reaching critical mass for boredom.

"Don't be silly, dearest," his mother told him wearily, jogging the screaming baby on her shoulder.

"I'm not! They're flying up behind us and they're going to get us! Look!"

Nobody bothered to look except Smith, who turned on his high crate to glance over his shoulder. To his astonishment, he saw some five or six winged forms in the air behind them, at a distance of no more than a mile or two. He turned completely around, bracing his feet on the edge of the cart, and shaded his eyes for a good look.

"The dragons will get us!" chorused the Smiths' other children, beginning to wail and cry.

"No, no, they won't," Smith shouted helpfully, looking down into their cart. "Dragons won't hurt you. And anyway, I don't think—"

"The lord in the black tent says they do," protested the little boy. "I went in when the big lady came out to eat so I could see if he was really a vampire like the runner said, and he told me he wasn't, only he'd been bit by a dragon when he was a little boy for making too much noise and it made him half-dead forever but he was lucky 'cause most dragons just eat children that make too much noise, they fly overhead on big wings and just catch them and eat them up like bugs!"

"Now, Wolkin—" said his father.

"I told you not to bother that man!" said his mother.

"Well, that just isn't true," yelled Smith, mentally damning Lord Ermenwyr. "Dragons don't do that kind of thing, all right, son? They're too small. I've seen 'em. All they do is fly over the water and catch fish. They build nests in cliffs. People make umbrellas out of their wings. No, what we've got here are gliders." He pointed up at the winged figures, who were much nearer now.

"Yes, Wolkin, you see? Perfectly harmless," said his father.

"Just people with big wings strapped on," explained Smith. "Sort of. They carry letters sometimes."

"And they have, er, flying clubs and competitions," added his father. "Nothing to be afraid of at all."

"Of course not," Smith agreed. "Look, here they come. Let's all wave."

The children waved doubtfully.

"Look," said the Smiths' little girl. "They've got pistol-bows just like you have, Caravan Master."

"What?" said Smith, as a bolt thunked into his left thigh.

The gliders were raking the caravan with boltfire. The result was screaming confusion and an answering barrage of shot from the caravans. Smith, firing both his weapons, glimpsed Parradan Smith standing, snarling, balancing as he sent boltfire from an apparently inexhaustible magazine into the nearest gliders. He saw Balnshik hanging out the side of the palanquin, bracing her feet on an immense old hunting weapon, and firing with deadly accuracy.

It was over in seconds. The closest of the gliders veered off, dropped something beside the road, and went down in a tangle of snapping struts and collapsing green fabric. The others wheeled. They lifted and floated off to the east, rapidly vanishing. The thing that had been dropped coughed, spurted dust, and exploded, throwing liquid flame in all directions. Fortunately the carts were well clear by the time it went off.

"Stop," gasped Smith, but the keymen were already applying the brakes. The carts shuddered to a stop, their iron wheels grinding in the stone ruts and sending up a flare of sparks the whole length of the caravan. He jumped from his high seat and fell, clutching his wounded leg. Scrambling up painfully he saw Parradan Smith already out and running for the fallen glider, holding a freshly cocked weapon upright over his head as he ran. Burnbright had turned and was racing back toward them, looking terrified.

"Anybody hurt?" Smith shouted, leaning against the cart as he tried to stanch the flow of blood down his leg.

It was some moments before he could get a coherent answer. Luckily, he had been the only one to sustain a wound. One of the Keymen Smiths had been slightly stunned by a bolt striking his steel pot-helmet, deflected by its wide brim; another shot had ricocheted and hit Keyman Crucible sidelong on his upper arm, leaving a welted bruise the size of a handball. Lord Ermenwyr was unharmed, but his luggage was struck through with a dozen bolts at least, and he had leaped from the palanquin and was screaming threats, in surprisingly full voice, at the remaining gliders, now only distant specks on the horizon.

"So much for his being a vampire," Smith muttered to himself. He was binding up his leg with a rag when Parradan Smith approached him, his face stony.

"You'd better come see this," he said.

"Is he dead?" Smith inquired, limping forward. The other man just nodded.

The glider was certainly dead. His neck had been snapped when his aircraft crashed, and lay at a distinctly unnatural angle; but it was obvious he'd been dead well before the impact. His quilted flight suit was torn and bloody in a dozen places.

"Damn," said Smith.

"Those are my bolts," said Parradan Smith, pointing out a scatter of small black-centered wounds. "Custom-made. Those two would be yours, probably."

"You're a lucky, lucky man," Lord Ermenwyr told the corpse, coming up to stare at it balefully. "If you were still alive, after what you've done to my best shirts—well, I wouldn't want to be you, that's all." He prodded the body with his boot. "No weapons. I suppose he was the one designated to drop the incendiary device."

"Probably."

"Good job Nursie nailed him before he managed it." He poked at the man's left arm, from which a big barbed steel projectile protruded.

"So these are hers too?" Parradan Smith pointed at two others, one in the dead man's right leg and one between his ribs.

"Yes. They're designed to take down elk."

"And these are mine, and these are Caravan Master's, so—" Parradan Smith stooped and pulled three feathered darts from the body. "Who the hell fired these?"

Lord Ermenwyr's eyes widened, seemed, in fact, at the point of starting out of his face.

"I'd be careful with those, if I were you," he said faintly.

They were little tubes of cane, tipped with what appeared to be thorns and fletched with small curling green feathers.

"Poisoned?" inquired Smith.

"Aren't all darts that mysteriously appear out of nowhere smeared with deadly poison?" said Lord Ermenwyr. Parradan Smith tossed them away.

"Do you know who fired them?"

"No!"

"Well, somebody fired them," said Smith. "What I'd like to know is, what was this one trying to do? He and his friends?"

"Trying to kill me, obviously," said Lord Ermenwyr.

"Have you enemies, my lord?"

"Dozens of them," Lord Ermenwyr replied. "And they're nothing to Daddy's enemies. In fact, I wouldn't put this past Daddy. He's never been fond of me." His rage had burned quickly down to ash, and he was pale, beginning to shake.

"Don't be ridiculous, Master," said Balnshik, appearing behind them suddenly. She looked over the battered corpse with a cold eye. "You know perfectly well that if your lord father had wanted you dead, you'd be dead by now." She stooped and pulled her steel points from the body. Some of the clothing tore as she retrieved the last one, and Smith leaned forward with an exclamation.

"Look, he's got a tattoo!"

"So he has." Balnshik glanced down at it. "One of those nasty little assassins' gangs, isn't it? There you are, Master, you see? Nothing to worry about."

"Nothing to worry about?" cried Lord Ermenwyr, his eyes bugging out again. "When I might have been riddled with boltfire and burned into the bargain? By the Nine Hells, what do you think's worth worrying about?" His voice rose to a scream. "You're going to let me die in this horrible featureless wilderness and I'll have no tomb, not even a proper funeral—"

He broke off with an *oof* as Balnshik seized him and threw him over one shoulder.

"You'll have to excuse his lordship," she said. "It's time for his fix. Come along, darling." She turned and strode back to the caravan.

Smith stared after her; then his attention was drawn back to the corpse, as Parradan Smith bent and methodically dug his bolts from the wounds.

"Is that an assassins' tattoo?" he asked.

"How should I know?" said Parradan Smith tonelessly, not looking up.

~

They scraped out a grave in the dry ground and covered the body with a thin layer of earth and stones. The green wings were laid over all.

Speed once they'd started up again was limited because Keyman Crucible's arm became swollen and painful. It was well after dark by the time they were able to make camp; by then Smith's leg was throbbing and fairly swollen too. As the fires were lit, as the tents were being set up, he limped slowly to the hut and waited for Ronrishim Flowering Reed to emerge.

"You're an herbalist, aren't you?" he said, when the Yendri came out.

Flowering Reed looked him up and down with distaste.

"Are you going to ask me for healing?" he asked.

"Yes, if you can help me."

"In the name of the Unsullied Daughter, then," he said, "I will require clean water. Have your minions fetch it."

The only person available to be a minion was Burnbright, who obligingly fetched a bucket of water from the pump and stayed to watch as Smith reclined before Flowering Reed's tent and submitted to having his trouser leg sliced open.

"Aren't you going to cauterize it with something?" she inquired, wincing as Smith's wound was probed. Smith grunted and turned his face away.

"Do you use a sword to cut through flowers?" replied the

Yendri, extracting the bolt and regarding it critically. "Ah, but I forget; you people do. It may surprise you to learn that the most violent solution to a difficulty is not always the best one."

"I was just asking, for goodness sake!" said Burnbright, and stormed away.

"Got anything for pain?" Smith asked through clenched teeth. Flowering Reed shook his head.

"I do not keep opiates for my personal use," he said. "I believe it is better to learn to bear with inevitable suffering."

"I see," said Smith.

"When you and all your people learn to see, there will be rejoicing and astonishment through the worlds," said Flowering Reed.

Smith endured in silence as his wound was cleaned, and the Yendri took a pungent-smelling ointment from his pack and anointed the wound. As Smith shifted so the bandage could be wound about his leg, he looked over at Flowering Reed.

"What do you make of the attack today?" he inquired.

Flowering Reed shrugged again. "One of your people's interminable quarrels. Filth slew filth, and so filth lusted after vengeance."

Smith decided there was no point attempting to defend the blood feud as part of his cultural heritage. "But who do you think they were after?"

"I have no idea, nor any interest in the matter," said Flowering Reed. "Though if I cared to speculate on such a thing, I might begin by observing who defended himself most viciously."

He tied off the bandage, and Smith sat up awkwardly. "Parradan Smith?"

"Perhaps. On the other hand, your people are always ready to unleash violence upon others. He may simply have been the best prepared."

"Nice to get an unbiased opinion," said Smith, getting to his feet.

"Leave me now. I must pray and cleanse myself."

"Go ahead." Smith limped away, and Burnbright came running to lend her shoulder for support.

"Isn't he awful?" she hissed. "Now he'll put his nose in the air and meditate on how much better he is than anybody else."

"At least he was willing to fix my leg," Smith said.

"Only because you asked him. They have to if they're asked; it's part of their religion or something. Don't think for a minute he'd have offered on his own."

"You don't like the Yendri very much, do you?"

"They're always raping runners," Burnbright informed him. "Not so much caravan runners like me, but the solos, the long-distance messengers, all the time."

"That's what I'd always heard, but I thought it was just stories," said Smith. "Since they're supposed to be so nonviolent."

Burnbright shook her head grimly.

"*They* say it's an act of love, not violence, and their girls take it as a compliment, so why shouldn't we? Self-righteous bastards. We learned all sorts of defenses against them at the mother house."

"Nice to know," said Smith. "How's Crucible's arm?"

"It's huge, and it's turning all sorts of colors," she said. "I don't think he'll be able to crank tomorrow. That means you'll have to take his place on the key. That's what Caravan Masters do."

"Oh," said Smith, who had been looking forward to a day of riding stretched out on the shipment of flour from Old Troon Mills.

"Funny about the dead glider," Burnbright said.

"What was funny about him?"

"He was from Troon." She helped him to a seat beside the fire. "I recognized him. He used to hang out at the Burning Wheel. That's the bar where all the gamblers go."

"You think Lord Ermenwyr's a gambler as well as a vampire?" Smith asked her wryly.

She flushed. "Well? I never saw him any other time but after dark until today, did you? And he never eats anything, and he looks just terrible! But he's not a gambler. He's somebody's ambassador, was what I heard, and he's been called off the job because he's sick so they're sending him to the spa. What, you think the gliders were after *him*?" She looked surprised.

"He thinks so."

"Hmmm." Her face was bright with speculation. Just then Mrs. Smith called for her, and she ran off to the kitchen pavilion.

⌐

No one slept particularly well that night. The Smith's baby screamed for two hours instead of the usual one. Smith divided watches with the keymen, taking the first shift, so he was up late anyway, getting stiffer and more chilled before Keyman Bellows took his place. Just as Smith had got himself drunk enough to pretend his wounded leg belonged to somebody else so he could doze off, he found himself sitting up, his heart pounding. He turned his head, staring into the west beyond the ring of carts. The faintest of touches on his face, a trace of moisture in the air, a scent as powerful and distinct as the sea's but certainly not the sea.

Across the fire from him, Mrs. Smith leaned up on one elbow in her bedroll.

"Wind's shifted," she muttered. "That's the Greenlands. We'll see it, tomorrow."

Smith lay back, wondering what she meant, and then he remembered the dark mountain.

⤷

He had forgotten it next morning, in the haze of his hangover and the confusion of breaking camp. He took Keyman Crucible's place on the key, crowding beside him as Crucible pedaled, and the effort of winding for the push-off alone was enough to make Smith's biceps twinge. By the time they were three hours on their way he had mentally crossed *keyman* off the list of possible careers for himself.

Busy with all this, Smith did not glance up at the horizon until the noon meal was handed along the line, and then he saw it: a rise of forested land to the northwest, and above it a black jagged cone. It didn't seem very big until his mind grappled with a calculation of the distance. Then his eyes wouldn't accept how immense it must be.

He put it out of his mind and attempted to unwrap his lunch with one hand. It was a pocket roll stuffed with highly spiced meat. He chewed methodically, looking back along the line of cars, and wondered again what the purpose of the glider attack had been. Robbery seemed unlikely, at least of the cargo. The most valuable thing they were carrying was Lady Seven Butterflies's holistic eggs, and the mental image of a corps of gliders attempting to fly, bearing between them perhaps a cargo net full of big violet eggs, was enough to make him grin involuntarily.

What if one of the passengers had something they wanted? The fact that the dead man had an assassin's tattoo didn't necessarily mean he wasn't also a thief. One man may in his time take many professions, as Smith knew too well.

He looked forward at the cart where the Smiths rode. They were jewelers; were they carrying any of their wares?

He turned back to look at the cart that Parradan Smith and the Yendri shared. They rode in mutual silence. Parradan Smith watched the eastern horizon. Flowering Reed's uneasy stare was fixed on the black mountain to the northwest. Smith ruled out the Yendri, who was carrying very little luggage and had no trunks at all. His race disdained personal possessions and produced nothing anyone would want, traded in nothing but medicinal herbs and the occasional freshwater pearl.

Parradan Smith, on the other hand, was couriering something. What? The instrument case he carried didn't seem heavy enough to be loaded with gold, as Burnbright had speculated.

Which left Lord Ermenwyr. Drugs, money, jewelry: The Lordling undoubtedly had plenty that would interest a thief.

Smith cranked again on the key, scanned the sky. No wings, at least.

But the black mountain grew larger as the hours went by; and after the following day, when they came to the divide and took the northern track, it loomed directly ahead of them.

⤚

"Smith."

He opened his eyes blearily. It seemed to him he had only just closed them; but the east was getting light. He turned and looked at Mrs. Smith, who was crouching beside him.

"We'd a visitor in the night, Smith, or so it seems. Still with us. I'd appreciate your assistance in removing it."

"What?" He sat up and stared, scratching his stubble.

She pointed with her smoking tube. He followed with his eyes and saw a mass of something on the ground in the center of camp, dimly lit by the breakfast cookfire.

"What the hell—?" Smith crawled out and stood with effort, peering at the thing. It didn't invite close inspection, somehow, but he lurched nearer and had a good look. Then he threw up.

If you took a gray-striped cat, and gave it the general size and limb configuration of a man, and then flayed it alive and scattered its flayed fur in long strips all over the corpse— you'd have something approximating what Smith saw in the pale light of dawn. You'd need to find a cat with green ichor in its veins, too, and remarkably big claws and teeth.

It was a demon, one of the original inhabitants of the world. Or so they themselves said, claiming to have been born of the primeval confusion at the beginning of time; for all Smith had ever been able to learn, it might be the truth. Certainly they had wild powers, and were thought to be able to take whatever solid forms they chose. This had both advantages and disadvantages. They might experience mortal pleasures, might even beget children. They might also die.

Smith reeled back, wiping his mouth. The thing's eyes were like beryls, still fixed in a glare of rage, but it was definitely dead.

"Oh, this is bad," he groaned.

"Could be worse," said Mrs. Smith, putting on the teakettle. "Could be you lying there with your liver torn out."

"Is its liver torn out?" Smith averted his eyes.

"Liver and heart, from the look of it. Doesn't seem to have got any of us, though. I didn't hear a thing, did you?" said Mrs. Smith quietly. Smith shook his head.

"But what is it? Is that a demon?"

"Well, there aren't any tribes of cat-headed men listed in the regional guidebooks," Mrs. Smith replied. "The principal thing with which we ought to concern ourselves just now is getting the bloody body out of sight before the guests see it, wouldn't you agree?"

"Right," said Smith, and limped away to the carts to get rope.

He made a halter, and together they dragged the body away from the camp, out onto the plain. There wasn't much there to hide it. They returned, and Smith found a shovel, and was going back to dig a grave when he saw the body convulse where it lay. He halted, ready to run for his life, game leg notwithstanding. The body flared green, bursting into unclean flame. It became too bright to bear looking at, throwing out a shower of green sparks, then something brilliant rose screaming from the fire and shot upward, streaking west as though it were a comet seeking to hide itself in the last rags and shadows of the night.

The flames died away and left nothing but black ashes blowing across the plain in the dawn wind.

"That was definitely a demon," Mrs. Smith informed him when he returned, leaning on his shovel. "Going off like a Duke's Day squib that way. They do that, you see." She handed him a tin cup of tea.

"But what was it doing here?" Smith accepted the cup and warmed his hands.

"I'm damned if I know. One doesn't usually see them this far out on the plain," said Mrs. Smith, spooning flatcake batter onto a griddle. "One can assume it came here to rend and ravage some or all of our company. One can only wonder at why it didn't succeed."

"Or who killed it," Smith added dazedly. "Or how."

"Indeed."

"Well well well, what a lovely almost-morning," said Lord Ermenwyr, emerging from his pavilion and pacing rapidly toward them. He looked slightly paler than usual and was puffing out enough smoke to obscure his features. "Really ought to rise at this hour more often. What's for breakfast?"

"Rice-and-almond-flour flatcakes with rose-apricot syrup," Mrs. Smith informed him.

"Really," he said, staring around at the circle of tents. "How delightful. I, er, don't suppose you're serving any meat as well?"

"I could fry up sausages, my lord," said Mrs. Smith.

"Sausages? . . . Yes, I'd like that. Lots of them? Blood rare?"

"Sausages only come one way, my lord."

"Oh. They do? But what about blood sausage?"

"Even blood sausages come well-done," Mrs. Smith explained. "Not much juice in a sausage."

"Oh." For a moment Lord Ermenwyr looked for all the world as though he were going to cry. "Well—have you got any blood sausage anyway?"

"I've got some imported duck blood sausage," said Mrs. Smith.

"Duck blood?" Lord Ermenwyr seemed horrified. "All right, then—I'll have all the duck blood sausage you've got. And one of those flatcakes with lots and lots of syrup, please. And tea."

Mrs. Smith gave him a sidelong look, but murmured, "Right away, my lord."

"You didn't notice anything unusual in the night, did you, my lord?" asked Smith, who had been watching him as he sipped his tea. Lord Ermenwyr turned sharply.

"Who? Me? What? No! Slept like a baby," he cried. "Why? Did something unusual happen?"

"There was a bit of unpleasantness," said Smith. "Something came lurking around."

"Horrors, what an idea! I suppose there's no way of increasing our speed so we'll be off this plain any quicker?"

"Not with one of our keymen down, I'm afraid," Smith replied.

"We'll just have to be on our guard, then, won't we?" said Lord Ermenwyr.

"You know, my lord," said Mrs. Smith as she laid out sausages on the griddle, "you needn't stand and wait for your breakfast. You can send out your nurse to fetch it for you when it's ready."

"Oh, I feel like getting my own breakfast this morning, thank you." Lord Ermenwyr flinched and bared his teeth as the Smiths' baby began the morning lamentation.

"I see," said Mrs. Smith. Smith looked at her.

He watched as, one by one, the keymen and the guests emerged from their tents alive and whole. Parradan Smith sniffed the air suspiciously, then shrugged and went off to wash himself. Burnbright crawled out of her bedroll, yawned, and came over to the kitchen pavilion, where she attempted to drink rose-apricot syrup from the bottle until Mrs. Smith hit her across the knuckles with a wooden spoon. The Smith children straggled forth and went straight to the mess of green slime and strips of fur where the demon's body had been and proceeded to poke their little fingers in it.

Ronrishim Flowering Reed stepped from his tent, saw the mess, and looked disgusted. He picked his way across the circle to the kitchen pavilion.

"Is it possible to get a cup of clean water?" he inquired. "And have you any rose extract?"

"Burnbright, fetch the nice man his water," said Mrs. Smith. "Haven't any rose extract, sir, but we do have rose-apricot syrup." Burnbright held it up helpfully.

Flowering Reed's lip curled.

"No, thank you," he said. "Plain rose extract was all I required. We are a people of simple tastes. We do not find it necessary to cloy our appetites with adulterated and excessive sensation."

"But it's so much fun," Lord Ermenwyr told him. Flowering Reed looked at him with loathing, took his cup of water, and stalked away in silence.

Lord Ermenwyr took his breakfast order, when it was ready, straight off to his palanquin and crawled inside with it. He did not emerge thereafter until it was time to break camp, when he came out himself and took down his pavilion.

"Is Madam Balnshik all right?" Smith inquired, coming to lend a hand, for the lordling was wheezing in an alarming manner.

"Just fine," Lord Ermenwyr assured him, his eyes bulging. "Be a good fellow and hold the other end of this, will you? Thanks ever so. Nursie's just got a, er, headache. The change in air pressure as we approach the highlands, no doubt. She'll be right as rain, later. You'll see."

In fact she did not emerge until they made camp that evening, though when she did she looked serene and gorgeous as ever. Mrs. Smith watched her as she dined heartily on that night's entrée, which was baked boar ham with brandied lemon-and-raisin sauce. Lord Ermenwyr, by contrast, took but a cup of consommé in his pavilion.

∽

"That's two murder attempts," said Mrs. Smith, as the fire was going down to embers and all the guests had retired.

"You don't think it's been robbery either, then," said Smith. She exhaled a plume of smoke and shook her head.

"Not when a demon's sent," she said. "And that was a sending, depend upon it."

"I didn't think there were any sorcerers in Troon," said Smith.

"What makes you think the sending came out of Troon?" Mrs. Smith inquired, looking dubious. He told her about Burnbright's recognizing the dead glider. She just nodded.

"You don't think the two attacks are unrelated, do you?" asked Smith. "Do you think the demon might have been sent by—" He gestured out into the darkness, toward the black mountain. Mrs. Smith was silent a moment.

"Not generally his style," she said at last. "But I suppose anything's possible. That would certainly complicate matters."

"I like trouble to be simple," said Smith. "Let's say it's somebody in Troon. It's my guess they're either after Parradan Smith or the little lord. Couldn't get them in town without it being an obvious murder, so they waited until we were far enough out on the plain that we couldn't send for help. Eh?"

"Seems reasonable."

"But the first attack didn't come off, thanks to there being a lot more people able to fight back here than they bargained for," Smith theorized. "Now we're getting farther out of range and they're getting desperate, so they hired somebody to send a demon. That costs a lot. I'm betting they've run out of resources. I'm betting we'll be left in peace from here on."

‿

And for the next two days it seemed as though he might be right, though the journey was not without incident. The Smith children began to grow gray fur on their hands, and nothing—not shaving, not plucking, not depilatory cream—could remove it. Moreover it began to spread, to their parents' consternation, and by nightfall of the second day they sat like a trio of miserable kittens while their mother had hysterics and pleaded with Smith to do something about it.

Such commotion she made that Lord Ermenwyr ventured from his bed, glaring and demanding silence; though when he saw the children he howled with immoderate laughter, and Balnshik had to come drag him back inside, scolding him severely. She came out later and offered a salve that looked like terra-cotta clay, which proved effective in removing the fur, though the children wept and whined that it stung.

Still, by the next morning the fur had not grown back.

～

The Greenlands rose before them, now, in range upon range of wooded hills. Beyond towered the black mountain, so vast it seemed like another world, perhaps one orbiting dangerously close. Its separate topography, its dark forests and valleys, its cliffs brightened here and there by the fall of glittering rivers and rainbowed mists, became more distinct with every hour and seemed less real.

Though the road skirted the hills in most places, the ground did climb, and the keymen grunted with effort as they pedaled. Smith worked so hard, his wound opened again and Keyman Crucible had to help him, winding with his good arm. The air was moist, smelling of green things, and when they made camp their first evening in a tree-circled glade there was not the least taste of the dust of Troon left in anyone's mouth.

～

Two days into the Greenlands, they were attacked again.

They had scaled a hill with sweating effort, and cresting saw a long straight slope before them, stretching down to a gentle shaded run through oaks beginning to go golden and red. Burnbright whooped with relief, and sprinted down the road before the caravan as it came rattling after. The Smith children raised a shrill cheer as the carts picked up speed, and bright leaves whirled in the breeze as they came down.

But near the bottom of the incline, there were suddenly a great many leaves, and acorns too, and then there was an entire tree across the road. A very large and fairly ugly man stepped out and stood before them, grinning.

He was doing it for effect, of course. He had the sashes, the golden earring, the daggers that went with a bandit, and he had, moreover, the tusks and thundercloud skin color that went with a demon hybrid. There was no need for him to shout, "Halt! This is an armed robbery!" and with his tusks he might have found it a little difficult to enunciate anyway. His job was to terrify and demoralize the caravan, and he was well suited for it.

However, it is not a good idea to terrify a little girl whose legs can run fifty miles in a day without resting. Burnbright screamed but, unable to stop given her momentum, did what had been drummed into her at the Mount Flame Mother House for Runners: She leaped into the air and came on heels first, straight into the bandit's face. He went over with a crash, and she went with him, landing on her feet. She proceeded to dance frenziedly on his head, as behind her the carts derailed and before her other bandits came howling from the forest.

Nor is it a good idea to lose the element of surprise. Smith and the others had enough warning, in the time they were hurtling toward the tree, to prepare themselves, and when the moment of impact came they were poised to leap clear. Smith landed hard on his hip but got off a pair of bolts into the bandit who was rushing him, which bought him enough time to scramble to his feet and draw his machete. The key-men had produced dented-looking bucklers and machetes from nowhere, and charged in formation, a pot-headed wall of slightly rusty steel.

One of the bolts had got Smith's opponent in the throat, so he was able to cut him down in a moment. As he swung to meet another shrieking assailant he had a glimpse of the tumbled caravan. The Smiths were desperately attempting to get their children into the shelter of an overturned cart, and a bandit who was advancing on them found his head abruptly caved in by a heavy skillet wielded by Mrs. Smith. Giant violet eggs were rolling everywhere, spilling free of their cargo netting, and Balnshik was kicking them aside as she leaped forward, a stiletto blade in either hand. She slashed at a bandit who backed rapidly from her, though whether he was intimidated more by the wicked little knives or the gleam of her white teeth, bared in a snarl of blood-thirsty joy, it would have been difficult to say.

Lord Ermenwyr, astonishingly, was up and on his feet, and had just taken off an assailant's head with a saber. Par-radan Smith had emptied his pistolbows, mowing down at least five attackers, and was locked in a hand-to-hand strug-gle with the sixth. That was all Smith was able to see clearly before he became far too preoccupied with his own survival to look longer.

His opponent was not, as the tusked bandit had been, hideous. He was lithe, slender, beautiful; but for the ram's horns that curved back from his temples and the fact that his skin was the color of lightning, he might have graced any boy prostitute's couch in the most elegant of cities. This did not impress Smith, but the youth fought like a demon too, and that painfully impressed him.

Blade blocked blade—*whipp*, a dagger was in the youth's free hand, and he'd laid open Smith's coat just over his heart. Smith's hand moved too fast to be seen and would have taken off the boy's head, but he was suddenly, magically, four paces back from where he ought to be. He smiled into Smith's eyes and lunged again, and Smith, jumping back, was unable to free his boot knife before they locked blades once more. The boy had all the advantage of inhuman speed and strength, and Smith began to get the cold certain feeling in his gut that he was going down this time.

All he had on the boy was weight, and he threw it into a forward push. He managed to shove the other one back far enough to grab his knife at last and they circled, the boy dancing, Smith limping. He knew vaguely that the bandits were getting the worst of the fight, but they might have been in another world. His world was that locked circle, tiny and growing smaller, and his opponent's eyes had become the moon and the sun.

The demon-boy knew he was going to win, too, and in his glee threw a few little eccentric capers into his footwork, strutted heel to toe, swung his dagger point like a metronome to catch Smith's gaze and fix it while he ran him through—

But he didn't run him through, because his own gaze was caught and held by a figure advancing from Smith's right.

"Hello, Eshbysse," said Mrs. Smith.

The boy's face went slack with astonishment. Into his eyes came uncertainty, and then dawning horror.

"Yes," said Mrs. Smith. "Fenallise."

He drew back. "Fenallise? But—you—"

"It's been thirty years, Eshbysse," she said.

"No!" he cried, backing farther away. "Not that long! You're lying." Averting his gaze from her, he dropped his weapons and put his hands to his face. It was still smooth, still perfect.

"Every day of thirty years," she assured him.

"I won't believe you!" Eshbysse sobbed. He turned to flee, wailing, mounting into the air and running along the treetops, and the red and golden leaves fluttered about his swift ankles as though they had already fallen. His surviving men, seeing the tide had turned, took to their heels along the ground with similar rapidity.

Smith dropped his weapons and sagged forward, bracing his hands on his thighs, gulping for breath.

"What the hell," he said, "was that all about?"

"We were an item, once," said Mrs. Smith, looking away

into the sea of autumn leaves. "You wouldn't think I was ever a little girl to be stolen out of a convent by a demon-lover, would you? But we did terrible things together, he and I."

"What'd he run off for?" asked Smith.

She shook her head.

"He was always afraid of Time," she said thoughtfully. "It doesn't get their kind as quickly as it gets us, but it does do for them sooner or later. Seeing me reminded him. One day he won't be pretty anymore; he can't bear that, you see."

Smith stared at her and saw in her face the girl she had been. She turned and looked at the aftermath of battle.

"Bloody hell," she said. Parradan Smith was staggering toward them, death-pale, supported by Flowering Reed.

"He's hurt," Flowering Reed cried.

↬

They made temporary camp by the side of the road and assessed the damage.

Parradan Smith was indeed hurt, had taken a stab wound in the chest, and though it was nowhere near his heart, he was in shock, seemed weakened on his left side. Flowering Reed advised that he shouldn't be moved for the present, so they made him as comfortable as they could in one of the tents.

Burnbright was bruised and crying hysterically, but had taken no other harm. Smith's ribs were scratched, and the keymen had taken assorted cuts, none serious. The Smiths and their children were unharmed. Balnshik was unharmed, as was Lord Ermenwyr. There were, however, nine dead bandits to be dragged into a pile and searched, and there was an oak tree to be cleared from the road, to say nothing of 144 giant eggs to be collected and a dozen carts to be righted and put back on track.

"So thanks a lot, Master of the Mountain," Smith muttered, as he was having his ribs taped up. Mrs. Smith, who was tending to him, shook her head.

"Have you taken a good look at the bodies?" she asked. "Three of 'em are our own people. The others look like half-breeds. Poor Eshbysse had got himself a band of threadbare mercenaries and thieves. When the old man attacks, you'll know; his people are all demons, and a good deal more professional than these feckless creatures. We'd have had no chance at all against him."

"That's encouraging," growled Smith.

"Would you believe it?" said Lord Ermenwyr brightly, approaching with an armful of violet eggs. "Not one of the damned things broke!"

Mrs. Smith looked scornful. "I suppose all that tripe about the perfect holistic packing shape had some sense in it, then."

"Are they supposed to be a perfect holistic shape?" Lord Ermenwyr looked intrigued. He tossed his armful into the air and, before Smith had time to yell, began to juggle them adroitly.

"My lord, could I ask you to put those back in the cart?"

Lord Ermenwyr tossed the eggs, one after another as they came out of their spinning circle, into the cart. "Shall I volunteer to search the bodies? Might be a purse or two on them."

"Do you think they were from the Master of the Mountain?" said Smith.

Lord Ermenwyr gave a short bark of a laugh. "Not likely! *His* men all wear mail and livery. Or so I've heard."

"Why does everybody know more about this than me?" Smith wondered, as the young lord went off to loot corpses.

"Well, you're not from around here, are you, dear?" Mrs. Smith tied off his bandage. "If you weren't from Port Black-rock or wherever it is, you'd have heard these stories all your life."

Smith was disinclined to tell her whether or not he was

from Port Blackrock, so he looked up at Keyman Bellows, who saluted as he approached. "How are we doing?" he inquired.

"Carts are righted, Caravan Master, and no damage to the wheels or gears. Old Smith and New Smith are taking axes to the roadblock now. Parradan Smith's asking for you."

"Right," Smith said, getting to his feet and pulling on his slashed coat. "I'll go see what he wants. When they're done with the tree, tell them to dig a grave pit."

His first thought, when he parted the tent flap and peered inside, was that he was looking at a dead man. But Parradan Smith's eyes swiveled and met his.

"Talk to you," he said.

"He shouldn't talk," said Flowering Reed, who sat beside him. Parradan Smith bared his teeth at the Yendri.

"Get out," he said.

"Easy!" Smith ducked his head and stepped in. "You'd better go; I won't let him wear himself out," he told Flowering Reed, who looked offended and left without a word.

When they were alone, Parradan Smith gestured awkwardly with one hand at the gang tattoo on his chest. "Know this?" he gasped.

"You're a Bloodfire," Smith replied.

He nodded. "Courier. Collected debt in Troon. He tried to get it back."

"Who did?" Smith leaned closer. Parradan Smith gulped for breath.

"Lord Tinwick. Gambler. His gliders." He watched Smith's face closely to see if he understood.

"The gliders were trying to kill you and take back what you'd collected?"

Parradan Smith nodded. He made a groping gesture toward his instrument case. Smith pulled it close for him. He pressed a key into Smith's hand.

"Open."

Smith worked the complicated locks and opened it, and caught his breath. Nested in shaped packing was a jeweled cup of exquisite workmanship, clearly very old.

"Heirloom. All he had to pay with. My lord wants it bad. You deliver—" Parradan Smith looked up into Smith's eyes. "And tell him. Pay well. Lord Kashban Beatbrass. Villa in Salesh. Find him."

A shadow shifted across the outside of the tent and moved away. Parradan Smith followed it with his eyes and smiled bitterly.

"He stopped listening," he said.

"Look, you aren't wounded that badly," said Smith, feeling he ought to say something encouraging. "I'm sure we can get you to Salesh."

Parradan Smith looked back at him.

"Turn me," he ordered.

"What?" said Smith, but he obeyed, lifting and half-turning the wounded man. He caught his breath; there was a red swelling on his back like an insect bite but immense, beginning to blister, and in its center a dark speck.

"See?" said Parradan Smith, breathing very hard. "Poisoned."

Smith said something profane. He drew his knife and scraped gently, and the black thing came out of the wound. He turned Parradan Smith on his back again and held up the object on his knife blade, squinting at it. It looked like the tip of a thorn, perhaps a quarter of an inch long.

"This is like those darts we took out of the glider," he said.

"In my back," said Parradan Smith. Smith groaned.

"Somebody in the party shot you," he said. "Maybe by accident?"

Parradan Smith looked impatient and drew a deep breath as though he was about to explain something too obvious to

Smith; but he never drew another breath after that and lay staring at Smith with blank eyes.

Smith sighed. He closed and locked the case. Flowering Reed approached him as he came out of the tent, and he told him, "He's dead."

"He might have lived if you'd listened to me," said the Yendri angrily.

"I don't think so," said Smith, and walked away to put the case in a safe place.

⤙

A while later he approached Lord Ermenwyr, who was puffing out rifts of purple weedsmoke as he watched the keymen digging the grave pit.

"We need to talk, my lord," he said.

"My master needs to rest," said Balnshik, appearing beside him as from thin air.

"I need to talk to him more than he needs to rest," said Smith stubbornly. Lord Ermenwyr waved a placatory hand.

"Certainly we'll talk, and Nursie can stand by with a long knife in case things take an unpleasant turn," he said. "Though I think we've seen the last of this particular band of cutthroats."

"Let's hope so, my lord," said Smith, drawing him aside. Balnshik followed closely, tossing her hair back in an insolent kind of way. Her shirt had been torn in the fight, giving him a peep at breasts like pale melons, and it was with difficulty that he drew his attention back to her young master. "You fought very well, if I may say so."

"You may," said Lord Ermenwyr smugly. "But then, I've had lots of experience fighting for my life. Usually against doctors. Today was a welcome change."

"Your health seems to have improved."

"I'm no longer rusticating in that damned dust bowl, am

I?" Lord Ermenwyr blew a smoke ring. "Bandits or no, the Greenlands does offer fresh air."

"What were you doing in Troon?" inquired Smith. Balnshik stretched extravagantly, causing one nipple to flash like a dark star through the rent in her shirt. Smith turned his face away and concentrated on Lord Ermenwyr, who replied, "Why, I was about my father's business. Representing his interests, if you must know, with Old Troon Mills and the other barley barons. Doing a damned good job, too, before the Lung Rot set in."

"Do you gamble, my lord?"

"Hell, no." Lord Ermenwyr scowled. "A pastime for morons, unless you've got an undetectable way of cheating. I don't need the money, and I certainly don't need the thrill of suspense, thank you very much. I've spent too much of my life wondering if I'd live to see my next birthday."

Smith nodded. "And the only reason you left Troon was for your health?"

"Yes."

"You'd made no new enemies there?"

Lord Ermenwyr's eyes glinted. "I didn't say that," he purred. "Though it wasn't my fault, really. I made the most amazing discovery."

"Master," said Balnshik, in the gentlest voice imaginable, but it was still a warning.

"Did you know," said Lord Ermenwyr, with barely suppressed glee, "that if you're very attentive to wealthy widows, they'll practically pay you to sleep with them? They'll give you presents! They'll take you nice places to eat! Good lord, I might have been a kitten on a string, and all I had to do was—"

"I'm sure the Caravan Master isn't interested, my lord," said Balnshik, putting an affectionate arm about his neck and locking it against his windpipe.

"How old is he?" Smith asked her.

"Sixteen."

"Twenty-five!" said Lord Ermenwyr, pushing back her arm. "Really!"

"Sixteen," Balnshik repeated.

"Seventeen," Lord Ermenwyr insisted. "Anyway, the only problem is, the ladies get jealous, and they won't share their toy. There was a Scene. A certain lady tried to do me an injury with her hairbrush. I only got out of it by pretending to have a seizure, and then I told her I was dying, which I am but not right then, and—"

"And his lord father thought it best my master have a change of air," Balnshik finished for him.

Smith rubbed his chin, scratching the stubble.

"So . . . would any of these ladies have felt strongly enough to hire a band of mercenaries to ambush you out here?" he said, without much hope.

"Well, I don't know—Lady Fristia was rather—"

"No," said Balnshik. "And now, I hope you'll excuse us? It's time his lordship had his drugs." She lifted Lord Ermenwyr bodily, threw him over her shoulder, and carried him off, protesting:

"It could have been Lady Fristia, you know! She was obsessed with me—"

⌒

They buried Parradan Smith in a separate grave and piled a cairn of stones to mark it, on Burnbright's advice, she being the nearest expert on Mount Flame City gang customs. They felt badly leaving him there, in the shadow of the black mountain. Still, there is only so much one can do for the dead without joining them.

⌒

Two days more they rolled on, fearful at every blind turning, but the fire-colored forest was silent under a mild blue sky. No picturesque villains jumped out from behind the mossy boles nor arose from the green ferns.

On the third day, Crucible told Smith, "We'll come to a Red House today. Might want their blacksmith to have a look at that rear axle."

"Red House, right," said Smith, nodding. "That would be one of the way station chain? I saw one on the map. Well, that'll be a relief."

Crucible laughed like a crow. "You haven't tasted their beer," he said.

↩

By afternoon, when the long shadows were slanting behind the oaks, they saw the Red House. It stood on a bluff above the road, in a meadow cleared and stump-dotted, with high windowless walls of red plaster turreted at the four corners where watchmen in pot-helmets leaned. Burnbright announced the caravan's approach on her trumpet, but they had already seen it from afar. By the time the keymen slowed for the turnout, the great gates were already opening.

Fortified as it was, an effort had been made to give the Red House a welcoming appearance. There was a quaint slated mansard built above the gate, bearing a sign of red glass that was illuminated after hours by lanterns: JOIN US HAPPY TRAVELER, it said. On either gatepost were carved the massive figures of folk heroes Prashkon the Wrestler and Andib the Axman, scowling down in a way that might be hoped to frighten off demons or any other ill-intentioned lurkers without the gates. As if that were not enough, the Housekeeper himself came running forward as the carts rattled in, screaming "Welcome! Welcome to Red House, customers!"

"Thank you," said Smith cautiously, climbing from his

cart and staring around. They were circled in an open courtyard of herringbone brick. To one side a high-vaulted hall
stood, with blue smoke curling from its big central chimney.
Built into the opposite wall were other long rooms: they
might be storerooms and barracks for the watchmen. There
was also a forge with a fire blazing, throwing on the dark
wall the darker shadow of the blacksmith, who was clanging
away lazily at a bit of glowing iron.

"You'd be out of Troon, Caravan Master, am I correct?"
asked the Housekeeper, coming up to slap Smith's arm
heartily. He winced.

"That's right," he replied. "And it hasn't been an easy
trip. We've been attacked twice. No, three times, and lost a
passenger."

"Ah! Demons, was it?" The Housekeeper shuddered.
"Horrible, horrible! But you'll be all right here. We're a
bright speck of safety in a hostile land. Salves for your
wounds and cheer for your heart. Everything for the traveler.
Smithy, trading post with unique curios, dining hall with
fine cuisine, splendid accommodations! Even baths. No
shortage of water. You'll dine with me, I trust?"

"Yes, thank you." Smith glanced at the caravan, but the
keymen were already wheeling the lead cart to the forge,
covering the cargo and locking things down with practiced
efficiency. "Hot baths for everybody first, though, I guess.
Have you got a doctor here? Some of us are wounded, and
there's a Yendri passenger who's helped out a little, but—"

"As it happens," said the Housekeeper, lowering his
voice, "Our medic is a Yendri. You won't mind him, I
promise you. Splendid fellow, knows his place, expert in all
kinds of secret remedies his people use. Eminently trustworthy. Many of them are, you know. We've had him here for
years. Never a mishap. I'll send him to you in the bathhouse, shall I?"

The last thing Smith wanted at that moment was to have to deal with another supercilious green person, but his leg hurt badly, so he just nodded, and said, "Great."

He was sitting in a long stone trough full of hot water, wishing it was deep enough to submerge himself, when the Yendri doctor entered the narrow stall and edged toward him. Like Flowering Reed, he was tall and regal-looking; but he wore a simple white robe and did not seem quite so superior.

"You are the wounded man?" he inquired, setting down a basket.

"It's mostly me," said Smith, sitting upright. "But the keymen are more important. They've got some bad gashes. In the name of the Unsullied Daughter, will you patch them up?"

The Yendri raised his eyebrows. "For the sake of the Unwearied Mother," he said, laying a peculiar emphasis on the title, "they have been tended to. They asked me to see you next. You took a bolt in the leg?"

Smith nodded, raising his leg from the water. The Yendri hissed softly when he saw the bolt wound.

"This is inflamed. Dry yourself and step out to the massage table, please."

He retreated, and Smith got hastily from the tub and toweled himself off. When he emerged from the stall, he saw that the Yendri had laid out a number of unpleasant-looking tools and bottles.

"You could just slap some salve and a bandage on it," he suggested uneasily.

"Not if you wish to keep your leg," the Yendri replied, helping him up on the table. Smith lay back and gritted his teeth, and for the next few minutes thought very hard about a cozy little bar in a seaside town, where from a window table one could watch blue dusk settling on the harbor and the yellow lamps blooming one after another on the ships and along the peaceful quay . . .

After far too long a time the Yendri was applying a bandage, and telling him, "The cut on your thorax will heal easily, but you'll have to keep the leg elevated. Can they make a pallet for you on one of the carts?"

"I think so," said Smith, unclenching his jaw with effort. "It was just a flesh wound. Did you really have to dig like that?"

"It had become—" The Yendri paused in tying off the bandage and looked at him. "Hm. Let me explain it like this: There are tiny demons who feed on wounds. They're so tiny you can't see them, but they can get into a cut and make you very, very sick, do you understand?"

Smith thought it sounded like the most idiotic superstition, but he nodded. "Tiny demons. All right. What's keeping my leg up supposed to do?"

"Well, there are—hm—tiny warriors in your heart, you see? And they'll do battle with the demons if they can get to them, but if you constrict the—hm—the river of your blood so they can't row their tiny warships along it—" The Yendri, observing Smith's expression, threw his hands in the air. "Let's just say you need to keep off your feet and rest, will that do? And perhaps it won't scar too badly."

"I'm too old to care about scars," said Smith, rubbing his leg.

"You're fortunate, then," said the Yendri, eyeing him critically. "Given the number you've got. You're a mercenary, I take it?"

"Have been," Smith replied warily.

"You've survived a great deal. You must be sensible enough to follow a doctor's advice." The Yendri bundled up his instruments.

"I'll do my best," said Smith. "Thank you. Thanks for being polite, too. Flowering Reed sounded like he hoped I'd die, even when he was putting on the bandage."

The Yendri looked at him sharply. "Another of my people treated you?"

"He's one of our passengers."

"Hm. Would that be where you learned the expression 'Unsullied Daughter,' by any chance?"

"Yes. I thought it was something we had to say so you'd treat us."

"No," said the Yendri quietly. "Any true follower of the Lady in question must heal the sick and the wounded, whether or not they invoke Her name. And regardless of who they are. Good evening, Caravan Master."

He took his basket and left. Smith pulled on his clothes and limped out of the bathhouse. It was twilight, with one star in a purple sky above the red walls, and the firelight from the forge threw his tottering shadow out black beside him as he made his way across the courtyard to the high hall.

⌒

"Caravan Master!" cried the Housekeeper, descending on him with a drink in either hand. "Come, sit with me. Your bath was enjoyable, yes, and you've had your leg seen to? Excellent. You'll enjoy a complimentary beverage and our unique regional cuisine while relaxing around the blazing warmth of our fire."

"Sounds wonderful," said Smith dazedly.

He let himself be led to a seat by the central fire pit, and sank into it with a grateful sigh, as a drink was pressed into his hand. Utter bliss. His state of euphoria lasted until he took a sip of his drink.

"What—what's this?" he gasped, turning to the House-keeper in disbelief.

"That's our special acorn beer," said the Housekeeper, a little defensively. "It's made nowhere else. We don't even brew enough to export."

"It's very unusual," said Smith.

"You'd really like it if you had a chance to get used to it," the Housekeeper told him. "It has a marvelous subtle complex bouquet."

Like a burning barn, thought Smith. He swirled the flat sour stuff, and said, "Delicate carbonation, too."

"Exactly," the Housekeeper said, and drank heartily. "None of your nasty gassy flatlands ale!" He wiped his mouth on the back of his hand and leaned toward Smith with a gleam in his eye. "Though I'm always interested in news from the flatlands, you understand. We've got almost everything here—fresh air, fine water, radiant health—of course it's a little dismaying at first, always looking over one's shoulder at the, er, mountain up there, but one soon grows used to that—still, we're a little out of touch, I have to admit. Almost miss the flatlands, sometimes."

"Really," said Smith, having another mouthful of his beer in the hope that it would improve upon acquaintance. It didn't.

"Yes," said the Housekeeper, staring into the fire. "Not so much at this time of year—the forest isn't so bad, the leaves look like flames now, and soon the branches will be bare so you can *see* things, good clean honest open spaces. Not like in summer when there's this smothering blanket of impenetrable green and anything could be hiding out there, anything could steal up behind you and—one gets a little edgy in the summer, yes. Demon-country, after all."

Smith nodded. "Do you get attacked much?"

"Attacked? No, no, not in here, this is a fine safe outpost. The odd demon over the wall now and again, but I think they're only after our beer."

Smith thought that very unlikely indeed.

"One just doesn't want to venture outside the walls, into all that—green," said the Housekeeper, and shuddered. "Well! Tell me of your travels, Caravan Master. Tell me the news of Troon."

Smith obliged, for the next quarter of an hour, and while he talked he surveyed the high hall. Other guests of the Red House, a mixed lot of Children of the Sun, Yendri and unclassifiable half-breeds, sat here and there eating, or drinking, or settling down for the night.

Across the fire pit, the keymen were lined up on a long settle, basking in the warmth in happy mutual silence. In the dining area, Mrs. Smith and Burnbright were sitting at a table, though they were not eating: Mrs. Smith had pushed away her laden trencher and sat smoking furiously, glaring at it. Burnbright was sawing away at a piece of meat with great difficulty. So formidable did it seem to be that it slipped out of the trencher now and then and had to be stabbed and dragged back by main force.

In the quiet area at the back of the hall, the Smiths had made up a couple of beds, and the children sat upright in one, chattering like starlings, while their mother rocked the screaming baby in the other and their father attempted to erect a makeshift curtain to screen them from the firelight. Other guests, having bedded down for the night, were rising now and then on their elbows to look threateningly at the little family.

Ronrishim Flowering Reed sat alone at a table, a carafe of something that looked like rainwater in front of him. Smith gazed at it longingly and rinsed his mouth with more of the beer. As he gave detailed descriptions of all the costumes he'd seen at Troon's Festival of Masks to the Housekeeper, Smith observed a hooded stranger rise from a seat in the shadows and approach Flowering Reed.

The stranger leaned over him and said something in a low voice. Flowering Reed looked interested, made a reply. The stranger sat down across from him and, taking out a long rolled envelope of supple leather, spread it open on the table to display some kind of small wares packed inside.

"But the ladies," said the Housekeeper. "Tell me about the ladies in Troon. I dream about sophisticated feminine graces, you know, day in, day out, as the caravans come and go. Ladies and their brocades. Their perfumes. Their tiny little jeweled sandals. Their refined accents!"

"Don't have the bloody Mixed Grill plate, whatever you do," muttered Mrs. Smith out of the corner of her mouth, dropping heavily into a chair beside Smith. "It's unspeakably horrid." She stuffed more amberleaf into her smoking tube and, leaning forward, lit it from the fire pit.

"I always thought inland men had lots of Yendri mistresses," said Smith to the Housekeeper. "Or half-demonesses or something. Wild forest girls who won't keep their clothes on, with breasts like . . ." Words failed him, as an image of Balnshik's bosom rose before his eyes.

"Don't tell *me* that thing was a kidney," Mrs. Smith growled, exhaling a cloud of smoke. "Grilled handball is more like it. And those creamed woodpeas! Inedible."

The Housekeeper was shaking his head sadly. "Oh, Caravan Master, I can see you're a stranger to the Greenlands. The Yendri women keep to themselves. As for any wild forest girls, well, first you've got to persuade them to bathe on a regular basis, and then you'd better keep a weapon under your pillow. And when you've had the bad luck to take up with one who's got some shapeshifting blood! No, no; one soon learns that a female and a lady are not necessarily one and the same. How I crave the sight of a real lady! The delicate ankles. The gauzy underthings. The cosmetics—" He had to pause to wipe saliva from the corner of his mouth.

"Ladies," said Smith to the Housekeeper. "Well—We're carrying cargo for Lady Seven Butterflies."

"Seven Butterflies!" The Housekeeper was ecstatic. "What a charming name. Is she delicate and fair, as it suggests?"

"I guess so," said Smith, remembering the mask with its black tongue. "I couldn't see her very well for her costume. But it was a pretty costume." He was distracted as Balnshik entered the high hall, evidently fresh from the bath. Her damp shirt clung to her breasts, which stood up proudly, as she carried on her head an elaborate construction of wood and canvas, with both hands up to steady it.

Behind her Lord Ermenwyr strutted, with his wet hair curling over the lace collar of his long nightshirt. He wore embroidered slippers and a matching nightcap, and carried a bedroll. His long smoking tube was still clenched between his teeth.

Balnshik selected a suitably remote section of the hall and set down her burden. In a moment she had it all unfolded and standing: a camp cot of ingenious design, complete with its own attached insect tent of gauzy netting, surmounted by a gilded cherub blowing a tiny trumpet. At least, it looked like a cherub. Was that a tiny tail it sported? Lord Ermenwyr passed her the bedroll and as Balnshik leaned between the curtains to arrange it on the cot, he wandered over to the fire.

"Good evening, all," he said, puffing out a great rift of purple weedsmoke that mingled a moment with Mrs. Smith's white amberleaf fumes, turning a sickly lavender before vanishing up the draft of the fire hood. "Splendid baths, Housekeeper. Not quite deep enough to have satisfying sex in, but all the hot water one could ask for."

"And this young man would be?" inquired the Housekeeper, mildly affronted.

"This is Lord Ermenwyr of the House Kingfisher," Smith explained, and the Housekeeper leaped to his feet.

"My lord! Honor, honor, all possible honor to your house!
Delighted to receive you at Red House. Please, here's a cushion, sit by the fire. A drink for the lord," he shouted to the bar.

"Er—he's very young," said Smith. "And an invalid
besides. I don't think beer would be a good idea."

"Oh, if he's an invalid, he must try our acorn beer," said
the Housekeeper earnestly, settling Lord Ermenwyr in his
own chair and arranging pillows around him. "It's got
plenty of health-giving qualities. Very tonic. And, begging
your pardon, Caravan Master, but any fellow with a beard is
surely old enough for strong waters."

"Of course I am," said Ermenwyr complacently. "Pray,
Caravan Master, don't trouble yourself. Is this the famous
acorn beer?" He accepted a cup from the slavey who had
hastened up to present it to him. "Thank you so much. To
your good health, Housekeeper," he said, and drank.

Smith cringed inwardly, watching as Lord Ermenwyr's
eyes popped wide. He swallowed, bared his teeth, turned the
grimace into a fearsome smile and said, "How original. I
wonder—could I purchase a barrel of this stuff? It'd make a
perfect gift for my older brothers."

Tears of joy formed in the Housekeeper's eyes. "Oh! The
honor you do us! My lord, it's in short supply, but for you—"

"Name your price," said Lord Ermenwyr.

"Please, accept it as a gift! And grant only that I may
claim the honor of your patronage," gushed the Housekeeper. Lord Ermenwyr frowned at that, and some of the
glittering nastiness went out of his eyes.

"You have my patronage," he said seriously. "There. See
that a barrel is packed with my trunks before we leave."

The Housekeeper twittered so that Smith was afraid he
was going to flap his arms and fly into the rafters. Mrs.
Smith watched the scene in disbelief until Burnbright came
wandering up forlornly.

"I can't find my bedroll," she said. "I think one of those strangers took it. Come help me look."

"They won't rape you, for heaven's sake," said Mrs. Smith. "Not with all these people here anyway."

"But they look like bandits," whined Burnbright, twisting her hands together. "Please?"

Grumbling and puffing smoke, Mrs. Smith hauled herself out of her chair and stamped off with Burnbright. At that moment the Yendri doctor entered, carrying his basket, making for the dining area where a guest was doubled up with indigestion. Smith nodded at the doctor, who did not notice, because his eyes were tracking across the room as he walked. He spotted Flowering Reed. Smith thought he looked disgusted, and wondered briefly if the Yendri disliked one another as much as they seemed to dislike all other races.

The doctor's gaze slid off Flowering Reed and he turned to go on, but paused again as he saw Lord Ermenwyr, who was laughing at something the Housekeeper had just said and tilting back his head to blow a smoke ring. The doctor halted, stared a long moment before going on to his patient.

Smith's attention was drawn away as a slavey came bustling up with a tray.

"Your supper at last, Caravan Master," said the Housekeeper. "I'm proud to present our local specialty: Huntsman's Mixed Grill with creamed woodpeas!"

"Oh. Thank you," said Smith. He sat straight, putting his drink aside gladly, and accepted a trencher and a rolled napkin full of utensils from the slavey. As he looked around for a place to set one of them down, he saw out of the corner of his eye the hooded man staring at him. He turned to meet his gaze. The man jumped to his feet, starting toward him.

"You! You're the Caravan Master. Those are your people, right? Can't you tell them to shut their damned baby up?"

"Well—I can try, but—" said Smith, awkwardly juggling utensils and thinking that the stranger was yelling louder than the baby.

"Wait a minute. I know you from somewhere," announced the stranger, raising his voice even more as he approached. "You're that thief they were looking for in Karkateen this summer!"

"What?" Smith gaped at the stranger, who had come up on him so rapidly they were now face-to-face. "No. You're mistaken. I've never been in Karkateen—"

"Are you calling me a liar?" shouted the stranger. His arm flashed out, and Smith's trencher went flying as he tried to fend him off, but there was no weapon in the stranger's hand. Instead there was a small bag of purple-dyed leather palmed there, and the stranger made a snatching motion at Smith's belt and held up the bag as though he'd just pulled it loose. "This is mine! Damn you, here's my mark on it!"

But he played the game a second too long, holding up the bag in righteous indignation for all to behold, because Smith saw him going for his knife with his other hand. That gave Smith time to drive his fork into the stranger's leg and roll forward out of his chair, under the stranger's guard. He came up behind him as the stranger was turning, and hip-checked him so he fell forward across Smith's empty chair with a crash.

"I'm not a thief, I'm not from Karkateen, and I didn't take that pouch from you because you had it in your hand the whole time," Smith babbled, drawing both his pistolbows and stepping back. "What the hell's going on?"

But even as the stranger turned, yanking the fork from his leg with a murderous glare, Smith knew what was going on. Burnbright, over in the sleeping area, screamed as four shadowy figures leaped to their feet and came forward. Surprisingly for men who had retired to their blankets, each was fully clothed and armed with a cocked pistolbow.

Smith gulped and retreated a pace farther, as the foremost stranger drew his knife and hurled it at him. Smith dodged the blade and fired both bolts straight into the stranger's chest, and couldn't imagine why the man looked as surprised as he did when he fell.

Then there were bolts whistling through the air toward him. Smith threw himself flat behind a table and chairs, heard the bolts plunking home into wood and into plaster, and heard more screams and inarticulate shouting, the loudest of which was the Housekeeper calling for his watchmen.

Reloading, Smith peered through table and chair legs and saw that Lord Ermenwyr had sensibly thrown a table down and got behind it on his hands and knees. Balnshik was in the act of flying to him, bounding over the scattered furniture. Smith leaned up to see where his assailants were and beheld to his astonishment that one was down, tackled from behind by Mrs. Smith and Burnbright, who were shrieking like mismatched furies and clubbing him on the head with trenchers. The keymen had as one risen to their feet, grabbed a wide settle, and made a shield of it as they blocked two of the other attackers.

The fourth man came on, however, reloading as he ran, evading the keymen and actually vaulting across the fire pit to get to Smith. Smith jumped up, kicking a stool toward the man to foul his legs as he landed, and the stranger managed to avoid the stool but stumbled on his fallen companion. Smith fired at him, one bolt skittering off into the debris and one smacking home into the man's side.

His assailant cursed, but lurched to his feet anyway and drew a short sword. He stood swaying, waving it at Smith, though his face was ashen. Smith grabbed up the stool and swung it at the man, knocking the sword out of his fingers. Another blow with the stool, and the man collapsed backward, bleeding from his mouth.

Smith backed away, hearing a commotion behind him that was perhaps the arrival of the Red House watchmen. He looked up and was amazed to see that the two remaining strangers had turned from the keymen and were engaging Balnshik, attempting to pinion her. They weren't succeeding very well; in fact, Smith heard the distinctive sound of snapping bone and a gibbering scream from one of the men; but they had successfully drawn her attention.

Behind her, Flowering Reed was moving quietly along the wall. His face looked odd. Was that something in his mouth? And what a strange look in his eyes, too, fixed as they were on Lord Ermenwyr, who was making himself as small a target behind his table as he could, and whose lips were moving in—prayer? But he could not see Flowering Reed advancing on him.

Smith knew the truth, suddenly, without understanding. Bawling "My lord!" he ran around the table to block Flowering Reed's advance, pulling his machete.

Something white was flowing toward him from his left with tremendous speed. The Yendri doctor? Something was coming thunderously up behind him. Flowering Reed looked at Smith with purest hatred in his eyes, and grimaced around the tube between his clenched teeth.

Then Smith was down, he was hit and he seemed to have struck his head on something, because it hurt a lot, and there was some other injury but minor, a little stinging in his arm. Smith turned his head and saw three tiny feathered darts sticking out of his wrist. Knowing that he must get the thorns out, he raised his machete to scrape them away; but the room blurred in bloody darkness before he could tell if he'd succeeded. *Oh*, he thought, *I'm dead.*

⤴

He was listening to Lord Ermenwyr talk, smoothly, persuasively, and what a silky manner the lordling could summon when he wanted to!

". . . assassins, without a doubt hired by my father's enemies. Professionals, artfully disguised. Why, you hadn't any idea they weren't simple traders, had you?"

The Housekeeper was moaning apologies.

Smith opened his eyes and looked up at the Yendri doctor, who was stitching up Smith's scalp. At least, that was what he looked as though he were doing. Smith could neither feel the jab of the needle nor any other sensation. He tried to speak and discovered that he was limited to fluttering his eyelids. The Yendri noticed his panic.

"You can't move because the darts in your arm were poisoned. We got them out, and I gave you an antidote. The paralysis will go away, in time. You're a fortunate man," he said, and resumed his task.

"A *very* fortunate man," agreed Balnshik, looming at the doctor's elbow. "Do hurry and recover, Caravan Master. I'm going to thank you personally for your act of heroism." She caressed him in a way that suggested something very nice indeed, and Smith's heartbeat quickened.

"What, is he conscious?" Lord Ermenwyr leaned over him from the other side. "Bravo, Caravan Master! Yes, you certainly don't want to die before you've been personally thanked. Nursie's quite talented. Have you ever heard of the Dance of Two Feathers and One Piece of String?"

Balnshik smiled gently and, placing her open palm on the lordling's face, shoved him backward. The doctor looked horrified. She leaned low into Smith's line of sight, and he almost felt the weight of her breasts.

"You have the gratitude of his lord father," she crooned, and kissed Smith. *Of all times to be paralyzed*, he thought. That was all he knew for a while.

∿

"The boys have sworn up and down you've been our caravan master for years and that you've never even been near Karkateen, so all that rubbish about a charge of theft has been dropped," Mrs. Smith told him, exhaling smoke.

"What about Flowering Reed?" Smith asked, speaking with difficulty.

"Not a trace of him," she replied in disgust. "Slithered out into the night like a snake and must have gone over the wall like a shadow. Bloody backstabbing greenie. No way to tell if it was him set those assassins on you, as they're all dead, but it seems likely. You've made some enemies in your day, haven't you, dear?"

"They were all members of the Throatcutters, did you know?" Burnbright said. "I saw their tattoos. They cost an awful lot to hire. That's why I can't think they were after you, see; they must have been after whatever Parradan Smith had in his case!"

"Were the carts broken into?"

Mrs. Smith shook her head. "The boys had a good look. Everything's secure. Nobody else hurt but you, and at least you were spared the Mixed Grill and creamed woodpeas."

"So, you see? Everything turned out all right," Burnbright concluded cheerfully. "The Yendri says you'll be on your feet again in another day or two, and we can push on. And think how much more room there'll be in the carts, now we're down two passengers!"

⌒

However, a solitary traveler came forward on the day Smith was well enough to leave and bought a passage to Salesh-by-the-Sea. His name was given as Mr. Amook, his occupation was given as Mercenary, his race was indeterminate, and he gave no address. He was very large and said very little. He took a seat in the cart just forward of Lord Ermenwyr's baggage cart and slouched there with his arms folded, and the screaming of the Smiths' baby didn't seem to bother him in the least.

Smith staggered out to the cart leaning on the Yendri doctor, who helped him up to a sort of couch the keymen had made out of the flour bags from Old Troon Mills.

"You must continue to take the infusion each night until the new moon," the doctor told him. "Your cook has the mixture; she promised me she'd make it up for you. When you reach Salesh, go to the hot baths in Anchor Street and ask for Levendyloy Alder. Tell him you need a detoxification, the full treatment. You should feel much better afterward."

"What'll it cost me?" Smith asked crossly, trying to find a comfortable position. He had just settled accounts with the Housekeeper, and was very glad his cousin had a business expense letter of mark.

"You can pay for it with this," the doctor replied, pressing something into his hand. Smith squinted down at it. It was a pendant of some kind, a clay disk on a woven cord. He slipped it about his neck.

"Thank you," he said.

"Be careful, Smith," said the doctor.

"I will be," Smith assured him. "Flowering Reed's still out there somewhere. You know, for all your people's talk about how much nicer you are than us, I always thought you were probably right. It's a real disappointment to find out you've got hypocrites just the same as we do. Or does your religion permit murder?"

The doctor made a wry face. "Hm. Not *my* religion, Caravan Master."

"How's a man like Flowering Reed become a killer, then?"

After a long silence the doctor answered sadly, "Who knows what is in his heart? But love can leave more death in its track than the most ardent hatred."

Smith nodded. He had learned that lesson elsewhere, long since.

"Go in peace, Caravan Master," said the doctor, and touched Smith's forehead briefly in blessing.

The carts jolted forward as the keymen hauled them into the ruts. The watchmen worked the gate capstans. There was a last-minute boarding scramble. Burnbright trumpeted their departure from the Red House. They rolled away into the forest of bright leaves and left that place of smoke and death behind them.

⤳

It was rough going, uphill and down, and the keymen pedaled until their bulging calves seemed ready to burst outright. The red stone road was uneven here and there too, or buckled and cracked from the roots of trees, imperfectly patched with cement. Sometimes it crossed the faces of high hills, hairpinning and skirting breathtaking drops into gorges far below; sometimes it ran through the bottoms of valleys, following watercourses, and cool air flowed with them as they shuttled along through willows going bronze in the frosts.

The black mountain loomed still above the red leaves. Smith, watching it from his elevated position mile after mile, had the eerie feeling that it was watching him in return.

Sometimes he thought he could make out structures at its peak, when no slate clouds obscured it: black walls and battlements, sharp obsidian spires, megalithic giants scowling blind in the sunlight. Sometimes he could see nothing but tumbled stone, a high field of basalt and fallen stars above the tree line.

But no one descended howling from that vast height, and when they made camp at night a profound stillness ringed them in. Even the Smiths' baby seemed subdued. Smith took to sleeping by day as much as he could, to watch the shadows beyond the trees after dark. Only once, one night, was there a distant scream that cut off abruptly. It might have been an animal. There was no sign of anything untoward having happened when they broke camp next morning.

Mr. Amook neither said nor did anything suspicious, but rode in stolid silence. He had no tattoos that Burnbright could spot, no matter how much she lingered near the watering huts. She was half-mad with curiosity about him.

⌒

The day came when the road began to slope downward again, a little obscured by drifts of leaves, and there was undeniably more light and air getting through the ancient branches. Not only that, the black mountain began to diminish behind them. They could glimpse the smoke of distant cities below on the plain, and far off a level horizon so perfect, it could be none but the sea itself.

⌒

Smith was roused from his jolting nap by Burnbright signaling with her trumpet. He leaned up on his elbow to peer along the road, and sought in his memory for the signal codes. As she trumpeted again he identified the message: another caravan sighted. In the next few seconds he sighted it too, racing along the floor of the valley into which they were just descending.

It was immense, fully sixty carts long, coming on with speed and power. The runner pacing before it was a sleek muscular goddess, the steel hats of the keymen (and there were dozens of keymen) were polished, the carts were freshly painted with a flying dragon logo and loaded with cargo of every kind. Even the passengers looked prosperous, gazing out from blank dust-goggled eyes with cool indifference.

They came charging smoothly up the hill toward Smith's caravan seemingly without the least effort! And there was their caravan master, sitting tall in the foremost cart, arms folded on the front of his long duster. No pistolbows for him; a long-range bow was displayed in its own rack on the side of his high seat, and a quiver just visible over his shoulder showed the red feathers of professional-quality hunting arrows. Smith gaped, and the caravan master acknowledged him with a majestic bow of the head as they came up on him and sped by.

The Smith children shrieked with excitement and waved. Even Mr. Amook turned his head to watch. Nobody could take their eyes off the grand spectacle, it seemed; and so everybody saw the last cart hurtling toward them with its outsize load, construction beams bound athwart the cart, protruding outward over its side just far enough to catch the protruding cargo net full of violet eggs on their last cart.

"Hey—" said Smith, watching in horror over his shoulder, and then it happened.

With a sound like a bowstring snapping the net was yanked away, the cart was jerked completely out of its ruts and came down at an angle so it toppled over, dragged along on its side after the rest of the caravan flaring sparks, and the eggs it had held went spilling, bouncing, tumbling out and down the embankment.

"STOP!" howled Smith, but the keymen had already seen and were manfully braking. The other caravan, meanwhile, had cleared the top of the hill and gone racing on all unmindful. The cargo net fluttered after it like a handkerchief waving good-bye.

As soon as the carts had ground to a halt, Smith slid down from his couch and staggered, groaning as he saw the extent of the damage. Lady Seven Butterflies's holistic containers were bobbing end over end down the hill into the bushes. The cart lay on its side, still disgorging eggs at a slow trickle. Under its wheels one egg had smashed, and lay flattened on the road. Smith hobbled over and picked it up. Fragments of bright glass sifted out, bits of iridescent wing fragile as a dry leaf, colored like a rainbow.

Smith said something unprintable. He slumped against the cart and stared at the wreckage.

Crucible and the other keymen leaped from their seats and came running back to inspect the cart, hauling it upright.

"Watch out for the eggs, you lot!" shouted Mrs. Smith, making her way along the line. "Oh, no, did they break? Bloody hell."

"That's it," muttered Smith. "We broke goods in transit. My cousin will lose Seven Butterflies Studios as a client. Two passengers gone and a client lost! So much for this job."

"Now, now, young Smith, this sort of thing happens all the time," Mrs. Smith told him, but there was a certain awe in her face as she looked around at the devastation. She took out a small flask, uncapped it, helped herself to a good shot of its contents, and passed it to Smith. "Drink up, dear. Despicable Flying Dragon Lines! I saw the way they had those beams loaded. Rampant heedlessness."

"Don't hang yourself yet, Caravan Master," Lord Ermenwyr told him, approaching in a cloud of purple weedsmoke.

"You'll find yourself another job in no time."

"Thanks," said Smith numbly, taking a drink from the flask. The liquor burned his throat pleasantly, with a faint perfume of honey and herbs.

"Let's just get this mess collected, shall we?" said Lord Ermenwyr, peeling off his tailcoat. He draped it over the next-to-last cart and started down the embankment, then turned to look balefully up at the passenger carts. "You! Horrible little children. Get off your infant bottoms and be of some use. We've got to find all of these eggs for the poor caravan master!"

With yells of glee, the three older Smith children jumped from the cart and ran obediently down the embankment to him. Burnbright came running back to help them. They set about hunting through the bushes for the remaining violet eggs, most of which had stopped rolling around by then.

"The wheel assembly's undamaged, sir," Crucible reported. "Both axles sound, but the hitch is wrecked." He held up a hook-and-rod twisted like a stick of Salesh Sweetvine. "We've got spares, of course. We'll just replace it, sir, shall we?"

"Go ahead," said Smith. He had another gulp from Mrs. Smith's flask, watching the children following Lord Ermenwyr about like puppies. He had stripped off his shirt, and they were putting all the eggs they found in it. "This is good stuff. What is it?"

"It's a cordial from the Abbey at Kemeldion," Mrs. Smith informed him. "The Father Abbot's own private receipt. We invented it together, he and I, when we were a good deal younger and less spiritually inclined than we are now." She groped in her pocket for her smoking tube and lit it. "Lovely man. Always sends me a barrel at the holidays. Nothing like it for a restorative when one travels, I find."

"Think it'll stick glass butterflies back together?" Smith wondered. "Maybe if we pray a lot?"

"I suppose it wouldn't hurt to pray. Don't worry, Caravan Master." Mrs. Smith kissed his cheek. She smelled of amber-leaf, and food, and good drink. It was a comforting kind of smell. "Whatever happens, I'll fix you a dish of fried eel when we get to Salesh. You've certainly earned it."

"My cousin won't think so," said Smith morosely, and had another drink as Lord Ermenwyr clambered up the bank toward them, accompanied by the Smith children with their arms full of violet eggs. He carried a great number of eggs in his shirt. His bare skin was pale and fine as a girl's, though he was otherwise quite sinewy and masculine.

"You know, Caravan Master, I don't believe this is quite as bad as we thought at first," he said. "None of these seem to be broken at all."

"So maybe only that one smashed?" Smith felt his mood lifting, or perhaps it was the cordial.

"I saw a man get his foot crushed in a wheel rut in Mount Flame City once, and there was just nothing left of it even to be amputated," said Burnbright encouragingly. "No wonder that one egg broke! I'll bet the rest are fine, though."

"Perhaps it's Lady Seven Butterflies's ballocky holistic packing method saving the day yet again," said Mrs. Smith.

Lord Ermenwyr threw his head back and laughed, in the fox-yipping way he had. Smith felt Mrs. Smith stiffen beside him and catch her breath. He looked at her, but she had turned her head to stare intently at the young man as he emptied his shirtful of eggs into the righted cart. When he had added Burnbright's and the Smith children's contributions, they started back down the embankment again for more, and Smith leaned over and murmured, "What's the matter?"

"Remarkable thing," Mrs. Smith said, more to herself

than to him. She followed Lord Ermenwyr with her eyes as he waded through the bushes, barking orders to the children. "May not be important. I'll tell you later."

⬿

To Smith's immense relief, it turned out that only the egg that had been ground beneath the wheels had broken. The remaining violet eggs, all 143 of them gathered from the embankment, proved to be whole without so much as a crack. The cart was repaired, a spare cargo net tied down over the surviving eggs, and they were on their way again.

⬿

That night at the camp, after the passengers had retired and the fire was beginning to think about settling down to coals, Smith edged over to Mrs. Smith. She sat regarding the autumn stars in silence, sipping a drink. She had been uncharacteristically silent all that evening.

"What did you see today?" Smith inquired in a low voice.

She glanced aside at him. "It had been nagging at me the whole journey, to be perfectly truthful," she told him. "Something about that big strapping wench. Something about that dreadful young man. Rather amazing sense of déjà vu, though I could not, simply could not place what was so familiar. This afternoon it all came back to me."

"What came back to you?"

Before she replied she fished out her smoking tube and packed it expertly, one-handed, and lit it. Exhaling smoke, she said, "It must have been fifteen years ago. I was working for the Golden Chain Line then; they ran the Triangle Route, from Salesh to Port Blackrock to Konen Feyy-in-the-Trees and back to Salesh. So just skirting the Greenlands, you see? Close enough to have that mountain glowering down at us half the trip.

"We took on new passengers in Konen Feyy. A family. Just like the Smiths over there, in a way. Father and mother and a handful of little children, one of them a babe in arms. Bound for Salesh-by-the-Sea, too. But they were quite wealthy, these people. A whole retinue of nurses and servants and bodyguards they had with them. Dozens of trunks! And a private pavilion that was quite outrageously grand.

"They called themselves Silverpoint. He was a big bearded blackavised man, didn't speak much, but you should have seen his servants leap to his least word. And she was—well, she was simply the most beautiful woman anyone in the rest of the caravan had ever seen. She wore a veil, but even so, half the men in the party fell in love with her. Even with a little screaming child on her shoulder the whole way."

"Their baby cried too?"

"Incessantly," Mrs. Smith said, with a grim look across the fire. "Half the night, every night. Until he stopped breathing altogether."

"He died?"

"Nearly. Four or five times, in the course of the journey. I don't know what was the matter with the poor tiny wretch. Perhaps he simply wasn't strong. Sickly, whey-faced little thing with limp curls, he was. Big wide eyes that looked at you as though he knew he wasn't long for this world and was keenly aware of the injustice of it all.

"It was the fifth night out it happened. The child had some sort of fit, turned quite blue, and died. Not a breath in him. Their servants howled like mad things, drew their own knives and started hacking at themselves! The other children woke and started to cry, and their mother reached out a hand to them, but in a distracted sort of way because she was praying, quite calmly you'd think from the look on her face.

"I was awake—half the camp was, with that tumult, but

I'd got up and was coming to see if there was anything to be done. And I tell you I saw the father come running up from wherever he'd been, grab a knife from a servant, shoulder his way into the lady's pavilion, and *cut the throat of his own child.*

"Thought I'd pass out where I was standing. But before I could scream, the baby trembled, kicked its legs and drew in a breath, hideous whistling sound. The mother bent over him and I couldn't see more, but I heard him begin crying in a feeble kind of way. The servants all threw themselves flat on their faces in the dust and began moaning. I backed away, but not before I saw the father come out with that knife in his hand. I shall never forget the look in his black eyes. He didn't say two words, but one of the servants jumped up at once and ran to fetch a basin of water and a box from their trunks.

"She was a tall girl, the servant. Buxom. Hair black as a raven's wing. Splendid-looking creature," said Mrs. Smith, laying emphasis on the word *creature*. "Well. Nothing more to see, as the City Guard are so fond of saying. I crept off to my bed and had nightmares. Next morning the child's as peevish as ever, though a good deal more quiet, picking at the bandage about his bitsy windpipe. Not a word about what had happened from his parents, though the lady did apologize for all the noise.

"We took them to their hotel in Salesh, as per contract. Last I saw of the child he was peering over the servant's shoulder with those big eyes, looking as though he was thinking about throwing another tantrum and winding his little fist in her black hair.

"She hasn't aged a day. A few other details gave her away, as well. I'd bet a month's salary she was hurt fighting off that cat-sending. She's a demoness; and I know of only one man in the world with the power to bind demons reliably.

"The baby's grown, and he goes by the name Kingfisher now; but he's still got the scar on his throat," Mrs. Smith added. "I saw it this afternoon, when he laughed."

"I ought to have kept my shirt on," said a smooth voice from out of the shadows.

Smith jumped. Mrs. Smith set her drink down, and with great care and deliberation drew a pistolbow from inside her coat. It was larger than either of Smith's and, to judge from the size of the gears and the bolt, much more powerful.

"Oh, now, surely there's no need for unpleasantness," said Lord Ermenwyr, stepping into the circle of firelight. "Aren't we all friends here? Aren't we fellow travelers? Have I done anything evil at all?"

"You're the son of the Master of the Mountain," said Mrs. Smith, training the weapon on him. In the dim light of the fire his skin had an unearthly green pallor, for he had dropped the glamour that disguised him. Eyes wide, he held out his open hands.

"Can I help that? Let's be reasonable about this. You've such a remarkable memory, dear Mrs. Smith; can you recall Daddy and Mummy being anything but perfectly law-abiding passengers? I'm sure we even tipped handsomely when we left the caravan."

There was a black mist flowing along the ground, out of the darkness, and it began to swirl behind him in a familiar outline.

"To be sure you did, on that occasion," agreed Mrs. Smith. "But your family has quite a reputation amongst the caravans, and not for generous tips."

"Oh, Daddy hasn't taken a caravan in years," said Lord Ermenwyr. "Really. Mummy made him give it up. I can't vouch for my brothers not engaging in some light raids now and then, one of those stupid masculine rite of passage things I suppose, but they're brutes, and what can one expect?"

Behind him, Balnshik materialized out of the night, regarding Mrs. Smith and Smith with eyes like coals. She too had dropped the glamour. Her skin was like a thundercloud, livid with phantom colors, glorious but hard to look at.

"Put your weapon down," she said.

Mrs. Smith looked at her thoughtfully.

"Certainly, when his lordship gives me his word we'll come to no harm," she replied.

"You have my word, as my father's son, that neither I nor mine will injure you nor compass your death in any way," said Lord Ermenwyr at once. Mrs. Smith laid the pistolbow aside.

"That's the formula," she told Smith. "We should be safe enough. I'm pleased to see you did contrive to grow up after all, my lord."

"Thank you," he replied. "It's been touch-and-go, as you can see, but I've managed." Throwing out his coattails, he sat down cross-legged by the fire and took out his smoking tube. Balnshik remained on her feet, hovering over him watchfully. He continued:

"Just *you* try living the life of a normal young man when people are always lurking about trying to kill you. It's not fair," he said plaintively.

"Correct me if I'm wrong, but aren't you a demon?" inquired Smith.

"Only one-quarter," the lordling explained, angling his smoking tube like a pointer. "Half at most. Daddy was a foundling, you see, so we're not sure. But what does it matter? When all's said and done, I'm not that different from the rest of you. Do you know why we were all going to Salesh on that memorable occasion, Mrs. Smith? Daddy was trying to give us a holiday by the sea. Buckets, spades, sand castles, all that sort of thing."

"Perfectly innocent," said Mrs. Smith with measured irony.

"Well, it was! And Mummy felt the sea air would do me good. We were just like any other family, except for a few things like Daddy's collection of heads and the fact that half the world wants us all dead."

"That was why Flowering Reed was after you," Smith realized. "He knew who you were."

Lord Ermenwyr sighed. "It's not easy being an Abomination. Saints aren't supposed to get married and have children, you see. It's sacrilegious. Anyone who can kill a walking blasphemy like me gains great spiritual merit, I understand. Of course, Flowering Reed disdained to do the job himself; wouldn't get his pure hands dirty. But his hired killers kept failing, thanks to you and the late Parradan Smith being so good at defending us all," he added, looking at Smith with affection.

"Was that why Flowering Reed shot him in the back?"

"Exactly. Nasty little darts. Flowering Reed's people rationalize any guilt away by saying that it's the poison on the thorn doing the killing, not them. Charming, isn't it?"

"But that greenie doctor was quite respectful to you," objected Mrs. Smith. "Even reverent."

"Well, madam, there are greenies and greenies. Flowering Reed belongs to a particularly vicious fundamentalist sect sworn to avenge my mother's, er, sullying, by whatever means necessary." Lord Ermenwyr lit his smoking tube with a small blue fireball and took a deep drag. "Mummy's disciples, on the other hand, were willing to admit that she knew what she was doing when she married Daddy and brought all of us semidevine semidemonic brats into the world." He blew smoke from his nostrils.

"I'm intrigued, young man," said Mrs. Smith. "Are your parents happily married?"

"I suppose so," he replied. "I won't say they haven't had their quarrels, but love conquers all. I believe that was Mummy's point in bedding the old bastard."

"You're being disrespectful, Master," crooned Balnshik, winding her hand into his hair. "You know that's not allowed."

"Ow! All right. Well, anyway—you can see, can't you, that there's no need to be alarmed by my presence in your caravan? All I want is to get to Salesh-by-the-Sea for a nice long stay at the spa, so I can recover what passes for my health," Lord Ermenwyr assured them.

"Your father's supposed to be the most powerful mage who ever lived," said Smith. "Can't he just magick you well?"

"My mother can heal the sick and raise the dead, but nothing she tries works on me either," retorted Lord Ermenwyr. He yelped in protest as Balnshik got a grip on his collar and hauled him to his feet.

"My master has the blood of two planes fighting in his heart," she told them. "It makes him unstable. Unreasonable. Rude. But there are advantages to being under his protection, dear Children of the Sun, and dreadful disadvantages to harming the least hair on his wicked little head. You understand, don't you?"

"Don't mind the death threats," Lord Ermenwyr told them. "It's her job to protect me. I'm sure you'd never do anything so stupid as to betray me to my enemies."

"No," said Smith hastily.

"I won't, either. But I shall refrain from doing so because I find the idea of your parents' love match rather sweet (*somebody* ought to have a happy marriage now and then) and not"—Mrs. Smith looked up severely at Balnshik—"because of your threats, my girl."

Balnshik smiled, showing all her gleaming teeth.

"Lady, I am seven thousand years old," she said.

"Well, I *feel* seven thousand years old," Mrs. Smith replied. "Let's leave it at that, shall we, and remain friends all around?"

"You are as wise as you are skilled in the arts of cuisine," Lord Ermenwyr assured her. "You won't regret it. And now, will you excuse me? The night damps are settling in. Terrible for the lungs, you know."

"Bid them good night, Master," said Balnshik, dragging him off.

"Bye-bye!" he called, waving his smoking tube at them.

Smith sagged backward, shaking.

"What the hell do we do now?" he murmured.

"Oh, we'll be quite safe," Mrs. Smith said, picking up her drink. "As long as we keep our mouths shut. I know demons."

～

And after all nothing had changed. Next morning both Lord Ermenwyr and Balnshik had resumed their ordinary appearance and made no reference whatever to the previous night's conversation. Breakfast was served, camp was broken, the carts got back on the road again as usual. It was so mundane that Smith, resuming his couch on the flour bags, wondered if he hadn't had a bizarre nightmare.

That day they came down out of the Greenlands at last, onto the plain. The caravan seemed to skim like a bird, speeding along the flat miles. They began to spot other cities lifting towers above secure walls, other roads crossing the distance and even intersecting their road, and now and then they passed caravans bound for regions unknown or dull merchants' carts rattling along. The Smith children waved and shrieked happily at them all. Mile after mile fell away, and every mile brought nearer the gray hills of Salesh-by-the-Sea, the only interruption of the expanding steel horizon.

They spent one last night at a way station, though it was so palatial it scarcely seemed to fit the name. There was a shop there selling sweets and fruit, biscuits and wine; there were all of three stone watering huts (no waiting!); there was even a booth with a scribe who would, for a price, copy out a map of your immediate destination, guaranteed to be accurate for any city precinct. In the dark the wind shifted and brought them the strong rank salt smell of the tides. Smith felt as though he had come home.

⤶

Salesh, like most cities on the sea, had only a half circle of city wall, a high curve of white flints at its back that gleamed in the sun like a shell mound, when the dense fogs now and then parted to let any sun through. There the resemblance to anything so formless as a mound stopped, however, for the wall was neatly laid with mile-castles along its top, patrolled by watchmen whose armor was enameled in a pattern like fish scales. Within the wall the city was laid out in a fan of long streets, each terminating on the seafront.

The city gate was standing wide when they arrived, and Burnbright trumpeted their arrival with glee, pausing only to flash the license and manifest at the city guard. As soon as they were waved through she leaped into the lead cart next to Pinion and flung both her fists toward the sky.

"We made it," she shouted, dancing. "We're safe! I'm great, I'm the fastest runner in the world, and Mount Flame City rules!"

"Oh, sit down and watch your mouth," said Pinion, but he was grinning too. He steered them down the long hill in splendor, riding the brakes, and the iron wheels shot sparks like a fireworks display celebrating their arrival. Expertly he took them around the sharp turn at Capstan Street, and they rocketed into the vast echoing hall of the Salesh-by-the-Sea caravan depot.

It was crowded and very loud, for another caravan had arrived just before them. Porters were lined up along the arcades, displaying their muscles as they awaited employment. The runners had taken an entire arcade for themselves and sat or leaned there, gossiping together, a blaze of scarlet uniform in the shadows. Clerks worked their way along the line of carts with manifest checklists, recording the arrival of goods and overseeing their unloading. Smith slid hastily from the flour bags and turned to collide with the Smiths and their baby.

"Well, here we are at last," he said.

"At last," Mr. Smith agreed. "And I must say I—Children! Come back here right now! I must say I've never beheld such personal bravery in a caravan master. Both my sons have told me they want to be just like you when they grow up, isn't that right, boys?"

"No," said the smaller of the boys. "He gets hurt all the time."

"That man is stealing our trunks!" screamed the little girl.

"No, no, that's our porter! Meefa, stop kicking the nice man! I—will you excuse us? Thank you so much," said Mr. Smith, and hastened away. Just beyond him, Mr. Amook was shouldering his one bag. He slipped off into the crowd and disappeared.

"Safe haven at last, eh?" said Lord Ermenwyr, emerging from his palanquin and yawning. "Good old Salesh-by-the-Sea. What memories of innocent childhood! Burying one's brothers in the sand. Watching all the nude bathers. How I used to love toddling up to pat their bottoms! You can get away with it when you're three," he added ruefully.

"Master, the porters are here," announced Balnshik,

swaying up at the head of a line of massive fellows who followed her with stunned expressions.

"Right. You! Four of you on the palanquin poles, all the same height, please, and if you can get me to the spa without making me motion sick you'll get a bonus. Mind those trunks! Now, Caravan Master," Lord Ermenwyr said, turning back to Smith. "Here's for your efforts in the line of duty." He took Smith's hand and set a purse in it, quite a heavy purse for its size. Then he leaned close and spoke in an undertone. "For your efforts beyond the call of duty, will you come be my guest at the spa tonight? Dinner, drinks, and general fun. Eh? Nursie would still like to thank you personally, you know." He elbowed Smith meaningfully.

"Honor on your house, my lord," said Smith. Lord Ermenwyr hooted in derision.

"Talk about impossibilities! I should tell you about the time—"

"Master, we don't want to keep the gentlemen waiting," said Balnshik. She caught him by his collar and the seat of his trousers and forcibly assisted him up into the palanquin, which had been hoisted onto the shoulders of four stolid porters. Having shoved him inside and closed the curtain on him, she turned to Smith with a dazzling smile. "Do come tonight, please."

"Yes, ma'am," Smith stammered.

"Until this evening, then," she said, and, turning to the porters, she ordered them follow her in a voice that lashed like a whip, and strode from the caravan depot, breasts jutting arrogantly. They followed her, needless to say.

Smith stared after her until his attention was pulled away by a clerk approaching him.

"Caravan Master"—the clerk peered over his spectacles at the manifest—"Smith? What's this I hear about damaged goods?"

"It's only one unit of one consignment," Smith explained. "The flour and the mineral pigments are fine."

"Yes, they're already claimed. But the shipment to Lady Katmile?"

"There was an accident," said Smith, sweating slightly as he turned and rummaged in his pack for the broken egg. "Minor collision. Not our fault. Just this one, see? But all the others are intact!" He waved at the 143 violet eggs reposing under their cargo net.

"Eggs?" The clerk frowned. "Most irregular. Who on earth authorized packing containers like that?"

"The sender, if you must know," said Mrs. Smith, bustling up to Smith's rescue. "All her own design. We hadn't a thing to do with it. Bloody nuisance the whole trip. She's lucky it's only the one!"

"We were attacked a lot, sir," Smith told the clerk. The clerk's eyes widened behind his spectacles, which magnified the expression freakishly.

"You'd better fill out an Assault, Damage and Loss form," he said.

"He's going to get off his feet and have a drink first," stated Mrs. Smith, linking her arm through Smith's. Behind her, the keymen and Burnbright assembled themselves to glare at the clerk. "Aren't you, Caravan Master? Anybody wants to see us, we'll be in the Stripped Gear over there." She pointed to a dark doorway set invitingly at the back of an arcade.

"That's right," said Crucible. "This is a wounded man, you know."

"And if he dies, there'll be all kinds of trouble, because he's the owner's cousin," said Burnbright, pushing forward assertively. "So there."

"Come along, boys," said Mrs. Smith, and, towing Smith after her, she made for the Stripped Gear, with Burnbright and the keymen flanking them. "You'll like this.

Charming little watering hole for the trade. Doesn't try to foist one off with plonk, and, moreover, rents rooms quite inexpensively."

"And we get our own bloody palanquin," said Burn-bright, which made no sense at all to Smith until they got through the dark doorway and he saw the rows of booths built to resemble big palanquins, complete with curtains and thickly padded seats. Apart from that bit of theatrics, the Stripped Gear was just what a bar should be: cozy, dark but not too dark to spot an attacker, crowded but not too loud for conversation. Smith felt his spirits rising as the keymen vaulted into the booth one after another and pulled him in after them. Mrs. Smith and Burnbright followed.

"My treat," he said.

"No, no; at least, not the first round," admonished Mrs. Smith. "Pray, allow us. We're really quite pleased with you, Caravan Master, aren't we, boys?"

They keymen all chorused agreement.

"Coming on at the last minute like you did after poor old Smelterman took that bolt," said Pinion.

"Considering it was your first time and all," agreed one of the other Smiths.

"I had my doubts, but you held up," said Crucible. "You're no coward, I'll say that for you."

"And a good man in a fight, too," said Bellows.

"I never saw anybody bleed the way you did and live," offered Burnbright. At that moment the publican came up.

"Mrs. Smith! Charmed to see you again," he said, bowing. She extended a regal hand, and he kissed it.

"Delighted to have returned, Mr. Socket. Six of your best Salesh Ambers for the gentlemen, a peach milk for the young lady, and I shall have a dry Storm Force Nine with a twist," she said. "Later we'll need to inquire regarding suitable accommodations for the night."

He hurried away, and after a pleasantly short interval returned with their order. When he had departed, Burnbright held up her peach milk. "Here's to our caravan master," she yelled, hammering on the table with her little fist. "Death to our enemies!" They all clinked glasses and drank.

"I have dreamed of this moment," said Mrs. Smith, lighting her smoking tube and filling the booth with amberleaf fumes at once. "I shall take in a show along the Glittering Mile."

"I'm off to the Winking Tit," said Crucible, and the other keymen nodded in emphatic unison.

"Are there any places like that for ladies?" Burnbright asked.

"Not at your age, you silly thing," said Mrs. Smith. "What you'll need to do is get yourself over to the local mother house to clock in your mileage. You should be very nearly certified by now. What will you do, Caravan Master?"

Smith had been thinking in bemusement about the Winking Tit, but roused himself, and said, "I've got something I have to deliver, so I guess I'll do that first. Tonight I'm supposed to go see Lord Ermenwyr where he's staying."

"And Nurse Balnshik too?" Pinion dug him in the ribs.

"You'd better order up some oysters," chortled Bellows.

"You know what you really ought to do first," said Mrs. Smith, pointing at the disk Smith wore about his neck, "is go over to the baths in Anchor Street and redeem that thing the greenie doctor gave you. You'll feel much better afterward, fit for the lists of love or whatever you get up to after dark."

"That's a good idea," agreed Smith, thinking of hot water and clean towels. "I've still got Troon dust places I don't want to think about."

"It's awfully hard to get it out of your ears," said Burnbright seriously.

At this moment Smith glanced over and saw that the clerk

had come into the bar with another person, and was staring about. He spotted Smith and the others and pointed, and the other person followed his gesture. Then she started toward Smith, and her attractive countenance was made less appealing by her expression of murderous rage.

"Uh—" said Smith.

"Caravan master! Can you sit and brazenly drink after such perfidy?" she hissed at him. Everyone in the booth drew back from her. She was clearly wealthy, with embroidered robes. Her hair was done up in an elaborate chignon held in place by jeweled pins. One expected to see her palanquin shopping or in a stage box at the theater, but certainly not leaning into a booth in the Stripped Gear, let alone with the veins in her neck standing out like that.

"Lady Katmile of Silver Anvil House?" guessed Smith. "Look, it was only one butterfly. Accidents happen and—"

"If it were only one!" she cried, and the clerk wrung his hands.

"Damage more extensive than reported," he said. "Contents examined with certified witness present. Every egg opened contained broken merchandise. Estimate fully half shipment in unacceptable condition."

"What d'you mean, damage?" shouted Mrs. Smith. "None of the damned things had so much as a crack in 'em, except the one we squashed!"

"Outer casings intact," admitted the clerk. "But inside—"

"What did you do, play handball with them?" demanded Lady Katmile. Smith closed his eyes, remembering Balnshik kicking violet eggs from her path as she ran, remembering Lord Ermenwyr juggling with them, remembering them bouncing down the high embankment. He said something profane.

Lady Katmile reared back like a snake about to strike.

"You wantonly destroy irreplaceable works of art, and

you have the insolence to use that kind of language too?" she said. "Well. This matter goes to the Transport Authorities, Caravan Master, do you understand me? I'll have your certification. I'll have the certifications of your underlings. I'll have your owner's house and lands and movable chattel. No fiend of the desert has thirst great enough to drink dry the sea of your debt!"

She turned and swept out, drawing her furred cape about her. The clerk lingered long enough to shake his finger at them menacingly. He muttered, "Complaint will be filed immediately," and scurried after Lady Katmile.

Stunned silence at the table for a long moment.

"Did she mean she was going to get *us* sacked too?" said Bellows at last.

"That's what she said," Smith told him.

"But—she can't do that. We've got a union!" he said.

"It won't do you any good if she has your keyman's certification canceled," said Smith. "Or my cousin goes out of business. Both of which seem pretty likely right now."

"I never even got my certification," Burnbright squeaked, and began to cry. She fell over against Mrs. Smith, who stared into the palpable gloom.

"Damn them all," she said at last. "I was planning on retiring soon anyway. May as well do it here. I've set aside a little money. Perhaps I'll open a hotel. Don't despair, boys. We'll think of something."

"Could you use a message runner?" asked Burnbright, wiping her nose on her sleeve.

"Perhaps. They're going to be hardest on you, young Smith." Mrs. Smith turned to him. "I'm sorry."

"It's not so bad," said Smith, still numb with shock. "It's not like I've got any money anyway. I can just disappear again."

"Again?" Crucible lifted his head from the table.

"It's a long story," Smith said. An idea occurred to him. "Look. Parradan Smith gave me something I was supposed to deliver for him—"

"We have been carrying around gangster loot, haven't we?" Burnbright looked awed.

"I might get a reward. If I do, you can have it for opening your hotel. Less whatever I need to buy a ticket to—to wherever I'm going next," said Smith.

"That's extraordinarily good of you," said Mrs. Smith quietly, tipping ash.

"Aw, Nine Hells," said Crucible. "Why is it the best caravan masters either die or leave the business?"

Smith remembered the purse Lord Ermenwyr had given him and pulled it out. "Here. I'll go make that delivery. You get us rooms with this, get our stuff out of the carts and stowed away before the Transport Authorities seize it all. I'll be back tonight after I visit his lordship."

"Maybe he'll help us too!" said Burnbright.

"Never count on a favor from the great, child," said Mrs. Smith. She drew the pouch toward her and squinted into it. "Even if they are remarkably generous. Well! We are resolute. I'll just step over and have a word with dear Mr. Socket. Boys, leap hence to secure what is ours. Burnbright, stay here and blow your nose, for heaven's sake."

She stood ponderously in the booth. "And you, young Smith. If you're able to rejoin us, there's a back door to the lodgings here on Fish Street, seldom watched after dark. If circumstance dictates otherwise—" She leaned forward and patted his cheek. "I'll make good on that fried eel dinner sometime or other. Go now, dear."

⌒

Having taken Parradan Smith's instrument case, Smith asked one of the porters where he might find the villa of

Lord Kashban Beatbrass. Upon discovering that it was at the residential end of Anchor Street, he crossed over a block and descended the long hill. He could look down on the roofs of the grand town houses, almost see into their private gardens, though around him was all the windy bustle of the poor end of the street. Fry vendors with their carts shouted their wares, beggars hobbled or rolled along bearing signs listing famous sea battles in which they'd lost various body parts, shabby-looking men went in and out of lodging houses and ship's chandlers'.

The sea gleamed out beyond all his misery, under a band of middle air clear of fog. White sails moved on the horizon, making for Port Ward'b across the bay. Smith reflected that he'd probably head that way himself in the morning and sign on to a ship, preferably one about to leave on an extended voyage, under a new assumed name. Flint? Stoker? Ironboot?

An icy wind hit him, piercing his worn clothes, making his wounds ache, and fluttering before his eyes a green poppysilk banner. He peered at the writing on it. Yendri characters, advertising something.

Turning, he saw the shop flying the banner bore a large sign with the word BATHS. He groped and found the clay disk on its cord inside his shirt.

"Might as well," he told himself, and went in.

The warm air hit him like a blast from a furnace, but it felt heavenly, rich with steam and Yendri perfumes that made him think of wild forest girls who wouldn't keep their clothes on. Smith could hear a fountain tinkling somewhere and the splash of water echoing on tile. He made his way to the counter, which was almost hidden behind hanging pots of ferns and bromeliads. A Yendri in a white robe leaned at the counter, reading a city broadside. He did not look up as he inquired, "You have come for a bath, sir?"

"Actually—" Smith pulled the clay disk off over his head. "I'm supposed to find Levendyloy Alder and ask for, uh, detoxification. The full treatment." He held out the disk. The Yendri looked up and focused on him intently.

"I am Alder," he informed Smith. "You have been ill? You have been, hm, wounded." He leaned over and took the disk. He passed it under his nostrils and scowled. "Poisoned. Hm. Please. Come inside."

He led Smith behind the counter into a changing room with shelves. "Your clothes and belongings in there," he said. He vanished behind a curtain as Smith stripped down and filled a shelf, setting all his knives in his right boot and resting Parradan Smith's case on top of the pile with great care. Peeling off his bandages too, he considered his battered body and sighed. *One of these days*, he told himself, *I won't be able to run fast enough*.

When the Yendri returned, he was carrying a teapot and small cup. "This way," he said, gesturing with the cup, and Smith followed him through the curtain and into a tiled corridor. They passed arched entrances to rooms with hot and cold pools, where other people swam or lounged in the water and talked. The Yendri led him to a room with a heavy door, handed him the teapot and cup, and worked the valve lock that opened the door. Steam billowed out, hot enough to make the hall seem chilly by comparison. Smith peered in and caught a glimpse of boulders and swirling water.

"Go in," said the Yendri, "Sit, and drink the tea. All of it, as quickly as you can. It will cleanse you. In an hour I will bring you out."

"All right," said Smith, and stepped in cautiously. The door closed behind him, and in a moment the air cleared enough for him to see that the room was tank-shaped, with a drain at the bottom. Water gushed from a tap in the ceiling and streamed down the rock walls, which radiated intense heat, and splattered and swirled off the boulders before finally cycling down the drain. There was one curved stone seat, awkward to sit on.

"Drink the tea," said a disembodied voice. Smith looked up and saw a grate in the wall, high up. He could just discern the Yendri's face behind it.

"You're going to watch me?" he asked.

"Sometimes your people faint," the Yendri replied. "The tea, please."

"All right." Smith sipped it grudgingly, but found it surprisingly good, hot and spicy. He drank it all and only when he had emptied the teapot did he notice the aftertaste.

"This isn't a purge, is it?" he asked.

"Yes," the Yendri replied. Smith groaned.

In the next hour a great deal of nasty stuff went down the drain, including a couple of old tattoos, exuding from his frantic skin like black syrup. Smith saw dirt from every place he'd ever lived coming to the surface, the yellow dust of Troon, the red dust of Mount Flame City, some gray residue he didn't want to think about. Occasionally jets of hot water shot from the ceiling, flooding the filth down the drain and almost washing Smith away with it. He clung to the stone perch and cursed the Yendri steadily. The Yendri watched him, impassive; and at the end of the hour shut off the water and came to let Smith out.

Smith had planned to throttle him the minute he could reach him, but collapsed on him instead. He let the Yendri support him back down the hall to a room with a tepid pool. The Yendri toppled him in and told him to swim. Smith decided to drown, but found to his astonishment that his strength was returning, and with it an extraordinary sense of well-being. After he had splashed about a while a pair of hulking bath attendants came to haul him out, slap him with cold towels, and make him drink a lot of plain water.

They led him at last to a massage chamber, where he was soaped and rinsed and oiled and kneaded. Then they applied fresh bandages to his wounds.

By that time Smith felt wonderful and no longer wanted to kill anybody. This made the events of the next few moments all the more unfortunate.

When the attendants had done with him, they indicated he should dress himself again. He floated out to the changing room, seemingly ten years younger than he had been when he left it.

A bulky man in very fine clothes was removing them in there, and three other men stood attendance on him, taking his garments one by one and folding them with care. Smith nodded as he passed them and went to his shelf. It didn't occur to him until his hand was on his clothes that he knew one of the men. Apparently it occurred to the other man at the same moment.

Smith heard the muttered exclamation and grabbed frantically in his right boot. He turned with a knife in his hand in time to see the other man advancing on him, drawing a blade fully ten inches long.

"This is for my cousins, you pig," snarled the man, preparing to slash at Smith. Before he could do so, however, Smith acted without thinking and threw his little knife.

Acting without thinking was something he generally did under circumstances such as the one in which he presently found himself. The details of circumstance might vary, but the result was always the same: a corpse at his feet and a great deal of trouble.

He looked down now at the body that had his knife hilt protruding from its left eye socket, then looked at the other three men. Was that his heartbeat echoing off the tiled walls? The fight had taken place in almost complete silence.

"I'm sorry," he gasped. "I'm dead, aren't I?"

The bulky man nodded, staring at him with mild amazement. "Nice work, though," he said. "Striker was one of my best." He gestured, and his remaining vassals seized Smith, and forced him to his knees. He turned to draw a blade from his clothes. Smith spotted a tattoo on his bare back.

"You're a Bloodfire," he stammered. "You wouldn't be Lord Kashban Beatbrass, by any chance?"

"I am," the lord replied, turning with a curved ceremonial blade.

"I've got something of yours!"

"And I'll have something of yours in a minute." Lord Kashban grabbed him by the hair.

"No! Listen," cried Smith, and hurriedly explained what had happened to Parradan Smith.

"That's his case on the shelf," he said, tilting his head in its direction with some difficulty. "I promised him I'd deliver it to you. He said you'd pay well. I was on my way to your house, I swear."

The lord paused, looking thoughtful. He got the case down from the shelf and opened it. Lord Tinwick's cup gleamed at him. He lifted it out, examined it, checked the inscription on the base.

"What did you do with Parradan's body?" he inquired.

"It's in a stone cairn on the north side of the road from Troon, about two days' journey from the Red House up there," said Smith.

"All right," said Lord Kashban. He looked down at Smith, studying him. "You worked in Port Chadravac for a while, didn't you? Weren't you one of the Throatcutters?"

"Not exactly," said Smith miserably. "I was sort of a consultant for them. A specialist."

"Yes, you were," the lord agreed, and awe came into his

face, though his voice remained level and quiet. "Artist is more like it. Nine Hells! *Nobody* ever saw you coming. They said you could vanish out of a locked room. What are you doing running from anyone?"

"I didn't want to do it anymore," Smith explained. "Just because a man's good at something doesn't mean he enjoys it."

Lord Kashban shook his head. "Unbelievable. All right; Parradan said I'd reward you, so I will. You have your life. Let him go," he told his men, who dropped Smith's arms at once.

"Honor on your house," said Smith, staggering to his feet. He grabbed his clothes and pulled them on.

"What do we do about Striker, my lord?" one of the men wanted to know.

"What do we do about Striker?" Lord Kashban pulled at his lip. "Good question. I've lost a good man. All right, wrap a towel around his head and carry him out to the palanquin. Tell the greenie he's sick. We'll give him a nice funeral in the garden tonight. You." He looked at Smith. "Had enough of retirement yet? Getting a little tired of looking threadbare? It pains me to see a man of your talents in the gutter. You could come work for me."

"You do me tremendous honor, my lord," said Smith, feeling his heart sink. "Though I have some other problems I have to take care of, and I don't—"

"Understandable," said Lord Kashban, making a dismissive gesture. "You don't have to decide right now. But you think about it, understand? And come talk to me when you're ready. You know where I live.

"Here," he said, turning to his men, who had slung Striker's corpse between them and were preparing to take it out. He dropped the case with Lord Tinwick's cup on Striker's chest. "Take that home, too, and lock it up. I'm going to have a massage."

Smith pulled on his coat hurriedly and exited first. He walked quickly through the outer room, with the two that carried the dead man close behind him, and the Yendri turned to look at them. His eyes widened but he made no sound; only shook his head sadly as they stepped out into the street.

Not caring to watch the body being stowed away in Lord Kashban's palanquin, Smith faded into the crowd and put some distance between himself and the bathhouse. It was getting dark, just the blue time of twilight he had always found comforting, and yellow lamps were being lit in every street and along the seafront. He found little to comfort him now, however.

He hated to think that he would have to accept Lord Kashban's offer, but it was the answer to his current predicament. He'd be able to stop running, he'd have protection from the law. He'd have money. More than enough to compensate Mrs. Smith and the others for the loss of their jobs. All he'd have to do was kill people, though he had promised himself he'd never earn his living that way again.

Not that there was any societal stigma involved in professional killing, at least among the Children of the Sun. Murder in the cause of a blood feud was honorable, and murder in the service of one's sworn lord a sure way for a bright young person to advance. Other races had difficulty understanding this cultural tradition, though one crabbed Yendri philosopher had advanced the opinion that, since the Children of the Sun seemed incapable of practicing any form of birth control, perhaps it was best to let them indulge their need to slaughter themselves as a means of keeping their population at manageable levels.

Smith respected tradition as much as the next man. He just didn't like to kill.

But it was what he was best at, and he had no other options that he could see.

Other than a dinner date with demons.

◞

He had nearly reached the bottom of the hill, and was in the neighborhood of the grand hotels, the gracious private houses fronting on the sea. Cold waves boomed on the empty beach, but along the Glittering Mile it might have been summer, so many lights were lit, so many well-dressed people were out and promenading on the seafront or being jogged from one fashionable address to another in open palanquins.

Smith hurried through them with his ragged coat collar turned up, looking for the spa. It was easy to find: it covered several square blocks. Everything was on a grand scale, with a lot of white marble and soaring columns and domes. The main entry hall was lit with barrel-sized lanterns brilliant enough to have guided ships at sea, and Smith felt dreadfully conspicuous as he scuttled in out of the night. The desk clerk stared at him in disbelief.

Fortunately, however, he was expected, and so the clerk led him out through the scented gardens to the grandest suite in the complex. It looked like a temple from the outside. It looked like a temple from the inside, too, as Smith was to discover.

"It's our old friend the caravan master, Nursie," Lord Ermenwyr yowled in delight, flinging the vast double doors wide. The clerk paled and vanished into the night. Lord Ermenwyr was stark naked except for a flapping dressing gown of purple brocade and what appeared to be a pair of women's underpants on his head. His smoking tube was clenched in a ferocious grin, and his pupils were tiny. Behind him, a prostitute was attempting to depart discreetly, in evident distress at lacking a certain item of her attire.

"Welcome, Caravan Master!" The lordling flung his arms around Smith. "My, you smell a *lot* better. Come in, it's a catered affair, don't you know! Lots of lovely excess. What?" he snapped at the girl, who had timidly pulled at his elbow. "Oh, you've no sense of romance at all."

He yanked off the underpants and handed them to her, then turned with aplomb and took Smith's arm in his, towing him from the hall. "Look at it all," he said, waving a hand at the vaulted ceiling with its mural of fluttering cherubs. "Pretty grand after all those nights of wretched wilderness, eh? Of course, a Yendri would purse his sanctimonious lips and say the glorious immensity of the stars was a far more splendid canopy for one's repose, but you know what I say to that?" He blew a juicy raspberry. "Oh, I love, love, *love* decadent luxuries! Look at this!"

Dropping Smith's arm he ran to the immense canopied bed and hurled himself into the middle of the scarlet brocade counterpane, where he began to leap up and down. The canopy was a good fifteen feet in the air, held aloft on a gilded finial, so he ran no risk of bouncing into it.

"I—despise—Nature," he panted. "Whoopee!"

"Master, did you pay that poor girl?" Balnshik came into the room, attired in a white robe demurely tied shut. "You've left the door open, darling. Hello, Smith." She turned and caught his head in both her hands, giving him a kiss that left his knees weak. "Don't mind him. He's overexcited. You haven't even offered him a drink, have you, you little beast?"

"Eeek! What was I thinking?" Lord Ermenwyr scrambled down and raced into the next room, reappearing a moment later with a bottle and a glass. "Here you go, Smith. This cost an awful lot of money. You're sure to like it." He poured a glass and offered it to Smith with a deep bow.

"Thank you," said Smith. Behind him he heard Balnshik slam and bolt the great doors, and realized that it was far too late to run. *What the hell*, he thought, and sampled the wine. It was sparkling and tasted like stars. Lord Ermenwyr drank from the bottle.

"Mm, good. Come on, let's dine," he said, and pulled Smith into the next room.

"Oh," said Smith, starting forward involuntarily. He hadn't eaten in hours and was abruptly aware of it at the sight of the feast laid out on the table. There were a couple of huge roasts, a hen, oysters, a whole baked fish in wine sauce, various covered tureens, hot breads and butter in several colors, more bottles, a pyramid of ripe fruit and another of cream buns and meringues, as well as a large cake sulking in a pool of liqueur. As is usual for feasts, candied kumquats and cherries decorated nearly everything.

"Room service," said Lord Ermenwyr dreamily, lifting the lid on a tureen. "Floating islands! My favorite. Don't stand on ceremony, Smith." He plunged his face into the tureen, only to be collared and dragged back by Balnshik.

"Sit down and put your napkin on, Master," she ordered. "Look at you, you've got meringue in your beard. Simply disgusting. Please be seated, dear Smith, and pay no attention to his lordship. I shall serve."

And this she proceeded to do, carving the meats and arranging a plate for Smith with the best of everything, the most prime cuts, the most melting fruit, ignoring Lord Ermenwyr as he happily drank custard sauce straight out of the tureen. Then she loaded a plate for herself, filled Smith's wineglass and her own, and sat down tête-à-tête with him as though they were alone.

"You followed that doctor's advice, I note, and were detoxified," Balnshik said, shaking out her napkin. "Quite a good idea. It's a nasty poison on those little darts, just like its inventors. Devious. Lurking. It can lie dormant in the flesh, even if one is treated with an antidote, and leap out into the blood unexpectedly later on."

"So—excuse me for asking, but—you really are a nurse, then," Smith said, trying not speak with his mouth full.

"Well, I know a great deal about death," she admitted. "That helps, you see."

"Hey! He can't pay no attention to me," protested Lord Ermenwyr belatedly, lifting his dripping beard from the tureen. "He's my guest."

"It's the other way around, darling," Balnshik informed him. "You're supposed to pay attention to him."

"Oh. How's the food, Caravan Master?"

"Wonderful, thanks," said Smith earnestly.

"You should see what we have for the orgy afterward." Lord Ermenwyr giggled. "Salesh Primo Pinkweed. What fun!" He stuck his head in the tureen again.

"I really must apologize for his lordship's manners," said Balnshik. "It's a reaction. The journey was quite stressful for him."

"I guess we're all lucky to be alive," said Smith. "Have those people tried to get him before?"

"Mm." She nodded, taking a sip of her wine. "But seldom so persistently. His lord father had no idea they'd have the audacity to make an attempt within sight of his own house. There are probably going to be some rather horrible reprisals. Whatever my master may say, his lord father loves him."

"Are the rest of the children like that?"

"No, fortunately." Balnshik looked amused. "My master is unique."

Lord Ermenwyr fell off his chair with a crash.

"Excuse me a moment, won't you?" Balnshik requested, and, rising, she fetched a cushion and tucked it under the lordling's head where he lay unconscious. She took the tureen from his hands and set it back on the table.

"Is he all right?" asked Smith, alarmed.

"It's just the sugar hitting the drugs. He'll sleep for half an hour, then he'll be up and bouncing around again," Balnshik said offhandedly, sitting back down and picking up a chop bone, which she proceeded to gnaw with unsettling efficiency. Smith noticed that there was nothing on her plate but meat, all of it blood-rare.

"Uh . . . I don't mean to be rude, but . . . young as he is, and sick as he is, why was he sent to Troon in the first place?" Smith inquired. "Shouldn't he be kept at home?"

Balnshik rolled her eyes.

"A joke got out of hand. One of his brothers and several of his sisters tried to kill him. Not very hard, you understand, but enough to cause terrible conflicts in the servants' hall. When you are bound by oath to slaughter any who attack one of his lord father's getting, and then the wretched little gets attack each other—well, what are you to do? It plays havoc with the semantics of one's geas. Very inconsiderate of them, and their lady mother"—Balnshik bowed involuntarily—"told them so, too. We were all very grateful.

"In any case, his lord father thought the responsibility of a diplomatic mission would be good for him. My master managed the business very well, but once he'd done what he was sent for he became bored." She glanced over at him in affectionate contempt. "He got into trouble, then he got sick. But, not being allowed home just yet, he was sent here."

Smith felt a wave of sympathy for the lordling. "It's hell not being able to go home. They ought to reconsider."

"It'll all blow over in time." Balnshik shrugged. "And he loves Salesh-by-the-Sea. So much to do here."

"That's good anyway," said Smith. "Should he really have all the drink and drugs and sex he wants, though? Maybe his problem is that he's been spoiled."

"That, and repeatedly raised from the dead," Balnshik replied. "You have no idea how difficult that makes instilling proper values in a child."

They ate for a while in silence. Despite its vast size, the dining room was warm, and Balnshik's robe didn't do much to conceal her bosom when she leaned forward. His other appetites having been handsomely assuaged, Smith found himself contemplating matters of the flesh.

If he thought too hard about who and what she was, his brain began to gibber and tell him to finish his wine, thank her, and leave with all possible speed. He found that he could ignore his brain if he gazed into her eyes and let her refill his wineglass. After the third glass his brain had stopped gibbering and lay in a quiet stupor in the back of his head, which suited him fine.

"Mmm." Balnshik pushed aside her plate, stretched luxuriously, and rose to her feet, smiling down at Smith. "I seem to recall making you a promise, Caravan Master. Shall we retire to the adjoining chamber? I'd love to see if you're a master at other jobs."

"That's right, the orgy!" cried Lord Ermenwyr, sitting up abruptly. He staggered to his feet, grabbed a bottle from the table, and lurched off into the adjoining chamber. Balnshik and Smith followed him. Smith paused to stare.

This was the private Temple of Health offered in every suite, as promised in the spa's brochures. It was an oval room with a domed ceiling of glass, through which the stars burned distantly. More white marble columns held up the dome, and between them tall stained-glass windows stood dark and opaque, except when someone passed through the garden beyond carrying a lantern. In the center a blue pool glimmered softly, giving off a fine vapor of sulfurous steam.

To counteract the smell, censers were suspended here and there from the lamps, sending up long blue trails of perfumed smoke. All the steam and sweetness made it unlikely anyone would feel like using the exercise equipment that was dutifully set up on the far side of the pool. On the near side, the shallow end, were piled silken cushions, and a water pipe was set up beside them.

"Hey nonny no!" Lord Ermenwyr writhed out of his robe and plunged into the pool. "Light the hubblebubble, Nursie dearest."

"Light it yourself," ordered Balnshik, turning to Smith with an expression of radiant tenderness and opening his shirt. "I have a reward to bestow, you ungrateful little sot."

"To be sure, you do," Lord Ermenwyr replied, leering, and leaned up out of the water and lit the pipe with another blue fireball.

Smith was self-conscious about his various cuts, but once Balnshik threw off her robe he utterly forgot about his own body. They joined Lord Ermenwyr in the pool and shared the water pipe with him. After that things became somewhat confusing, but quite pleasant if one wasn't easily shocked.

Lord Ermenwyr swiftly became so intoxicated he was in danger of drowning, but refused to leave the pool for the silk cushions. Instead he yelled an incantation, and from the suddenly roiling water a swim bladder emerged, of the whimsical sort generally provided for children. Instead of being a swan or seahorse, however, it was a mermaid with immense pneumatic breasts. He clambered into her embrace and bobbed about for a while making rude remarks until he passed out, tethered to the side only by the umbilical cord of the water pipe's hose clutched in his fist.

"Now then, my lovely Smith," whispered Balnshik, gliding with him to the far end of the pool. She wound her arms around him and kissed him, and they plummeted to the bottom of the pool in a long embrace. Smith could have happily drowned then, but she bore him to the surface again and set him against the coping.

"Just you lean there, darling, rest your arms," she told him. She kissed his throat, kissed his chest, kissed her way down to the waterline. Then she went below the waterline.

Moaning happily, he leaned his head back and closed his eyes. In addition to Balnshik's other talents, she was evidently able to breathe underwater.

Though not to hear underwater, apparently; which was why Smith was the only one to notice the struggle taking place outside the nearest stained-glass window.

Dragging his attention back from sweet delight with profound reluctance, he opened his eyes. Yes. Even stoned as he was, he could tell that was unmistakably a fight out there. Blade clanging on blade, scuffling boots, a muffled curse. He was gazing up at the stars in the roof and wondering if he ought to do anything about it when the question became academic.

Something blocked the stars and then the glass dome shattered inward, as two hooded figures dropped through on ropes like a pair of spiders. Before Smith could react, something else crashed through the window behind him, sending blue and green and violet glass panes everywhere. Smith gulped, aware that he had no weapons of any kind.

But it seemed he didn't need any.

There was a new roiling in the water, and something rose roaring to the surface. It was not a toy mermaid. It was gigantic, serpentine, scaled, writhing, monstrous, and it was the color of a thundercloud. Its teeth were a foot long. It snarled up at the men who had come through the ceiling, regarding them with eyes like glowing coals. They screamed.

Smith swam for his life to the shallow end of the pool, where Lord Ermenwyr still drifted unconscious.

"Up! Up! Out!" he shouted incoherently, grabbing for the first thing he could reach, which happened to be the lordling's beard. It came off in his hand, loosened by its long immersion in custard sauce and bathwater. He stood, staring at it stupidly. Lord Ermenwyr opened outraged eyes. Then he saw what was happening over Smith's shoulder, and his little naked punk's face registered horror.

"You wear a fake beard," said Smith in wonder.

"It's a facial toupee," Lord Ermenwyr told him furiously, rolling to the side as something hissed through the air from behind them. It smacked into one of the mermaid's breasts, which began to deflate. Smith looked down and saw a feathered dart.

Turning, he beheld Ronrishim Flowering Reed in the act of drawing breath for another shot. A wounded man was dragging himself along the coping after Flowering Reed, stabbing at the Yendri's ankles.

Smith acted without thinking. He had a false beard instead of a knife in his hand, so the effect wasn't as drastic as it usually was, but satisfying all the same. The sodden mess slapped full into Flowering Reed's face with such force it knocked the little blowpipe down his throat. He choked and fell backward. The man on the coping grabbed him and pulled him close, running the dagger into him several times. A wave broke over the coping and obscured them in bloody foam. Smith tried not to look at what was happening in the deep end of the pool.

Lord Ermenwyr had splashed out and was running for the dining room, and Smith raced after him. He barely made it through before the double doors slammed. Lord Ermenwyr leaned against them, gasping for breath.

"Better to leave Nursie alone when she's working," he told Smith.

"What are you, ten?" Smith inquired. Lord Ermenwyr just looked at him indignantly.

≈

After a while the horrible noises stopped, and they opened the door far enough to see Balnshik lifting the wounded man in her arms. There was no sign of Flowering Reed or the other intruders.

"Bandages NOW," she panted, and Smith grabbed napkins from the table. She carried Mr. Amook (for it was he) into the bedroom and bound up his side. Lord Ermenwyr stood by, wringing his hands.

"Please don't die!" he begged Mr. Amook. "I can't bring you back if you die!"

Mr. Amook attempted to say something reassuring and passed out instead.

There came a thunderous hammering and shouts from the front door. Lord Ermenwyr wailed and ran to stick on a fresh beard. Smith, in the act of pulling on his trousers, stumbled into the hall to face the clerk and several members of the City Guard.

"About time you got here," he improvised. "We just chased off the thieves. What kind of hotel is this, anyway?"

≈

After profuse apologies had been made, after crime scene reports had been filed, after Lord Ermenwyr's baggage had been transferred to another suite and a Yendri doctor in Anchor Street sent for to see to Mr. Amook—

Smith, Balnshik, and Lord Ermenwyr sat around a small table in varying degrees of comedown and hangover.

"You promise you won't tell anybody about the beard?" Lord Ermenwyr asked for the tenth time.

"I swear by all the gods," repeated Smith wearily.

"It will grow in one of these days, you know, and it'll be just as impressive as Daddy's," Lord Ermenwyr assured him. "You haven't seen Daddy's, of course, but—anyway, what's a mage without a beard? Who'd respect me anymore?"

"Damned if I know."

"Fortunately, the witnesses aren't likely to blab. Horrible Flowering Reed is finally dead, and what a consolation that is! And those other two probably didn't see me, and if they did, they're dead anyway. You're certain they're dead, Nursie?"

"Oh, yes." She closed her eyes and smiled blissfully. "Quite dead."

"So that just leaves you, Caravan Master, and of course you won't tell."

"Uh-uh."

"I'll make it worth your while. Honestly. Anything you've always wanted but never had? Any personal problems you'd like some assistance with? You should have explained about your 'special talents' sooner! Daddy always needs skilled assassins, *he'd* give you a job in a second," chattered Lord Ermenwyr, whose mind was racing like a rat in a trap.

Smith's mind, however, suddenly woke to calm clarity.

"Actually," he said, "there is something you can help me with. I need a lot of money and a good lawyer to defend me against the Transport Authorities."

Lord Ermenwyr whooped and bounced in his chair. "Is that all? Daddy *owns* the Transport Authorities! There are more ways of making money off caravans than robbing them, you see, even when you're forced to become law-abiding. Mostly law-abiding anyway. Name the charges, and they're dropped."

"It's more complicated than that," said Smith. Settling himself comfortably in his chair, he began to tell the long story of everything that had happened since they bade him good-bye at the caravan depot.

〜

"Terrace dining with a splendid view of the sea," said Mrs. Smith thoughtfully, waving a hand at a bare expanse of concrete. She had a drag at her smoking tube and exhaled. "We shall deck it over quaintly, and put up latticework with trumpet vines to make it gracious. Tables and striped umbrellas." She turned and regarded the old brick building behind them. "And, of course, an interior dining room for when the weather's horrid, with suitably nautical themes in its décor."

"Are you sure you want this property?" inquired Lord Ermenwyr. Behind him, the keymen were methodically pacing out room dimensions.

Burnbright stuck her head out an upstairs window and screamed, "You should see the view from up here! If we fix the holes in the roof and put in some walls, it'll be great!" She waved a small dead dragon, mummified flat. "And look what I found in a corner! We could hang it over the street door and call ourselves the Dead Dragon!"

Lord Ermenwyr shuddered.

"No, silly child, it'll be the Hotel Grandview: Fried Eel Dinners A Specialty," decided Mrs. Smith.

"The real estate agent said there was a much better location on Windward Avenue," said Lord Ermenwyr. "Surely you'd rather do business somewhere a bit less crumbling?"

"I like this. It's got potential," Smith assured him.

"Some people enjoy a challenge, Master," Balnshik told Lord Ermenwyr, draping a furred cloak about his shoulders.

"But it's so weather-beaten," he fretted.

"I should prefer to say it has character," said Mrs. Smith. "One can go a long way on character. Wouldn't you say so, Mr. Smith?"

"Yes," he said, slipping an arm about her and looking up at the improbable future shining in the clouds. "I'd say so."

HOW beautiful is Salesh, that white city by the sea, in festival time!

Her broad ways are strung with bright lanterns, and banners of purple and crimson stream from her high towers. Slender Youth runs laughing in gilded sandals through her gardens, pulling fragrant roses down to scatter the petals, and Age lies sated on cushions by her winepresses, tonguing the goblet of life for its last drop of pleasure. Smoke of sweet incense rises from her braziers, rises with the music of sistrums, citherns, tambours, lyres, and trumpets brazen-throated. Here lovers come as bees to the comb, rolling in honey of unbridled excess, for in Festival time in Salesh nothing is forbidden. The god of the flesh raises his staff in benign blessing on his votaries, and sweet Delight leads the merry dance!

Or so it says on the brochure put out by the Festival Guild. Needless to say, it's hard to find a hotel room in Salesh at that time of year.

In anticipation of the busy holiday, Smith was cleaning out the drains at the Hotel Grandview.

It was the first time he'd done it in all the months he'd been the hotel's proprietor. The Children of the Sun tended to be forgetful in matters regarding ecosystems both large and small, and he had been content all this while to send the Grandview's waste down its main flush pipe without ever wondering where it went afterward.

However, when he had received a notice that the Grandview was due for its first safety inspection, and noted that drains were foremost on the list of things to be inspected, it occurred to him that he'd better have a look at them first. On prising up the iron trap just outside the hotel's kitchen, he was astonished to discover that the barrel-wide pipe below was almost completely blocked with a solid greenish sludge, leaving an aperture for flow no bigger around than an average drinking straw.

Smith knelt on the paving stones, staring at it in bewilderment, while his staff stood looking on unhelpfully.

"You know, some of the gentlemen and ladies been complaining their washbasins drain slow," offered Porter Crucible. "I'll bet that's why."

"What do I do now?" said Smith plaintively. He looked up at the porters. "I guess we'll just have to get scrapers and take turns digging it out."

The porters took a step back, in perfect unison.

"That's as much as our Porters' Union certificates are worth, you know," said Crucible. "We're already on ten-year probation from transferring out of the Keymen's Union."

"Anyway, we couldn't get our shoulders down that pipe," added Pinion. "And you couldn't either, come to that."

"Somebody small and skinny could, though," added Bellows, and they turned to stare at Burnbright. She backed away, looking outraged.

"There's a Message Runners' Union too," she protested. "And I would not either fit down there! I've got breasts now, you know. And hips!"

Which was true; she had recently grown those very items, and filled out her scarlet uniform snugly enough to be ogled by gentlemen guests when she raced through the hotel bar.

"Nine Hells," muttered Smith, and clambered to his feet. "I'll dig it out as far as I can. Where's a shovel?"

"What were you on about just now?" Mrs. Smith, emerging from the kitchen, inquired of Burnbright. She wiped her hands on her apron and peered down at the opened drain. "Great heavens! What a disgusting mess. No wonder the drains are sluggish." She pulled out a smoking tube and packed it with fragrant amberleaf.

"It's got to be cleared before the safety inspectors get here," said Smith, who had found a shovel and now stuck it experimentally into the sludge. The sludge, which was roughly the consistency of hard cheese, fought back.

"Oh, you'll never get rid of it like that," Mrs. Smith advised, flicking the flint-and-steel device with which she lit her amberleaf. She took a drag, waved away smoke, and explained: "There's a fearfully caustic chemical you can buy. You just pour it down the drain, leave it to dissolve everything away, and Hey Presto! Your drains are whisper-fresh by morning. Or so the chemists claim."

"Doesn't that pipe drain into the open ocean?" asked Crucible.

"Haven't the slightest idea," said Mrs. Smith. She eyed Burnbright. "You're young and agile; jump up there, child, and investigate."

Burnbright scrambled up on the edge of the parapet and hung the upper part of her body over, peering down the cliff.

"Yes!" she cried. "I can see where it comes out! Big trail of slime goes right into the sea!"

"No problem, then!" said Smith cheerfully, putting back the shovel. "Can we buy that stuff in bulk?"

❦

By midafternoon the porters had brought back ten barrels of tempered glass marked SCOURBRASS'S FOAMING WONDER, with instructions stenciled in slightly smaller letters underneath that and, smaller still, a scarlet skull and crossbones followed by the words: *POISON. Use caution when handling. Not to be added to soups, stews, or casseroles.* Smith mixed up the recommended dosage for particularly long-standing clogs and poured it into the drain. He was gratified to see a jet of livid green foam rise at once, as though fighting to escape from the pipe, then sink back, bubbling ominously. He stacked the opened barrel next to the hotel's toolshed, beside the nine unopened ones, and returned to the kitchen in a happy mood.

"Looks like that stuff's working," he said to Mrs. Smith, who was busy jamming a small plucked and boned bird up the gaping nether orifice of a somewhat larger boned bird. "Er—what's this?"

"Specialty dish of the evening," she panted. "Hard-boiled egg in a quail in a rock hen in a duck in a goose in a sea dragon, and the whole thing roasted and glazed in fruit syrup and served with a bread sauce. Miserably complicated to make, but it's expected at Festival time, and besides"— she gave a final shove and the smaller bird vanished at last, "—rumor hath it there's some sort of journalist has booked a table for this evening, and it always pays to impress the restaurant critics."

Smith nodded. The Hotel Grandview was an old building with uncertain plumbing in a distinctly unfashionable part of town, but its restaurant had a steadily growing gourmet clientele that was keeping them in business. That was entirely due to Mrs. Smith's ability to turn a sausage or a handful of cold oatmeal into cuisine fit for anybody's gods, let alone the gastronomes of a seaside resort.

"So I shall need Burnbright to run down to that Yendri

shop for a sack of those funny little yellow plums, because they'll fit in the sea dragon's eye sockets after it's cooked and give it a fearfully lifelike air," Mrs. Smith added.

"I'll send her now," said Smith, filching a piece of crisply fried eel from a tray and wandering out in search of Burnbright.

He was expecting a certain amount of whining. He was right.

"I *hate* going into Greenietown!" wailed Burnbright. "They always look at me funny! They're all a bunch of oversexed savages."

"Look, they're not going to rape you," Smith told her. "They have to take a vow they won't do anything like that before they're allowed to open shops in our cities."

"Well, they're always lying in wait by the mountain roads and raping our long-distance messengers," claimed Burnbright. "At the Mount Flame Mother House for Runners—"

"Do you know anybody that's ever actually happened to?"

"No, but everybody knows—"

"You can run all the way back," Smith told her, slipping a coin into her hand and gently ushering her toward the hotel's front door.

"Why can't Smith or Bellows or one of them go?" Burnbright persisted.

"Because they've gone up to the caravan depot to pick up Lord Ermenwyr's trunks," said Smith.

"Eeew," said Burnbright, and sped out the door.

She did not particularly care for Lord Ermenwyr either, despite the fact that he was the Hotel Grandview's patron. Burnbright's immediate disfavor was due to the fact that Lord Ermenwyr consistently made overtures of an improper nature to her during his frequent visits, and she thought he was a creepy little man, patron or no.

Smith ducked into the bar to see if all was going well, took a brief detour through the indoor section of the restaurant (silent as a temple at that hour, with its folded napkins and crystal set out expectantly) and slipped behind his desk to look over the guestbook. The Grandview was full up with reservations, as he'd hoped it would be for the holiday. His eye fell on the name just below Lord Ermenwyr's: Sharplin Coppercut.

Smith knit his brows, thinking the name was familiar. Some kind of journalist? Maybe the food critic Mrs. Smith was expecting? As he wondered, a thin shadow moved across the doorway and a thin and elegantly dressed man followed after it. Behind him a city porter struggled with a ponderous trunk.

The elegant man came straight to the desk, moving silent as his shadow, and in a quiet voice said; "Sharplin Coppercut."

Smith blinked at him a moment. "Oh!" he said belatedly, "You have a reservation. Right, here you are: Room 2. It's just up those stairs, sir, first door on the left. Come to have fun at the Festival, have you?"

"I do hope so," said Coppercut, stamping the ledger with his house sign. He replaced his seal in its pendant box and swept the lobby with a penetrating gaze. "Have you a runner on the premises?"

"Yes, sir, we're a fully equipped hotel. We can send your correspondence anywhere in the city. She's stepped out for a moment, but I'll be happy to send her up as soon as she gets back, sir," Smith offered.

"Please do," said Coppercut, showing his teeth. He went upstairs as quietly as he had done everything else, though the porter thumped and labored after him, cursing under the weight of the trunk.

Then there was a commotion of another kind entirely, for in through the street door came two of the biggest men

Smith had ever seen. They were built like a pair of brick towers. That they managed to get through the doorway side by side was extraordinary; it seemed necessary to bend time and space to do it. They had to come in side by side, however, for they bore on their massive shoulders the front traces of a costly looking palanquin. Into the lobby it came, and two more giants bearing the rear traces ducked their heads to follow. They were followed by a tall Yendri, who wore the plain white robe of a physician. Behind them came Porters Crucible, Pinion, Old Smith, Bellows, and New Smith, bearing each no less than three trunks.

"*Smith*," hissed a voice from within the palanquin. "Is the lobby empty?"

"At the moment," Smith replied.

In response, the palanquin's curtains parted, and Lord Ermenwyr slid forth, nimble as a weasel. He straightened up and stood peering around warily. He wore an inky black ensemble that contrasted sharply with the unnatural pallor of his skin. He wore also a pomaded beard and curled mustaches, and clenched between his teeth a jade smoking tube from which a sickly green fume trailed.

"Safe at last," he muttered. "Hello, Smith; we're traveling incognito, you see, I mean even more so than usual, hence all the cloak-and-dagger business, and I don't suppose you've got my suite key ready, have you, Smith?"

"Right here, my lord," said Smith, handing it over the counter. Lord Ermenwyr took it and bolted for the stairs, with the tails of his coat flying out behind him. His palanquin-bearers gaped after him; then, exchanging glances, they hoisted the palanquin after them and lumbered toward the staircase. They got it up into the hall with inches to spare, tugging awkwardly. The Yendri bowed apologetically to Smith.

"His lordship is somewhat agitated," he said.

"That's all right," Smith assured him. "As soon as you give him his fix, he'll calm down."

The Yendri looked shocked. Smith realized that he was quite a young man, slender and smooth-faced, and though his features would undoubtedly one day be as harshly angular as the others of his race, he had at the moment a certain poetic look. His stammered reply was cut short by a shriek from upstairs:

"*Willowspear! For Hell's sake, my medication!*"

"See?" said Smith. The Yendri hurried upstairs.

"What was all that?" demanded Mrs. Smith, emerging from the kitchen with a frown, wiping her hands on her apron.

"Lord Ermenwyr's arrived," Smith explained.

"Oh," she said. "Who was that he was yelling after?"

"He's got a doctor with him," said Smith.

"Instead of Madam Balnshik, this time? I never saw such a hypochondriac in my life," stated Mrs. Smith. "Do you suppose the doctor knows about . . . ?"

"He'd have to, wouldn't he?" said Smith. "By the way, I think your food critic's arrived."

"Ah!" Mrs. Smith edged sidelong behind the desk to look at the register. She studied it a moment. "Let's see . . . Coppercut?" she scowled. "No, no. That man doesn't write restaurant reviews. Far from it! He's a—"

"Here we are!" caroled Lord Ermenwyr, sliding gracefully down the banister of the staircase. The four giants hurried after him, taking the stairs, however, and followed at a slight distance by the Yendri doctor.

"My lord—" he gasped.

"All together again!" Lord Ermenwyr landed with a crash and skittered across the lobby. His pupils had gone to pinpoints. "Good old Smith! You've had the drains cleaned since I was here last, haven't you? And Mrs. Smith, how charming to see you! Nursie sends her best, she'd have been here but Mother had another damned baby"—here the giants and the Yendri doctor bowed involuntarily—"and Nursie adores babies, obsessed with the horrible little things in all their lace and woolies and whatnot—I keep warning everyone that they'll find a cradle full of tiny gnawed bones one of these days, but nobody listens. Smith! Good to see you! Have I checked in yet?"

"No, Master," one of the giants reminded him, in a terrifyingly deep voice with slightly odd enunciation. Smith looked at him sharply and exchanged a glance with Mrs. Smith.

"How careless of me." Lord Ermenwyr took out his seal and stamped HOUSE KINGFISHER in five places on the register's page. "And I haven't done introductions yet, have I? Smith, Mrs. Smith, these are my bodyguards: Cutt, Crish, Stabb, and Strangel. Aren't those great names? And this is my personal physician." He waved a hand at the Yendri. "Agliavv Willowspear. A man who knows his antidepressants!"

Willowspear bowed.

"Yes, yes, I know he's a greenie, but he's utterly trustworthy," said Lord Ermenwyr in a stage whisper. "Known him all my life. Mother's always succoring defenseless orphans, alas. Anyway, I had to bring him; he's one of Mother's disciples and he's on a vision quest or something, isn't that right, Willowspear?"

"In a manner of speaking, my lord," said Willowspear.

"A vision quest to Salesh at festival time?" said Mrs. Smith, regarding him keenly.

"Yes, lady." Willowspear drew himself up and met her gaze. "My father, Hladderin Willowspear—"

Burnbright entered clutching a small bag presumably containing yellow plums, and, seeing Lord Ermenwyr at the desk, did her best to tiptoe through to the kitchen unobserved. About three paces on, however, her gaze riveted on

Willowspear. Her mouth fell open, but she made no sound and kept moving forward, though her gaze remained on the Yendri. The result was that she walked straight into a chair and fell over it with a crash.

Everyone turned to stare at her.

"And it's little Burnbright!" yodeled Lord Ermenwyr, vaulting the back of a sofa to land beside her and pull her to her feet. "Nine Hells, you've grown *tits!* When did that happen?"

"Girls grow up overnight, they say," Smith explained, moving between them quickly, closely followed by Willowspear.

"Don't they, just? Burnbright, runner dearest, you'll have to come recite the latest news for me tomorrow, eh?" Lord Ermenwyr leered around Smith at her. "Private little tête-à-tête in my chamber? I like the morning report over my tea and pastry. I have breakfast in bed, too. Wouldn't you like—"

"Her knee is bleeding," Willowspear pointed out.

Burnbright took her eyes from him for the first time and peered down at her leg dazedly. "Oh," she said. "It is."

"Well!" Lord Ermenwyr cried. "I'll allot you the services of my personal physician to tend to it, how about that? Off to the kitchen with her, Willowspear, and plaster up that gorgeous leg, and make sure the other one's undamaged, while you're at it. She earns her living with those, after all."

"That would be beautiful—I mean—nice," said Burnbright.

"And as soon as he's done, you've got a customer in Room 2," Smith told her.

"Right," she said, wide-eyed, as Willowspear took her hand and led her away.

"I'm talking too much, aren't I?" said Lord Ermenwyr, looking around with an abrupt change of mood. "Oh, God, I need to get laid. Not safe, though. Smith, might we have a cozy chat in the bar? Just you and I and the bodyguards?

There are a few little things you need to know."

Mrs. Smith rolled her eyes. Smith muttered a silent prayer to his ancestors, but said, "Right away, lord."

At that moment another guest arrived with some fanfare, a well-to-do lady who had apparently donned her festival costume early and seemed to be going as the Spirit of the Waters, to judge from the blue body paint and strategically placed sequins. Two goggle-eyed city porters followed her, with trunks that presumably contained the clothes she was not wearing.

Smith braced himself, expecting Lord Ermenwyr to engage in another display of sofa-vaulting; to his immense relief, instead the lordling gave the woman an oddly furtive look and plucked at Smith's sleeve.

"I'll just step into the bar now, if you don't mind," he muttered. "Pray join me when you've got a minute."

He slunk away, with the bodyguards bumping into one another somewhat as they attempted to follow closely.

Smith stepped behind his desk to register the Spirit of the Waters, or Lady Shanriana of House Goldspur as she was known when in her clothes. Mrs. Smith lingered, seemingly loath to go back to the kitchen just yet.

When Lady Shanriana was safely on her way upstairs to her room, Mrs. Smith leaned close and said quietly, "Those are demons the lordling's got with him."

"That's what I thought," Smith replied. "With a glamour on them, I guess."

"I can always tell when somebody's talking around a pair of tusks, no matter how well they're hidden. The accent's unmistakable," said Mrs. Smith. "But perhaps they'll mind their manners. Nurse Balnshik was capable of civilized behavior, as I recall."

Smith shivered pleasurably, remembering the kind of behavior of which Nurse Balnshik had been capable.

"She didn't have tusks, of course," he said irrelevantly.

At that moment Burnbright and Willowspear returned from the kitchen. She seemed to be leaning on his arm to a degree disproportionate to the tininess of the sticking plaster on her knee.

"I've never heard of using hot water and soap on a cut," she was saying breathlessly. "It seems so simple! But then, you probably said some sort of spell over it too, didn't you? Because there's really no pain at all—"

"There you are, Willowspear," said Lord Ermenwyr edgily, popping out of the bar. "I need you to check my pulse. Where's Smith?"

"Just coming, lord," said Smith, stepping from behind the counter. "And, Burnbright? You need to step up to Room 2."

"Oh. All right," she said, and climbed the stair unsteadily.

Smith and Willowspear followed Lord Ermenwyr into the bar, where he retreated to the farthest darkest booth and sat looking pointedly back and forth between Smith and the barman. Smith took the hint.

"Seven pints of Black Ship Stout, Rivet, then go mind the front desk for a bit," he said. Rivet looked bewildered, but complied.

When they were settled in the booth (all but the bodyguards, who would never have fit in there anyway but made a solid wall in front of it) Lord Ermenwyr had a gulp of his pint, leaned forward in the gloom, and said, "I'm afraid I'm in certain difficulties, Smith."

Smith groaned inwardly, but had a bracing quaff of his own pint, and said merely, "Difficulties, you say."

"Yes, and it's necessary I . . . hem . . . lie low for a while. That's why I'm here."

Smith thought to himself that his lordship could scarcely have chosen a more public place to go to ground than a resort hotel at Festival time, but he raised an eyebrow and said, "Really?"

"Yes, yes, I know what you're thinking, but I have my reasons!" Lord Ermenwyr snapped. "I'd better explain. I belong to certain, shall we say, professional organizations? Hereditary membership, thanks to Daddy. The AFA, the WWF, NPNS, BSS—"

"And those would be?"

"Ancient Fraternity of Archmagi," Lord Ermenwyr explained impatiently. "World Warlocks' Federation. Ninth Plane Necromancers' Society. Brotherhood of Sages and Seers. To name but a few. And I, er, seem to have made an enemy.

"It all started when I attended this banquet and wore all my regalia from all the groups of which I'm a member. Well, apparently that wasn't considered quite in good taste, as some of the societies aren't on the best of terms, but I'm new at this so how was I supposed to know? And several people took offense that I was wearing the Order of the Bonestar on the same side of my chest as the Infernal Topaz Cross *and* carrying the Obsidian Rod in my left hand.

"Just a silly little misunderstanding, you see? But one gentleman was rather more vocal than the rest of them. He'd been drinking, and I'd been, mmm, self-medicating, and I might have been clever at his expense or something, because he seems to have developed a dislike for me quite out of all proportion to anything I may or may not have said."

Smith drank the rest of his pint in a gulp. "Go on," he said, feeling doomed already.

"And then we ran for the same guild office, and I won," Lord Ermenwyr. "I even won fairly. Well, reasonably fairly. But evidently this gentleman had wanted all his life to be the Glorious Slave of Scharathrion, and that I of all people should have dashed his hopes was too much. Rather silly, considering that all the title amounts to is being treasurer to a fraternity of pompous idiots obsessed with power; but there it is, and he's decided to kill me."

"All right," said Smith patiently. "And that's not against the club rules?"

Lord Ermenwyr squirmed in his seat. "Not as such, because he's filed a formal declaration of intent to challenge me to a duel. Out of all the interminable number of fraternal bylaws, he got hold of one that'll permit him to take my office if he defeats me in formal combat.

"Of course, he's got to find me to do that," he added, snickering.

"And so you're hiding out here?"

"Exactly," Lord Ermenwyr replied. "Perfect place for it! Magi are an antisocial lot, because they think they're cleverer than everyone else, so what better place for me to dodge him than in the midst of the mundane mob he so detests? These duels always take place on a blasted heath or a mountaintop or somewhere equally dramatic. He won't want to stoop to showing off his wizardly prowess in Salesh High Street, not he!"

"You haven't touched that beer," Smith said to Willowspear. "Don't you drink?"

"No, sir, not alcohol," Willowspear replied, pushing the glass toward him. "Please, help yourself."

"Thanks." Smith took the stout and drank deep before asking Lord Ermenwyr, "You haven't tried to buy your enemy off?"

"That was the first thing I did, when I saw how he was taking it," Lord Ermenwyr admitted, his gleam of glee fading somewhat. " 'Here,' I said, 'you can take your old staff of office, I don't want it. Be the Glorious Slave of Scharathrion, if it means that much to you!' But he insists it has to be bought in blood. Mine, I need hardly add. So I took to my heels."

"What about—" Smith looked around furtively. "What about your lord father?"

All four of the bodyguards genuflected, slopping their drinks somewhat.

"He's no use at all," said Lord Ermenwyr bitterly. "He said that any son of his ought to be able to make mincemeat of a third-rate philtermonger like Blichbiss, and it was high time I learned to stand on my own and be a man, et cetera et cetera ad infinitum, and I said, 'I hate you, Daddy,' and ran like hell. And here I am."

"Master, you mustn't speak of the Master of Masters that way," Cutt growled gently. "He is confident his noble off-spring will bring swift and hideous death to his enemies, fol-lowed by an eternity of exquisite torment."

"Oh, shut up and watch the door," Lord Ermenwyr told him.

"So—you didn't come here because you want me to kill this man for you," Smith ventured.

"*You?*" Lord Ermenwyr gave a brief bark of laughter. "Oh, no no no! Dear old Smith, you're the best at your trade (I mean, your former trade) I've ever seen, but Blich-biss is a mage! Way out of your league. No, all I need you to do is keep my visit here a secret. I'm just going to lurk in my suite until the problem goes away. I'll have my meals sent up, and a courtesan or two, and if the luscious little Burn-bright will keep me posted on local news and go out for my prescriptions now and then, I ought to get along famously. And . . . er . . . if you could manage to find a sheep for the boys to kill every couple of days, that would be nice too," he added.

"When you do you think it'll blow over?" Smith asked. "I'd always heard magi had long memories."

"He'll have to give up eventually," Lord Ermenwyr assured him. "Don't look so worried! It's not as though there's going to be a battle, with bodies scattered all over your nice clean hotel."

"And you can keep him healthy?" Smith asked Willowspear.

"As healthy as I ever am," said Lord Ermenwyr.

"I do the will of the Unwearied Mother," said Willowspear, bowing his head. "And I will die, if necessary, to protect Her child."

"I am *not* a child, I'm a slightly underage playboy, and there's no need to get histrionic about it," said Lord Ermenwyr testily. "We're simply going to have a pleasant and very low-profile holiday by the sea."

"Good, then," said Smith, draining the second stout. "Because the hotel's up for having its first safety inspection soon. It would be nice if nothing happened to queer things."

"Oh, what could happen?" said Lord Ermenwyr breezily, lifting his glass.

Smith just shook his head, watching the lordling drink. He supposed that benign heavenly beings who incarnated into the flesh with the purpose of defeating worldly evil knew best how to go about their divine jobs; but surely there had been a better way to do it than singling out a Lord of Evil, marrying him, and forcing him to behave himself? Let alone bringing a lot of highly unstable and conflicted children into the world.

At least Lord Ermenwyr was only *half* a demon. Maybe only a quarter.

⁓

By evening the hotel was full and so was the restaurant, especially the outdoor terrace overlooking the bay, for Festival was scheduled to begin with a grand fireworks extravaganza. In keeping with the theme of unbridled sexual license to celebrate the primordial union of the First Ancestors, the fireworks really should have come at the end of Festival; but by that time the populace of Salesh was generally too sore and hungover to pay proper attention to further pyrotechnics.

The guests, resplendent in their body paint and masks, whooped and applauded as the bright rockets soared upward with a thrilling hiss, exploded into flowers of scarlet and emerald fire, and drifted down into the afterglow of sunset. Ships in the harbor ran colored lanterns up into their riggings and fired charges of colored paper from their cannons, so that streamers and confetti littered the tideline for days afterward. Partygoers rowed back and forth on the black water, occasionally colliding with other little boats and exchanging interesting passengers.

Barely audible all the way out on Salesh Municipal Pier, musicians played songs of love and longing to entice those who had not already paired off into the Pleasure Houses. The night was warm for spring, and the white waxen blossoms of Deathvine perfumed the air wherever they opened; so there were few who resisted the call to yield up their souls to delight.

"Where the hell are all our servers?" demanded Smith, struggling out to the center buffet with an immense tray that bore the magnificent Ballotine of Sea Dragon. Diners exclaimed in delight and pointed at its egg-gilded scales, its balefully staring golden eyes.

"The servers? Whanging their little brains out in the bushes, what do you think?" Crucible replied sourly. He took the ballotine from Smith and held it aloft with the artificial smile of a professional wrestler, acknowledging the diners' cheers a moment, before setting it down and going to work on it with the carving knife.

"We've got to get more people out here! Where's Burn-bright?"

"She ran off crying," said Crucible, sotto voce, producing the first perfectly stratified slice of dragon-goose-duck-hen-quail-egg and plopping it down on the plate of a lady who wore nothing but glitter and three large artificial sapphires.

"What?"

"Asked her what was the matter. She wouldn't tell me. But I saw her talking to that doctor," muttered Crucible, sawing away at another slice. He gave Smith a sidelong sullen glare. "If that bloody greenie's been and done something to our girl, me and the boys will pitch him down the cliff. You tell his lordship so."

"Hell—" Smith turned wildly to look up at the lit windows of the hotel. Lord Ermenwyr, like most of the other guests, was seated on his balcony enjoying the view of the fireworks. Cutt and Crish were ranged on one side of him, Stabb and Strangel on the other, and behind his chair Agli-avv Willowspear stood. Willowspear was gazing down onto the terrace with an expression of concern, apparently searching through the crowd.

"Smith!" trumpeted Mrs. Smith, bearing a five-tiered cake across the terrace with the majesty of a ship under full sail. "Your presence is requested in the lobby, Smith." As she drew near she added, "It's Crossbrace from the City Wardens. I've already seen to it he's got a drink."

Smith felt a wave of mingled irritation and relief, for though this was probably the worst time possible to have to pass an inspection, Crossbrace was easygoing and amenable to bribes. Dodging around Bellows, who was carrying out a dish of something involving flames and fruit sauce, Smith paused just long enough to threaten a young pair of servers with immediate death if they didn't crawl out from under the gazebo and get back to work. Then he straightened his tunic, ran his hands through his hair, and strode into the hotel, doing his best to look confident and cheerful.

"Smith!" Crossbrace toasted him with his drink, turning from an offhand examination of the hotel's register. "Joyous couplings. Thought I'd find you joyously coupling with some sylph!"

"Joyous couplings to you, too," said Smith heartily, noting that Crossbrace was in uniform rather than Festival undress. "Who has time to joyously couple when you're catering the orgy? You've got a drink? Have you dined? We've got a Sea Dragon Ballotine out on the terrace that's going fast!"

"Business first," said Crossbrace regretfully. "Little surprise inspection. But I expect you're all up to code, eh, in a first-class establishment like this?"

"Come and see," said Smith, bowing him forward. "What are you drinking? Silverbush? Let me just grab us a bottle as we go through the bar."

The inspection was cursory, and went well. No molds were discovered anywhere they didn't belong. No structural deficiencies were found, nor any violations of Salesh's codes regarding fire or flood safety. Crossbrace contented himself with limiting the upstairs inspection to a walk down the length of the corridor. Then they went back down to the kitchen, by which time they'd half emptied the bottle of Silverbush and some of the guests on the restaurant terrace were beginning to writhe together in Festival-inflamed passion.

"And you've got to see the drains, of course," Smith insisted, opening the door into the back area. Crossbrace followed him out readily, and looked on as Smith, with a flourish, flung the trap wide.

"Look at that!"

"Damn, you could eat out of there," said Crossbrace in admiration. He took down the area lamp and shined it into the drain, as the distant sound of erotic enchantment drifted across the water. "Beautiful! And that's an old pipe, too. City records says this place was built back in Regent Kashlar's time."

"S'right," affirmed Smith, refilling Crossbrace's glass and having a good gulp himself from the bottle. "But they built solid back then."

Somewhere close at hand, hoarse panting rose to a scream of ecstasy.

"Didn't they, though?" Crossbrace had another drink. "What's your secret?"

"Ah." Smith laid a finger beside his nose. "Scourbrass's Foaming Wonder! See?" He waved a hand at the ten canisters neatly stacked against the wall.

"That's great stuff," said Crossbrace, and stepped close to read the warning.

Smith heard, ominous under all the giggling and groaning, the sound of someone running through the kitchen. The area door flew open, and Pinion stared out at him, looking panic-stricken.

"Boss! Somebody's gone and died in—"

Crossbrace straightened up abruptly and turned around. Pinion saw him and winced. "In Room 2," he finished miserably.

"Oh, dear," Crossbrace said, sobering with alchemical swiftness. "I suppose in my capacity as City Warden I'd better have a look, hadn't I?"

Smith ground his teeth. They went back upstairs.

"He'd ordered room service," Pinion explained. "Never called to have the dishes taken away. I went up to see was he done yet, and nobody answered the knock. Opened the door finally and it was dark in here, except for the light coming in from the terrace and a little fire on the hearth. And there he sits."

Smith opened the door cautiously and stepped inside, followed by Crossbrace and Pinion. "Mr. Coppercut?" he called hopefully.

But the figure silhouetted against the window was dreadfully motionless. Crossbrace swore quietly and, finding a lamp, lit it.

Sharplin Coppercut sat at the writing table, sagging backward in his chair. His collar had been wrenched open, and he stared at the ceiling with bulging eyes and a gaping mouth, rather as though he was about to announce that he'd just spotted a particularly fearsome spider up there.

On the table across the room were the dishes containing his half-eaten meal. The chair had been pushed back and fallen, the napkin dropped to the floor, and a small table midway between the dinner table and the desk lay on its side, with the smoking apparatus it had held scattered across the carpet.

"That's *the* Sharplin Coppercut, isn't it?" said Crossbrace.

"He's the only one I know of," groaned Smith, going to the body to feel for a pulse. He couldn't find one.

"Saw his name in the register. Dear, dear, Smith, you've got a problem on your hands," stated Crossbrace.

"Oh, gods, he's stone dead. Crossbrace, you know it wasn't our food!"

"Sat down to eat his dinner," theorized Crossbrace, studying the dining table. "Had his appetizer; ate it all but a bit of parsley. Drank half a glass of wine. Working his way through a plate of fried eel—that's your house specialty, isn't it?—when he comes over queer and needs air, so he loosens his collar and gets up to go to the window. Bit clumsy by this time, so he bumps over the smoking table on his way. Makes it to the chair and collapses, but dies before he can get the window open. That's the way it looks, wouldn't you say?"

"But there was nothing wrong with the eels," Smith

protested. "I had some myself this aftern—" He spotted something on the table and stared at it a moment. Then his face lit up.

"Yes! Crossbrace, come look at this! It wasn't food poisoning at all!"

Crossbrace came around to look over the corpse's shoulder. There, scrawled on a tablet bearing the Hotel Grandview imprimis, were the words AVENGE MY MURD.

"Oh," he said. "Well, this puts a different light on it."

"Somebody *killed* him," said Smith. "And he took the trouble to let us know!" He felt like embracing Coppercut. An accidental death by food poisoning could wreck a restaurant's reputation, but a high-profile revenge slaying in one could only be considered good publicity.

"So some*body* killed him," said Crossbrace thoughtfully. "Gods know he had a lot of enemies. Poison in his wine? Poisoned dart through the window? Could have been a mage hired to do the job with a sending, for that matter. Look at the coals in the fireplace, what'd he want with a fire on such a warm night? Suspicious. Maybe a smoke efrit suffocated him? Lucky break for you, Smith."

"Isn't it?" Smith beamed at the corpse.

"But it makes a lot more work for me." Crossbrace sighed. "I'll have to get the morgue crew up here, then I'll have to investigate and question everybody, which will take all bloody night. Then I'll have to file a report in triplicate, and there's his avengers to notify, because he must have kept some on retainer . . . and here it is Festival time, and I had an alcove booked at the Black Veil Club for tonight."

"That's a shame," said Smith warily, sensing what was coming.

"It cost me a fortune to get that alcove, too. My lady friend will be furious. I think I'm going to do you a favor, Smith," Crossbrace decided.

"Such as?"

"It's Festival. I'm going to pretend this unfortunate incident hasn't yet happened to stain your restaurant's good
name, all right? We both know it wasn't food poisoning, but
rumors get out, don't they? And the funniest things will
influence those clerks in the Permit Office." Crossbrace
swirled his drink and looked Smith in the eye.

"But we do have a famous dead man here something's
got to be done about. So I'll come back in two days' time,
when Festival's done and everything's business as usual.
You'll have a body for me and not only that, you'll have
found out who, where, when, how, and why, so all I have to
do is arrest the murderer, if possible, and file the paperwork.
I'll have a Safety Certificate for you. Everybody wins.
Right?"

"Right," said Smith, knowing a cleft stick when he saw
one.

"See you after Festival, then," said Crossbrace, and finished his drink. He handed the glass to Smith. "Thanks."

↶

Having sworn Pinion to secrecy and sent him down to serve
food, Smith finished the bottle of Silverbush and indulged in
some blistering profanity. As this accomplished nothing, he
then proceeded to examine the room more closely, while the
sounds of a full-scale orgy floated up from the terrace below.

There was no trace of anything suspicious on the uneaten
food, nor anything that his nose could detect in the wine.
The empty appetizer plate had held some sort of seafood, to
judge from the smell, but that was all. No hint of Scourbrass's Foaming Wonder, which relieved Smith very much.

He dragged Coppercut's body to the bed, laid it out, and
examined him with a professional's eye for signs of subtle
assassination. No tiny darts, no insect bites, no wounds in

easily overlooked places; not even a rash. Coppercut was turning a nasty color and going stiff, but other than that he seemed fine.

Straightening up, Smith looked around the room and noticed that the low coals were smoking out in the fireplace. He approached it cautiously, in case there really was an efrit or something less pleasant in there, and bent down to peer in. The next moment he had grabbed a poker and was raking ashes out onto the hearth, but it was just about too late: for of the gray ruffled mass of paper ash there, only a few blackened scraps were left intact. Muttering to himself, he picked them up and carried them out to the circle of lamplight on the table. Writing. Bits of scrolls?

Spreading them out, turning them over, he found that some were in what was obviously a library scribe's neat hand; others in a rushed-looking backhand that consistently left off letter elements, like the masts on the little ship that signified the *th* sound, or the pupil of the eye that stood for the suffix *ln*. Two hands, but no sense: He had the words *journeyed swiftly to implore* and *so great was his* and *unnatural*, also *ghastly tragedy* and *swift anger* and *they could not escape*.

Only one offered any clue at all. It said *to the lasting sorrow of House Spellmetal, he—*

The name *Spellmetal* was vaguely familiar to Smith. He knit his brows, staring at the fragment. *House* Spellmetal. Somebody wealthy, some dynasty that had suffered notoriety. When had that been? Ten years ago? Fifteen? More? Smith attempted to place where he'd been living when the name was in the news. And there had been a scandal, and the son and heir of House Spellmetal had died. A massacre of some kind, not a decent vendetta.

Smith turned and stared at the fireplace again. Now he noticed the scribe's case sitting open in a chair. He went over and peered into it. Three-quarters empty, though it had clearly held more. Someone had pulled out most of the case's contents and burned them.

"Blackmail," he said aloud.

He looked speculatively at Sharplin Coppercut. Closing the scribe's case and tucking it under his arm, Smith went out and locked the door behind him.

The dead man lay on his bed, staring up in horror. Below his window bosoms jiggled, thighs danced, bottoms quivered, tongues sought for nectar, and slender Youth kicked off its golden sandals and got down to business. Life pulsed and shivered, deliciously, deliriously, in every imaginable variation on one act; but it had finished with Sharplin Coppercut.

⌢

Mrs. Smith had retired when he went to her, and was sitting up in bed smoking, calmly reading a broadside. The staff inhabited the long attic that ran the length of the hotel, divided into several rooms, far enough above the garden for the sounds of massed passion to be a little less evident as it filtered up through the one narrow gabled window.

"Not going out, Smith?" she inquired. Her gaze fell on the case he carried, and she looked up at him in sharp inquiry. "Dear, dear, have we had a contretemps of some kind?"

"You said Sharplin Coppercut isn't a food critic," said Smith. "What kind of journalist is he, then?"

"He's a scandalmonger," Mrs. Smith replied. "Writes a column that runs in all the broadsides. A master of dirty innuendo and shocking revelation. He's done some unauthorized biographies of assorted famous persons, too, instant best-sellers if I recall correctly. I've read one or two. Racy stuff. Mean-spirited, however."

"He dressed pretty well, for somebody living on a writer's salary," said Smith.

"You're speaking of him in the past tense," observed Mrs. Smith.

"Well, he's dead."

"I can't say I'm surprised," said Mrs. Smith, taking a drag and exhaling smoke. "I assume you mean he's been murdered?"

"It looks that way." Smith sagged into a chair.

"Hmph." Mrs. Smith regarded the scribe's case. "My guess would be, he blackmailed the wrong person. They do say he made more money being paid *not* to write, if you understand me. Had a network of spies in every city digging up dirt for him. Did his research, too. It was what made his stuff so entertaining, you see—never indulged in empty insinuation. When that man threw mud, it stuck."

"Why would he have been writing about the House Spellmetal scandal?" Smith wondered. Mrs. Smith's eyes widened.

"He was fool enough to blackmail those people? They're still angry about it, and they've got a long reach. How d'you know that was who did for him?"

Smith explained how the body had been found and about the scroll fragments that had survived the fire. "I've been trying to remember what the scandal was all about," he said. "I was working on a long-run freighter back then, and we didn't put into port much, so I don't think I ever heard the whole story."

Mrs. Smith made a face. "I believe it requires a stiff drink, Smith," she said.

Getting out of bed, she pulled a dressing gown on over her voluminous shift and poured herself an impromptu cocktail from the bottles on her dresser. She poured one for Smith too, and when they were both settled again said, "I'll tell you as much as I know. It was in all the broadsides at the time; there were ballads, and somebody even attempted to mount a play on the subject, but House Spellmetal had it suppressed with breathtaking speed. D'you remember a self-proclaimed prophet, called himself the Sunborn?"

"Vaguely," said Smith. "Came to a bad end, didn't he?"

"Very. That was at the end of the story, however. It all started out in wine and roses, as they used to say. He was a charismatic. Could charm the birds down out of the trees and anyone's clothes off. Preached deliverance through excess; with him it was Festival all year long, every day. If he'd confined himself to having a good time, he might still be with us.

"Unfortunately, he really believed what he taught." Mrs. Smith shook her head.

"He was the one House Spellmetal went after," Smith recalled.

"So he was."

"And there was a massacre, wasn't there? Why?"

Mrs. Smith had a long sip of her drink before answering.

"He had a band of followers," she said at last. "Like any charismatic. One of the things he advocated was free love between the races, so he had quite a mixed bag of people at his, ahem, services. They were driven out of every place they settled in. At last the Sunborn had a vision that he and his lovers were to found a holy city where all might live according to his creed, greenies included.

"And then, somehow or other, the heir to House Spellmetal fell under his influence."

"That was it," Smith said. "And the Spellmetals disapproved."

"Of course they did. The boy was young and thick as two planks, but he adored the Sunborn and he was, of course, rich. So he offered the Sunborn and his followers a huge estate House Spellmetal owned, up near their marble quarries, to be the site of the new holy city. Away they all went and moved into the family mansion there. The boy's father was beside himself.

"You can guess the rest. House Spellmetal raised an army and went up there to get the boy back and forcibly evict the rest of them, with the exception of the Sunborn, whom they intended to skin alive. They didn't get him alive, however. They didn't get anybody alive. There was an armed standoff and finally a massacre."

Smith shook his head. Mrs. Smith finished her drink.

"I have heard," she said, "that Konderon Spellmetal strode in through the broken wall and found his son dead in the arms of an equally dead Yendri girl, pierced with one arrow in the very act itself. I've heard he swore eternal vengeance on any follower of the Sunborn, and hasn't thought of another thing since that hour."

"But they all died," said Smith.

"Apparently there were a few who fled out through the back, just before the massacre." Mrs. Smith shrugged and stared into her empty glass before setting it aside. "Women and children, mostly. The Spellmetals had a body they said was the Sunborn's skinned, but there have always been rumors it wasn't really him, and he's supposed to have been sighted over the years here and there. One couple, a man and his wife and baby, went straight to the law and turned themselves in. They weren't mixed-race, and it turned out they hadn't really been part of the cult; they'd just been the Sunborn's cousins or something like that.

"They were acquitted. They hadn't got five steps out of the Temple of the Law when an assassin hired by House Spellmetal put a pair of bolts right through their hearts. Needless to say, any remaining survivors stayed well underground after that."

"So they must have fabulous prices on their heads," Smith mused.

"I imagine so. Konderon Spellmetal's still alive."

"So Coppercut might have tracked one of them down and

threatened him or her with exposure," said Smith. "Or he might have been proposing to rake it all up again in a book, against House Spellmetal's wishes."

"Occasionally the broadsheets like to do Where-Are-They-Now retrospectives," said Mrs. Smith.

"But whoever killed him went through his papers and burned anything to do with the scandal," Smith theorized. "I wonder if they got it all?"

He opened the scribe's case and drew out those papers that remained inside. Mrs. Smith watched him as he shuffled through them.

"They must have been interrupted before they could finish. Anything of note?"

Smith blinked at the pages. They were notes taken in the hasty backhand, apparently copied from city files, and they appeared to trace adoption records for an infant girl, of the house name Sunbolt. She'd been made a ward of the court of the city of Karkateen. There were brief summaries of depositions from persons involved, and then the note that the venue for the child's case had been changed to Mount Flame. There, after medical certification that she was likely to grow up into the necessary physical type for such work, the infant had been placed in the Mount Flame Mother House for Runners.

The next few pages were all notes of interviews with various persons, concerning the five young runners who had entered active service in the twelfth year of the reign of Chairman Giltbrand.

The very last page was a list of five names, none of them Sunbolt, with four of them crossed out. The remaining name was underlined. It was Teeba Burnbright.

Under that was written: *Present employment: house messenger, Hotel Grandview, 4 Front Street, Salesh-by-the-Sea.*

"I didn't know her first name was Teeba," said Smith distractedly.

"Burnbright?" Mrs. Smith scowled at him. "What's she got to do with it?"

Smith waved the handful of papers, thinking hard.

"The first thing he asked when he got here was if he could see our house runner," he said. "I sent Burnbright up to him as soon as she got back. I haven't seen her since. Crucible said she'd run off crying about something. Oh, hell—"

"She's asleep in her room," Mrs. Smith informed him. "I went into the cellar for some apricot preserves for the Festival Cake, and she was hiding down there, sniveling. She'd opened a bottle of orchid extract and gotten herself into a state of messy intoxication. I gave her a dose of Rattlerail's Powders and a thorough telling-off, and sent her to bed. Smith, that child's far too scatterbrained to pull off a murder!"

"But she knows something," said Smith.

"Well, you're going to have to wait until morning to question her," said Mrs. Smith, "with the condition she was in."

"I guess so." Smith stuffed the papers back in the scribe's case and set them aside. Suddenly he felt bone-tired and very old. "All this and Lord Ermenwyr under the roof, too. I've had enough of Festival."

"Two days yet to go of exquisite orgiastic fun," said Mrs. Smith grimly.

⤙

Far too early the next morning, Smith was crouched at his desk in the lobby, warming his hands on a mug of tea. Most of the hotel's guests were either passed out in their rooms or in the shrubbery, and it would be at least an hour before anyone was likely to ring for breakfast. He had already spotted Burnbright. She was sitting in the deserted bar, deep in quiet conversation with the young Yendri doctor. He was holding both her hands and speaking at length. Smith was only waiting for Willowspear to leave so he could have a word with her in private.

While they were still cloistered together, however, Lord Ermenwyr and his bodyguards came down the staircase.

"Smith." Lord Ermenwyr looked from side to side and caught his sleeve. "Are you aware you've got a . . . er . . . deceased person in Room 2?"

"Not anymore," Smith told him. "We carried him down into the cold storage cellar an hour ago."

"Oh, good," said the lordling. "The smell was making the boys restless, and there was a soul raging around in there half the night. Came through my wall at one point and started throwing things about, until I appeared to him in my true form. He turned tail at that, but I was looking forward to a bit of fun tonight and don't want any apparitions interrupting me. Who was it?"

Smith explained, rubbing his grainy eyes.

"Really!" Lord Ermenwyr looked shocked. "Well, I wish I'd been the one to send him to his deserved reward! Coppercut was a real stinker, you know. No wonder Burnbright's in need of spiritual comfort."

"Is that what they're doing in there?" Smith peered over at the bar.

"She and Willowspear? Of course. He's a Disciple, you know. Has all the sex drive of a grain of rice, so skittish young ladies in need of a sympathetic shoulder to cry on find him irresistible." Lord Ermenwyr sneered in the direction of the bar. "Perhaps she'd like a bit of slightly more robust consolation later, do you think? I'll listen to her problems *and* give her advice she can use next time she has to kill somebody."

"You don't think she did it?" Smith scowled.

"Oh, I suppose not. Say, did you have plans for the

body?" Lord Ermenwyr turned back and looked at him hopefully.

"Yes. The City Warden is coming for it after Festival."

"Damn. In that case, what about sending out for a sheep?" The lordling dug in his purse and dropped a silver piece on the desk. "That ought to take care of it. Just have the porter lead it straight up to my suite. I'm going back to bed now. Would the divine Mrs. Smith be so kind as to send up a tray of tea and clear broth?"

"I'll see it done, lord," said Smith, eyeing the silver piece and wondering where he was going to get a live sheep during Festival.

"Thanks. Come along, boys." Lord Ermenwyr turned on his heel and headed back toward the stairs, with his body-guards following closely. At the door of the bar he leaned in and yelled: "If you've *quite* finished, Willowspear, I believe my heartbeat's developing an alarming irregularity. You might want to come along and pray over me or something. Assuming you've no objection, Burnbright dearest?"

There was a murmur from the bar, and Willowspear hurried out, looking back over his shoulder. "Remember that mantra, child," he said, and turned to follow his master up the stairs.

"Burnbright," Smith called.

A moment later she came through the doorway, reluctant to look at him. Burnbright was in as bad a shape as a young person can be after a night of tears and orchid extract, which was a lot better than Smith himself would have been under the same circumstances. She dug a knuckle into one slightly swollen eye, and asked, "What?"

"What happened, up there with Mr. Coppercut?"

Her mouth trembled. She kept her gaze on the floor as she said; "I thought he wanted me to run him a message. He didn't have any messages. He told me he knew who I really was. Told me all this story about these people who got themselves killed when I was a baby, or something. Said he knew who fostered me out to my mother house. Said I had guilty blood and some big noise House Smeltmetal or somebody would pay a lot of money for my head. Said he could set bounty hunters after me with a snap of his fingers!"

She looked up at Smith in still-simmering outrage. "I told him it was a lot of lies. He said he could prove it, and he said he was going to write about me being one of the survivors, so everybody'd know who I am and where I live. Unless I paid him. And I said I didn't have any money. And he said that wasn't what he wanted."

"Bastard," said Smith. "And . . . ?"

"What d'you think he wanted?" Burnbright clenched her little fists. "And . . . and he said there were other things he wanted me to do. I got up to run at that, and he couldn't stop me, but he told me to think it over. He said to come back when I'd calmed down. Said he'd be waiting. So I ran away."

"You went downstairs to hide?"

"I needed to think," said Burnbright, blushing. "And Mrs. Smith caught me and gave me what for because I was drinking. So I went upstairs, but I'd been thinking, well, it's Festival after all and maybe it's not so wrong. But it seemed awfully unfair, now of all times! But then I thought maybe he'd leave me alone after—and nobody'd ever know if I . . . well anyway, I went in to see him. But—" She paused, gulped.

"He was dead?"

Burnbright nodded quickly, giving him a furtive look of relief. "Sitting there in the firelight, just like in a ghost story. So I left."

"You didn't have anything to do with getting him killed? Didn't put drain cleaner in his food?" asked Smith, just to have it said and done with. Burnbright shook her head.

"Though that would have been a really good idea," she

admitted. Her eyes widened. "Did somebody do that? Eeeew!! It must have eaten through him like—"

"We don't know how he died," said Smith. "I'm trying to find out."

"Well, it wasn't me," Burnbright maintained. "As mean as he was, he probably had lots of enemies. And now he can't hurt anybody else!" she added brightly.

"Did you touch anything in the room when you were there?"

"Nothing," Burnbright said. "You're not supposed to, are you, at a murder scene? There were lots of murders in Mount Flame City; everyone there knows what to do when you stumble on a body. Leave fast and keep your mouth shut!"

"All right. So you haven't told anybody?"

Burnbright flushed and looked away. "Just that . . . doctor. Because I . . . he asked me what was the matter. But he won't tell. He's very spiritual."

"For a greenie, eh?"

"I never met one like him," said Burnbright earnestly. "And he's *beautiful*. Don't you think? I could just stare at that face for hours."

"Well, don't," Smith told her, too weary to be amused. "Go help the porters cleaning up the terrace."

"Okay!" Burnbright hurried off. Smith watched her go, pressing his tea mug to the spot on his left temple where his headache was worst. The heat felt good.

He was still sitting like that, mulling over what he'd just learned, when a man came running in from the street.

Smith straightened up and blinked at him suspiciously, not because of the stranger's precipitate appearance but because he wasn't sure what he was seeing. There was a blurred quality to the man's outline, an evanescent play of uncertain colors. For a moment Smith wondered whether Coppercut's ghost wasn't on the loose, perhaps objecting to his body being laid out on three blocks of ice between a barrel of pickled oysters and a double flitch of bacon.

But as he neared the desk, stumbling slightly, the stranger seemed to solidify and focus. Tall and slender, he wore nothing but an elaborately worked silver collar and a matching ornament of a sheathlike nature over his loins. It being the middle of Festival, this was nothing to attract attention; but there was something unsettlingly familiar about the young man's face.

His features were smooth and regular, handsome to the point of prettiness. His hair was thickly curling, and there was a lot of it. His wide eyes were cold, glittering, and utterly mad.

"Hello," he said, wafting wine fumes at Smith. "I understand this is a, er, friendly hotel. Can I see your thing you write people's names in?"

His voice was familiar too. Smith peered at him.

"You mean the registration book?"

"Of course," said the youth, just as three more strangers ran through the doorway and Smith placed the likeness. If Lord Ermenwyr were taller, and clean-shaven, and had more hair, and didn't squint so much—

"There he is!" roared one of the men.

"Die, cheating filth!" roared another.

"Vengeance!" roared the third.

The youth said something unprintable and vanished. Smith found himself holding two mugs of tea.

The three men halted in their advance across the lobby.

"He's done it again!" said the first stranger.

"There he is!" The second pointed at the tea mug in Smith's left hand.

"Vengeance!" repeated the third man, and they resumed their headlong rush. But they were now rushing at Smith.

They were unaware of Smith's past, however, or his particular talent, and so, ten seconds later, they were all dead.

One had Smith's left boot knife embedded in his right eye to the hilt. One had Smith's right boot knife embedded in his left eye, also to the hilt. The third had Smith's tea mug protruding from a depression in his forehead. Looking very surprised, they stood swaying a moment before tottering backward and collapsing on the lobby carpet. No less surprised, Smith groaned and, getting to his feet, came around the side of the desk to examine the bodies. Quite dead.

"That was amazing! Thanks," said the youth, who had reappeared beside him.

Smith's headache was very bad by then, and for a moment the pounding was so loud he thought he might be having a stroke; but it was only the thunder of eight feet in iron-soled boots descending the stairs, and behind them the rapid patter of two feet more elegantly shod.

"*Master*!" shouted Lord Ermenwyr's bodyguards, prostrating themselves at the youth's feet.

"Forgive us our slowness!" implored Cutt.

"What in the Nine Hells are you doing here?" hissed Lord Ermenwyr furiously, staring at the youth as though his eyes were about to leap right out of his head.

"Hiding," said the youth, beginning to grin.

"Well, you can't hide here, because *I'm* hiding here, so go away!" said Lord Ermenwyr, stamping his feet in his agitation. Willowspear, who had come up silently behind him, stared at the newcomer in amazement.

"My lord! Are you unhurt?" he asked.

The youth ignored him, widening his grin at Lord Ermenwyr. "Ooo! Is the baby throwing a tantrum? Is the poor little stoat scared he's going to be dug out of his hole? Here comes the scary monster to catch him!"

"Stop it!" Lord Ermenwyr screamed, as the youth shambled toward him giggling, and as the youth's graceful form began to run and alter into a horrible-looking melting mess. "You idiot, we're in a city! There are *people* around!"

Smith drew a deep breath and leaped forward, grabbing the thing that had been a youth around its neck and doing his best to get it in a chokehold. To his amazement, Cutt, Crish, Stabb, and Strangel were instantly on their feet, snarling at him, and Willowspear had seized his arm with surprisingly strong hands.

"No! No! Smith, stop!" cried Lord Ermenwyr.

"Then . . . this isn't the mage Blichbiss?" Smith inquired, as the thing in his grip oozed unpleasantly.

"Who?" bubbled the thing.

"This is the Lord Eyrdway," Willowspear explained. "The Variable Magnificent, firstborn of the Unwearied Mother, heir to the Black Halls."

"He's my damned brother," said Lord Ermenwyr. "You'd better let him go, Smith."

Smith let go. "A thousand apologies, my lord," he said cautiously.

"Oh, that's all right," gurgled the thing, re-forming itself into the handsome youth. "You did just save my life, after all."

This brought Smith's attention back to the three dead men lying in front of the desk. Lord Ermenwyr followed his gaze.

"Dear, dear, and I promised you there wouldn't be any bodies lying around your nice hotel, didn't I? Boys, let's get rid of the evidence. Who were they?" He turned a gimlet eye on Lord Eyrdway, as the bodyguards moved at once to gather up the dead. They carried them quickly up the stairs, chuckling amongst themselves.

"Who were they? Just some people," said Lord Eyrdway, a little uncomfortably. "Can I have a drink?"

"What do you mean, *'just some people'*?" demanded Lord Ermenwyr.

"Just some people I . . . cheated, and sort of insulted their mothers," said Lord Eyrdway. "And killed one of their brothers. Or cousins. Or something." His gaze slid sideways to Smith. "Hey, mortal man, want to see something funny?"

He lunged forward and grabbed Lord Ermenwyr's beard, and gave it a mighty yank.

"*Ow!*" Lord Ermenwyr struck his hand away and danced back. Lord Eyrdway looked confused.

"It's a *real* beard now, you cretin!" Lord Ermenwyr said, rubbing his chin.

"Oh." Lord Eyrdway was nonplussed for a moment before turning to Smith. "See, he's got this ugly baby face and he was worried he'd never grow a real mage's beard like Daddy's, so he—"

"Shut up!" raged Lord Ermenwyr.

"Or maybe it was to hide his pimples," Lord Eyrdway continued gloatingly, at which Lord Ermenwyr sprang forward and grabbed him by the throat. Willowspear and Smith managed to pry them apart, and managed only because Lord Eyrdway had made a ridge of thorns project out of the sinews of his neck, causing his brother to pull back with a yelp of pain. He stood back, nursing his hands and glaring at Lord Eyrdway.

"Those had better not be venomous," he said.

"Curl up and die, shorty," Lord Eyrdway told him cheerfully. He looked around. "Is there a bar in here?"

"Maybe we should all go upstairs, lord?" Smith suggested.

"Er—no," said Lord Ermenwyr. "I don't think you want to go into my rooms for the next little while." He looked at the entrance to the bar. "It's private in there."

It would be hours yet before Rivet came in to work, so

Willowspear obligingly went behind the bar and fetched out a couple of bottles of wine and glasses for them.

"Is anybody else likely to come bursting in here in pursuit of you?" Lord Ermenwyr inquired irritably, accepting a glass of wine from Willowspear.

"I don't think so," said Lord Eyrdway. "I'm pretty sure I scared off the rest of them when I turned into a giant wolf a few streets back. You should have seen me! Eyes shooting fire, fangs as long as your arm—"

"Oh, save it. I'm not impressed."

"Are you a mage also, lord?" Smith inquired, before they could come to blows again.

"*Me*, a mage?" Lord Eyrdway looked scornful. "Gods, no. I don't need to do magic. I *am* magic." He drained his wine at a gulp and held out his glass to be refilled. "More, Willowspear. What are you doing down here, anyway?"

"Attending on your lord brother," Willowspear replied, bowing and refilling his glass. "And—"

"That's right, because Nursie's busy with the new brat!" Lord Eyrdway grinned again. "So poor little Wormenwyr needs somebody else to start up his heart when it stops beating. Did you know my brother is practically one of the undead, mortal? What was your name?"

"Smith, lord."

"The good Smith knows all about *me*," said Lord Ermenwyr. "But I never told him about you."

"Oh, you must have heard of me!" Lord Eyrdway looked at Smith in real surprise.

"Well—"

"Hear, mortal, the lamentable tragedy of my house," Lord Ermenwyr intoned gloomily. "For it came to pass that the dread Master of the Mountain, in all his inky and infernal glory, did capture a celestial Saint to be his bride, under the foolish impression he was insulting Heaven thereby. But, lo! Scarce had he clasped her in his big evil arms when waves of radiant benignity and divine something-or-other suffused his demonic nastiness, permanently reforming him; for, as he was later to discover to his dismay, the Compassionate One had actually *let* him capture her with that very goal in mind. But that's the power of Love, isn't it? It never plays fair.

"And, in the first earthshaking union of their marital bliss, so violent and so acute was the discord across the planes that a hideous cosmic mistake was made, and forth through the Gates of Life issued a concentrated gob of Chaos, and nine months later it sort of oozed out of Mother and assumed the shape of a baby."

"My lord!" Willowspear looked anguished. "You blaspheme!"

"Stuff it," Lord Eyrdway told his brother. "It's all lies, mortal. Smith? Yes. I was a beautiful baby, Mother's always said so. And I could change shape when I was still in the cradle, unlike you, you miserable little vampire. You know how he came into the world, Smith?"

"Shut up!" Lord Ermenwyr shouted.

"Ha, ha—it seems Mother and Daddy were making love in a hammock in a gazebo in the garden, and because they were neither on the earth, nor in the sky, nor under earth or in the sea, nor indoors nor out, but suspended—"

"Don't tell that story!"

"I forget exactly what went wrong, but seven months later, Mother noticed this wretched screaming little thing that had fallen out under her skirt, and she had pity on it, even though *I* told her she ought to give it away because we didn't need any more babies, but I guess being the Compassionate One she had to keep it, and unfortunately it grew up, though it never got very big." Lord Eyrdway smiled serenely at his brother.

"You pus-bucket," Lord Ermenwyr growled.

"Midget."

"Imbecile!"

"Dwarf."

"You big walking string of shapeless snot from the nose of a diseased—"

"I know you are, but what am I?"

"You—!" Lord Ermenwyr was on the point of launching himself across the table at his brother when Smith rose in his seat, and thundered, *"Shut up, both of you!"*

The brothers sat back abruptly and stared at him, shocked.

"You can't tell us to shut up," said Lord Eyrdway in wonderment. "We're *demons.*"

"Quarter demons," Willowspear corrected him.

"But I killed three men for you, so you owe me," said Smith. "Don't you? No more fighting as long as you're both here."

"Whatever you like," said Lord Eyrdway amiably enough, taking a sip of his wine. "I always honor a debt of blood."

"I still want to know what you're doing off the mountain," said Lord Ermenwyr sullenly. "To say nothing of why you chose to bolt into my favorite hotel."

"Oh," said Eyrdway, looking uneasy. "That. Well, I made a little mistake. It wasn't my fault."

"Really?" Lord Ermenwyr smiled at him, narrowing his eyes. "Whatever did you do, might one ask?"

"I just raided a caravan," said Lord Eyrdway.

"Hmmm. And?" Lord Ermenwyr's smile showed a few sharp teeth.

"Well—you know, when caravans are insured, they really ought to be required to carry signs or something saying who insured them, so everybody will know," said Lord Eyrdway self-righteously.

Lord Ermenwyr began to snicker.

"You raided a caravan that was insured by Daddy's company," he stated gleefully. "And Daddy had to pay the claim?"

"Your father runs an insurance company?" Smith inquired.

"And makes a lot more money than by being a brigand," Lord Ermenwyr replied. "There are only so many ways you can keep your self-respect as a Lord of Evil when you can't break any laws."

"And there wasn't even any nice loot," complained Lord Eyrdway. "Nothing but a lot of stupid bags of flour. So I cut them all open in case there was anything valuable inside, which there wasn't, so we just threw the stuff around and danced in it and came home white as ghosts, and then it turned out the flour had been going to a village where the people were starving, so that got Mother mad at me too."

"You sublime blockhead!" Lord Ermenwyr rocked to and fro, hugging himself.

"So Daddy told me I was banished until I could repay him the value of the caravan," said Lord Eyrdway. "And Mother reproached me."

"Ooh." Lord Ermenwyr winced. "That's serious. And you haven't a clue how to get money, have you?"

"I do so!" snarled Lord Eyrdway. "I stole some from a traveler when I was coming down the mountain. But he didn't have nearly enough, so I asked the next traveler I robbed where there was a good gambling house, and he said there were a lot of them in Salesh-by-the-Sea."

"Oh, gods."

"Well, you're always on about how much fun you have here! So I got over the city wall and found a nice gambling house, and at first I won lots of money," Lord Eyrdway said. "And they served me a lot of free drinks. So I drank a little more than I should have, maybe. So some of what happened I don't remember too well. But there was a lot of shouting."

"You must have killed somebody," said Smith.

"Yes, I think I did," Lord Eyrdway agreed. "Not only did I not win any more money, they wanted money from *me*! And so I left, and changed into a few things to throw them off the chase. But they figured out I was changing, somehow, and kept after me. So I ran down to the harbor and turned myself into a seagull. Wasn't that clever of me?" He turned to his brother, bright-eyed. "Nobody can pick one seagull out of a crowd!"

"You're brilliant," drawled Lord Ermenwyr. "Go on."

"So I spent the night like that, and all the lady seagulls fell in love with me. But I was thirsty by this morning, so I turned back into me and went walking along the harbor looking for a place to get a drink. Then I heard a yell, and when I turned around, there were those people again, and they had other people with them, and they were all coming after me with weapons drawn."

"You booby, they'd had time to circulate your description," Lord Ermenwyr told him.

"Really?" Lord Eyrdway looked dismayed. "What are they so upset about? I thought nothing was forbidden in Salesh in Festival time."

"They're talking about sins of the flesh, not manslaughter," Smith pointed out.

"Oh. Well, it ought to say so on those brochures, then! Anyway I remembered you had a safe house somewhere hereabouts, so I went looking for it, but—"

"You were coming to me for *protection*?" Lord Ermenwyr smiled, showing all his teeth.

"No, I wasn't!" said Lord Eyrdway at once. "I don't need your protection! I just thought, you know . . ." He opened and shut his mouth a few times, seeking words.

"Well, that's done it; his brain's seized up with the effort,"

Lord Ermenwyr said to Smith. "While we're waiting, let me apologize for this unsightly complication. As for you, brother dearest, I shall be happy to offer you refuge. It's what Mother would want me to do, I'm sure."

"Go explode yourself," said Lord Eyrdway pettishly. "I just thought I could borrow enough money from you to pay Daddy back."

"Ah, but then you'd miss the instructive discipline Daddy was meting out by your temporary banishment, wouldn't you?" said Lord Ermenwyr. "And I'm certain Mother was hoping you'd learn some sort of moral lesson from the experience, as well."

"Does that mean you won't lend me the money?"

"You fool, it's ridiculously easy to get money from mortals without stealing it from them," Lord Ermenwyr said.

"It is?" Large brass wheels and gears appeared in the air above Lord Eyrdway's head, turning slowly. "People do that, don't they?"

"Quite. For example, Smith, here, used to kill people for money," said Lord Ermenwyr.

"Used to," Smith said. "I keep a hotel now. I don't recommend the assassin game, lord. It's a lot harder than it sounds."

"Well, I don't want to do anything hard," said Lord Eyrdway, frowning. The gears above his head metamorphosed into a glowing lamp, and he turned to his brother. "I know! Haven't you been peddling your ass to the mortals?"

"I'm a junior gigolo," Lord Ermenwyr corrected him. "And it's much more subtle than mere peddling. You have to romance them. You have to wheedle presents. You have to know the best places to unload presents for cash. But, yes, you can get mortals to pay you ever so much for having sex with them, if you're young and beautiful."

"How'd you manage it, then?" Lord Eyrdway chortled.

"Smith, shall I tell you about the time Eyrdway here was beaten up by our sister?"

"Don't tell him that story!"

"Then watch your mouth, you oaf. A male prostitute has to be charming." Lord Ermenwyr stroked his beard and considered his brother through half-closed eyes. "There are certain streets where one goes to linger. You make yourself look young and vulnerable, and I always found it helped to let a little of my glamour down, so mortals could just get the tiniest glimpse of my true form."

"I can do that," Lord Eyrdway decided.

"Then you wait for someone to notice you. You want somebody older, somebody well dressed. Usually they offer to buy you a drink."

"Got it."

"And then you go to bed with them and make them as happy as you possibly can. The customer is always right, remember."

"Are you sure this is what you used to do?" Lord Eyrdway looked dubious as he ran back over the details.

"Why, of course," said Lord Ermenwyr silkily. He had a sip of his wine.

"And you can really get money this way?"

"Heaps," Lord Ermenwyr assured his brother.

"Well, then, I ought to be a famous success!" said Lord Eyrdway happily. "Because I'm lots more attractive than you. I think I'll start today."

"You won't get anybody to pay for sex during Festival," said Smith.

"That's true," Lord Ermenwyr agreed. "You'll have to start next week. You can stay with me until then. You can't practice here in Smith's hotel, because he's having a bit of trouble already. But there are public orgies scheduled all over town tonight." He looked his brother up and down. "I'd recommend going in a different shape. You're still wanted by the City Wardens, remember."

"Right," said Lord Eyrdway. "Thanks."

"What are brothers for?" said Lord Ermenwyr.

"Bail," said Lord Eyrdway. He looked curiously at Smith. "You're having trouble? Anything I can help with? You did save my life, after all."

Smith explained the circumstances, so far as he knew them, surrounding the murder of Sharplin Coppercut.

"Well, if things turn nasty, I'll let little Burnbright hide in my room until she can be smuggled out," said Lord Ermenwyr. "Is she really one of the massacre survivors?"

"Coppercut thought so," said Smith. "And he'd gone to a lot of trouble to dig up evidence. But she can't have been much more than a newborn when it all happened."

"Mother took in somebody's orphan from the Spellmetal thing, didn't she?" said Lord Eyrdway. He pointed at Willowspear. "In fact, it was you, wasn't it?"

Lord Ermenwyr grimaced. Smith looked at Willowspear. "Is that true?"

"You've just implicated him, you moron," Lord Ermenwyr told his brother.

"Yes, sir, it's true," Willowspear replied. "I lost my parents in the massacre."

"But he can't kill anybody, Smith," said Lord Ermenwyr. "He's one of Mother's disciples. They don't do that kind of thing."

"He was on the same floor as Coppercut at the time the murder happened," Smith explained patiently. "He's connected to the Spellmetal massacre. He's a doctor, so he knows herbs and presumably poisons. Wasn't he in the kitchen at one point? When he fixed up Burnbright's knee? And he was standing *behind* your chair on the balcony during the fireworks display; I saw him. He might have slipped away without you noticing."

"Smith, I give you my word as my father's son—" protested Lord Ermenwyr.

"What about it?" Smith asked Willowspear. "Coppercut was a damned bad man. He was using his knowledge to hurt innocents. A lot of people would have considered it a moral act to take him out. Did you?"

"No," said Willowspear. "As a servant of the Compassionate One, I may not judge others, nor may I kill."

"Coppercut couldn't have had anything on him, anyway," said Lord Ermenwyr. "No records to trace. Yendri adoptions aren't done through your courts."

"Somebody in rags showed up one day at the front battlement, carrying a baby," Lord Eyrdway affirmed. "Which was you, Willowspear. Mother took the baby in, the beggar went away. End of story."

"It's a coincidence," stated Lord Ermenwyr. "It could have been anybody here."

Smith nodded, not taking his eyes from Willowspear's face. The young man met his gaze unflinchingly. "I'll interview the guests, then, as they become conscious."

Lord Eyrdway remembered his drink and emptied it in a gulp. "By the way, Ermenwyr, somebody else came round to the front gate asking for you. Just before Daddy threw me out."

"What?" Lord Ermenwyr started. "Who?"

"Said his name was . . . oh! That funny name you said." Lord Eyrdway gestured at Smith. "Bitchbliss?"

"Blichbiss!"

"Whatever. The gate guards told him you'd gone abroad and weren't expected back for a while. You'd better get in touch with him."

"I'm not about to get in touch with him!" said Lord Ermenwyr, and explained why. Eyrdway listened, puzzled at first, then frowning.

When his brother had finished, he said, "You mean this man wants to challenge you, and you're ducking him?"

"Of course I'm ducking him, you half-wit!"

"What are you, a coward?" Lord Eyrdway looked outraged.

"Yes! And if you'd died as often as I have, you'd be a coward too!" said Lord Ermenwyr.

"But you can't refuse a challenge," said Lord Eyrdway. "What about the honor of our house?"

"*Honor?* Hello! Eyrdway, are you in there? Remember who Daddy is?" Lord Ermenwyr yelled in exasperation. "And anyway, you ran like a rabbit yourself when those mortals were after you."

"Oh, that. Well, they were nobodies, weren't they? Just some people who wanted to kill me, for some reason. But you have to accept a challenge," said Lord Eyrdway reasonably.

"No, I don't, and I won't," announced Lord Ermenwyr, tugging at his beard. Hands trembling with vexation, he drew out his smoking tube and packed it full of weed from a small pouch. "Look at me, look what you've done to my nerves!"

"Poor baby," jeered Lord Eyrdway, and then his manner changed. "Oo. Is that pinkweed? Can I have a hit?"

"No." Lord Ermenwyr lit the tube with a small fireball.

"Not in here!" Smith cautioned.

"Sorry." Lord Ermenwyr ostentatiously pantomimed waving out a nonexistent straw and setting it down, as he puffed out aromatic fumes in a thick cloud. "I'm going to go upstairs now and have my breakfast, which I never got because you arrived right in the middle of it, and if you promise not to bring a certain subject up again, I'll share some of this."

"What subject?" asked Lord Eyrdway.

"Oh, and Smith?" Lord Ermenwyr stood and edged out of the booth. "The sheep won't be necessary."

⌐

The first of the hotel guests to appear, wandering in with a bewildered expression from the shrubbery, was Lady Shanriana of House Goldspur. She had lost several rather necessary sequins and her blue body paint needed strategic touching up.

Smith hastened forward with a complimentary robe and wrapped it around her, inquiring, "Lady, will you be pleased to take breakfast in the room or in the indoor dining area?"

"In my room, I suppose," she said. "I'm not sure I recall checking in here last night. Did I have servants with me?"

"No, lady, you came alone." Smith escorted her up the stairs, for she was wobbling slightly as she walked. "You're in Room 3. May I suggest hot tea and a sweet roll?"

"Three or four of them," she replied. "And send someone up to draw me a hot bath. Someone handsome."

"We'll send our most attractive porter, madam," said Smith, mentally noting that New Smith was slightly less weather-beaten than his fellow porters. "Though all our porters are more noted for their strength than their handsomeness, I must warn you."

"Hmm." Lady Shanriana dimpled in several locations. "Strength is nice. I like strength."

"I hope you weren't disturbed at any time last night," Smith went on. "We had a mild vendetta problem, it appears."

"Oh, well, that happens," said Lady Shanriana, waving a

dismissive hand as she wandered past Room 3. Smith, on pretext of leaning close to whisper in her ear, caught her shoulder and steered her gently back around to her door.

"But it's rather a scandal, I'm afraid, though of course they do say a scandal is good for business," Smith murmured, watching Lady Shanriana's face. A gleam of avid interest came into her eyes.

"Who got killed?" she inquired.

"Well—I've been asked to keep it quiet, but—" Smith leaned closer still. "It was Sharplin Coppercut, the writer."

He watched her face closely. The gleam vanished at once, to be followed by a look of disappointment and chagrin. "Oh, no, really? I never missed his columns! He did that wonderfully steamy unauthorized biography of Lady What's-her-name, the shipping heiress, didn't he? *The Imaginary Virgin?* Oh, how awful!"

"Was he a personal acquaintance of yours?"

"Heavens, no. One doesn't associate with writers," said Lady Shanriana, looking even more dismayed. She fumbled with the latch on her door. Smith opened it for her and bowed her in.

"On the other hand, once the news is made public, you'll be able to tell people you had the room across from the one Sharplin Coppercut was in when he died," Smith pointed out. She seemed distinctly pleased at that. "I hope you weren't inconvenienced when it happened?"

"No; I was out on the terrace all night. At least, I think I was. Yes, I'm sure I must have been, because there was a whole party of officers from somebody's war galleon, and they all claimed me because they serve the Spirit of the Waters, don't they, you see? So we had a lovely time all evening. I must have missed the killing. I suppose it was a dreadfully bloody affair? Assassins all in black leather, hooded?" Her eyes glazed with a private fantasy.

"Something like that," Smith said.

"Ooh. Send up that porter quickly, please. And a plate of sausage." Lady Shanriana rubbed her hands together.

Descending the staircase, Smith crossed her off his mental list of suspects. In his previous line of work, he had developed the knack of reading people's expressions fairly well. Lady Shanriana might have a kink for bloodshed, but she had been genuinely startled to hear of Coppercut's death.

He caught New Smith in the lobby and gave him Lady Shanriana's breakfast order, just as a naval officer came stumbling in from the terrace, struggling into his tunic.

"What time is it?" he demanded wildly, as his face emerged from the collar.

"First Prayer Interval was an hour ago," Smith told him. He calmed down somewhat.

"Where's the nearest bathhouse?" he inquired. "I've got blue stuff all over me."

"The Spirit of the Waters . . . ?" Smith prompted him, mentally adding the word *alibi* next to Lady Shanriana's name.

"Oh! That's right." The officer grinned as memory returned to him. "Gods! She started with the midshipmen at sundown and worked her way through to the admiral by midnight. Drowned us all. Joyous couplings! Great food here, too."

"We get a lot of celebrity clientele," Smith said. "Sharplin Coppercut, for example."

"Who's that?" The officer dug a sequin out of an unlikely place.

"The writer."

"Really? Never heard of him. Say, did I ask you where there was a bathhouse?"

"There's one around the corner on Cable Street," Smith said. "Joyous couplings."

"You too," said the officer, striding across the lobby. At the door he turned back, a look of inquiry on his face.

"It has a prophylaxis station, also," Smith assured him. Beaming, he saluted and left.

In the course of the next hour, Smith worked his way through the surviving hotel guests as they became conscious. The occupants of Room 4 were an elderly married couple from Port Blackrock who were in their room all evening, except for a foray onto the balcony to watch the fireworks. They had only vaguely heard of Sharplin Coppercut, being under the impression he was somebody who'd run for dictator of their city three terms ago, or was it four? They bickered about whether it was three or four terms ago for several minutes, until abruptly deciding they were both wrong and that Sharplin Coppercut had been the name of their grandson's first rhetoric tutor, the one who'd had such bad teeth.

"You didn't happen to hear anything unusual last night, did you?" Smith inquired, whereupon they got into a debate over what could be considered unusual in a hotel like this at Festival, with a lengthy reminiscence on how Festival had been celebrated in the old days, followed by a rumination on hotels both general and specific. Half an hour later, Smith thanked them and left. He was fairly confident they were not Coppercut's killers.

The occupant of Room 5 was a thickset, sullen businessman who had to be retrieved from under a table on the terrace and revived with a dose of hangover powders. He was profoundly surly even after the powders had taken effect, was missing his purse and sandals and threatened to beat Smith to a pulp if they'd been stolen, and was barely more gracious when Crucible located them safely tucked away under the chair he'd been sitting in the night previous. He ostentatiously checked the contents of the purse, threatening to fracture Crucible's jaw if anything had gone missing.

When it proved that nothing had been stolen, he ordered breakfast and threatened to break Smith's legs if it wasn't delivered to his room in fifteen minutes.

Not the sort of man to employ poison as a means of killing someone.

Returning down the corridor, Smith saw pink smoke curling out from under the door of Lord Ermenwyr's suite and heard terrifying laughter coming from the room beyond. Shuddering, he walked on and went back to the kitchen.

". . . *much* more digestible," Mrs. Smith was saying as he walked in. She and Burnbright were bending over another sea dragon, but this one was a dessert with a fruit bombe forming its body and a curved neck and head of marzipan. Lined up on trays on the table were row upon row of sugar scales, like disks of green glass, and Mrs. Smith was carefully applying them to the sea dragon's back with a pair of kitchen tweezers.

"Hello, Smith," she said, glancing up at him. "Any progress?"

"Some," said Smith. He pulled out a kitchen stool and sat down, staring glumly at the sea dragon. "This is our entry for the Festival cooking contest?"

"The Pageant of Lascivious Cuisine for the Prolongation of Ecstasy'," Mrs. Smith informed him. "I've got a good chance of winning, or so my spies tell me. The chef over at the Sea Garden failed to get in a special shipment of liqueurs he was counting on, and the chef at the spa's entry is simply an immense jam roll frosted to look like a penis. Ought to be quite a subliminal qualm of horror amongst the judges when it's sliced up and served out, wouldn't you think?"

"Yes," said Smith, wincing and crossing his legs.

"We'll do the wings next," Mrs. Smith told Burnbright. "Melon sugar, pomegranate dye, and rum, boiled to a hard syrup the same way. I'll show you the shapes I want it cut once it's cooled. How's our little mystery going?" she inquired of Smith.

"None of the other guests did the murder," said Smith, rubbing his temples.

"It still wasn't me," said Burnbright, clouding up.

"Silly child, nobody ever thought it was you for a minute. You know, Smith, anyone might have wandered in from the street and done for Coppercut, in all that pullulating frenzy of lust going on last night," Mrs. Smith remarked, setting scales in a ring around the dragon's eye. "And it's not as though there's any shortage of people with motives. After the way he told all about the scandalous lives of the well-to-do? Especially Lady Quartzhammer, who, as I believe, was depicted in the best-selling *The Imaginary Virgin* as having a passionate affair with a dwarf."

"And a bunch of goats," added Burnbright, stirring pomegranate dye into sugar syrup.

"Something dreadfully unsavory, in any case. To say nothing of the exposé he did on House Steelsmoke! I shouldn't think they particularly cared to have it known that Lord Pankin's mother was also his sister, and a werewolf into the bargain." Mrs. Smith turned the sea dragon carefully and started another row of scales.

"Didn't he say that all the Steelsmoke girls are born with tails, too? That was what I heard!" said Burnbright.

"He interviewed the doctor who did the postnatal amputations," Mrs. Smith said. "Thoroughly ruthless, Sharplin Coppercut, and ruthlessly thorough. When his demise is made public, I imagine a number of highborn people will drink the health of his murderer in sparkling wine."

"But he went after lowborn people too," Burnbright quavered.

"Quite so. It seems unlikely you'll solve this, Smith."

Mrs. Smith leaned back and lit her smoking tube. She blew twin jets of smoke from her nostrils and considered him. "Perhaps Crossbrace could be persuaded with a bribe, instead of a likely suspect? Unlimited access to the bar? Or I'd be happy to cater a private supper for him."

"It all depends on how—" Smith looked up as he heard a cautious knock at the kitchen door.

"Come in," said Mrs. Smith.

Willowspear entered the kitchen and stopped, seeing Smith. "I beg your pardon," he said, a little hoarsely. His eyes were watering and inflamed.

"Was the pinkweed getting to you?" Smith inquired.

Willowspear nodded, coughing into his fist. Burnbright, who had spun about the moment she heard his voice, came at once to his side.

"Would you like to sit down?" she asked, in a tone of concern Smith had never heard her use. "Can I get you a cup of water?"

"Yes, thank you," said Willowspear. Smith and Mrs. Smith exchanged glances.

"Are their lordships getting along?" Smith inquired.

"Reasonably well," Willowspear replied, sinking onto the stool Burnbright brought for him. "My lord Ermenwyr is reclining on his bed, tossing fireballs into the hearth. My lord Eyrdway is reclining on a couch and has transformed himself into a small fishing boat, complete with oars. They are past speech at the present time, and so are unlikely to quarrel, but are still in fair control of their nervous systems. Thank you, child." He accepted a cup of water from Burnbright, smiling at her.

"You're awfully welcome," said Burnbright, continuing to hover by him.

"It's very kind of you," he said.

"Not at all!" she chirped anxiously. "I just—I mean—you're not like them. I mean, you looked like you needed—er—"

"A drink of water?" prompted Mrs. Smith.

"That's right," said Burnbright.

"I did," said Willowspear. He took a careful sip. "I'm not accustomed to pinkweed smoke in such concentration. I don't indulge in it, myself."

"Well, but it's full of nasty fumes in here!" said Burnbright, pointing at Mrs. Smith's smoking tube.

"Nothing but harmless amberleaf," said Mrs. Smith in mild affront. Burnbright ignored her.

"Would you like to step out in our back area until you feel better?" she asked Willowspear. "There's lovely fresh air, and—and a really nice view!"

"Perhaps I—"

"Would you like me to show you?"

They stared into each other's eyes for a moment.

"I—yes," said Willowspear, and Burnbright led him out the back door.

Mrs. Smith blew a smoke ring.

"Well, well," she remarked.

"I didn't think she had a sex drive," said Smith wonderingly.

"It's Festival, Smith," Mrs. Smith replied.

"I guess she had to fall in love sooner or later," said Smith. "I just never thought it'd be with a Yendri."

Mrs. Smith shrugged.

"They taught her to despise greenies at the mother house, from the time she was old enough to stagger around on her little legs. That would only make the attraction more powerful, once it hit," she said. "The thrill of the forbidden, and all that."

She paused a long moment, her gaze unreadable, and took

another drag on her smoking tube. "Besides," she added, exhaling smoke, "it's in her blood."

At that moment a small pan on the hearth hissed as its contents foamed up, and Mrs. Smith leaped to her feet. "Hell! She's gone and left that syrup on the fire!" Muttering imprecations, she snatched it off and dumped its molten contents on the marble countertop, where the red stuff ran and spread like a sheet of gore.

"What on earth?" Smith scrambled to his feet, staring.

"It's the candy glass for the dragon's wings," Mrs. Smith explained, glaring at the door through which Burnbright and Willowspear had disappeared. "Grab a spatula and help me. If we don't pull this mess into wing shapes before it hardens, it'll be wasted. Gods and goddesses, I could wring that child's neck sometimes!"

Smith, being a wise man, grabbed a spatula.

⌐

By that afternoon, Smith was too busy to continue his investigation.

Salesh had stretched on her silken couch and awakened once again, blinking through wine-fogged eyes at her lover Festival. After a brief moment of confusion and search for headache remedies, she had recollected who he was and taken him back into her insatiable embrace with renewed vigor.

The solemn bells for Third Prayer Interval signaled the start of the grand Parade of Joyous Couplings along Front Street. Its staging area was just around the corner on Hawser, so guests at the Hotel Grandview had a fine view of the proceedings.

With a shrill wail of pipes, with a chime and rattle of tambourines, here came the first of the revelers, clad in a shower of rose petals and very little else! They danced, they tossed their wild hair, they bounded athletically for the edification of the assembled crowd along the street's edge. Winsome girls rode the shoulders of bull-mighty boys, and from small baskets the girls tossed aphrodisiac comfits to onlookers.

Behind them, a team of men costumed as angels towed a wide flat wagon. Riding in it were some two dozen nurses who bore in their arms the bounty of last year's Festival, pretty three-month-olds decked in flowers. The babies stared around in bewilderment, or wept at all the noise, or slept in sublime indifference to the passion that had created them.

Following after, likewise crowned in flowers, were scores of little children born of previous Festivals, marching unevenly behind the foremost, who carried a long banner between them reading: LOVE MADE US. They trotted doggedly along, pushing back wreaths that slipped over their eyes. They stared uncertainly into the sea of adult faces, searching for their mothers, or waved as they had been told, or held hands with other children and laboriously performed the dance steps they had been taught for this occasion.

Next came the Salesh Festival Orchestra, blaring with enthusiasm a medley that began with "Burnished Beard on My Pillow," continued into "The Lady Who Could Do It Thirty Times Without Stopping" and concluded with a rousing arrangement of "The Virgins of Karkateen." After them came the parade floats sponsored by the different businesses and guilds of Salesh.

Here, steering badly as it lumbered along, for all that it was driven with ingenious gear ratios by its clockwork rowers, was a thirty-foot gilded galley bearing the Spirit of Love, in her scarlet silks. Her breasts were the size of harbor buoys, and puppeteers worked her immense languid hands as she blessed the crowd.

Here was a float presenting the Mother of Fire in her garden, a towering lady wreathed in red and yellow scarves,

which were kept in constant motion by concealed techni-
cians working a series of bellows under the float. Their
scrambling legs were just visible under the skirts of the pageant wagon, and now and then a hand would flash into view
as it tossed a fistful of incense onto one of the several braziers that were housed in giant roses of flame-colored enameled tin.

Here was a float representing the Father Blacksmith, presented at the Anvil of the World, his sea-colored eyes great
disks of inset glass with lanterns behind them, and his left
arm articulated on a ratcheting wheel cranked by a techni-
cian who crouched under his elbow, so that it rose and fell,
rose and fell with its great hammer, beating out the fate of
all men, and more incense smoke streamed upward from his
forge.

After his wagon came a dozen clowns dressed as phal-
luses, running to and fro on tiny spindly legs and peering
desperately through tiny eyeholes as they tried to avoid
falling over one another. They were great favorites with the
little children in the audience.

Next came rolling a half-sized replica of the famous war
galley *Duke Rakut's Pride*, its decks crowded with sailors
and mermaids, waving cheerfully at the crowd despite their
various amatory entanglements. Halfway down the block
between Hawser and Cable its topmast became entangled in
an advertising banner stretched across Front Street at roof
level, and the parade had to be halted long enough for a
sailor to disengage, scramble up the mast with his knife, and
cut the banner's line, for which he received cheers and
applause.

After that, more musicians: the Runners' Trumpeting
Corps, long-legged girls resplendent in their red uniforms
and flaring scarves, lifting curiously worked horns to blare
the Salesh Fanfare with brazen throats. Behind them came

the drummers of the Porters' Union, thundering mightily on steel drums with their fists, so that the din rolled and echoed between the housefronts for blocks. And after them, a contingent from the Anchor Street Bakery came pulling a giant cake on wheels, from the top of which children costumed as cherubs threw sweet rolls to the crowd.

Male jugglers marched after, miraculously keeping suggestively painted clubs in the air without stopping their forward momentum, though each bore a female acrobat with her legs twined about his waist in mimicked intimate union. The girls occasionally leaned far backward and walked with their hands, or juggled small brass balls.

More floats, more Spirits of This or That relating to the procreative act, more bands, a few civic leaders borne along in decorated carts to applause or execration. Brilliant streamers flew, and confetti in every color, and bird kites towed on ribbons, and banners that flared like the ice lights in northern kingdoms where sunlight came so seldom there were a hundred different words for darkness.

When it had all gone by at last, the throng of merrymakers followed it down the hill, shedding clothing as they went, donning masks, seizing flowers from hedges that grew over walls, lighting scarlet lamps; and it was Festival!

Though householders less inclined to revel at Pleasure's fountains issued out into the street and swept up the stepped-on bits of sweet roll, or complained bitterly about the flowers torn from their hedges.

"Damned Anchor Street Bakery," said Mrs. Smith, as she and Smith retreated through the lobby. "I may have some competition! With all those bloody cherubs throwing free treats to the crowd, the voting in the dessert category may be swayed."

"Are you worried?"

"Not particularly," she said, lighting her smoking tube.

"Free treats or not, the master baker at Anchor Street uses nothing but wholemeal flour. I'd like to see anybody make a palatable fairy cake out of a mess of stone-ground husks!"

She swept upstairs, trailing smoke, to don her finery for the contest. Smith followed her as far as the landing, where he rapped cautiously at the door to Lord Ermenwyr's suite.

"Come in, damn you," said a deathly voice from within.

Smith opened the door and peeked inside. Lord Ermenwyr was sprawled on the parlor couch with his head hanging backward off the edge and his eyes rolled back, so that for one panicky moment Smith thought he needed to be resuscitated.

"My lord?" He hurried inside. But the ghastly figure on the couch waved a feeble hand at him.

"Assist me, Smith. What time is it?"

"Halfway between Third and Fourth Prayer Interval," said Smith, lifting Lord Ermenwyr into a sitting position.

"Doesn't tell me a lot, does it, since I don't worship your gods, and I wouldn't pray to them even if I did," moaned Lord Ermenwyr. "Is it drawing on toward evening, or are my eyes simply dying in their sockets?"

"It'll be sunset in half an hour," Smith said, fetching him a carafe of water and pouring him a cup.

"I wish I really was a vampire; I'd be feeling great about now." Lord Ermenwyr looked around sourly. "But I am alone, abandoned by all who ever claimed they loved me."

"We are still here, Master," said a slightly reproachful voice. Smith turned, startled to note the four bodyguards lined up against the wall on either side of the balcony window. The glamour was off them and their true nature was quite evident; they resembled nothing so much as a quartet of standing stones with eyes and teeth, looming in the shadows.

"Well, aren't you the faithful ones," said Lord Ermenwyr, sipping from his cup. "Careful where you sit, Smith. The

Variable Magnificent's undoubtedly lurking around in the shape of an especially ugly end table or hassock."

"No, I'm not," said a voice from the bedroom, and Lord Eyrdway stepped into view. Smith had to stare a moment to be certain it was really he; for he had altered his height, appearing several inches shorter, and lengthened his nose, and moreover was wearing a full suit of immaculate formal evening dress.

"Hey!" Lord Ermenwyr cried in outrage. "I didn't say you could wear my clothes! You'll get slime all over them."

"Ha-ha, you fell for it," Lord Eyrdway said. "I wouldn't wear your old suits anyway; the trouser crotches wouldn't fit me. I only copied them. It's all me, see?" He turned to display himself. "I'm going to go out and find a party. Who'll recognize me with clothes on?"

"Want to hear me waste advice, Smith?" said Lord Ermenwyr. "Listen: Eyrdway, don't drink. If you do, you will begin to boast, and as you're not at home in the land of spoiled darlings, someone will take offense at your boasting and call you out, and then you'll kill him, and then the bad people will chase you again. You don't want that to happen, do you, Way-way?"

"It won't happen, Worm-worm," his brother told him, grinning evilly. "I'm going to be clever. I'm going to be brilliant, in fact."

"Of course you will," Lord Ermenwyr repeated, sagging back on the cushions. "How silly of me to imagine for a moment you'll get yourself into trouble. Go. Have a wonderful time." He sat forward abruptly and his voice sharpened, "But those had better not be my pearl earrings you're wearing!"

"No, I copied those too," said Lord Eyrdway, shooting his neck forward out of his collar a good two yards so he could dangle the earrings before his brother's eyes. "You think I'd touch something that had been in your ears? Ugh!"

"Retract yourself! The last thing I need in my condition is a close-up of your face," said Lord Ermenwyr, swatting at him with one of the cushions. "Perfidious princox!"

"I know you are, but what am I?"

"Get out!"

"I'm going," Lord Eyrdway said, dancing to the door, colliding with it, then flinging it wide. "Look out, Salesh; you've never seen true youth and beauty until tonight!"

Lord Ermenwyr gagged.

"Open a window, Smith. I'd rather not vomit all over your carpets."

"You could do with a little fresh air," Smith said, opening the window and letting out some of the smoke. "No wonder you stop breathing all the time."

"It's not my fault I'm chronically ill," said Lord Ermenwyr. "I was born sickly. It's Daddy's fault, probably. He didn't infuse me with enough of the life force when he begot me. And the rest is Eyrdway's fault. He used to try to smother me in the cradle when Nursie wasn't looking, you know."

"I guess these things happen in families," said Smith. He took up a sofa cushion and used it as a fan to wave smoke out the window.

"Oh, the horror of siblings," Lord Ermenwyr said, closing his bloodshot eyes. "You're an orphan, aren't you, Smith? Lucky man. Yet you've got people who love you. Nobody would shed a tear if I gasped out my irrevocable last."

"You're just saying that because you haven't had your medication," said Smith encouragingly. "Where's Willowspear, anyway?"

"Vision questing, I assume," Lord Ermenwyr replied. "Do you know how to give an injection?"

"A what?" Smith frowned in puzzlement.

"Where you shoot medicine into someone's arm through a needle?"

Smith blanched. "Is that a demon thing?"

"I'd forgotten your race is dismally backward in medical practice," Lord Ermenwyr sighed. "Fetch me the green box on my dresser, and I'll show you."

Smith found the box, and watched in horrified fascination as Lord Ermenwyr drew out a glass tube shaped like a hummingbird, with a long needle for a beak. Removing a tiny cartridge of something poison-green from the box, he flipped up the hummingbird's tail feathers and loaded the cartridge; then opened and shut its tiny wings experimentally, until a livid green droplet appeared at the end of the needle.

"And Mr. Hummyhum is ready to play now," said Lord Ermenwyr, rolling up his sleeve. Taking out an atomizer, he squeezed its bulb until a fine mist of something aromatic wet his arm; then, with a practiced jab, he gave himself an injection. Smith flinched.

"There. My pointless life is prolonged another night," said Lord Ermenwyr wearily. "What are you looking so pale about? You're an old hand at sticking sharp things into people."

"It's different when you're killing," said Smith. "But when you're *saving* a life . . . it just seems perverse, somehow. Stabbing somebody to keep them alive, brr!"

"Remind me to tell you about invasive surgery sometime," said Lord Ermenwyr, ejecting the spent cartridge and putting the hummingbird away. "Or trepanning! Think of it as making a doorway to let evil spirits out of the body, if it'll help."

"No, thanks," said Smith fervently. He couldn't take his eyes off the glass bird, however. "You could shoot poison into somebody with one of those things to kill them, and it'd barely leave a mark, would it?"

"You wouldn't even need poison," Lord Ermenwyr told him, rubbing his arm. "A bubble of air could do it. It's not the sort of murder you could do by stealth very easily, though. Well, maybe *you* could. What, are you still trying to find out who killed that wretched journalist?"

Smith nodded.

"I know who didn't kill him, and I know what he didn't die of. That's about it."

"What did he die of, by the way?"

"I've no idea. There's not a mark on him."

"You haven't done an autopsy?" Lord Ermenwyr turned to stare at him. Smith stared back. "Oh, don't tell me you people don't do autopsies either!"

"I don't think we do," Smith admitted. "What's an autopsy?"

Lord Ermenwyr explained.

"But that's desecrating the corpse!" yelled Smith. "Ye gods, you'd have the angry ghost and every one of his ancestors after you in this world and the next!"

"All you have to do is tell them you're conducting a forensic analysis," said Lord Ermenwyr. "I've never had any trouble."

"I still couldn't do it," said Smith. "That's even worse than sticking needles into somebody. Cutting up a corpse in cold blood's an abomination."

"Oh, I wouldn't know anything about abominations, not me," said Lord Ermenwyr, beginning to grin as his medication took affect. "Look here, why don't I do the job for you? I take it the idea of a demon fooling around with a corpse doesn't violate your sense of propriety quite as badly?"

"I guess it would be different for you," Smith conceded.

"Well then!" Lord Ermenwyr sprang to his feet. "I've even got a set of autopsy tools with me. Isn't that lucky? One ought never to travel unprepared, at least that's what Daddy says. The restaurant's closed tonight, isn't it? We can just open him up in the kitchen!"

"No!" Smith protested. "What if he decided to haunt in there, ever after? The restaurant's our whole reputation. We could be ruined!"

"And it wouldn't be terribly sanitary, either, I suppose," Lord Ermenwyr said, rummaging in a drawer. "Where did I leave that bone saw? No matter; we'll just wait until everyone's gone off to Festival, and we'll bring him up here. More privacy!"

⌐

Smith went downstairs and waited, nervously, as one by one the guests came down in their Festival costumes and walked out or ordered bearers to take them into the heart of town, where most of the evening's Festival activities were going on. Mrs. Smith emerged from the kitchen, followed by Crucible and Pinion bearing between them the Sea Dragon Bombe on a vast platter. It was glorious to see, spreading wings like fans of ruby glass, and light glittered on its thousand emerald scales.

Mrs. Smith herself was no less resplendent, swathed in tented magnificence of peacock-blue satin and cloth of gold, her hair elaborately coifed, her lips crimsoned. A wave of perfume went before and followed her.

"We're off to the civic banqueting hall. Wish me luck, Smith," she said. "I'll need it. I've just been informed the Anchor Street Bakery got a shipment of superfine manchet flour from Old Troon Mills this morning."

"Good luck," said Smith. "They use too much buttercream, anyway."

"And the bombe is loaded with aphrodisiacs," said Mrs. Smith, pulling out her best smoking tube—black jade, a foot long and elaborately carved—and setting it between her teeth. "So we must hope for the best. Be a dear and give us a light?"

Smith gave her a light and a kiss. As he leaned close, Mrs. Smith murmured; "Burnbright's gone out with young Willowspear."

"You mean to the Festival?" Smith started.

"They spent ages out there together on the parapet," she said. "When I went into the bar to get a bottle of passion-fruit liqueur for the serving sauce, they came sneaking through. Thought I didn't see them. But I saw their faces; I know that look. They ran out through the garden and went over the wall. I don't expect they'll be back until morning, but you might leave the side door unlocked."

Smith was trying to imagine Willowspear doing something as earthly as scrambling over a wall with a girl. "Right," he said, nodding slowly. "Side door. Well. Return victorious, Mrs. Smith."

"Death to our enemies," she replied grimly. Pulling her yards of train over one arm and puffing out clouds of smoke, she strode forth into the night, and Crucible and Pinion followed her with the bombe.

⤻

Leaving Bellows on duty in the lobby and the two other Smiths in the bar to deal with any late-night emergencies, Smith hurried upstairs and rapped twice on Lord Ermenwyr's door. It was immediately flung wide by Lord Ermenwyr, who stood there grinning from ear to ear.

"All clear?"

"All clear."

"Come on, boys!" He shot out of his room past Smith and went clattering down the stairs, and the four bodyguards thundered after him.

"Er—" Smith waved frantically, attempting to direct

attention to the fact that Cutt had his head on backward. Lord Ermenwyr turned, spotted the problem, giggled, and corrected it with a wave of his hand.

"Sorry," he said in a loud stage whisper. "Come on, where's the you-know?"

Smith hurried down to join them and led the party back to the kitchen, where they descended into the cold cellar. Coppercut was gray and stiff as a board, which put smuggling him upstairs in an empty barrel out of the question. At last, after a certain amount of grisly hilarity and impractical, not to say criminal, suggestions, they settled for draping the corpse in sacking and carrying him out. Smith prayed there wouldn't be any guests in the lobby, and there weren't; after Bellows gave them the all clear and waved them through, they took the body up the stairs, tottering under it like a crowd of mismatched ants toting a dead beetle.

Thoroughly unnerved by the time they were back in Lord Ermenwyr's suite, Smith was relieved to see neither black candles nor dark-fumed incense lit, but only bright lamps arranged around a table that had been tidily covered with oilcloth. On a smaller table close at hand were laid out edged tools of distressingly culinary design.

"Let's just plop him down over there," said Lord Ermenwyr, slipping out from under the corpse to shut the door. "Boys, cut his clothes off."

"Don't *cut* them, for gods' sake," said Smith. "I've still got to hand him over to Crossbrace tomorrow. If he's naked with a big hole in him, that'll raise some questions, won't it?"

"Too true," Lord Ermenwyr said. "All right; just get the clothes off him somehow, boys."

The bodyguards set to their task obligingly, and though Coppercut's body went through some maneuvers that could best be described as terribly undignified, his clothes came off at last.

"It's like one of those puzzles," growled Crish happily, holding up Coppercut's tunic. "You can do it; you just have to think really hard."

"Good for you," said Lord Ermenwyr, removing his own jacket and shirt. He stripped a sheet from the bed and tied it around his neck like an immense trailing napkin. Smith paced nervously, watching the proceedings and silently apologizing to Coppercut.

"Now then." Lord Ermenwyr stepped up to the corpse and studied it. "What have we got? A male Child of the Sun, dead roughly a day and a half. Looks to be in the prime of life. No signs of chronic illness present. Well-healed scar on the right side, between the third and fourth ribs. Someone once took a shot at you with, hm, a pistol bolt? Missed anything vital, though. Otherwise unscarred and well nourished. Some evidence of initial processes of putrefaction."

Smith groaned. "Get on with it, please!"

"You want me to find out what killed him, don't you?" Lord Ermenwyr replied. He peered into Coppercut's eyes and ears, felt gingerly all over his skull. "No evidence of head injury. Nobody sneaked up and coshed him from behind. Signs of asphyxia present. Internal suffocation? I'm betting on poison. Let's see the stomach contents."

He selected a small knife from the table at his elbow and made a long incision down Coppercut's front. Smith, watching, felt himself break out in a cold sweat.

"Let's see, where does your race keep their stomachs? I remember now . . . here we go. Come and help me, Smith. Oh, all right! Strangel, hand him the lamp and *you* come help me. Honestly, Smith, what kind of an assassin were you?"

"A quick one," Smith panted, averting his face. "Even on the battlefield you have to hack off arms and heads and things, but—but it's all in the heat of the moment. It's nothing like this. I guess you learned how from your lord father?"

The bodyguards started to genuflect and narrowly stopped themselves, as lamplight flickered crazily in the room and Crish nearly dropped what Lord Ermenwyr had given him to hold.

"Steady," warned Lord Ermenwyr. "No . . . I learned it from Mother, if you want to know the truth. It's her opinion that if you study the processes of death, you can save other lives. Don't imagine she trembles over the dissecting table either, Smith. She has nerves of ice. *Real* Good can be as ruthless as Evil when it wants to accomplish something, let me tell you."

"I guess so." Smith wiped his brow and got control of his nerves.

"He didn't eat much. I'd say his stomach was empty when he got here. Had . . . wine, had Mrs. Smith's delightful fried eel . . . looks like a bit of buttered roll . . . what's this stuff?"

"He ate his appetizer," Smith stated. "I think it was fish."

"Fish, yes. Those dreadful little raw fish petits fours Salesh is so proud of? That's what these are, then. I can't imagine how you people manage to eat them, especially with all those incendiary sauces . . . oh."

"Oh?"

"I think I've found what did for him, Smith," said Lord Ermenwyr in an odd voice. He reached for a pair of tweezers and picked something out of the depths of Coppercut, and held it out into the lamplight, turning it this way and that. Smith peered at it. It was a small gray lump of matter.

"What the hell is that?"

"Unless I'm much mistaken—" Lord Ermenwyr took up a finely ground lens in a frame and screwed it into his eye. He studied the object closely. "And I'm not, this is a bloatfish liver."

"And that would be?"

Lord Ermenwyr removed the lens and regarded him. "You were a weapons man, weren't you? Not a poisons man. I'd bet you've never sold fish, either."

"No, I never did. Bloatfish liver is poisonous?"

"Deadly poisonous." Lord Ermenwyr spoke with an unaccustomed gravity. "The rest of the fish is safe to eat, but the liver is so full of toxin most cities have an ordinance requiring that it be removed before the fish can be sold. Perhaps Salesh isn't as safety-conscious. In any case, this got into his fish appetizer. He had three minutes to live from the moment he swallowed it down."

Smith groaned. "So it was his dinner. Not Scourbrass's Foaming Wonder."

"Yes, but I don't think you have to worry about losing your catering license," said Lord Ermenwyr, setting aside the liver and beginning to replace Coppercut's organs. "This wasn't negligence. It was deliberate murder. The liver was incised laterally to make sure the poison was released. Anyway, you don't just stick a whole bloatfish liver inside a Salesh Roll by mistake!"

Smith bowed his head and swore quietly.

Coppercut had been sutured up and was having his garments wrestled back on when there came a sharp knock at the door.

"What?" demanded Lord Ermenwyr, removing his makeshift apron and reaching for his shirt.

"It's me," said Lord Eyrdway from the hallway.

"Bathroom," hissed Lord Ermenwyr to his bodyguards, gesturing at the corpse. They grabbed it up and carried it off. "He tends to get overexcited if he sees cadavers," he explained to Smith in an undertone, then raised his voice. "You're back early. What's the matter? Wasn't Salesh impressed with your beauty?" he inquired, buttoning up his shirt.

"Oh, I made a big splash." Lord Eyrdway's voice was gleeful. "And I stayed sober, too, nyah nyah! But the most amazing thing happened. Are you going to let me in? I've brought you a present."

Lord Ermenwyr's eyes narrowed to slits as he shrugged into his jacket.

"Really," he said noncommittally. In an undertone, he added; "Smith, would you be so kind as to open the door? But do it quickly, and stand well back. He's up to some ghastly practical joke."

Smith, who was sitting on the floor having a stiff drink, struggled to his feet and went to the door. He opened it and stood back. There on the threshold was Lord Eyrdway, his formal appearance a little disheveled. Behind him in the hall stood another gentleman, whose evening dress was still perfectly creased and immaculate.

"Hello, Smith," Lord Eyrdway said. "Look who I met in the Front Street Ballroom, brother!"

Lord Ermenwyr's eyes went perfectly round with horror. The other gentleman strode past Lord Eyrdway into the room, looking grimly triumphant.

"Glorious Slave of Scharathrion," he said in the resonant voice of a mage, "I hereby challenge you to thaumaturgical combat."

"You'll have to fight him now," added Lord Eyrdway, shutting and bolting the door behind them. "For the honor of our house."

"Despicable coward!" said Deviottin Blichbiss. He was a tall portly man, or at least was wearing the shape of one, with neatly parted hair and a sharp-edged mustache. "Did you really think I wouldn't hunt you down amongst these wretched mundanes? Now you'll die like a rat in a wall, as you richly deserve."

"I'm not a well man," said Lord Ermenwyr in a faint voice. "I'm afraid I'm not up to your challenge."

"You're afraid!" gloated Blichbiss. "And whether you're well, sick, or dead, we're going to duel in this room tonight. It's not a customary combat location, but mundane cities are within the permitted areas."

"Oh, you're lying," said Lord Ermenwyr, pulling at his beard in agitation.

"I most certainly am not. And if you were any kind of scholar, instead of the spoiled scion of a jumped-up Black Arts gladiator, you'd know that!"

"Are you going to let him talk about Daddy that way?" demanded Lord Eyrdway.

"I quote as precedent the *Codex Smagdaranthine*, fourth chapter, line 136: 'And it came to pass that in the mundane city of Celissa, in the seventh year of Fuskus the Tyrant's reign, Tloanix Hasherets was done grave insult by Prindo Goff, and therefore challenged him to wizardly battle, whereupon they dueled in the third hour after midnight in the central square of the city, and Hasherets smote Goff down with a bolt of balefire, and scattered his ashes in the fountain there,' " recited Blichbiss in a steely voice.

"But you haven't got a second," Lord Ermenwyr pointed out.

"I'll be his second," said Lord Eyrdway. "Smith can be yours."

"You traitor!"

The bodyguards came shuffling into the room and stopped, staring at Blichbiss. A low growl issued from Cutt's throat. All four of them began to drool. Lord Ermenwyr put his hands in his pockets, smirking.

"And then again, my gentlemen here just might tear you into little pieces," he said.

"No, they won't," Lord Eyrdway assured Blichbiss. "They take orders from my family, and I've got precedence over my little brother. You can't kill this man, boys, do you understand? That's a direct order. He's insulted Lord Ermenwyr, and so he's Lord Ermenwyr's kill alone."

The bodyguards drew back, looking at one another in some confusion. There was a taut silence in the room as they worked out the semantics of their terms of bondage, and finally Cutt nodded and bowed deeply, as did the other three.

"We respectfully withdraw, Masters," he said.

Smith shifted his grip on the bottle he was holding, just the slightest of movements, but Lord Eyrdway turned his head at once.

"Don't try it, Smith, or I'll kill you," he said. "And I'd really be sorry, because I like you, but mortals shouldn't get mixed up in these things."

"Thank you for the thought, however, Smith," said Lord Ermenwyr, with a hint of returning bravado. "Way-way, you are going to be in so much trouble with Mother."

Lord Eyrdway blanched.

"I'm doing you a favor, you whiner," he said plaintively. "You can't always run from everything that scares you. Fight the man!"

"Yes," said Blichbiss, who had been standing there with his arms folded, looking on in saturnine triumph. "Fight me."

"Very well." Lord Ermenwyr shot his cuffs and drew himself up. "I assume I get choice of weapons, as is customary?"

Blichbiss nodded, hard-eyed.

"Then, given the fact that we're indoors and my second here has personal property at risk, I think we'll just avoid incendiary spells, if you've no objection?"

"None."

"So, under the circumstances, I think . . . I choose . . . Fatally Verbal Abuse!" cried Lord Ermenwyr.

Blichbiss's eyes flashed. "Typical of you. And I accept!"

Smith racked his brains, trying to remember what he'd ever heard of mages and their preferred means of killing one another. He vaguely recalled that Fatally Verbal Abuse was considered a low-caliber weapon. It had none of the glamour or impact of, say, a Purple Dragon Invocation or a Spell of Gradual Unmaking. In fact, there was some dispute as to whether it constituted an actual *magickal* weapon at all, given the propensity of people to believe what they are told about themselves anyway, and their tendency to fulfill negative expectations. There were those on the fabled Black Council who held that only the process of accelerated impact qualified it as a valid means of score-settling between arcanes.

This was not to say that Fatally Verbal Abuse could not produce dramatic results, however, or that strategy was not required in its use.

Blichbiss cleared his throat. He stood straight. "The first assault is mine, under the ancient rules of combat. Prepare yourself."

Lord Ermenwyr stiffened. Blichbiss drew a deep breath.

"You," he said, "are a twisted, underdeveloped dwarf with a bad tailor!"

Lord Eyrdway chortled. Smith gaped as, before his eyes, Lord Ermenwyr began to warp and shrink, and his suit seemed to become too long in one leg and too short in one arm.

Lord Ermenwyr bared his teeth and replied; "No, I am a handsome and exquisitely dressed fellow of somewhat less than average height while *you* are a squawking duck with gas!"

Blichbiss shuddered all over and dwindled, farting explosively, as Lord Ermenwyr and his suit returned to their normal proportions. Through the emerging bill that was replacing his teeth, Blichbiss managed to quack out the counterspell; "No, I am a gas-free man with neither wings nor bill who speaks in pure and persuasive tones, whereas you are a streak of black slime in a crack in the floor, soon to be scrubbed into oblivion!"

And like an expanding balloon he resumed his original shape, as Lord Ermenwyr seemed to dissolve, to darken, to sink down toward a crack in the floor . . .

"No!" he gurgled desperately. "I am a straight sound mage, mildew-resistant and clean in all my parts, but you are a one-legged castrated blind dog with mange!"

Whereupon he became the upright mage he said he was, and the black fungus that had begun to cover his face vanished; but Blichbiss toppled to the floor, clutching at his groin with swiftly withering arms, and turning his blind scabrous furry face he howled; "No! I am a man, full and complete and strong upon both my legs, clearly seeing that you are a toad whose teeth have grown together, preventing your speech!"

"Whoops," said Lord Eyrdway gleefully, for both he and Smith had caught the fallacy: Toads have no teeth. "Tried too hard to be clever!"

Lord Ermenwyr jerked back, an agonized look on his face as his teeth snapped shut. He struggled to get out words as he began to shrink and change color; as his mouth widened, the rest of the incantation cycled through and the teeth vanished. He made a horrible noise, just perceptible as words, "No! I am no toad but a man, with perfect and flawless dentition, clearly capable of stating that you are a mere giant mayfly with no mouth at all!"

"No!" gasped Blichbiss, as gauzy wings burst from the back of his dinner jacket. "I am a"—her reached up and tore at his elongating face to prevent his mouth from sealing before he could finish the counterspell—"a man with a mouth such as all men have, and no wings nor any brief life span, whereas you are a cheap tallow taper, your mouth wide with molten wax, your tongue the black wick, awrithe with living flame!"

"No!" Lord Ermenwyr screamed, spitting fire. "I am a man, and my tongue is supple, alive and flameless, no tallow to block my loud pronouncement that you are no man at all but a hanging effigy of old clothes stuffed with paper, your face a painted sack, your mouth a mere painted line, incapable of utterance!"

"Gurk!" exclaimed Blichbiss, as a noose appeared from nowhere and hoisted him up by the neck. "No! I am not hanging and—" He ripped his sealing mouth open again. "I am a mage whose curses are swift and always deadly, with a quick mouth to pronounce that *you*,"—and a terrible gleam came into his eyes—"are a pusillanimous little half-breed *nouveau-arcane* psychopath who richly deserves the inescapable blast of witchfire that is about to electrocute him where he stands!"

"Hey!" said Smith in dismay, and Lord Eyrdway looked confused as he played the spell back in his head; but Lord Ermenwyr, his eyes bugging from their sockets, stared up at the crackling circle of white-hot energy that had just begun to circle his head. He shrieked the first thing that came to mind;

"I know you are, but what am I?"

With his last syllable the witchfire reached critical mass and shot out a ravening tongue of lightning, hitting Blichbiss square in the middle of his waistcoat. That gentleman had just time to look outraged before he made a sizzling noise, his sinuses discharged copiously, and the fire engulfed him in a crackling blaze for the space of three seconds before vanishing with a loud popping sound.

Blichbiss fell backward with a crash, smoke and steam rising from his slightly charred mustache. He had been felled by the deadliest of counterspells, the one against which there is no appeal. So simple is its operative principle, even little children grasp it instinctively; so puissant is it in its demoralizing effect, grown men have been driven to inadvertent self-destruction, as Blichbiss now was evidence. Oddly enough, his clothes were almost untouched.

"That was cheating, that last one," said Lord Eyrdway. "Wasn't it? I thought you said no incendiary spells."

Lord Ermenwyr turned on him in fury. "Of course he cheated, you dunce! But it wouldn't have mattered if he'd managed to kill me."

"Of course it would have," Lord Eyrdway said reasonably. "Then Smith could have appealed his victory to the Black Council, as your second."

"A lot of good that would have done *me*, wouldn't it?" Lord Ermenwyr said, trembling in every limb as the reaction set in. He staggered backward and, like a landslide, his bodyguards surrounded him and caught him before he fell. Cutt set him gently into an armchair.

"Master is drained," he said solicitously. "Master is exhausted. What Master needs now, to restore his strength, is to eat his enemy's liver fresh-torn from his miserably defeated body, while it's still warm. Shall I tear out the liver for you, Master?"

"Gods, no!" cried Lord Ermenwyr in disgust.

"But it's good for you," said Cutt gently, "and you need it. It's full of arcane energies. It will replenish you with the life force of your enemy. Your lord father—" pause for group genuflection—"always consumes the livers of those so rash as to assail him. If they have been particularly offensive, he eats their hearts as well. Come now, little Master, won't you even try it?"

"He's right, you know," Lord Eyrdway said. "And think of the publicity! Nobody's ever going to challenge *your* right to be guild treasurer again. I wouldn't mind a bit of the bastard's heart, myself."

"Can I get it cooked?" asked Lord Ermenwyr.

"No!" said all the guards and Lord Eyrdway together.

"That would destroy much of its arcane wholesomeness," Cutt explained.

"Then I'm damned well having condiments," Lord Ermenwyr decided. "Smith, can you get me pepper and salt and a lemon?"

"Right," said Smith, and fled.

At least the sorcerous duel seemed to have passed unnoticed by anyone else, though Bellows gave him an inquiring look as he raced back from the kitchen with the condiments Lord Ermenwyr had requested. He just rolled his eyes in reply and hurried back upstairs.

When he reentered the suite, Blichbiss's body had been laid out on the dissecting table, and Lord Ermenwyr was attempting to wrench open the waistcoat and dress shirt.

"He shouldn't be exhibiting rigor mortis this early," he was complaining. "Unless that's the effect of the spell. Hello, Smith, just set those down anywhere. Damn him, these buttons have melted!"

"Rip it open," Lord Eyrdway suggested.

"Tear apart your vanquished enemy," Cutt counseled. "Slash into his flesh and seize the smoking liver in your mighty teeth! Wrest it forth and devour it, as his soul wails and wrings its hands, and let his blood run from your beard!"

"I don't think I'm quite up to that, actually," said Lord Ermenwyr, sweating. He cut the garments apart, laid open Blichbiss with a quick swipe of a knife, and peered at the liver in question. "Oh, gods, it looks vile."

"You didn't mind slicing up Coppercut," Smith remarked.

"Autopsying people is one thing. Eating them's quite another," said Lord Ermenwyr, gingerly cutting the liver out. "Eek, damn—look, now it's got on my shirt, that stain'll never come out. Hand me that plate, Smith."

Smith, deciding he would never understand demons, obliged. Lord Ermenwyr laid Blichbiss's liver out on the plate and began cutting it up, turning his face away. "Oh, the smell—Did you bring a juicer with that lemon, Smith? I'll never be able to keep this down—"

"What are you doing?" said Lord Eyrdway, looking on scandalized.

"I'm fixing Liver Tartare, or I'm not eating this thing at all," his brother snarled. "And the rest of you can just get those offended looks off your faces. Smith, you'd better go before you pass out."

Smith left gratefully.

He went downstairs, where Old Smith and New Smith were dozing in a booth, and woke them and sent them off to bed. Then he fixed himself a drink and sat alone in the darkened bar, sipping his drink slowly, reviewing the events of the last two days.

∽

When he heard Mrs. Smith returning with Crucible and Pinion, he emerged from the bar. "How did it go?" he inquired.

Crucible and Pinion, who were staggering slightly, threw their fists into the air and gave warrior grunts of victory. Mrs. Smith held up her gold medal.

"A triumph," she said quietly. She looked into Smith's eyes. "Boys, I think you'd best go to bed."

"Yes, ma'am," said Pinion thickly, and he and Crucible staggered away.

"Why don't we go talk in the kitchen?" Mrs. Smith suggested. She started down the passageway, and Smith followed, carrying his drink.

In the kitchen, Mrs. Smith removed her medal and hung it above the stove. She considered it a moment before turning and drawing out a chair. She draped her gown's train over one arm and sat down; and, with leisurely movements, took out and filled her smoking tube.

"A light, please, Smith," she requested.

He lit a straw at the stove, digging in the banked coals, and held it out for her. She puffed until the amberleaf lit and sat back.

"Well?" she said.

"How would I get hold of a bloatfish liver, if I wanted one?" Smith asked her.

"Simple," said Mrs. Smith. "You'd just walk down to the waterfront when the fishermen were sorting through their catches, before the fish-market dealers got there. You'd find a fisherman and ask if he had any nice live bloatfish. You might play the foolish old woman, a bit. And you'd listen very carefully when the fisherman told you how to filet the fish once you'd got it home, and thank him for his warning about the nasty liver. Then you'd carry the bloatfish home in a pail.

"And," she went on composedly, "if there was a particularly wicked man asking for an early dinner . . . and if you knew he'd ruined a few innocent people in his time and even driven a couple of them to suicide . . . and if you knew a little girl was crying her eyes out because he'd threatened her with what amounts to a death sentence unless she slept with him, even though she'd just fallen in love with someone else . . . and moreover this wicked man wanted her to give him information that would betray certain other persons . . . Well, then, Smith, I expect something rather dreadful might find its way into the appetizer he'd ordered.

"Mind you, I admit to nothing," she added. "But I have absolutely no regrets."

Smith sat in silence a moment, turning his drink in his hands, watching the ice melt. "Information that would betray certain other persons," he echoed. "He wasn't sure about you yet, but if he'd scared Burnbright badly enough, he'd have had you; and you've got a restaurant and a reputation to lose. Much better prospect for blackmail.

"You sneaked up there in the dark and burned most of his notes, but someone—probably Burnbright—interrupted you before you finished. You had the feast to get on the table, and Burnbright to calm down, so you never got back in there to burn the rest of the papers before Pinion discovered the murder."

Mrs. Smith exhaled smoke and watched him, silent. At last he said,

"Tell me how you got mixed up in the Spellmetal massacre."

She sighed.

"Years ago," she said, "I was working for the old Golden Chain caravan line. We got a party of passengers bound for the country up around Karkateen.

"It was the Sunborn and his followers. They'd just been thrown out of one town, so they'd chartered passage to another. But the Sunborn had already begun to talk of founding a city where all races would live together in perfect amity.

"When they left the caravan at Karkateen, I went with them."

"Had you become a convert?" Smith asked. She shook her head, her eyes fixed on something distant, and she shrugged.

"I was just a bad girl out for a good time," she said. "I didn't believe the races could live together in peace. I didn't believe one man could change the world. But the Sunborn asked me to come, and . . . if he'd asked me to jump from the top of a tower, I'd have done it. You never heard him speak, Smith, or you'd understand.

"He had the strangest gift for making one *clean*, no matter what he did in bed with one: He carried innocence with him like a cloak he could throw about your shoulders. With him, you felt as though you were forgiven for every wrong thing you'd ever done . . . and love became a sacrament, meant something far more than grappling for pleasure in the dark.

"Well. There were nearly thirty of us, of mixed races. Of the Children of the Sun there were a few boys and girls from well-to-do families. There was me; there were a couple of outcasts, half-breeds, and one girl who was blind; and there was a young man who always seemed uncomfortable with us, but he was the Sunborn's kinsman, and so he followed him out of a sense of family duty. Ramack, his name was. The greenies were all a wild lot, nothing like the ones you meet here running shops. Gorgeous savages. Poets. Musicians.

"It was a mad life. It was wonderful, and stupid, and exhausting. We committed excesses you couldn't begin to imagine. We starved, we wandered in the rain, we danced in our rags and picked flowers by the side of the highway. It was everything Festival is supposed to be, but with a *soul*, Smith!

"The Sunborn joined me to a Yendri man, and blessed our union in the name of racial harmony. I suppose I loved Hladderin well enough; greenies make reasonably good lovers, and he was drop-dead beautiful too. But I loved the Sunborn more.

"When Mogaron Spellmetal joined us, he suggested we all go live on his family's land. Away we went, dancing and singing. I bore Hladderin a child . . . what can I say? He was a pretty baby. I was never the motherly type, but his father thought the world of him.

"He was just six months old the day House Spellmetal showed up with their army."

"You don't have to talk about this part, if it's painful," said Smith.

"I won't talk about it. I still can't . . . but during the fighting, a grenade blew out the back wall of the garden. And when it was over, I ran like mad through the break, and so did a lot of others. I looked back and saw Hladderin fall with one of those damned long black arrows through his throat. Right after him came Ramack carrying the blind girl, her name was Haisa, she'd been a special favorite of the Sunborn's because he said she was a seeress. She was in labor at that very moment. Her baby picked that time of all times for its inauspicious birth!

"Ramack and Haisa got out alive, though. I waved to them, and Ramack spotted the ditch where I'd taken cover, and they joined me there. We managed to crawl away from the slaughter, and by nightfall we were safe. I don't know what happened to the others.

"Haisa had her baby that night. It was a little girl."

"Burnbright?" asked Smith. Mrs. Smith nodded.

"We hid in the wilderness for a couple of weeks, weeping and trying to think what to do. It was hard to get our brains engaged again, after all that long ecstatic time. Ramack decided at last that the best thing to do was to throw ourselves on the mercy of the authorities. We hadn't heard yet about how Mogaron had died, you see, or his father's blood oath, and since Ramack had never really been a believer in the Sunborn, he didn't mind recanting. In the end he and Haisa went off to Karkateen and gave themselves up. You know what happened to them. At least the assassins missed the baby."

"Why didn't you go?" Smith asked.

"I wasn't willing to recant," Mrs. Smith replied. "And I had my child to think of. But what kind of life would he have had with me, under the circumstances, being the color he was? I'd heard the stories of the Green Witch, as we used to call her on the caravan routes. Our nasty little lord's sainted Mother. Hladderin had told me she took in orphans.

"So I carried him up to the Greenlands, and I climbed that black mountain. I came to a fearful black gate where demons in plate armor leered at me. But a disciple in white robes came down, practically glowing with reflected holiness, and took the child off my hands and promised to keep him safe. And that was that.

"I went down the mountain and took sanctuary myself for a while, in the Abbey at Kemeldion. When the scandal had become old news, I changed my name to Smith and got a job cooking for your cousin's caravan line. It was work I knew, and, besides, it seemed like a good idea to keep moving.

"I kept track of what the Karkateen authorities had done with Burnbright, which was the alias they had sensibly given her. When your cousin needed a runner to replace one that had quit, I suggested he pick one up in Mount Flame. By sheer good luck he got little Burnbright. I've looked out for her ever since, for her father's sake."

Loud in the sleeping house, they heard the sound of footsteps approaching. A moment later the kitchen door opened, and Lord Ermenwyr looked in. He was very pale.

"I wonder whether I might get something for indigestion?" he inquired. "But I see I'm interrupting serious talk."

"Fairly serious," Smith said.

"Yes, I thought you'd have to have a certain conversation sooner or later." The lordling pulled out a stool and sat down at the table. "May I respectfully suggest that no one do anything rash? If by some silly chance somebody accidentally happened to, oh, I don't know, commit a murder or something—which I'm sure would have been completely justified, whatever the circumstances—well, you wouldn't believe the unsavory incidents my family has hushed up."

"I'll bet I would," said Mrs. Smith. She got up and fetched a bottle of after-dinner bitters, and mixed a mineral-water cocktail, which she presented to Lord Ermenwyr. She sank heavily into her chair again. He lifted his glass to her.

"Consider this a gesture of trust in your excellent good sense,' he said, and drank it down. "Ah. Really, I'm very fond of you both, and I'm not about to let truth and justice prevail. We'll sweep the odious Coppercut under the carpet somehow—"

More footsteps. The door swung open, and Burnbright and Willowspear stood there, holding hands. They were pale too. They looked scared.

"We—" said Burnbright.

"That is, we—" said Willowspear.

They fell silent, staring at the party around the table. Lord Ermenwyr's mouth fell open. After a moment of attempted speech, he finally sputtered: "*You?* Damn you, Willowspear, I wanted a piece of that! Burnbright, my love, if you thought he was a jolly romp, wait until you've danced the three-legged stamp with me!"

"No," said Burnbright, as Willowspear put his arm around her. "I'm in love with him. I—I don't know how it happened. It just happened!"

"I don't know how it happened," Willowspear echoed. "It just happened. Like lightning dropping from the sky."

"Like a big ship bearing down on you out of the fog," said Burnbright.

"There was nothing we could do," said Willowspear,

seeming dazed. "I had my duty—and my vows—and I always thought that She was the only love I would ever need, but—"

"I never wanted to fall in love," said Burnbright tearfully. "And then—the whole world changed."

Mrs. Smith shook her head.

"And you both look perfectly miserable," said Lord Ermenwyr smoothly. "But, my dears, you're both getting all upset over nothing! You're forgetting that it's Festival. This is a momentary fever, an illusion, a dream! Tomorrow you'll both be able to walk away from each other without regrets. And if not tomorrow, the next day, or soon after. Trust me, darlings. It'll pass."

"No," said Willowspear, his voice shaking. "It will never pass. I won't blaspheme against Love." He looked at Mrs. Smith. "I had had a dream, lady. I was an infant hidden in a bush. Another child was laid beside me, tiny and lost. I knew she was an orphan, a child of misfortune, and I wanted to take her in my arms and protect her.

"When I woke, I went to the Compassionate One and begged Her for my dream's meaning. She told me I must find my life where it began."

Awkwardly he came to her, leading Burnbright by the hand, and knelt. "Lady, I mean to marry Teeba. Give me your blessing."

He reached out his hand and touched her face. Mrs. Smith flinched; a tear ran down her cheek.

"Now you've done it," she said hoarsely. "Now we're both caught." She reached up and took his hand.

"Marry?" cried Lord Ermenwyr. "Are you mad? Look at the pair of you! Look at the world you'll have to live in! I can tell you something about mixed marriages, my friend! You've no idea how hard it is to be Mother and Daddy's son."

Willowspear ignored him. "I never would have troubled

you," he told Mrs. Smith. "But word came to us that there was a man like a jackal, seeking out anyone who had followed the Sunborn. I knew he would hunt down my mother.

"The Compassionate One bid me go with Her son to this city. I meant to warn you. But then, the man was slain . . . and I saw Teeba, and it was as though I had known her all my life."

"That's not her real name," said Mrs. Smith. "Her name is Kalya."

"Really?" Burnbright squeaked. "Oh, that's wonderful! I've always *hated* Teeba!"

"Use the old name at your peril, child," Mrs. Smith told her. "You're not safe, even after all these years. And how do you think you'll live?" She looked from one to the other of them in despair. "What do you imagine you'll do, open a shop in Greenietown? You think you'll be welcome even there, the pair of you?"

"I could still be a runner here," said Burnbright. "And—" She looked at Smith in desperate appeal. "Wouldn't it be a good idea if we had a house doctor? My friend Orecrash at the Hotel Sea-Air says all the really elegant places have a doctor on the premises, like at the spa. And rich people like to go to—to Yendri doctors, because they're exotic and have all this mystic wisdom and like that. He could teach them meditation. Or something. Please?"

"We could try," said Smith.

"Madness," Lord Ermenwyr growled. "Sheer madness."

"It isn't either!" Burnbright rounded on him. "We won't need anything else, if we have each other."

"You have no idea what you're doing," said Mrs. Smith sadly. "Either of you. You can't imagine how hard it'll be. But it can't be helped now, can it? So you have my blessing. And I wish you luck; you'll need it."

"Nobody's asking for *my* blessing," complained Lord Ermenwyr. "Or even my permission."

Willowspear stood and faced him. "My lord, your lady Mother—"

"I know, I know, this was all her doing. She knew perfectly well what would happen when she sent you down here," said Lord Ermenwyr wearily. "Meddling in people's lives to bring them love and joy and spiritual fulfillment, just as she's always doing. Didn't bother to tell *me* anything about it, of course, but why should she? I'm just miserable little Ermenwyr, the only living man in Salesh who hasn't had sex this Festival."

"That's not true," said Smith.

"Well, that's a comfort, isn't it? All right, Willowspear, you're formally excused from my service. Go be a mystic holy man house doctor to a people who'd as soon stone you as look at you. You'll have to register with the city authorities, you know, as a resident greenie, and take an oath not to poison their wells or defile their wives. You'll come running back up the mountain the next time there's a race riot—if you can run fast enough."

"Anybody who tried to hurt him would have to kill me first!" said Burnbright, putting her arms around Willowspear and holding tight.

"I see," said Lord Ermenwyr. "I suppose in that case there's not the slightest chance you'd be willing to give me a quick tumble before the wedding? A little bit of Lord's Right, you know, just so you can say you shopped around before you bought?"

"Dream on," she retorted.

"Well, you'll never know what you missed," Lord Ermenwyr grumbled. "Oh, go to bed, both of you. I'm ready to puke from all the devotion in here."

"My lord." Willowspear bowed low. He turned to Mrs. Smith, took her hand, and kissed it. "Madam."

"Go on," she said.

He clasped hands once again with Burnbright, and they went out. Burnbright's voice floated back, saying:

". . . bed's too narrow, but that's all right; we can just move it out and sleep on the floor!"

"Smith, however shall they manage?" cried Mrs. Smith. "That child hasn't got the brains the gods gave lettuce!"

"We'll look after them, I guess," said Smith. "And she's sharper than you give her credit for."

"She's every inch the fool her father was," said Mrs. Smith.

A silence followed her statement, until they once again heard the sound of footsteps approaching. Slightly unsteady footsteps.

The kitchen door opened, and Lord Eyrdway leaned in, grinning. His ruffled shirtfront was drenched in gore.

"I have to tell you, you're missing a great party," he informed his brother. "Did you know there was another corpse in your bathroom?"

Smith groaned and put his head in his hands.

"Eyrdway, they needed that body!" Lord Ermenwyr sprang to his feet.

"Oops." Lord Eyrdway looked at Smith and Mrs. Smith. "Sorry."

"Don't worry," Lord Ermenwyr told them. "He'll make it up to you. Won't you, Variable Nincompoop?"

"Oh, drop dead again," his brother replied. He looked at Smith. "Seriously, though, is there anything I can do to help?"

↪

Salesh in the aftermath of Festival is a quiet place.

Laughing Youth isn't laughing as it shuffles along, wishing its golden sandals weren't so bright. Don't even ask about what Age is doing. It's too gruesome.

City Warden Crossbrace had spent much of the last two days in a darkened alcove, so he found the sunlight painfully brilliant as he tottered up Front Street toward the Hotel Grandview. His uniform had the same wrinkles and creases it had had before he'd thrown it off, shortly after bidding Smith a good evening. His head felt curiously dented, and all in all he'd much rather have been home in bed. But a sense of duty drove him, as well as an awareness of the fact that corpses don't keep forever and that the worse shape they were in when reported at last, the more questions would be asked.

Still, by the time he stepped through the Grandview's street entrance, he was wondering how big around Coppercut's body was in relation to that nice capacious drainpipe, and how much of a bribe he might get out of Smith for suggesting that they just stuff the dead man down the pipe and forget he'd ever been there.

When his eyes had adjusted to the pleasant gloom of the lobby, he spotted Smith sitting at the desk, sipping from a mug of tea. He looked tired, but as though he felt better than Crossbrace.

"Morning, Crossbrace," he said, in an offensively placid voice.

"Morning, Smith," Crossbrace replied. "We may as well get down to business. What've you got for me?"

"Well, something surprising happened—" Smith began, just as Sharplin Coppercut strode into the lobby.

"You must be the City Warden," he said. "Hello! I'm afraid I caused a fuss over nothing. Silly me, I forgot to tell anybody I occasionally go catatonic. I don't know why it happens, but there you are. I was sitting in my lovely room enjoying the sunset and, bang! Next thing I know I'm waking up on a slab of ice in this good man's storeroom. I was so embarrassed!"

Crossbrace blinked at him.

"You went catatonic?"

"Mm-hm." Coppercut leaned back against the desk and folded his hands, with his thumbtips making jittery little circles around each other. He cocked a bright parrotlike eye at Crossbrace. "Crash, blank, I was gone."

"But—" Even with the condition he was in, Crossbrace remained a Warden. "But in that case—why'd you write that note?"

"Note? What note?"

"That note you appeared to have been writing when you had your spell," Smith said helpfully. "Remember that you'd sat down at the writing desk? It looked like you wrote *Avenge My Murder*."

"Oh, that!" said Coppercut. "Well. I'm a writer, you know, and—I had this brilliant idea while I was eating, so I got up to write it down. It was—er—that I needed to get in touch with a friend of mine. Aven Gemymurd."

"Of House Gemymurd in Mount Flame City?" Smith improvised.

"Yes! That's it. They're, er, not very well known. Secretive family. So it occurred to me they must have something to hide, you see?" Coppercut squinted his eyes, getting into his role. "So I thought I'd just visit my old friend Aven and see if I could dig up any dish on his family! Ha-ha."

Crossbrace peered at him, still baffled.

"You look like you could use a cold drink, Crossbrace," said Smith, setting down his tea mug and sliding out from behind the desk. "It's nice and dark and cool in the bar."

The hell with it, thought Crossbrace. "I'd like that," he said. As he followed Smith to the bar, he addressed Coppercut over his shoulder: "You know, sir, you might want to invest in one of those medical alert tattoos people get. It might save you from being tossed on a funeral pyre before your time."

"Yes, I think I'll do that," said Coppercut, following them into the bar. "What a good idea! Because you know, Warden, that there are attempts on my life all the time, because I'm so widely hated, and anybody might make a mistake and think—"

"Coppercut?" A small scowling man appeared out of nowhere, twisting his mustaches. "You're late for our interview. I was going to give you all kinds of trashy details about the life of my late father, remember?"

"Oh, that's right!" exclaimed Coppercut, as the small man grabbed his elbow and steered him out of the bar. "How stupid of me—but I get like this, you know, when I've just waked up after a catatonic fit, very disorganized—nice meeting you, City Warden, sir!"

⌐

"So you got your Safety Certificate," said Lord Ermenwyr with satisfaction, exhaling green smoke. "And the Variable Magnificent is safely on his way home."

He was sitting with Smith and Mrs. Smith at their best terrace table, as they watched the first stars pinpricking out of the twilight. Like an earthbound echo, Crucible and Pinion moved from table to table lighting the lamps and oil heaters.

"I thought he couldn't go home until he'd got enough money to pay back your lord father," said Smith, dodging an elbow as Lord Ermenwyr's bodyguards genuflected.

Lord Ermenwyr snickered.

"Much as he was looking forward to joining the Boys' Own Street Corner Brigade, it doesn't look as though it'll be necessary. The late unlamented Mr. Coppercut carried his private accounts book with him, as it turns out. Had more gold socked away in the First Bank of Mount Flame than Freskin the Dictator! Eyrdway's quite taken with pretending to be a famous scandalmonger. Plans to masquerade as Coppercut a bit longer."

"Is that safe?" Mrs. Smith inquired. "Given the enemies Mr. Coppercut had?"

"Probably not," said Lord Ermenwyr. "If he's sensible, he'll hit the bank first, pay back Daddy, then party the rest of the fortune away before anyone suspects he's an imposter. That's what *I* told him to do. Will he listen? Or will I run into him in some low bar in six months' time, ragged and grotesquely daubed with cosmetics, vainly attempting to interest potential buyers? I can but hope." He exhaled a cloud of smoke and smiled at it beatifically, as though he beheld a vision of fraternal degradation therein.

"You must have been horrible little children," said Mrs. Smith, shaking her head.

"Utterly, dear Mrs. Smith."

"Did your lord brother clean out your bathroom before he left?" Smith inquired cautiously.

"Of course he didn't," said Lord Ermenwyr. "He never cleans up any mess. That's for law-abiding little shrimps like me, or so I was informed when I attempted to get him to at least take a sponge to the ring in the tub. I just smiled and offered him the contents of Mr. Coppercut's traveling medicine chest. He was delighted, assuming it was full of recreational drugs. Since bothering to read labels is also only for law-abiding little shrimps, he'll be unpleasantly surprised to learn that Mr. Coppercut suffered from chronic constipation."

"So your bathroom . . ."

"Oh, don't worry; I had the boys scrub down the walls. Only a medium could detect that anything unpleasant happened there now," Lord Ermenwyr said.

"And the . . ."

"Got rid of them last night. We collected all the, er, odds and ends and crept down to your back area drain under cover of darkness. Dumped them in and pitched most of a barrel of Scourbrass's Foaming Wonder in after them. Poof!" Lord Ermenwyr blew smoke to emphasize his point. "All gone, except for a couple of indignant shades, and I gave them directions to the closest resort in Paradise, with my profound apologies and a coupon for two free massages at the gym. But, Smith, I meant to ask you—where does that drain empty out?"

"Oh, not on the beach," Smith assured him. "It goes straight into the sea."

"You're dumping sewage and caustic chemicals into the sea?" Lord Ermenwyr frowned.

"Everybody does," said Smith.

"But . . . your people swim in that water. They catch fish in it."

Smith shrugged. "The sea's a big place. Maybe all the bad stuff sinks to the bottom? It's never caused a problem for anybody."

"And maybe you're all being slowly poisoned, and you don't realize it," said Lord Ermenwyr. He looked panicked. "Nine Hells! I've been drinking oyster broth here!"

"Oh, it's perfectly wholesome," said Mrs. Smith.

"But don't you see—" Lord Ermenwyr looked into their uncomprehending faces. He groaned. "No; no, you don't. This is one of those cultural blind spots, isn't it? Mother's always on about this. She says you'll all destroy yourselves one of these days with just this sort of heedlessness, and then Daddy says 'Well, let them, and good riddance,' and then they start to quarrel and everyone runs for cover. Look, you can't just keep pouring poison into your ocean!"

"Well, where else can we put it?" Smith asked.

"Good question." Lord Ermenwyr tapped ash from his smoking tube. "Hmm. I could ensorcel your sewage pipes so they dumped into another plane. Yes! Though, to do any real good, I'd need to put the same hocus on all the sewer pipes in town . . ."

"But then the sewage would just back up in somebody else's plane," Mrs. Smith pointed out.

"Unless I found a plane where the inhabitants *liked* sewage," said Lord Ermenwyr, packing fresh weed into the tube and lighting it with a fireball. He puffed furiously, eyes narrowed in speculation. "This is going to take some planning."

"I'm sure you'll come up with something," said Mrs. Smith. "I'd imagine your lady mother will be very proud of you."

Lord Ermenwyr looked disconcerted at the idea.

Across the terrace, picking their way between the tables with some awkwardness because they seemed unable to let go of each other, came Willowspear and Burnbright.

"We need something," said Burnbright.

"That is—with your permission, sir—" said Willowspear.

"What he wants to know is, there's a dirt lot on the other side of the area where we keep the dustbins, and it's got nothing but weeds on it now, so couldn't we make a garden there?" said Burnbright. "To grow useful herbs and things? Him and me'd do all the work. I don't know anything about gardening, but he does, so he'll teach me, and that way we could have medicines without having to go to the shops in— in the quarter where Yendri live. Wouldn't that be nice?"

"I guess so," said Smith.

"Ha! Just try it," said Lord Ermenwyr. "The minute passersby spot a greenie planting exotic herbs here, there'll be rampant rumors you're growing poisons to kill off the good citizens of Salesh as part of a fiendish Yendri plot. You'll get lynched."

"No, we won't!" said Burnbright. "You're only saying that because I wouldn't sleep with you, you nasty little man. If people come to Willowspear when they're sick and his medicine makes them feel better, they won't be afraid of him!"

"Of course they will, you delectable idiot. They'll be intimidated by the idea that he has secret knowledge," Lord Ermenwyr explained. "Evil mystic powers! Scary mumbo jumbo!"

"Not if they get used to him," said Burnbright. Her eyes went wide with revelation. "That's the whole problem, is that nobody ever really gets to know anybody else, but if they did, they'd see that other people aren't so bad after all and a lot more like us than we thought and . . . and . . . sometimes everything you've been told your whole life is wrong!"

"You can't change the world, child," said Mrs. Smith.

"I'll bet we can change some of it," said Burnbright defiantly. "That bit with the weeds, anyway."

"If we don't try, how will anyone know whether it can be done?" said Willowspear to Mrs. Smith. She said nothing, watching as Burnbright gazed up at him in adoration.

"I'll have Crucible get you some gardening tools," said Smith.

"Thank you!" Burnbright threw her arms around his neck and kissed him.

"You won't regret it, sir," Willowspear assured him, terribly earnest. He took Burnbright's hand again.

They walked off together, into the fragrant twilight.

"A light, Mrs. Smith?" Lord Ermenwyr offered.

"Please." She angled her smoking tube, and he caused a bright fireball to flash at its tip. Smith waved away multicolored smoke.

"The boy seems to have turned out well. I'm very much obliged to your lady mother," Mrs. Smith told Lord Ermenwyr. He puffed and nodded, leaning back in his chair.

"You might have managed it yourself, you know, after all," he replied. "You've practically raised Burnbright, wretched little guttersnipe that she is. Why?"

She gave him a hard level stare.

"Because it's hard to let go of the past," she said. "You keep hoping you can make the story turn out with a happier ending, even when you've learned better. If those two children can escape the doom in their blood, maybe all that death and agony wasn't suffered for nothing. And . . ."

"And what?" Smith inquired.

Mrs. Smith set her hand on Smith's. "She's Kalyon Sunbolt's daughter, Smith. If I had it to do all over again tomorrow, I'd die at his side. Gods don't walk this earth very often, but one walked in him. I can't explain it any better than that."

She glanced across the terrace. Willowspear and Burnbright were poking around in the weeds behind the dustbin. The sound of their young voices floated back through the dusk as they made plans for their garden.

Smallbrass Enterprises Proudly Presents

THE PLANNED COMMUNITY OF TOMORROW!!!!

Leave your cares behind in the dark, crowded warrens of Mount Flame and breathe free in the delightful new seaside community of SMALLBRASS ESTATES. When completed, this sportsman's paradise will enclose a hundred acres of prime coastal and riverfront property behind secure fortifications, creating a happily safeguarded living area for its fortunate citizens.

Spacious residential quarters situated conveniently near business and shopping arcades will enable our latter-day pioneers to enjoy all the blessings of an unspoiled rural paradise without giving up any of the civilized comforts to which they are accustomed. A fully armed militia is already in place to guarantee that forest denizens keep a respectful distance from this new beachhead of our race.

Wide skies! Glorious prospects! Abundant game! Clean water! All these are your birthright, and you may claim them at SMALLBRASS ESTATES!

Inquire at the Sign of the Three Hammers, Chain Avenue, Port Ward'b.

FOREST denizens,' " says an angry voice. " 'Beachhead of *their* race?' " says another. "*Their* birthright!" says a third voice.

There is more muttered conversation in the darkness.

The stars wheel through the hours; the bright sun rises at last, and its slanting bars strike the wall where the real estate sign was pasted up only the day before. A city Night Warden, trudging home at last, stops and stares at the wall. From a crack in the pavement a green vine has sprouted and scaled the red stones with supernatural speed. It has thrust tendrils under the poster, spread and ripped and crumpled its fragments; and small green snails are crawling over what remains, greedily consuming the paper and its bright inks.

⤶

Smith looked broodingly through his guest ledger.

No question about it; bookings were down since the Month of the Sardine Runs. Business at the restaurant was better, but still less than what it had been formerly.

There were a lot of good reasons why, of course. Deliantiba and Blackrock were engaged in a civil war, which put something of a crimp in travel and trade along the coast; not many pleasure boats set out for vacation destinations when a warship was likely to attack first and sort out survivors later.

Also, the price of fish had skyrocketed lately, which drove up prices in the restaurants; and though it was common knowledge that there *was* no fish shortage, that it was all a plot by the fishermen to drive prices up, still the fish didn't seem to have heard that and stayed out of their customary waters. And now the new trouble . . .

As if on cue, Crossbrace of the City Wardens walked into the lobby, accompanied by two of his lieutenants. He assumed a stiff formal stance and avoided Smith's eyes as he said; "Citizen! In accordance with Salesh City Statute 1,135.75, all members of alien races are required to swear an oath of allegiance and obedience to Salesh City Law. They have within two days of notification to comply or file an appeal with the—"

"He already took the oath, Crossbrace, you know that—" began Smith in real annoyance. Crossbrace, still keeping his eyes averted, held up an admonitory finger.

"Ah! That was Salesh City Statute .63, you see?" he said in a normal tone of voice. "There's a new oath they have to take saying they won't vandalize our property."

"Oh." Smith was still annoyed. "Well, did you have to bring an arrest squad with you?"

"It's not an arrest squad," Crossbrace protested, looking hurt. "We thought we'd give him an escort. In case there's trouble. There has been trouble, you know."

Smith knew, but he muttered to himself as he slid from behind the front desk and led the way out onto the hotel's back terrace.

It was a nice place, a shaded garden with a dramatic view of the sea. Strange and gorgeous flowers bloomed in one area set apart by low stone balustrades. There six people stood with their faces turned to the sky, in various postures of rapture. They were all Children of the Sun. The seventh was not; and he was speaking to them, softly and encouragingly.

". . . and think of your own mothers, or any woman who was ever kind to you: some part of Her was in their hearts. Focus your prayers on that ideal of love and reach out to Her—"

He noticed Smith and the wardens.

"—and She must hear you, and She *will* help you. Now, we'll conclude for this afternoon; go home and continue the meditation exercise on Compassion."

Willowspear walked quickly toward Smith, murmuring "What is it?" as his students moved like sleepers waking.

"You have to—"

"It's my duty to inform you that—"

"What are the Wardens doing here?" demanded one of the students, shooting from Bliss to Righteous Indignation like a pistol bolt.

"You can't harass our *trevani!*" cried another student, grabbing up a gardening tool, and Willowspear grimaced and held out his hands to them in a placatory gesture.

"Please! Consider the First Principle of Patience in the Face of Aggression!" he cried. Somebody muttered something about a Trowel in the Face of Oppression, but in the trembling moment of peace that followed Smith said quickly, "It's just a new oath you have to take, saying you won't commit any acts of vandalism. All right?"

"I'll be glad to swear the oath," said Willowspear at once.

"What in the Nine Hells is a *trevani*?" demanded one of the Wardens, scowling.

"Shut up," Crossbrace told him.

"He's teaching 'em to worship the Green Witch," said the other Warden.

"The Green *Saint*! He's teaching us the Way of the Unwearied Mother, you unenlightened dog!" shouted another student.

"Not very successfully, either!" Willowspear cried, turning to face his students. "Put the shovel down, Mr. Carbon. Don't shame me, please. Go to your homes and meditate on the First Principle."

His students filed from the garden, glaring at the Wardens, who glared back, and Willowspear sighed and pressed his slender hands to his temples.

"Forgive them," he said. "May I take the oath here, Mr. Crossbrace?"

"We have to escort you to the Temple of Law for it," said Crossbrace, shifting from foot to foot. "Because of the trouble, see?"

"All right."

"And a couple of mine will go with you, how about that?" said Smith. The porters Crucible and Pinion, who had been watching in silence from the lobby doorway, stepped forward and flexed their big arms.

"That'd be capital!" said Crossbrace, with a ghastly attempt at heartiness. "Let's all go now and get it over with, eh?"

"Right," growled Pinion.

Smith saw them off, then went into the restaurant's kitchen. Mrs. Smith was pounding spices in a mortar, and Burnbright was peeling apples. She was perched on a tall stool, rather precariously given her present condition, and there were shadows of exhaustion under her eyes.

"So I said to him, 'Eight crowns for that puny thing? At that price it had bloody well better to be able to jump up and grant three wishes—'" Mrs. Smith paused to tip ash from her smoking tube into the sink, and saw Smith. In the moment of silence that followed, Burnbright looked up, looked from one to the other of them, and began to cry.

"Oh, oh, what's happened now?" she wailed.

"He's had to go down to the Temple of Law again," Smith told her. "He won't be long, though."

"But he hasn't *done* anything!" Burnbright wept. "Why can't they leave us alone?"

"It's just the way life is sometimes, child," said Mrs. Smith, mechanically going to a cabinet and fetching out a bottle of Calming Syrup. She poured a spoonful, slipped it into Burnbright's mouth between sobs, and had a gulp straight from the bottle herself. Having done that, she renewed her efforts with the mortar so forcefully that a bit of clove went shooting up and killed a fly on the ceiling.

"One goes through these dismal patches, now and again," she continued grimly. "War. Economic disaster. Bestial stupidity on the part of one's fellow creatures. Impertinent little men charging eight crowns for a week-old sardine. One learns to endure with grace." Another particularly violent whack with the mortar sent a peppercorn flying. It hit the bottle of Calming Syrup with a *ping*, ricocheted off and narrowly missed Smith's nose before vanishing out the doorway into the darkness of the hotel bar.

"He'll be all right," said Smith, patting Burnbright's shoulder. "You'll see. Everyone in this street will vouch for him—and after all, he's married to you! So it's not as though he could be ordered to leave the city or anything."

Burnbright thought about that a moment before her lip began to tremble afresh.

"You mean they could do that?" she said. "With our baby coming and all?"

"Of course they couldn't, child," said Mrs. Smith, looking daggers at Smith and reaching for the Calming Syrup again. "We just told you so. Besides, he's my son, isn't he? And it's my little grandbaby's future at stake, isn't it? And I'd like to see the City Factor foolhardy enough to throw miscegenation in *my* face."

I wouldn't, thought Smith, and exited quietly.

He heard the bell in the lobby summoning him. Someone was hammering away at it imperiously. He swore under his breath, wondering what else could go wrong with his day, or his week, or his life . . .

"Here he is! Oh, dear, doesn't he look cross?" said Lord Ermenwyr brightly. "Ow! What was that for?"

"Because you're an unsympathetic little beast, Master,"

Balnshik told him, and held out her hand. "Smith, darling! How have you been these last few months?"

Smith gulped. His brain ground to a halt, his senses shifted gears.

He knew she was an ageless, deathless, deadly thing; but there she stood in a white beaded gown that glittered like frost, with a stole of white fox furs, and she was elegant and desirable beyond reason.

Beside her stood Lord Ermenwyr, looking sleek and healthy for a change, loudly dressed in the latest fashion. How anyone could wear black and still be loudly dressed was a mystery to Smith. The lordling's hat bore some of the responsibility: it was a high sugar-loaf copatain, cockaded with a plume that swept the lobby's chandelier. Beyond him were Cutt, Crish, Stabb, and Strangel, heavily laden with luggage.

"Uh—I've been fine," Smith replied.

"Well, you look like you've been through a wringer," Lord Ermenwyr said. "Never mind! Now *I'm* here, all will be joy and merriment. Boys, take the trunks up to my customary suite and unpack."

They instantly obeyed, shuffling up the stairs like a city block on the move. Lord Ermenwyr looked Smith up and down.

"Business has been off a bit, has it? I shouldn't be at all surprised. But you needn't worry about me, at least! I'm simply here to relax and have a lovely time in dear old Salesh-by-the-Sea. Go to the theaters with Nursie dearest, visit the baths, sample the latest prostitutes—"

There was a rending crash from somewhere upstairs.

"Oh, bugger," said Lord Ermenwyr, glancing upward. "We forgot to give them a room key, didn't we?"

"I think poor Smith needs a cool drink on the terrace,"

said Balnshik, running one hand through his hair. "Let's all go. Fetch a bottle from the bar, Master."

~

He had to admit he felt better, sitting out at one of the tables while Balnshik poured the wine. All his other problems shrank in comparison to the prospect of a few weeks' visit by demons, even if they were pleasantly civilized ones. And Balnshik's physical attentions were pleasant indeed, though they stopped abruptly when Burnbright and Mrs. Smith joined them on the terrace. Instantly, the ladies formed a tight huddle and locked into a private conversation whose subject was exclusively pregnancy.

Lord Ermenwyr regarded them narrowly, shrugged, and lit his smoking tube with a fireball.

"Tsk; they won't even notice us for the next three hours, now, Smith. I suppose we'll have to sit here and find manly things to talk about. I detest sports of any kind, and your politics don't even remotely interest me, and the weather isn't really a gender-specific topic, is it? How about business? Yes, do tell me how your business is going."

Smith told him. He listened thoughtfully, exhaling smoke from time to time.

". . . And then there's the trouble in, in the quarter where the Yendri businesses are," Smith continued. "I can't understand it; everyone's always gotten along here, but now . . . *they're* all resentful and we're all on edge. The bathhouse keepers are up in arms, by all the gods! Rioting herbalists! I don't know where it will end, but it certainly isn't good for keeping hotel rooms occupied."

"Oh, I'll book the whole damn place for the summer, if that'll help," said Lord Ermenwyr. "That's the least of your worries. You know what's behind all this, of course."

"No," said Smith, with a familiar sense of impending doom. "What's behind it?"

"This stupid man Smallbrass and his Planned Community, naturally," Lord Ermenwyr replied. "Don't tell me you haven't seen the signs! Or perhaps you haven't. They're being defaced as soon as they go up."

"Oh. That place being built down the coast?" Smith blinked. "What about it? The Yendri always complain when we build another city, but it's not as though we were hurting anybody. We've got to have someplace to live, haven't we?"

"I don't know that the other races sharing the world with you would necessarily agree," said Lord Ermenwyr delicately.

"Well, all right. But why should they be so *especially* bothered now?"

Lord Ermenwyr looked at Smith from a certain distance, all the clever nastiness gone from his face. It was far more disconcerting than his usual repertory of unpleasant expressions.

"Perhaps I ought to explain something—" he began, and then both he and Smith were on their feet and staring across the garden at the hotel. There was shouting coming from the lobby, followed by the shatter of glass. Burnbright gave a little shriek that dopplered away from them as they ran, along with Mrs. Smith's cry of, "Stay here and keep down, for gods' sake!"

Smith, though older and heavier, got there first, for halfway through the garden Balnshik materialized in front of Lord Ermenwyr and arrested his progress with her formidable bosom. He hit it and bounced back, slightly stunned, and so Smith was the one to catch Willowspear as he staggered out into the garden. The Yendri was bleeding from a cut above one eye.

"It's all right," he gasped. "They ran away. But the front window is smashed—"

They haven't been here two hours, and I'm already down a door and a window, said an exasperated little voice in the back of Smith's head. Out loud he said, "Damn 'em anyway. Look, I'm sorry—"

"Oh, they weren't your people," Willowspear told him, pressing his palm to the cut to stop the bleeding. "They were Yendri, I'm afraid."

"What in the Nine Hells did you do that for?" Lord Ermenwyr demanded of Balnshik. "I think I've got a rhinestone in my eye!"

"I'm under geas to protect you, Master," she reminded him.

"Well, I'm supposed to protect anyone ever sworn to my service, and an oath is just as good as a geas any day—"

"Bloody greenies!" snarled Crucible, emerging from the lobby. "Are you all right, son?"

"Don't call him a greenie!" cried Burnbright, who had finally struggled across the yard. "Oh, oh, he's hurt!"

"Well, but he's *our* greenie, and anyway it was the other damn greenies—"

"I'm fine," Willowspear assured her, attempting to bow to Lord Ermenwyr. "It's a scratch. My gracious lord, I trust you're well? We were coming back up Front Street and we were accosted by three, er—"

"Members of the Yendri race," supplied Smith helpfully.

"—who demanded to know what I was doing in the company of two, er—Children of the Sun, and wanted me to go with them to—I think it was to attend a protest meeting or something, and when I tried to explain—"

"They started chucking rocks at our heads," said Pinion, dusting his hands as he stepped out to join them. "But halfway down the block the City Wardens caught sight of them and they took off, and the Wardens went after 'em like a gree—like something really fast. You want us to board up the window, boss?"

⌒

Fifteen minutes later they were back at their places on the terrace, somewhat shaken but not much the worse for wear. Balnshik had deftly salved and bandaged Willowspear's cut, and he sat with a drink in one hand. Burnbright perched in his lap, clinging to him. Mrs. Smith had been puffing so furiously on her jade tube that she was veiled in smoke, like a mountain obscured by mist.

"But you'd be safe up there, you young fool," she was telling Willowspear. She turned in appeal to Lord Ermenwyr. "You're his liege lord or something, aren't you? Can't *you* tell him to go, for his own good?"

"Alas, I released him from his vows," said Lord Ermenwyr solemnly. "Far be it from me to tell him that considerations of duty outweighed the vague promptings of a vision quest. Bet you're sorry now, eh? Ow," he added, almost absentmindedly, as Balnshik boxed his ear. "Besides, if a boy won't listen to his own dear mother, whomever else will he heed?"

"I can't go back to the Greenlands," said Willowspear. "I've planted a garden here. I have students. I have patients. My child will be born a citizen of this city. I'm doing no one any harm; why shouldn't I be safe?"

Mrs. Smith groaned and vanished in a fogbank of fume.

"And how would my love travel, so heavy laden?" Willowspear continued, looking down at Burnbright. "You can't have our baby in the wilderness; not a little city girl like you. You'd be so frightened, my heart."

"I'd go anywhere you wanted, if we had to," she said, knuckling away her tears. "I was born in the wilderness, wasn't I? And I wouldn't be scared of the Master of the Mountain or anybody."

"He doesn't really eat babies," Lord Ermenwyr told her. "Very often, anyway. Ow."

"And maybe everyone will come to their senses, and this whole thing will blow over when the weather turns cooler," said Smith.

"Ah—not likely," said Lord Ermenwyr. "Things are going to get rather nasty, I'm afraid."

"That's right; you were saying that when all hell broke loose." Smith got up and opened another bottle. "If my business is going to be wrecked, I'd at least like to know why."

Lord Ermenwyr shook his head. He tugged at his beard a moment, and said finally, "How much do you know about the Yendri faith?"

"I know they worship your mother," said Smith.

"Not exactly," said Lord Ermenwyr.

"Yes, we do," said Willowspear.

Lord Ermenwyr squirmed slightly in his chair. "Well, you don't think she's a—a goddess or anything like that. She's just a prophetess. Sort of."

"She is the *treva* of the whole world, She is the living Truth, She is the Incarnation of divine Love in its active aspect," said Willowspear with perfect assurance. "The Redeemer, the Breaker of Chains, the Subduer of Demons,"

"Amen," said Balnshik, just a trace grudgingly.

"Yes, well, I suppose she is." Lord Ermenwyr scowled. "All the Yendri pray to Mother, but she has someone she prays to in her turn, you know. You have to understand Yendri history. They used to be slaves."

"The Time of Bondage," sang Willowspear. "In the long-dark-sorrow in the Valley of Walls, in the black-filth-chains of the slave pens they prayed for a Deliverer! But till She came, there moved among the beaten-sorrowing-tearful the Comforter, the Star-Cloaked Man, the Lover of Widows."

"Some sort of holy man anyway," said Lord Ermenwyr. "Resistance leader, apparently. Foretold the coming of a Holy Child, then conveniently produced one. Daddy's always had his private opinion on how *that* happened."

Willowspear was shocked into speechlessness for a moment before stammering, "She miraculously appeared in the heart of a great *payraja* blossom! There were witnesses!"

"Yes, and I saw a man pull three handkerchiefs and a silver coin out of his own ear over on Anchor Street this very afternoon," Lord Ermenwyr retorted. "Life's full of miracles, but we all know perfectly well where babies come from. The point is, when she was three days old the Yendri rose in rebellion. The Star-Cloaked Man carried her before them, and she was their—"

"Their Shield, their Inspirer, that day in the wheatfield, that day by the river, when grim was the reckoning—"

"And evidently in all the uproar of overthrowing their masters, the Star-Cloaked Man cut his foot on a scythe or something, and the wound could never heal because he'd broken his vow of nonviolence to finally start the rebellion. So he limped for the rest of the big exodus out of the Valley of Walls, lugging Mother-as-a-baby the whole way."

"And flowers sprang up in the blood where he walked," said Willowspear.

"I remember hearing this story," Mrs. Smith murmured. "Oh, what a long time ago . . . There was supposed to have been a miracle, with some butterflies."

"Yes!" cried Willowspear. "The river rose at his bidding, the great-glassy-serpentbodied river, and for the earth's children it cut the way, the road to liberation! And they left that place and lo, after them came the souls of the dead. They would not stay in chains, in the form of butterflies they came, whitewinged-transparent-singing, so many flower petals drifting on the wind, the broken-despaired-of-lost came too, and floated above their heads to the new country."

"Which means they followed the annual migration path of some cabbage moths, I suppose. It added a mythic dimension to everything, to be sure, and eventually they got as far as where the river met the sea," said Lord Ermenwyr. "The 'sacred grove of Hlinjerith, where mist hung in the branches.' Just exactly what happened next has always been a matter of some speculation in our family."

"Everyone knows what happened," said Willowspear, looking at his liege lord a bit sternly. "The Star-Cloaked Man, the Beloved Imperfect, was sore afflicted of his wound, and his strength was faded, and his heart was faint. His disciples wept. But She in Her mercy forgave his sin of wrath."

"Oh, nonsense, she can't have been more than six months old—"

"She worked a miracle for his sake, and from the foam of the river his deliverance rose—"

> "It is made of the crystal foam,
> The White Ship,
> See it rise, and from every line and spar
> Bright water runs; the wild birds scream and sing
> To see it rise on the glassy-smooth wave.
> And it will bear us over
> To where all shame is washed away
> It will sail the new moon's path
> And it will bear us over
> To the Beloved's arms . . ."

The song rose seemingly from nowhere, warbled out in a profound and rather eerie contralto. It was a moment before

Smith realized that Mrs. Smith was singing, from within her cloud.

They all sat staring at her a moment before Balnshik pulled a handkerchief from Lord Ermenwyr's pocket and handed it to her.

"Thank you," said Mrs. Smith indistinctly. "You could top up my drink, too, if you don't mind. Your father used to sing that, young Willowspear." She blew her nose. "When he was stoned. Mind you, we all were, most of the time. But do go on."

"Daddy thinks that the Star-Cloaked Man died, and was quietly buried on that spot," said Lord Ermenwyr. "But most Yendri believe some magical craft bore him away across the sea. And all the white butterflies went with him. The Yendri crossed the river with Mother and the rest of the refugees, and they settled in the forests."

"But each year, in the season of his going, many of our people travel to that grove where the river meets the sea," said Willowspear. "There they pray, and meditate. In sacred Hlinjerith, it is said, healing dreams come to the afflicted, borne on the wings of white butterflies."

"And now, just guess, Smith, where your Mr. Smallbrass has decided to build his Planned Community," said Lord Ermenwyr.

"Oh," said Smith.

"No wonder the greenies are having fits," said Mrs. Smith, blowing her nose again.

"That's awful!" said Burnbright, appalled. She looked up at Willowspear. "We can't just go building houses all over somebody else's holy place! Why didn't you tell me what was going on?"

"My love, what could you do?" Willowspear replied. "You're not to blame."

"But it's *wrong*," she said. "And we're always doing it,

aren't we? Cutting down your trees and moving in? We don't know it's wrong, but no wonder you hate us!"

"How could I ever hate you?" he said, kissing her between the eyes. "You are my jewel-of-fire-and-the-sun. And you are not like the others."

"I am, though," Burnbright said. Lord Ermenwyr cleared his throat.

"To interrupt this touching moment of mutual devotion— I haven't told all yet."

"It gets worse?" asked Smith.

"Yes, it does," said Lord Ermenwyr. "As bad luck would have it, there was a prophecy made when Mother and Daddy got married, to the effect that one day the Star-Cloaked Man will return from over the sea, and that he'll set the world to rights again. Daddy says it was propaganda put about by reactionary elements who disapproved of Mother no longer being quite such a virgin as she used to be.

"Nevertheless—that prophecy's been dug out and dusted off. The Yendri are saying that the Star-Cloaked Man is coming back any day now. And when the White Ship comes sailing back and ties up at the Smallbrass Estates Marina, formerly Hlinjerith of the Misty Branches—well, the Star-Cloaked'll be pretty cheesed off to see what's happened to local property values."

"But it's only a legend, right?" said Smith.

"Not to all those denizens of the forest," said Lord Ermenwyr. "And the first of your people to set an axe to the sacred grove will get his head split open. It'll be all-out race war."

"But the Yendri are *nice*. They don't do things like that," said Burnbright miserably.

"Some of them do," said Balnshik. "Remember Mr. Flowering Reed?"

There was a silence at that.

"Of course," said Lord Ermenwyr in a terrifically casual

voice, "the *clever* thing to do would be to take a holiday in a happy seaside resort before all hell breaks loose and happy seaside resorts become a thing of the past, then skip out to a nice impenetrable mountain fortress ironclad with unbreakable protective spells.

"Even better would be persuading one's friends to join one in safety. So one could watch the smoke rising from the former seaside resorts without getting all upset about one's friends dying down there. You see?"

"Do you really think it'll come to that?" said Smith.

"It cannot," said Willowspear. He had another gulp of his drink and looked up from it with the fire of determination in his eyes. "My students listen to me. Perhaps I could form a delegation. If my people would only *talk* to yours—"

"What would it take to make anybody listen, though?" Smith looked uneasily at Willowspear. "And should you call attention to yourself? You've got a lot to lose if it goes wrong."

"I have more to lose if no one makes the effort!" said Willowspear.

"More than you realize," said Lord Ermenwyr. "There are other players in this game, my friend."

"What do you mean?"

The lordling looked shrewd. "The Yendri aren't the only people with colorful mythology. Burnbright, my sweet, have you ever told your husband the story of the dreadful Key of—"

His mouth remained open, forming the last syllable of what he had been about to say, his expression did not change in the slightest; but it was as though Time had stopped in a narrow envelope about his body. The others sat blinking at him for a moment, waiting for him to pick up his train of thought or sneeze.

"Master?" said Balnshik sharply.

"Is he having a seizure or something?" Mrs. Smith demanded.

"No, because he'd be jerking his arms and legs and foaming at the mouth and spitting out live scorpions," said Burnbright. "There was this holy man in Mount Flame who used to—"

"Should he be glowing?" Smith inquired, leaning close to look at him.

Whether he should or not, Lord Ermenwyr had certainly begun to glow from within, as though he were a lantern made of opaque glass. It was an ominous green in color, that light, edged with something like purple, though it was steadily brightening to white—

"Hide your faces!" ordered Balnshik, in a voice none of them considered disobeying even for a second, though Willowspear had already pulled Burnbright down and dropped with her.

Smith found himself staring bemusedly at a pair of skeletal hands silhouetted before his face, which was odd because his eyes were closed . . . understanding at last, he gulped and rolled blindly off his seat, burying his face against the garden flagstones. The horrible light was everywhere still, but it had taken on a quality that was more than visual. It had a scent, a painful perfume. It was sound, a hissing, insinuating crackling like . . . like fire or whispering . . .

Voices. Something was talking. He didn't understand the language. Was it being spoken, or played?

Abruptly it stopped, and the light went out. Smith heard Lord Ermenwyr say "Oh, damn," quite distinctly. Then there was a crash, as though he had toppled backward.

"What the bloody hell was that?" said Mrs. Smith, from somewhere at ground level nearby.

"What is it? What's the matter?" Willowspear sounded agonized.

"He's—ow—oh, the baby's kicking—" said Burnbright, somewhat muffled.

"Come now, Master, this won't do," said Balnshik quite calmly, though with a certain distortion in her voice that suggested she might have altered her appearance just the tiniest bit, and was speaking through, for example, three-inch fangs. "Sit up and collect your wits. You're not hurt at all. Stop frightening everyone."

Smith opened his eyes cautiously. He could see again. No glowing afterimages, no clouds of retinal darkness. It was as though the light had never been. He got to his feet and peered at Lord Ermenwyr, who was sitting up in Balnshik's arms. There was still a flicker of green light on the surface of his eyes.

"My lord has simply received a Sending," Balnshik explained.

"Oh, is *that* all," grumbled Mrs. Smith, struggling to stand.

"It's a message conveyed by sorcerous means," said Willowspear, helping her up. "My lord, are you well?"

Lord Ermenwyr had, in fact, begun to recover his composure and grope for his smoking tube; instead he sagged backward and closed his eyes.

"Feel—weak . . . Must . . . lie . . . down . . ." He moaned.

Balnshik pursed her lips.

"Smith . . . ," Lord Ermenwyr continued, "Willowspear . . . carry me up to my . . . my bed . . ."

Smith and Willowspear exchanged glances. Balnshik was perfectly capable of throwing her master over one shoulder like a scarf and carrying him anywhere he needed to be, and everyone present knew this, which was perhaps why Lord Ermenwyr opened one eye and groaned, with just an edge to his feebleness:

"Nursie dearest . . . you must see to . . . to . . . poor little Burnbright . . . Smith and Willowspear, are you going to let me die here on the damned pavement?"

"No, my lord," said Willowspear hurriedly, and he and Smith raised Lord Ermenwyr between them. The lordling got an arm over both of their shoulders and staggered between them. He continued to make pitiful noises all the way up the hotel stairs and down the corridor to his suite, where Cutt and Crish stood like menhirs on either side of the gaping door.

"Help me . . . to the bed . . . not *you*, I meant Smith and Willowspear," snapped Lord Ermenwyr. "So . . . weak . . ."

They dutifully carried him across the threshold and were well into the dark room before the ceiling fell in on them. At least, that was what Smith remembered it sounding like afterward.

⌒

Smith opened his eyes and blinked at the ceiling.

Ceiling? It looked like the underside of a bunk. It *was* the underside of a bunk, and it was pretty close to his face. In fact there didn't seem to be much room anywhere, and what there was, was pitching in a manner that suggested . . .

All right, he was in the forecastle of a ship. That might be a good thing. It might mean that the last twenty years had all been a dream, and he was going to sit up and discover he was youthful, flexible, and a lot less scarred.

Smith sat up cautiously. No; definitely not flexible. Youthful, either. Scars still there. And the cabin he occupied was a lot smaller than the forecastle of the last ship in which he'd served, though it was also much more luxurious. Expensive paneling. Ornamental brasswork. Fussy-patterned curtains at the portholes. Probably not a lumber freighter, all things considered.

He swung his legs over the edge of the bunk and stood up, unsteadily, trying to find the rhythm of the ship's movement and adjust. The immediate past wasn't a complete void: he remembered confusion, voices, torchlight, lamplight . . .

The ship heeled over in a manner that suggested it wasn't being crewed very well. Smith clung to the edge of the bunk, then lurched to the porthole, just in time to see a shapeless mass of nastiness falling past. On the deck immediately above his head, someone profoundly baritone attempted to make consoling noises, and an irritable little voice replied, "No, I don't give a damn. Just don't let go of the seat of my pants."

Mumble mumble mumble mumble.

"Don't be stupid, we can't be in danger. The sky is blue, it's broad daylight, and, anyway, the beach is right over there. See the surf?"

This remark, together with the realization that it had been spoken over a steady background din of clinking blocks and flapping canvas, sent Smith out of the cabin and up the nearest companionway as though propelled from a cannon's mouth.

"Master, the Child of the Sun has awakened," said Cutt in a solicitous voice, addressing Lord Ermenwyr's backside. Lord Ermenwyr was too busy vomiting to reply, and Smith was too busy hauling on the helm and praying to all his gods to comment either, so there was a moment of comparative silence. The ship heeled about, throwing Lord Ermenwyr backward onto the deck, and her sails fluttered free.

"You! Whichever one you are! C'mere and hold this *just like this!*" Smith shouted, seizing Strangel and fixing his immense hands on the wheel. The demon obeyed, watching in bemusement as Smith ran frantically about on deck, making sheets fast, dodging a swinging boom, and crying hoarsely all the while, "Lord-Brimo-of-the-Blue-Water save us from a lee shore, Rakkha-of-the-Big-Fish save us from a lee shore, Yaska-of-the-White-Combers save us from a lee shore, two points into the wind, you idiot! No! The other way! Oh, Holy Brimo, to Thee and all Thine I swear a barrel of the best and a silver mirror if You'll only get us out of this—"

"Rakkha-of-the-Big Fish?" Lord Ermenwyr mused from the scuppers.

Smith raced past him and grabbed the helm again.

"Wasn't I holding it right?" Strangel inquired reproachfully.

"—Holy Brimo, hear my prayer, You'll get a whole bale of pinkweed and, and an offering of incense, and, er, some of those little cakes the priests seem to think You like, anything, just get me off this lee shore *please*!"

"I think it's working, whatever it is you're doing," Lord Ermenwyr said. "We're not going wibble-wobble-whoops anymore. You see, lads? I told you Smith knew how to operate one of these things."

The next hour took a lot out of Smith, though the ghastly roar of the surf grew ever fainter astern. He had no time to ask the fairly reasonable questions he wanted to ask with his hands around Lord Ermenwyr's throat, but he was able to take in more of his surroundings.

The ship was clearly somebody's pleasure craft, built not for sailing but for partying, and she was a galley-built composite: broad in the beam and shallow of draft, operating at the moment under sail, but with a pair of strange pannierlike boxes below the stern chains and a complication of domes, tanks, and pipes amidships that meant she had the new steam-power option too. The boilers seemed to be stone-cold, however, so it was up to Smith to get her out of her present predicament.

Once the ship's movement had evened out, Lord Ermenwyr crawled from the scuppers and strolled up and down on deck, hands clasped under his coattails, looking on in mild interest as they narrowly avoided reefs, rocks, and Cape Gore before winning sea room. His four great bodyguards lurched after him. There was no one else on deck.

"Where's the crew?" Smith demanded at last, panting.

"I thought you'd be the crew," said Lord Ermenwyr, holding up his smoking tube for Crish to fill with weed. "I knew you used to be a sailor. Aren't these new slaveless galleys keen? I can't wait until we fire this baby up and see what she can do!"

Out of all possible things he might have said in reply, Smith said only, "What's going on, my lord?"

Lord Ermenwyr smiled fondly and lit his smoke. "Good old sensible Smith! You're the man to count on in a crisis, I said to Nursie."

"Is she here?"

"Er—no. I left her in Salesh to look after the ladies. They'll be absolutely safe, Smith, believe me, whatever happens. Do you know any other experienced midwife who can also tear apart armored warriors with her bare, er, hands? Lovely *and* versatile."

Smith counted to ten and said, "You know, I'm sure you gave me a thorough explanation of this whole thing and got my consent, too, but I seem to have lost my memory. Why am I here?"

"Ah." Lord Ermenwyr puffed smoke. "Well. Partly because you clearly needed a holiday, but mostly because you're such a damned useful fellow in a fight. We're on a rescue mission, Smith. Hope you don't mind, but I had a feeling you might have objected if I'd asked you first. And I *knew* I could never get Willowspear to listen to reason, so I had to knock him out too—"

There was a drawn-out appalled cry from below. Willowspear rushed up the companionway, staring around him.

"Oh, bugger; now I'll have to start the explanation all over again," said Lord Ermenwyr.

Willowspear was much less calm than Smith had been. The few inhabitants of Cape Gore looked up from mending their nets as his shriek of *"What?"* echoed off the sky.

⌒

"I don't know if I've ever told you about my sister, Smith," said Lord Ermenwyr, pouring out a stiff drink. He offered it to Willowspear, who had collapsed into a sitting position against the steam tanks and was clasping his head in his hands. Willowspear ignored him.

"No, I don't think you have," said Smith.

Lord Ermenwyr tossed back his cocktail and sighed with longing. "The Ruby Incomparable, Lady Svnae. Drop-dead gorgeous, and a gloriously powerful sorceress in her own right to boot. I proposed to her when I was three. She just laughed. I kept asking. By the time I was thirteen, she said it wasn't funny anymore, and she'd break my arm if I didn't leave off. I respected that; yet I still adore her, in my own unique way.

"And I would do anything for her, Smith. Any little gallant act of chivalry or minor heroism she required of me. How I've dreamed of spreading out my second-best cloak for her to foot it dryly over the mire! Or even, perchance, riding to her rescue. Suitably armed. With a personal physician standing by in case of accidents. Which is why I need the two of you along on this junket, you see?"

"So . . . the Sending was from your sister?" guessed Smith. "She's in trouble and she needs you to save her?"

"I believe the word she used was *Assist*, but . . . it amounts to the fact that *she needs me*," said Lord Ermenwyr.

"My wife needs me, my lord," said Willowspear hoarsely.

"She doesn't need to see you stoned to death or torn apart by an angry mob," Lord Ermenwyr replied. "And it was clear you were getting heroic ideas, so I just stepped in and did what was best for you. And look at this lovely boat I was able to get on an hour's notice, remarkably cheaply! I thought I'd call her the *Kingfisher's Nest*. Aren't those striped sails sporty? The kitchen's even stocked with delicacies. Cheer up; you'll be happily reunited once this is all over."

"Where is your sister, then?" Smith asked, keeping a wary eye in the coastline.

"Ah, this is the clever part," said Lord Ermenwyr, laying a finger alongside his nose. "She's at the Monastery of Rethkast. Which is on the Rethestlin, you see? So if we'd set out on foot to rescue her, we'd have had to have hired porters and spent weeks trudging across plains and mountains and other dreary things.

"*This* way, we just sail along the coast to the place where the Rethestlin flows into the sea, and float up the river until we're at the monks' back door. The Ruby Incomparable descends to her little brother's loving arms, he bears her off in triumph, and we all sail back to Salesh to pick up the supporting cast before going off on a pleasure cruise of indeterminate length."

Smith groaned.

"You don't have a problem with my beautiful plan, do you, Smith?" Lord Ermenwyr glared at him.

"No," said Smith, wishing Balnshik were there to give the lordling the back of her hand. "I have a lot of problems with your plan. See those sails on the horizon? The purple ones? Those are warships, my lord. They belong to Deliantiba. It's got a blockade on Port Blackrock just now. We can't sail through, or they'll board us and confiscate our vessel, if we're lucky."

"Oh. And if we're not lucky?"

"We'll hit a mine, or take a bucketful of clingfire or a broadside of stone shot," Smith told him.

Lord Ermenwyr stared at the purple sails a long moment.

"There's a ship merchant in Salesh who's going to find that seven hundred of his gold pieces have suddenly turned into asps," he said. "The smirking bastard. No wonder he had so many of these recreational vessels up for sale."

"And even if the blockade wasn't there," Smith continued, "what makes you think that the Rethestlin is navigable?"

Lord Ermenwyr turned, staring at him. "I beg your pardon?"

"He doesn't know about the falls. He can't read maps," said Willowspear with venom. "His lord father had a geographer captured especially to teach him, but he wouldn't learn. He was a spoiled little blockhead."

Now Lord Ermenwyr turned to stare at Willowspear, and Smith stared too. Willowspear looked back at them with smoldering eyes.

"Why, my old childhood friend and family retainer," said Lord Ermenwyr, "is that Resentment I see in your face at last? Yes! Let it out! Revel in the dark side of your nature! Express your rage!"

Without a word, and quicker than a striking snake, Willowspear stood up and punched him in the mouth. Lord Ermenwyr tottered backward and fell, and his bodyguards were beside him quicker than Willowspear had been, snarling like avalanches.

"You have struck our Master," said Stabb. "You will die."

But Lord Ermenwyr held up his hand.

"It's all right! I did ask for it. You may pick me up, however. I have to admit I was no good at maps," he added, as his bodyguards lifted him and dusted him off with solicitous care, "I just wasn't interested in them."

"Really?" said Smith, too struck by the surrealism of the moment to come up with anything better to say.

"He defaced his tutor's atlas," snapped Willowspear. "He crossed out the names of cities and wrote in things like *Snottyville* and *Poopietown*. I could not believe Her son would do such things."

"Neither could Daddy," said Lord Ermenwyr. "I thought he was going to toss me off a battlement when he saw what

I'd done. He actually apologized to the man and set him free. I had got it through my nasty little head that the blue wriggly lines meant water, though. And where there's water, you can float on it, can't you? So how do we have a problem, Smith?" He narrowed his eyes.

"Do you know what a waterfall is?" Smith watched the purple sails.

"Of course."

"How do you sail up one?"

Lord Ermenwyr thought about that.

"So . . . sailors don't have some terribly clever way of getting around the problem?" he said at last.

"No."

"Well, we'll figure something out," said Lord Ermenwyr, and turned to look at the warships. "Aren't those things getting closer?"

"Yes!" said Willowspear, undistracted from his fury.

"Do you think they've seen us?"

"It'd be a little hard to miss the striped sails," said Smith.

"All right, then; we'll just go around their silly blockade," Lord Ermenwyr decided. "It'll delay us, I suppose, but it can't be helped."

Smith was already steering a course out to sea, but within the next quarter hour it became clear that one warship was breaking from its squadron and making a determined effort to pursue them. Lord Ermenwyr watched its progress from the aft rail. Willowspear stalked forward and prayed ostentatiously, like a gaunt figurehead.

"I think we need to go faster, Smith," the lordling remarked after a while.

"Notice how they've got three times the spread of canvas we have?" said Smith, glancing over his shoulder.

"That's bad, is it?"

"Yes, it is."

"Well, can't we just do something sailorly like, er, clap on more sail?"

"Notice how they've got three masts, and we have one?"

"I know!" Lord Ermenwyr cried. "We'll light the boiler and get the invisible oarsmen going!"

"That would probably be a good idea," Smith agreed.

"Yes! Let them eat our dust! Or salt spray, or whatever."

Smith nodded. Lord Ermenwyr fidgeted.

"Ah . . . do you know how to get the mechanism working?" he asked politely.

～

The boiler took up most of a cabin amidships, and it had been cast of iron in the shape of a squatting troll, whose gaping mouth was closed by a hinged buckler. Fortunately for everyone concerned, its designer had thoughtfully attached small brass plaques to the relevant bodily orifices, marked LIGHT BURNER HERE and FILL WITH OIL HERE and RELIEVE PRESSURE BY OPENING THIS VALVE.

"How whimsical," Lord Ermenwyr observed. "If I ever have to transform a deadly enemy into an inanimate object, I'll know what form to give him." He shuddered as Smith yanked open the oil reservoir.

"Empty," Smith grunted. "Did your ship merchant sell you any fuel?"

"Yes! Now that you mention it." The lordling backed out of the cabin and opened the door to the cabin opposite, revealing it to be solidly stacked with small kegs. "See?"

Smith sidled through and pulled a keg down to examine it. "Well, it's full," he stated. "Good stuff, too; whale oil."

"You mean it's been rendered down from whales?" Lord Ermenwyr grimaced.

"That's right." Smith tapped the image stenciled in blue on the keghead, a cheery-looking leviathan.

"But, Smith—they're intelligent. Like people."

"No, they're not; they're fish," said Smith, looking around for a funnel. "Mindless. Here we go. You hold that in place while I pour, all right?"

"Promise me you won't throw the empties overboard, then," said Lord Ermenwyr, reaching out gingerly with the funnel. "Certain mindless fish have been known to stalk fishermen with something remarkably like intelligence. And a sense of injury."

Smith shrugged. When the oil reservoir had been filled, when the water pump had been opened, when the burner had been lit with a handy fireball and the troll's eyes begun to glow an ominous yellow behind their glass lenses, Lord Ermenwyr stood back and regarded the whole affair with an expression of dissatisfaction.

"Is that all?" he said. "I was expecting a rush of breath-taking speed."

"It has to boil first," said Smith.

There came a thump and clatter on the deck above their heads.

"Master," said a deep voice plaintively, "that ship threw something at us."

Smith swore and sped up the companionway.

The bodyguards were standing in a circle, staring down at a ball of chipped stone that rolled to and fro on the deck. Willowspear, who had retreated as far forward as he could get, pointed mutely at the warship that was by then just over an effective shot's length astern, close enough to see the blue light in the depths of the cabochon eyes of its dragon figurehead.

"Was that a broadside?" inquired Lord Ermenwyr, worming past Smith to glare at the ship.

"No. That was a warning," said Smith.

Cutt, Crish, Stabb, and Strangel all bent at once to pick up the stone ball, and butted heads with a noise like an accident in a quarry. After a moment of confused growling, Cutt got hold of the ball. He turned and threw it at the warship, in a titanic stiff-armed pitch that struck its foretop and broke the yard, sending it crashing to the deck in a tangle of rigging.

Lord Ermenwyr applauded wildly.

"That'll slow 'em down! *Good* Cutt!"

"What if all they wanted to do was speak with us?" cried Willowspear. "Do you realize we may have just lost any chance of resolving this peacefully?"

"Oh, you're no fun at all."

"The best we could have hoped for was being boarded anyway," said Smith. "They'd have confiscated the boat and stuck us in a holding prison for civilians while they sorted us out. If we were lucky, we'd have seen the light of day after the war's over."

"But—"

"They're cranking back their catapult for another shot," warned Lord Ermenwyr.

Smith saw that this was indeed the case, and that the warship's crew, which had been going about their business on deck in an unhurried way until the strike and only occasionally glancing out at their quarry, was now assembled all along the rail, staring at the *Kingfisher's Nest* as a hawk stares at a pigeon.

The fighters among them held up their oval shields, bright-polished, and began to tap them against their scaled armor in a slow deliberate rhythm, *clink* and *clink* and *clink*, and the common sailors took up the rhythm too, beating it out on the rail. On bottles. On pans. The ratcheting of the great arm echoed it too as it came back, and back—

"Hell! Here it comes," said Smith, and prepared to drop flat, but the shot went high and fell short, sending up a white gout of water.

"We don't have anything we can shoot back with," fretted Lord Ermenwyr.

"If you'd told me about this trip ahead of time, we might have," Smith retorted, watching the activity on the enemy's deck. Now there were sailors swarming in the rigging, hauling up a replacement yard and cutting lines free, and there was a team busy adjusting the placement of the catapult. The moment it was set again, however, all hands paused in their work, all faces turned back to the *Kingfisher's Nest,* and once again they began to beat out the rhythm, *clink* and *clink,* even the clinging topmen striking out their beat on the dull blocks and deadeyes.

But as the catapult's arm moved back, inexorable, there came a sound to counterpoint it: *clank*, and *splash*, and *clank* and *splash*, and *clanksplash clanksplash—*

"Hooray!" Lord Ermenwyr made a rude gesture at the warship. "We have oarsmen!"

And oars did seem to have deployed out of the panniers astern, jutting and dipping with a peculiar hinged motion, like a team of horses swimming on either side. The *Kingfisher's Nest* did not exactly surge ahead, but there was no denying it began to make way, in a sort of determined crawl over the choppy swell. Over on the warship they launched their shot, and it arched up again and hung for a moment in the white face of the early moon before plummeting down in another fountain, approximately where Smith had been standing two minutes earlier.

"*Now* they'll see," gloated Lord Ermenwyr. "We'll leave them all befuddled in our, er—"

"Wake," said Smith.

"Yes, and after dark they won't have a chance, because we'll slip silently away through the night and evade them!"

"I don't think we're going anywhere silently," said Smith,

shouting over the clatter of the mechanism. "And there'll be moonlight, you know."

"Details, details," Lord Ermenwyr shouted back, waving his hand.

They fled south, keeping the coastline just in sight, and the warship followed close. Its smashed yard was replaced in a disconcertingly short period of time, so the *Kingfisher's Nest* lost some of its lead again. The whole chase had a bizarre clockwork quality Smith had never seen in a sea battle before. The *Kingfisher's Nest* paddled on, puffing steam like a teakettle, while the warship's crew kept up its clattering commentary. Were they trying to intimidate? Were they being sarcastic?

They never gave it up in any case, all the way down the coast, past a dozen fishing villages, past Alakthon-on-Sea, past Gabekria. The sun sank red, throwing their long shadows out over the water, and the white foam turned red and the breasts of the seabirds that paced them turned red as blood. When the sun had gone they fled on through the purple twilight, still pursued, and the warship lit all its lanterns as though to celebrate a triumph.

"Aren't they ever giving up?" complained Lord Ermenwyr. "What did we ever do to them, for hell's sake?"

"They're chasing us because we're running," said Smith wearily. "I guess they think we're spies, now. It's a matter of money, too. We got off a shot at them and did damage, so we're a legitimate prize if we're taken."

Lord Ermenwyr lit his smoking tube with a fireball. "Well, this has ceased to be amusing. It's time we did something decisive and unpleasant."

"It has never occurred to you to pray to Her for assistance, has it?" said Willowspear in a doomed voice. His lord pretended not to hear him.

"It would help if we had a dead calm," said Smith. "That

would give us the advantage. Could you do something sorcerous, maybe, like making the wind drop?"

"Hmf! I'm not a weather mage. Daddy, now, he can summon up thunder and lightning and the whole bag of meteor-
ological tricks; but I don't do weather."

"In fact, I don't think I ever saw you praying at all, not
once!"

"Could you summon us up a catapult that's bigger than
theirs, then?" Smith inquired.

"Don't be silly," said Lord Ermenwyr severely. "Sorcery
doesn't work like that. It works on living energies. Things
that can be persuaded. I could probably convince tiny parti-
cles of air to change themselves into wood and steel, but I'd
have to cut a deal with every one of them on a case-by-case
basis, and do you have any idea how long it would take?
Assuming I even knew how to build a catapult—"

Smith hadn't heard the shot, but he caught the brief glint
of moonlight on the stone ball as it came in fast and low,
straight for the glowing point of the lordling's smoking
tube. Without thinking, he dropped and yanked Lord
Ermenwyr's feet out from under him. Lord Ermenwyr fell,
the ball shot past. It smashed into the nearest of the boiler
domes, where it stuck. The dome crumpled along one riveted seam and began to scream shrilly, as steam jetted
forth.

"Those *bastards*!" Lord Ermenwyr gasped. "That could
have been me!"

"It was meant to be," said Smith. "But please don't call
them names when they board us, all right? We might get out
of this alive."

"They're not boarding us," said Lord Ermenwyr, scrambling to his hands and knees. "I defy them!"

"Notice how we're slowing down?" said Smith. "See the
steam escaping from the boiler? It's like, er, blood. It's the

vital fluid that makes the clockwork oarsmen row. And, since it's leaking out—"

"*Dead meat!*" bellowed Crish, wrenching the ball loose. He turned and shot-putted it straight into the bows of the oncoming warship, where it did a lot of damage, to judge from the hoarse screaming that followed.

"This isn't helping—" groaned Smith.

"I'll show them dead meat," said Lord Ermenwyr, in a voice that made Smith's blood run cold. He looked up to see that the lordling had risen, and had thrown off the glamour that normally disguised him. His pallor gleamed under the moon; he seemed an edged weapon, a horrible surprise, and there was something corpselike and relentless in the stare he turned on the warship.

He leaned sidelong over the rail and reached a hand toward the water. Smith's eyes blurred, he winced and blinked and turned his face away: for Lord Ermenwyr was warping size and distance, somehow, effortlessly dipping his hand in the moon-gleaming sea though it lay far below his arm's reach, swirling the water idly, as though the sea were no more than a basin.

He said something that hurt Smith's ears. He called. He persuaded. Smith found himself compelled to look back and saw a light rising under the waves. The warship was perilously close, pistol bolts were hissing across the short space of water that they had not crossed, thudding and clattering home. The lordling ignored the bolts, though he turned his head slightly as the shadow of the bow loomed black in the moonlight. Smiling, he raised his hand full of water, and the light under the waves came closer upward, and grew brighter.

He spoke a Word.

Something emerged from the water and kissed the lordling's hand, and that was all Smith registered before his brain refused to accept the geometry of what he saw. But it was bright, glowing to outshine the moon with the green phosphorescence of the depths, and it had a sweetish scent, and it made a high fizzing kind of sound that might have been speech. Smith trembled, felt a seizure beginning, and shut his eyes tightly.

But he could hear the screaming on the other ship.

He heard the wrenching and snapping of wood, too, and the full-throated and triumphant howling of Cutt, Crish, Stabb, and Strangel. He heard Willowspear's footsteps swift on the companionway, and his pleading voice. Smith swallowed twice before he was able to mutter; "Have mercy on them, have mercy on them, o gods . . ."

The shouting was going on and on. There was a bubbling, a rush of air and displaced water. There was still shouting. The smell diminished, the bubbling too, but the shouting continued.

Smith opened his eyes and looked full into the moon. For a moment he glimpsed the double image of a towering shape below it that dwindled, solidified, patted its mundane form about it like a garment, and was only Lord Ermenwyr after all. Smith scrambled to his knees and peered over the railing.

The warship was still there, though falling astern and foundering. Its bowsprit with the dragon figurehead, in fact much of its forecastle, was missing. Boats were being flung over and men flung themselves too, swimming desperately to get free of the wreck and of the brightness under the water.

But the bright thing sank, and diminished, and a moment later there was no light but the moon and the now-distant lanterns of the ship, though they were going out one by one. No clattering any more, of any kind, for the first time in hours. Smith's ears rang in the silence.

"What was that?" he asked.

"Oh, you really don't want to know," said Lord Ermenwyr. "They broke my toy, so I broke theirs."

A wind came across the sea and bellied out their sails. The silence filled gradually with the long-familiar creaking of the ship under way. Lord Ermenwyr took up his smoking tube again and relit it, shielding it against the wind with both hands. Smith steadied his trembling legs, got to his feet.

"Thank you," he said, "for not having them all killed."

"Well, aren't you the magnanimous soul?" said Lord Ermenwyr, regarding him askance. "I couldn't see myself facing Mother again if I'd given them what they deserved. Her stare of reproach could take out a whole fleet of warships."

"My lord, we must go back and rescue them," said Willowspear.

"No!" Lord Ermenwyr bared his teeth. "What do you think I am, a *nice* man? It won't do them any harm to paddle across the briny deep looking fearfully over their shoulders for a while, expecting any moment some unspeakable creature to rear up out of the primordial oozy depths and . . . and . . . Oh, bugger all, I'm getting seasick again. Help me to my cabin, Willowspear. I want my fix, and I need to lie down."

Willowspear glowered at him.

"I'm doing this for your Mother's sake," he said, and helped Lord Ermenwyr to the companionway.

"Fine. Smith, you can stay up here and mind the steering-wheel thing. Boys, stand guard. Perhaps you can get Smith to teach you how to belay the anchor or some other terribly nautical business . . ."

His voice retreated belowdecks.

Smith staggered to the wheel and clung there, breathing deeply. Distant on the headland were the tiny yellow lights of a village. There was a fair wind; the stars were washed out by light, the night sky washed to a soft slate-blue, and the moon rode tranquil above the wide water. If anything unwholesome traveled below, it kept to its deeps and troubled the air no more

He brought his gaze back to the deck, and met eight red lights in a line. No; they were four pairs of eyes. Cutt, Crish, Stabb, and Strangel were watching him, unblinking as towers.

"What is an anchor, Child of the Sun?" asked Strangel.

What the hell, thought Smith.

"All right," he said. "You're going to learn to crew this ship. Understand?"

The demons looked at one another uncertainly.

⌒

Smith woke on deck in the morning, sprawled in a coil of hawser, and—sitting up—felt every year of his life in the muscles of his lower back. Gritting his teeth, he stood and surveyed the deserted bay wherein the *Kingfisher's Nest* lay anchored. It had seemed like a safe harbor by moonlight; he was gratified to see no other sail and a clear sky without cloud.

"Child of the Sun."

He turned his head (feeling a distinct grinding in his neck) and saw the four demons standing motionless by the rail, watching him hopefully.

"Are we to pull up the anchor now?"

Smith ran his hands over his stubbly face. "Not yet," he said. "See all these pistol bolts sticking in things? Pull 'em all out and collect 'em in a bucket. Find a wood plane and some putty and get rid of the splinters and the holes, all right? And I'll go see if I can find a wrench so I can start taking the boiler dome apart."

The demons looked at one another.

"What is some putty, Child of the Sun?"

It took no more than an hour to show them what to do. Smith had discovered that the demons were not actually stupid; just terribly literal-minded. By the time Lord Ermenwyr came on deck they were scraping and filling industriously, as

Smith sat in the midst of the disassembled boiler dome, tapping out the dent and realigning the seam.

"Oh, good, I hoped you'd be able to fix that," said Lord Ermenwyr, pacing forward and surveying the horizon.

"I can patch it together enough to work," Smith shouted after him. "It would be nice to have some solder, though."

"You'll manage," the lordling assured him.

"Where's Willowspear?"

"Fixing us breakfast." Lord Ermenwyr paced back in a leisurely fashion and stood regarding Smith's efforts with mild interest.

"Are you sure that's safe?" Smith said, around the rivet he was holding in his teeth at that moment. He spat it out, smacked it into place, and resumed tapping. "You've annoyed him a lot, you know. I didn't think he was capable of hitting anybody."

"Neither did he." Lord Ermenwyr snickered. "Another step in his journey toward self-knowledge. Now he's decided to make amends by cooking for us on this jaunt."

"Does he know how to cook?"

"He's dear Mrs. Smith's son, isn't he? Bound to have inherited some of her culinary genius." Lord Ermenwyr hitched up his trousers and squatted on the deck, staring in fascination as Smith worked. "And what a splendid job you're doing! It just comes naturally to you, doesn't it? You people are so good with—with hammers, and rivets, and anvils and things. It would really be a shame . . ."

Smith waited a moment for him to finish his sentence. He didn't. When Smith looked up he was staring keenly out to sea, pretending he hadn't said anything.

"Just before you got hit by the Sending," said Smith, "You were saying a lot of ominous stuff about the collapse of civilization and dropping dark hints about other people getting involved."

"Was I? Why, I suppose I was," said Lord Ermenwyr in an innocent voice.

"Yes, you were. And you said something about a Key."

"Did I? Why, I suppose I—"

"Breakfast, my lord," said Willowspear, rising from the companionway with a kettle. He sat down cross-legged on the deck and began to ladle an irregularly gray substance into three bowls. Smith and Lord Ermenwyr watched him with identical appalled expressions.

"What the Nine Hells is that stuff?" Lord Ermenwyr demanded.

"*Straj* meal, boiled with a little salt," Willowspear told him calmly. "Very healthy for you, my lord."

"But—but that's nursery food! We used to fling it at each other rather than eat it," said Lord Ermenwyr. "And when it dried on a wall, the servants had to scrape it off with wire brushes."

"Yes, I remember." Willowspear lifted his bowl and intoned a brief prayer. "Your Mother lamented the wastefulness of Her unappreciative offspring."

Smith stared at them, remembering the smiling inhuman thing that had summoned a horror from the deeps, and trying to imagine it as an infant throwing its porridge about. "Er . . . I usually have fried oysters for breakfast," he said.

"This is a wholesome alternative, sir. Better for your vital organs," Willowspear replied.

"All right, I know what you're doing," said Lord Ermenwyr. "You're punishing me, aren't you? In a sort of passive pacifistic Yendri way?"

"No, my lord, I am not." Willowspear lifted a morsel of the porridge on two fingers and put it into his mouth.

"And I'll bet the meal has been sitting in bins down there for months! There's probably weevils in it. Listen to me, damn you! I had that larder stocked with nice things to eat.

Everything the merchant could cram in there on an hour's notice. Jars of pickled sweetbreads and amphorae of rare liqueurs and candied violets. Fruit syrups! Plovers' eggs in brine! Runny cheeses and really crispy thin fancy crackers to spread them on! *That's what I want for breakfast!*" Lord Ermenwyr raged, his eyes bulging.

"Then I suggest, my lord," said Willowspear, "that you go below and prepare your own meal."

He raised his head and looked his liege lord in the eye. Smith held his breath, and for a moment it seemed that the very air between them must scream and burst into flame. At last Lord Ermenwyr seemed to droop.

"You're using Mother's tactics," he said. "That's bloody unfair, you know." He sagged backward into a sitting position and took up the bowl. "Ugh! Can't I even have some colored sugar to sprinkle over it? Or some syrup of heliotrope?"

"I could prepare it with raisins tomorrow," Willowspear offered.

"I haven't even got my special breakfast spoon." Grumbling, Lord Ermenwyr helped himself to the porridge.

Smith took a cautious mouthful. It was bland stuff, but he was hungry. He shoveled it down.

"My lord?" said a voice like a hesitant thunderstorm. Cutt, Crish, Stabb, and Strangel stood watching them eat.

"What?" Lord Ermenwyr snapped.

"We have not tasted blood or flesh in three days," said Strangel.

Lord Ermenwyr sighed and got to his feet, still dipping porridge from the bowl. As he ate, he scanned the horizon a moment. At last he sighted a fin breaking the water, and a pale shape gliding below the surface close to shore. He pointed, and through a full mouth said indistinctly, "Kill."

His bodyguards were over the rail and into the water so quickly that Smith barely saw them move.

Moments later, cosmic retribution caught up with a shark.

⌐

"So there was this Key you mentioned," said Smith, as he fitted the boiler dome back into place.

"So I did," said Lord Ermenwyr a little sullenly, staring out at the whitecaps that had begun to appear on the wide sea. He ignored Willowspear, who was carefully setting up a folding chair for him.

"Well? What were you talking about?"

"The Key of Unmaking."

Smith halted for a moment before picking up the wrench and going on with his work.

"That's just a fable," he said at last. "That's just, what do you call it, mythology."

"Oh, is it?" Lord Ermenwyr jeered. "It's in your Book of Fire. You're not a believer, then, I take it?"

Smith went on bolting down the dome. He did not reply.

"I am familiar with the Book of Fire," said Willowspear hesitantly. "Though I confess I haven't studied it. It's your, er, religious history, is it not?"

"It's the legends from the old days," said Smith, getting to his feet. He wiped his hands clean with a rag.

"You're *not* a believer," Lord Ermenwyr decided. "Very well; but you must have heard the story of the Key of Unmaking."

"*I* haven't," said Willowspear.

"I'll tell you about it, then. Long ago, when the World was uncrowded and the personified abstract archetypes supposedly walked around on two legs, there was a God of Smithcraft, which was a pretty neat trick given that blacksmithing hadn't been invented yet."

"Shut up," Smith growled. "He was the one who worked out how to make the stars go up and down. He made the swords and tridents for the other gods. He designed the aperture mechanism that rations out moonlight, or we'd all be crazy from too much of it."

"You do remember, then," said Lord Ermenwyr.

"And he . . . well, he fell in love," said Smith reluctantly. "With the fire in his forge. But he knew the flames were only little images of True Fire. He watched her blaze across the sky every day, but she never noticed him. So he put on his sandals and his cloak and his hat and he walked in the World following after True Fire, always going west, hoping to get to the mountain where she slept every night.

"He took his iron staff with him and, uh, things happened like, when he walked through the Thousand Lake country near Konen Feyy the ground was muddy, and his staff end left holes in the ground that filled up with water, and that's how the lakes got there. And up in a crater on top of a mountain he found True Fire at last.

"He courted her, and they became lovers. And they wanted to have children, but she—well, she was True Fire, see? So he made children for her, instead, out of red gold. And she touched them with holy fire and they became alive. Perfect mechanisms that could do anything other children could do, including grow up and have children themselves. And they were the ancestors."

"Some of *your* ancestors, Willowspear, on your mother's side," said Lord Ermenwyr. "Isn't that an odd thought?"

"And . . . True Fire made islands rise up out of the sea, and the Children of the Sun lived on them," said Smith. "Those were the first cities."

He threw down the rag and squinted up at the sky. "We should get moving again," he said. "Make sail and weigh anchor!"

The demons, who had been sprawled out in sated repose, clambered to their feet. Two set to with the capstan bars and the anchor jumped up from the depths like a fishhook, while two mounted into the dangerously creaking shrouds.

"There's more to the story, though, isn't there, Smith?" said Lord Ermenwyr.

"Yes," said Smith, taking the helm. "All right, you lot, remember where the anchor goes? Right. Coil the hawser like I showed you."

"Clever lads!" Lord Ermenwyr called out. "But Smith can't sail away from the story. Pay close attention, Willowspear, because this is where it all went wrong. If the Children of the Sun had stayed on their islands, all would have been well for the rest of us. Unfortunately, they were clever little clockwork toys and invented all this ship business. Halyards, lanyards, jibs, and whatnot. Which enabled them to spread out and colonize other people's lands."

"That was ages before the Yendri even came here, so you can't blame—"

"The demons were here, though. They matter too."

"We travel because our Mother travels," said Smith. "That's what the stories say. That's why we're always moving, the way She moves across the sky."

"Yes, but you don't exactly bring us light, do you?" said Lord Ermenwyr.

At the wheel Smith narrowed his eyes, but said nothing as he guided the ship out of the bay.

"Burnbright is the light of my world," said Willowspear. "They are capable of great love, my lord."

"And that's the other problem!" said Lord Ermenwyr. "They breed like rabbits. Even their own legends say that soon there were so many of them running about the world that the other personified abstract archetypes got upset that their own children were being crowded out, so they went to the Smith god and complained."

"There was a council of the gods," said Smith. "They told the Father he had to do something. So he made . . . so he is supposed to have made this Key of Unmaking."

"The opposite of a key that winds mechanisms up, you see, Willowspear?" said Lord Ermenwyr.

"No," said Willowspear.

"It shuts us off, all right?" said Smith. "Or it's supposed to. It's only a myth, anyway. The stories say that the gods used it to bring on calamities. The first time they used it was when the Gray Plague came. Everybody died but a handful of pregnant women hiding in a cave, that's what the story says. And then everything was all right for ages, and the cities came back.

"And then . . . Lord Salt is supposed to have used it when he burnt the granaries of Troon, and famine came, and the Four Wars broke out at once. In the end there was just a handful of fishing villages along the coast, because inland the ghosts massed on the plains like armies, there were so many angry dead. Nobody could live there for generations.

"And people say . . ." Smith's voice trailed off.

"What people *say*," said Lord Ermenwyr, "is that one day the Key of Unmaking will be used for the third time, if the Children of the Sun can't learn from their mistakes, and there will be no survivors."

"But it's just a story," said Smith stubbornly.

"I have news for you," said Lord Ermenwyr, taking out his smoking tube and tapping loose the cold ash. "It's real."

"No, it isn't."

"I beg to differ. What's the Book of Fire say about it? Let's see what I can recall . . . (Mother made us study comparative religions, and Daddy always said they were good for a laugh, so I applied myself to the subject) . . . 'The Father-Smith sorrowing sore, on the Anvil of the World, Forged his fell Unmaking Key, Deep in the bones he hid it there, Till Doomsday should dredge it up. Frostfire guards what Witchlight hides."

"It's a metaphor," said Smith.

"How can you disbelieve your own Scripture?" Willowspear asked him, dismayed.

"It's different for you," Smith replied. "Your history is still happening, isn't it? His mother is still writing letters to her disciples and running the shop, isn't she? If you have a question of faith, you can just go to her and *ask* her."

"Though Mother says nobody listens to her anyway," said Lord Ermenwyr parenthetically.

"But Hlinjerith of the Misty Branches will still be sacred though a thousand years pass, and the White Ship will still have put forth from its shores. The passage of time can't make truth less true," argued Willowspear.

"You're missing the point, my friend," said Lord Ermenwyr. "It doesn't matter whether Smith believes in the Key of Unmaking or not. Other people do, and they feel it's high time it was used again."

"What kind of people?" asked Smith, feeling a chill.

"Oh . . . certain demons have felt that way about your race for years," said Lord Ermenwyr, with an evasive wave of his hand. "But that's never been much of a threat, because no two demons can agree on the color of the sky, let alone a plan of action. I'm afraid this whole Smallbrass Estates affair has made things worse, though."

Smith shuddered. But, "So what?" he said. "There isn't actually any real literal Key."

"We'll see, won't we?" Lord Ermenwyr said. "If you don't think there's any real danger, Smith, why should we greenies worry?"

He leaned back in his chair and gazed out at the bright sea sparkling.

"I'm getting a headache from all this glare," he said after a moment. "Willowspear, fetch me a parasol. And perhaps my spectacles with the black emerald lenses."

⌒

The third day out dawned clear and bright, but far to the south was a glacier wall of fog, purple in the morning sun, blinding white at noon. By afternoon they had come close, and it loomed across half the world. Under it the blue sea faded to steel color and green, with a pattern like watered silk, and distance became confused. Rocks and islets swam into view, indistinct in the gloom.

Smith struck sails and proceeded with caution, relinquishing the helm to Willowspear every few minutes to take soundings from the chains. He sighed with relief when he spotted a marker buoy, a hollow ball of tin painted red and yellow, and ran aft to the wheel.

"We're at the mouth of the Rethestlin," he told the others. "And the tide's with us. This is where we go inland, right?"

"Yes! Turn left here," said Lord Ermenwyr. He shivered. "Chilly, all this damned mist, isn't it? Cutt, I want my black cloak with the fur collar."

"Yes, Master." Cutt went clumping down the companion-way.

"The water has changed color," observed Willowspear, looking over the side.

"That's the river meeting the sea," Smith told him, peering ahead. "Maybe we should anchor until this fog lifts . . . no! There's the next buoy. We're all right. You ought to thank Smallbrass Enterprises for that much, my lord; this would be a lot harder without the markers."

Willowspear scowled. "Surely they haven't begun their desecration!"

"No," said Smith, steering cautiously. "They can't have

got enough investors yet. These were probably put down for the surveying party. So much the better for us. Weren't we supposed to be racing to rescue your sister, my lord?"

"She'll hold off the ravening hordes until we get there," Lord Ermenwyr said, allowing Cutt to wrap him in the black cloak. "She's a stalwart girl. Once, when Eyrdway was tormenting me, she knocked him down with a good right cross. Bloodied his nose and made him cry, too. Happy childhood days!"

The tide swung them round the buoy, and another appeared. A smudge on the near horizon resolved into a bank of reeds; and the thump and wash of surf, muffled, fell behind them, and the cry of a water bird echoed. The roll and pitch of the sea had stopped. They seemed stationary, in a drifting world . . .

"We're on the river," said Smith.

The fog lifted, and they beheld Hlinjerith of the Misty Branches.

It was a green place, a dark forest coming down to meadows along the water's edge, cypress and evergreen oak hung with moss that dripped and swayed in long festoons in the faint current of air moving upriver. Deeper into the forest, towering above the green trees, were bare silver boughs where purple herons nested.

Three tall stones had been set up in a meadow. Yendri signs were cut deep into them, spirals of eternity and old words. Around their bases white flowers had been planted, tall sea poppies and white rhododendrons, and the bramble of wild white roses. Willowspear, who had been praying quietly, pointed.

"The shrine to the Beloved Imperfect," he said. "That was where he stood, with the Child in his arms. There he saw the White Ship, that was to bear him over the sea, rise from the water. *This* water!" He looked around him in awe.

Lord Ermenwyr said nothing, watching the shore keenly. Smith thought it was a pretty enough place, but far too dark and wet for Children of the Sun to live there comfortably. He was just thinking there must have been a mistake when they saw the new stone landing, and the guardhouse on the bank at the end of it.

"Oh," said Willowspear, not loudly but in real pain.

It was a squat shelter of stacked stones, muddy and squalid-looking. Piled about it were more of the red-and-yellow buoys and a leaning confusion of tools: picks, shovels, axes, already rusted. There were empty crates standing about, and broken amphorae, and a mound of bricks. There was a single flagpole at the end of the pier. A red-and-yellow banner hung from it, limp in the wet air.

The shelter's door flew open, and a figure raced out along the bank.

"Ai!" shouted a man, his hopeful voice coming hollow across the water. "Ai-ai-ai! You! Are you the relief crew?"

"No, sorry," Smith shouted back.

"Aren't you putting in? Ai! Aren't you stopping?"

"No! We're headed upriver!"

"Please! Listen! We can't stay here! Will you pick us up?"

"What?"

"Will you pick us up?" The man had run out to the end of the pier, staring out at them as they glided by. "We've got to get out of here!"

"We're on a bit of a schedule, I'm afraid," said Lord Ermenwyr. "Can't do it."

"Oh, please! You don't—look, the wood's all wet. We can't cook anything Bolter and Drill are sick. And at night—" The man cast a furtive glance over his shoulder at the forest.

Smith groaned. "Can't we give them some oil, at least?" he muttered.

"Would some oil help you?"

"What? Oil? Yes! Just pull in for a minute, please, all right?"

"Bring up a keg," Lord Ermenwyr ordered Stabb. He raised his voice again to call out in a bantering tone, "So I take it you're not happy in Beautiful Smallbrass Estates?"

"I wouldn't live here if you paid me a thousand crowns!" the man screamed, panic in his eyes as he realized that the *Kingfisher's Nest* was truly not going to stop.

"Maybe we can pick you up on the return trip!" Smith cried.

"Damn you!" The man wept. Smith grimaced and turned away, watching the river. He heard the splash as Stabb hurled the keg of oil overboard. Turning back, he saw the man wading into the shallows, grabbing desperately at the keg as the eddy carried it close. To Smith's relief he caught it, and was wrestling it ashore when the tide carried them around a bend in the river, and dark trees closed off the view.

"There, now, he can get a nice fire started with the oil," said Lord Ermenwyr, watching Smith. "And there'll probably be a relief crew arriving any day now."

"What's in those woods?" asked Smith. "Demons?"

"No!" said Willowspear. "This is a holy place. They brought their terrors with them. This is what happens when men profane what is sacred. The land itself rejects them, you see?"

Smith shrugged. He kept his eyes on the river.

⌇

They made hours and many miles upriver before the tidal bore gave out, then moored for the night in a silent backwater. In the morning they lit the boiler again, and thereafter the *Kingfisher's Nest* progressed up the river in a clanking din that echoed off the banks, as the dipping ranks of oars worked the brown water. Birds flew up in alarm at the racket, and water serpents gave them a wide berth.

⁓

On the fifth day, they ran aground.

Smith had relinquished the helm to Cutt while he downed a stealthy postbreakfast filler of pickled eel. He swore through a full mouth as he felt the first grind under the keel, and then the full-on shuddering slam that meant they were stuck.

He scrambled to his feet and ran forward.

"The boat has stopped, Child of the Sun," said Cutt.

"That's because you ran it onto a sandbank!" Smith told him, fuming. "Didn't you see the damned thing?"

"No, Child of the Sun."

"What's this?" Lord Ermenwyr ran up on deck, dabbing at his lips with a napkin. "We're slightly tilty, aren't we? And why aren't we moving?"

"What's happened?" Willowspear came up the companionway after him.

"Stop the rowers!" Smith ran for the boiler stopcock and threw it open. Steam shrieked forth in a long gush, and the oars ceased their pointless thrashing.

"You have hyacinth jam in your beard, my lord," Willowspear informed Lord Ermenwyr.

"Do I?" The lordling flicked it away hastily. "Imagine that. Are we in trouble, Smith?"

"Could be worse," Smith admitted grumpily. He looked across at the opposite bank. "We can throw a cable around that tree trunk and warp ourselves off. She's got a shallow draft."

"Capital." Lord Ermenwyr clapped once, authoritatively. "Boys! Hop to it and warp yourselves."

After further explanation of colorful seafaring terms, Smith took the end of the hawser around his waist and swam, floundering, to the far shore with it, as Cutt paid it out and Strangel dove below the waterline to make certain there were no snags. After four or five minutes he walked to the surface and trudged ashore after Smith.

"There is nothing sharp under the boat, Child of the Sun," he announced.

"Fine," said Smith, throwing a loop of cable about the tree trunk. He looped it twice more and made it fast. Looking up, he waved at those on deck, who waved back.

"Bend to the bloody capstan!" he shouted. Cutt, Crish, and Stabb started, and collided with one another in their haste to get to the bars. Round they went, and the cable rose dripping from the river; round they went again, and the cable sprang taut, and water flew from it in all directions. Round once more and they halted, and the *Kingfisher's Nest* jerked abruptly, as one who has nodded off and been elbowed awake will leap up staring.

"Go, boys, go!" said Lord Ermenwyr happily, clinging to the mast. "Isn't there some sort of colorful rhythmic chant one does at moments like these?"

The demons strained slightly, and the *Kingfisher's Nest* groaned and began to slither sideways.

"That's it!" Smith yelled. "Keep going!"

The *Kingfisher's Nest* wobbled, creaked, and—

"Go! Go! Go!"

—lurched into deep water with a splash, and a wave rose and slopped along the riverbank.

"Stand to," said Smith. As he bent to loose the cable, he became aware of a sound like low thunder. Looking up over his shoulder, he pinpointed the source of the noise. Strangel was growling, glaring into the forest with eyes of flame, and it was not a metaphor.

Smith went on the defensive at once, groping for weapons he did not have. As he followed Strangel's line of sight, he saw them too: five green men in a green forest, cloaked in green, staring back coldly from the shadows, and each man wore a baldric studded with little points of green, and each man had in his hand a cane tube.

Strangel roared, and charged them.

Their arms moved in such perfect unison they might have been playing music, but instead of a perfect flute chord a flight of darts came forth, striking each one home into Strangel's wide chest.

He kept coming as though he felt nothing, and they fell back wide-eyed but readied a second barrage, with the same eerie synchronization. The darts struck home again. They couldn't have missed. Strangel seemed to lose a little of his momentum, but he was still advancing, and smashing aside branches as he came. Not until the third flight of darts had struck him did his roar die in his throat. He slowed. He stopped. His arms remained up, great taloned hands flexed for murder. Their forward weight toppled him and he fell, rigid, and rolled over like a log rolling.

His snarling features seemed cut from stone. The lights of his eyes had died.

The Yendri stared down at him in astonishment.

Smith turned and dove into the river.

He was scrambling over the rail of the *Kingfisher's Nest* when the first dart struck wood beside his hand. He felt Willowspear seize his collar and pull him over, to sprawl flat on the deck, and he thought he saw Lord Ermenwyr running forward. Cutt, Crish, and Stabb gave voice to a keening ululation, above which very little else could be heard; but Smith made out the *clang* that meant someone had closed the stopcock, followed by a tinkly noise like silver rain. He looked up dazedly and saw poisoned darts hitting the boiler domes, bouncing off harmlessly, and Lord Ermenwyr on his hands and knees behind the domes.

"Rope! Rope!" he was shouting, and Smith realized what he meant. The *Kingfisher's Nest* had been borne backward on the current, stopped only by the cable that he had not managed to loose in time. It swung now on the flood, its cable straight as a bar. Smith dragged himself forward to the tool chest by the boiler domes, and, groping frantically, there he found a kindling hatchet.

He rose to his knees, saw two Yendri directly opposite him on the bank in the act of loading their cane tubes, and took a half dozen frenzied whacks at the cable before diving flat again. The darts flew without noise. But he heard them strike the domes again, and one dart bounced and landed point down on his hand. He shook it off frantically, noting in horror the tarry smear on his skin where the dart had lain. Someone seized the hatchet out of his hand and he rolled to see Willowspear bringing it down on the cable, bang, and the cable parted and they shot away backward down the river, wheeling round in the current like a leaf.

⤳

The oars had begun to beat again by the time Smith could scramble to the helm and bring her around, thanking all the gods they hadn't grounded a second time.

"Was anybody hit?" he cried. The demons were still howling, hurling threats palpable as boulders back upriver. "Shut up! *Was anybody hit?*"

"I wasn't," said Willowspear, picking himself up. "My lord? My lord!"

Smith spotted Lord Ermenwyr still crouched behind the boilers, his teeth bared, his eyes squeezed shut. Sweat was pouring from his face. Smith groaned and punched the wheel, and Willowspear was beside his liege lord at once, struggling to open his collar; but Lord Ermenwyr shook his head.

"I'm not hit," he said.

"But what's—"

"*I lost one of them,*" he said, opening sick eyes. "And Mother's right. It hurts worse than anything I've ever known. Damn, damn, damn."

"What can I do for you, my lord?" Willowspear lowered his voice.

"Help me up," Lord Ermenwyr replied. "They need me to do something."

"Who were those people? What happens now?" Smith asked, steering downriver.

The lordling did not reply, but steadied himself on his feet with Willowspear's help. He brushed himself off and marched aft to Cutt, Crish, and Stabb. By the time he reached them he was swaggering.

"Now, boys, that's enough! What good will shouting do?" he demanded.

They fell silent at once and turned to him meekly, and Smith was astonished to see their hideous faces wet with tears.

"Now we are no longer a set of four, Master," said Cutt.

"Of course you are. Look! I've caught old Strangel right here." Lord Ermenwyr held up a button he'd plucked from his waistcoat. "See? There's his living soul. I'll put it in a new body as soon as ever we're home. But what does he need now?"

The demons stared at him, blank. Then they looked at one another, blanker still.

"*Revenge!*" Lord Ermenwyr told them. "Lots of bloody and terrible revenge! And who's going to be the hideous force that dishes it out, eh?"

". . . Us?" Stabb's eyes lit again, and so did Cutt's and so did the eyes of Crish.

"Yes!" Lord Ermenwyr sang, prancing back and forth before them. "Yes, you! Kill, kill, kill, kill! You're going to break heads! You're going to rip off limbs! You're going to do amusing things with entrails!"

"Kill, kill, kill!" the demons chanted, lurching from foot to foot, and the deck boomed under their feet.

"Happy, happy, happy!"

"*Happy, happy, happy!*" The planks creaked alarmingly.

"Kill, kill, kill!"

"*Kill, kill, kill!*"

⤚

A while later they had come about and were steaming back up the river again, at their best speed.

"Half a point starboard!" Smith called down from the masthead. Below him, Willowspear at the helm steered to his direction cautiously, glancing now and then at the backs of his hands, where STARBOARD was chalked on the right and PORT on the left. On either side stood Cutt and Crish, shielding him each with a stateroom door removed from its hinges. Lord Ermenwyr sat behind him in a folding chair, shadowed over by Stabb with yet a third door. The lordling had his smoking tube out, but its barrel was loaded with poison darts gleaned from the deck, and he rolled it in his fingers and glared at the forest gliding past.

They drew level with the place where they had been attacked, and there was the cut cable trailing in the water; but of their assailants there was no sign.

"Two points to port," Smith advised, and peered ahead.

The fogbanks of the coast lay far behind them; the air was clear and bright as a candle flame. From his high seat he could see forest rolling away for miles, thinning to yellow savanna far to the north and east, and he knew that the grain country of Troon was out beyond there. Westward the land rose gradually to a mountain range that paralleled the river. Far ahead, nearly over the curve of the world perhaps, the mountains got quite sharp, with a pallor nastily suggestive of snow though it was high summer.

And in all that great distance he could see no house, no smoke of encampments, no castle wall or city wall, and no other ship on the wide river. He saw no green men, either; but he knew they would not let themselves be seen.

"One point to starboard," he cried, and his voice fell into vast silence.

~

By evening they had gone far enough, fast enough, for Smith to judge it safe to drop anchor off an island in the middle of the river. Crish and Stabb were left on deck to keep watch, and Cutt blocked the companionway like a landslide.

"This is *a good* wine," Lord Ermenwyr remarked, emerging from the galley with a dusty bottle. "Nice to know there are still a few honest merchants left, eh?"

Smith sighed, warming his hands at the little stove. He looked around the saloon. It was quite elegant. More polished brass and nautical curtains, bulkheads paneled in expensive woods, not one whiff of mildew. And nothing useful. No weapons other than in potential: a couple of pointless works of art in one corner, a dolphin and a seagull cast in bronze, slightly larger than life and heavy enough to kill somebody with. They didn't suit Smith's tastes, as art. He preferred mermaid motifs himself, especially mermaids with fine big bosoms like—

"Here," said Lord Ermenwyr, pressing on him a stoneware cup of black wine. "A good stiff drink's what you want, Smith."

"I'll tell you what I want," Smith replied, taking the cup and setting it down. "I want to know who killed Strangel."

Lord Ermenwyr shifted in his seat.

"He isn't really dead," he said hastily. "Not as we think of being dead. Really. With demons, you see—"

"They were the Steadfast Orphans," said Willowspear. "Those of our people who refused to accept the Lady's marriage and . . . and subsequent offspring. They are an order of fighters, Smith. They will kill if they believe it's justified."

"Like Flowering Reed," Lord Ermenwyr explained. "He was one of them."

"Hell," said Smith, with feeling. "Are they after you again?"

After an awkward pause, Lord Ermenwyr said, "I don't think so. They might have been on their way to Hlinjerith."

Smith thought of the pleading man on the landing, and his horror registered on his face.

"They wouldn't harm those men," Willowspear assured him. "Especially not if they were ill. The Orphans are stubborn and intolerant and—and bigoted, but they never attack unless they are attacked first."

"So as to have the moral edge," sneered Lord Ermenwyr. "Mind you, they have no difficulty hiring someone else to kill for them. And they'll go to great lengths to arrange 'accidents,' the hypocritical bastards."

"Strangel charged them, so they took him out," said Smith. "All right. But what'd they go after me for?"

"I think they'd probably spotted me on deck by then," the lordling replied, "and it's open season on me all year round, you know, what with me being an Abomination and all."

"But they worship your mother, don't they?" Smith knitted his brows. "I've never understood why they think she won't mind if they murder her children."

"They worship Her as a sacred virgin," Willowspear explained. "And it is thought that Her . . . defilement, hm, is a temporary state of affairs, and if, hm, if Her husband and children cease to exist, then the cosmic imbalance will be righted and She will be released from Her, hm, enslavement and return to Her proper consciousness."

"It doesn't help that Daddy's a Lord of Darkness," said Lord Ermenwyr. "Complete with black armor and other evil clichés. But the fact is, the Orphans simply don't like anybody. They despise people like Willowspear for not holding to the Old Faith. They don't like demons just on principle, because chaos isn't in line with their idea of cosmic harmony. And they *really* hate your people, Smith. Especially now. Which is unfortunate, because nobody else likes you much either."

"Oh, what did we ever do to anybody?" Smith demanded. He was cold, and tired, and starting to feel mean.

Lord Ermenwyr pursed his lips. "Well . . . let's start with acting as though you're the only people in the world and it all belongs to you. The rest of us get relegated to 'forest denizen' status, as though we were another species of beast, or maybe inconvenient rock formations. It never seems to occur to you that we might resent it.

"Then, too, there's the innocent abandon with which you wreck the world, and I say innocent because I really can't fathom how anybody but simpletons could pour sewage into their own drinking water. You cut down forests, your mines leave cratered pits like open sores, and—have you noticed how expensive fish is lately? You've nearly fished out the seas. I might add that the whales are not fond of you, by the way."

"And the other races never do anything wrong, I suppose," said Smith.

"Oh, by no means; but they don't have quite the impact of the Children of the Sun," said Lord Ermenwyr. "You're such ingenious artificers, you see, that's part of the problem. Yet I do so love your cities, and your clever toys, like this charming boat for example. I'd be desolated if I had to live in the forest like the Yendri. Do you know, they didn't even have fire until Mother taught them how to make it? I can't imagine dressing myself in leaves and living in a bush and, and having nasty tasteless *straj* for breakfast, lunch, and dinner." He glared at Willowspear, who rolled his eyes.

"It is a simple and harmonious life, my lord," he said. "And it harms not the earth, nor any other living thing."

"But it's damned boring," said Lord Ermenwyr. "Give me the Children of the Sun any day. If only they would learn to use birth control!" He looked back at Smith imploringly.

"Sex is good for you," said Smith. "And you don't get a baby every time, you know. If we have more than anybody else, it's because we're made better than other people, see? Physically, I mean, and no offense to any races present. But you can't ask people not to make love."

"But—" Lord Ermenwyr pulled at his beard in frustration. "You could use—"

"They don't know about it, my lord," said Willowspear.

"I beg your pardon?" The lordling stared.

"They don't know about it," said Willowspear quietly, gazing into his cup of wine. "My Burnbright was as innocent as a child on the subject. She didn't believe me when I explained. Even afterward, she was skeptical. And, of course, with our baby on the way, there has been no opportunity—"

"Oh, you're lying!"

"I swear by your Mother."

Lord Ermenwyr began to giggle uneasily. "So that's why prostitutes always seem so surprised when I—"

"What are you talking about?" Smith demanded, looking from one to the other of them. Lord Ermenwyr met his stare and closed his eyes in embarrassment.

"No, Smith, you're a man of the world, surely *you* know," he said.

"What?"

"Oh, gods, you're old enough to be my father, this is too—it really is too—you really don't know, do you?" Lord

Ermenwyr opened his eyes and began to grin. He set down his drink, wriggled to the edge of his seat, and leaned forward. Swiftly, in terse but admirably descriptive words, he told Smith.

Smith heard in blank-faced incomprehension.

"Oh, that'd never work," he said at last.

⌐

On the seventh day, they came to the falls.

Smith had been expecting them. He had heard the distant rumble, seen the high haze of mist and the land rising ahead in a gentle shelf.

"You'd better fetch his lordship," he told Willowspear, who was standing at the rail between Cutt and Crish, scanning the riverbank. So far there had been no sign of the Yendri.

"What is it?"

"We're going to run out of navigable river up ahead, and he'll have to decide what he wants us to do next."

"Ah. The Pool of Reth," said Willowspear.

"You knew about it?"

"The monastery is not far above. Three days' journey this way, perhaps. His Mother corresponds with them often."

"Fine. What are we going to do about the waterfall?"

Willowspear spread his slender hands in a shrug. "My lord assumed you would think of a way. You people are so clever, after all," he added, with only the faintest trace of sarcasm.

Smith spun the wheel, edging the *Kingfisher's Nest* around a dead snag. "Funny how everyone thinks we're the worst people in the world, until they need something done. *Then* we're the wonderful clever people with ideas."

Willowspear sighed.

"You mustn't take it personally."

"All I know is, if you put a naked Yendri and a naked

Child of the Sun down in a wilderness, with nothing to eat and nowhere to sleep, the Yendri would sit there and do nothing for fear of stepping on a blade of grass. The Child of the Sun would figure out how to make himself clothes and tools and shelter and—in ten generations the Child of the Sun would have cities and trade goods and—and *culture*, dammit, while the Yendri would still be sitting there scared to move," said Smith.

"If I were going to argue with you, I would point out that in ten more generations the Child of the Sun would have wars, famine, and plague, and the Yendri would still be there. And in ten more generations the Child of the Sun would be dead, leaving a wrecked place where no blade of grass grew; and the Yendri would still be there," said Willowspear. "So who is wiser, Smith?"

"I'm sure I don't know," said Lord Ermenwyr, climbing up on deck. Stabb followed him. "But the only way anyone would ever win this stupid experiment would be to make the naked Yendri and the naked Child of the Sun of opposite sexes. Then they'd think of something *much* more interesting to do. What's that noise up ahead, Smith?"

"You'll see in a minute," said Smith. They came around a long bar of mud alive with basking water snakes, yellow as coiled brass, and beheld the Pool of Reth.

It opened four acres of forest to the sun, and the water was clear as green glass endlessly rippling, save at the edge where the Rethestlin thundered down in its white torrent from the cliff, along a wide shelf the height of a house. Green ferns taller than a man leaned from the bank, feeding on the air that was wet with rainbows. Tiny things, birds maybe, flitted across in the sunlight, and now and then one of them would make an apparently suicidal plunge into the cascade.

Willowspear pointed silently. On the bank to one side was

an open meadow, and two tall stones stood there, carved with signs as the three at Hlinjerith had been carved. The same flowers had been planted about their bases, but in this more sheltered place had grown to great size. Rose brambles were thick as Willowspear's arm, poppy blooms the size of dishes, and the standing stones seemed smaller by comparison. A trail led from them to the base of the cliff, where it switchbacked up broadly, an easy climb.

"Here the Star-Cloaked faltered," said Willowspear. He drew a deep breath and sang: " 'Leading the unchained-lost-amazed, holding the Child, the blood of his body in every step he took; this was the first place his strength failed him, and he fell from the top of the cliff. The Child fell with him. The people came swift down running lamenting, and found Her floating, for the river would not drown the Blessed-Miraculous-Beloved; and in Her fist She held the edge of his starry cloak, as in Her hand She now holds the heavens and all that is in them.

" 'And so he was brought into the air, the Imperfect Beloved, and the people wept for him; but the Child pulled his hair, and he opened his eyes and lived. And he was stunned-silent-forgetful a long while, but when he spoke again it was to praise Her. And the people praised Her. In this place, they first knew She was the Mother of Strength and Mercy, and they knelt and praised Her.' "

Lord Ermenwyr grimaced, and in a perfectly ordinary voice said, "So, Smith, how do we get up the falls?"

"Oh, that'll be easy," said Smith, guiding the *Kingfisher's Nest* into the Pool. "You just arrange to have a team of engineers brought in, with a small army and heavy equipment. We could work out a system of locks and dams that'd get us up to the top in ten minutes. Shouldn't take more than a couple of years to build."

"Ha-ha," said Lord Ermenwyr. "No, Smith, really."

"Drop the anchor!" ordered Smith, and opened the stop-cock as the demons obeyed him. Steam shot forth white, adding more rainbows to the air as it gradually subsided. The ever-clanking sound of the oars stopped. "Really," he said.

"Look, I happen to know the Yendri get up this river all the time," said Lord Ermenwyr heatedly.

"Not in one of these galleys, they don't," said Smith.

"Well, can't you do something with one of those, what are those things called, levers? One of my tutors, another one of *your* people by the way, told me you could move anything with a lever."

"Why, yes. All we need is a lever, say, ten times the length of the keel, and a place to balance it, and a place to stand . . . oh, and tools and materials we don't happen to have," said Smith.

"You're being unnecessarily negative about this, aren't you?"

"Why don't you use sorcery, then, your lordship?"

Willowspear cleared his throat.

"The Yendri," he said, "travel in small light craft. When they arrive here, they get out and carry the boats up that path, and so along the bank above until they can set sail and push against the current again."

"Portage," said Smith. "The only trouble being, this vessel weighs a lot more than a canoe."

"Coracle."

"Whatever."

Lord Ermenwyr looked hopefully at his bodyguards. "What do you think, boys? Could you carry my boat up there?"

The three demons blinked at him.

"Yes, Master," said Cutt, and they all three dove overboard and a moment later the *Kingfisher's Nest* rocked in the water as her anchor was dragged along the bottom.

"No! Wait!" shouted Smith, tottering backward, for the bow was rising out of the water. "This won't work!"

"You don't know demons!" cried Lord Ermenwyr gleefully, wrapping his arms around the mast.

The stern was free of the water, and to Smith's astonishment the whole vessel lurched purposefully up the shore—

And abruptly there was a most odd and unpleasant noise, and her bow went down.

Willowspear, who had been clinging to the rail, peered over to see what had happened. He said something horrified in Yendri.

"Master," said a mournful voice from beneath them, "I am afraid that now Crish will need a new body too."

⌒

Lord Ermenwyr blew his nose.

"No," he said wretchedly, "it has to be me. But I'm damned if I'm going to do it with these clothes on."

He yanked at one of his boots manfully and ineffectively, until Willowspear arose and went to him and took the lordling's foot in his hands.

"Pull backward," he advised.

"Thank you."

They sat in the lee of the *Kingfisher's Nest*, looking vast as a beached whale where it had settled on the shore. Smith had built a small fire and was adding sticks to it now and then, but it wasn't able to do much against the damp and the growing darkness. Lord Ermenwyr disrobed quickly once his other boot was off. He stood shivering and pale in the purple twilight.

"Right," he said, and picked his way along the edge of the Pool until he found a broken branch of a good size. Stripping the leaves and twigs away gave him something that would pass for a staff. Muttering to himself, he walked a certain number of paces, turned, and began to sketch the outline of a body in the mud.

He worked quickly, and did not take great pains with detail. The result was a squared-off blocky thing that did not look particularly human, with a scored gash for a mouth and two hastily jabbed pits for its eyes. But it did look remarkably like Cutt and Stabb, who sat like boulders in the firelight, watching him.

"There's old Strangel," he said, nodding with satisfaction. "Now for Crish."

He marked out another figure of the same size and general appearance.

"So he can really . . . re-body them?" Smith asked Willowspear in a low voice. Willowspear nodded. "How's he do that?"

"It is his lord father's skill," said Willowspear, in an equally low voice, though Cutt and Stabb heard him and genuflected. "His lord father can speak with the spirits in the air. He binds them into his service, and in return he gives them physical bodies, that they may experience life as we do."

Smith poked the fire, thinking about that.

"Did his father, er, create Balnshik?" he asked.

"Long ago," said Willowspear. "Which is to say, he sculpted the flesh she wears."

"He's quite an artist, then, you're right," said Smith.

"My lord is still young, and learning his craft," said Willowspear, a little apologetically, glancing over his shoulder at Cutt and Stabb. "But he has the power from his father, and he is his Mother's son."

"So's Lord Eyrdway," said Smith. "How d'you reconcile somebody like him being the offspring of Goodness Incarnate?"

Willowspear looked pained. "My Lord Eyrdway was,

hm, engendered under circumstances that . . . affected his development."

"Too much magic, eh?"

"Perhaps. He is a *tragaba*, a . . . moral idiot. Like a beast, he cannot help what he does. Whereas my Lord Ermenwyr knows well when he is being an insufferable little—"

"I ought to make a couple of others, don't you think?" Lord Ermenwyr's voice came floating out of the darkness.

"Good idea," Smith called back, but Willowspear turned sharply.

"Is that wise, my lord?"

"It is if we want to get any farther upriver," was the reply.

"What's the matter?" asked Smith.

"It is no easy process," said Willowspear, "giving life."

They sat in silence for a while, and Smith let the fire die back a little so they could see farther into the darkness. They watched as the pale figure moved along the edge of the Pool, crouching in the starlight beside each of the figures he had drawn. One after another he excavated, digging with his hands along each outline, scooping away enough mud to turn a drawing into a bas-relief, and then into a statue lying in a shallow pit. Finally, they saw him wandering back. He was wet and muddy, and no longer looked sleek; his eyes were sunk back into his head with exhaustion.

"Wine, please," he said. Smith passed him the bottle from which he had been drinking, but he shook his head.

"I need a cup of wine," Lord Ermenwyr said. "And an athalme. A boot knife would do, I suppose."

Smith fished one of his throwing knives out of his boot top and handed it over hilt first, as Willowspear poured wine into a tea mug they'd brought out of the galley.

"Thank you," Lord Ermenwyr said, and trudged away into the night again. They heard him muttering for a while in the darkness, and could just glimpse him pacing from one muddy hole to the next. Willowspear averted his eyes and added more wood to the fire.

"He'll need warmth, when this is over," he said. "I wish, in all that indigestible clutter of pickles and sweets he brought, that there was anything suitable for making a simple broth."

The night drew on. They heard him chanting a long while in the darkness, and then as the late moon rose above the forest canopy they glimpsed him. He was standing motionless, his arms upraised, staring skyward. As the white light flowed down onto the bank and lit the Pool of Reth, his voice rose: smooth, imperative, somehow wheedling and desperate too. He was speaking no language Smith knew. He was making odd gestures with his hands, as though to coax the stars down . . .

The air crackled blue over the first pit. It became a mass of brilliant sparks that settled down slowly about the figure there. Smith held his hand up before his eyes, for the whole clearing was lit brighter than day, and hollow black shadows leaned away from the tree trunks clear across the Pool as another mass of light formed above the second pit, and then the third, and then the fourth. Flaring, they drifted down, and the four recumbent forms caught fire.

Whoosh. The fire went out. There was blackness, and complete silence. Even the sounds of the night forest had halted, even the relentless thunder of the falling water. Had the river stopped flowing? Then a shadow rose against the stars beside Smith, and he heard Willowspear call out in Yendri. Sound began to flow back, as though it were timid.

"It's all right," was the reply, sounding faint but relieved.

Willowspear sat down again but Cutt and Stabb rose, staring forward through the dark.

"Seems to have worked, anyway." Lord Ermenwyr's

voice was nearer. "Come along, boys. One-two-one-two. That's it."

By the returning moonlight Smith saw the lordling, staggering rather as he led four immense figures along the edge of the pool.

"See, boys? Here's our Crish and Strangel again," he said, laughing somewhat breathlessly. "Just as I promised you."

"Now we are a set of six!" said Cutt, in quiet pride.

"Master, what is our name?" said one of the giants.

"Yes, you must have names, mustn't you, you two newlings?" Lord Ermenwyr reached the *Kingfisher's Nest* and looked down sadly at the ashes of the fire. "Oh, bugger. No! No! Let's not name anybody that!"

Giggling, he turned back to his servants and raised a shaking hand to point at them in turn.

"Your name is, ah, Clubb! And your name is . . . Smosh, how about that?" His whole body was trembling now, as he whooped with laughter. "Isn't that great?"

Then his eyes rolled back in his head, and he pitched forward into the mud.

⤳

Nothing would rekindle the fire, so they made a bed for him in one of the tilted staterooms, stacking mattresses against what was for the moment a floor, and on Willowspear's advice swaddling him tight in blankets.

"He's taken a chill," said Willowspear, looking at him unhappily.

"He should have kept his clothes on," grumbled Smith, crawling along the bulkhead to fetch more blankets and another bottle of wine.

They bundled up on either side of the lordling, cramped and close but warm, and lay there in the dark listening to the night sounds.

"So . . . if something happens to him, what do we do?" said Smith at last. "Turn around and go home?"

He heard Willowspear sigh.

"If the Lady Svnae is truly in danger, it's my duty to come to her aid."

"But you're a married man," said Smith. "You've got a baby on the way. Don't you miss your wife?"

"More than you can imagine," Willowspear replied.

"Though I suppose it's a little cramped in that attic room with the two of you . . ." Smith did not add, *And the sound of Burnbright's voice would have me shipping out after a month.*

"No." Willowspear stretched out in the darkness, folding his arms behind his head. "It's a paradise in our room. In summer it's so hot . . . one night, we . . . there was a box of children's paints in the storeroom. A guest had left it behind, I think. We took it and painted each other's bodies. Orchids and vines twining our flesh. Unexpected beasts. Wings. Flames. Rivers. The stars shone down through the holes in the slates, and we pretended we were seeing them through the jungle canopy. The whole house slept silent in the heat, but we two were awake, exploring . . . the night insects sang and our sweat ran down and the paint melted on her little body, and she plundered me, she was a hummingbird after nectar . . . and afterward we ran downstairs hand in hand, naked as ghosts, and bathed in the fountain in the garden. We pretended it was a jungle pool. *Oh*, she said, *wouldn't it be awful if anybody saw us like this?* And her eyes sparkled so . . ."

He fell silent. Smith drank more wine, remembering.

"Have you ever been in love like that?" Willowspear inquired at last.

"Not really," said Smith. "I never stayed anywhere long enough. My mother died when I was a baby, so . . . my aunt's family took me in. And I had to work for my keep, so I was apprenticed out young. And one night I was coming back from delivering an order and . . . some thieves jumped me. I killed all three of 'em. Standing there with bodies all around, scared out of my wits at what I'd done. So I ran away to sea. And later I was in the army. And later still . . . so, I was never any place to meet the kind of girl you settle down with. Lots of women, but, you know . . . you both just get down to business. It isn't especially romantic."

A silence fell. Finally, Smith said, "You could go home. I could go on and rescue the lady. I haven't got as much to lose, and I'm better with weapons."

"I don't doubt that," said Willowspear. "But what would my mother say, Smith?"

"You think Fenallise would miss me?" Smith blinked. It had never occurred to him.

"Of course she would," Willowspear replied. "And I am still bound by honor. Lady Svnae's Mother raised me, Smith. She guided me on the path that brought me to my own mother and my wife. If Her daughter is in danger, how can I walk away?"

"I guess you couldn't," Smith agreed.

"It may even be," Willowspear said dreamily, "that this is a quest, and She means me to travel on. She knows the journey of each star in the heavens, and all the journeys of the little streams to the great sea; and each man's path through life, She knows, Smith. Even yours. Even mine."

A hollow voice spoke out of the darkness.

"You won't leave off worshipping her, will you?" said Lord Ermenwyr. "Give me some of that wine."

"Yes, my lord." Willowspear propped him up. Smith tilted the bottle. Lord Ermenwyr drank, and settled back with a sigh.

" 'Yes, my lord,' he says. Why should I be your lord? All

my life, even when I was a snotty little thing in long clothes, there you were all big-eyed watching my family like we were kings and queens," said Lord Ermenwyr hoarsely. "You and the servants. *Yes, my lord, Yes, Master, Kneel to your Lady Mother!* All her damn disciples climbing our mountain on their knees, expecting her to solve all their problems for them!"

"But She always did," said Willowspear.

"That's the worst part," Lord Ermenwyr replied. "She does. You know what it's like, growing up with a mother who knows everything? You, you look in her eyes, and you see—everything you really are—"

He went into a coughing fit. Willowspear scrambled away, returning unsteadily through the darkness with his medicine kit and the box containing Lord Ermenwyr's medication. He drew a sealed glass jar from the kit and gave it a vigorous shake. To Smith's astonishment, it at once began to glow with a chilly green light.

"I thought you couldn't do magic," he said.

"I can't," Willowspear replied. He fitted a medicine cartridge into the hummingbird needle and gave Lord Ermenwyr an injection. "Have you ever seen a phosphorescent tide? It works on the same principle. Lie still now, my lord."

The lordling subsided and lay breathing harshly, looking even more like a corpse in the unearthly light.

"Oh, put it out," he demanded. "I want to sleep."

"At once, my lord." Tight-lipped, Willowspear set the jar in the box and closed the lid.

"And you can just get that look off your face." Lord Ermenwyr's voice floated out of the abrupt darkness. "You know I have insomnia. Did you know that, Smith? Chronic insomniac, ever since I was a baby."

"Really." Smith lay down again, drew up his blanket.

"Nothing helped but sleeping with Mother and Daddy. I

hated the night nursery. Eyrdway came and took horrible shapes at the foot of my cot, until Svnae got up and hit him with her wooden dragon. I ran out the door, down the long dark halls, right between the legs of the guards. I scrambled into bed with Mother and Daddy.

"Daddy growled, but Mother was ever so gentle in that ruthless way of hers and explained I couldn't stop in their bed, but she'd take me back and stay with me until I was asleep. The servants made her up a bed by my cot. She told me we were going to go to sleep. I closed my eyes tight, but I could hear my heart beating, and that always scared me, because what if it stopped?

"So I opened my eyes at last. Mummy was asleep.

"And I thought: Mummy knows everything, even Daddy's servants say so, and she is all the Good in the world. *And she's asleep.* What happens to the world when Good sleeps?

"I'll bet you never wondered about that, did you, Willowspear?"

"No, my lord, I never did." Willowspear sounded exhausted.

"Well, I did. I've been scared to sleep ever since."

"My lord," said Smith. "We've got hard work to do tomorrow."

A sullen silence fell, and remained.

Once or twice there were screams in the forest, brief ones. Smith told himself it was animals, and went back to sleep.

⤚

He was cautious when he crawled out in the dawn, all the same.

"Child of the Sun."

Smith met the gaze of six pairs of red eyes, at the level of his own before he swung himself over the rail and dropped to the ground. He nearly landed on a motionless body, and staggered back; but it was only a wood deer, or had been, for its head had been torn off and it had been clumsily, if thoroughly gutted.

"We hunted," said Cutt. "Now our master can have broth."

"That was a good idea," said Smith, looking up at Cutt. He gaped as he saw the single green dart that protruded from between Cutt's eyes. "Hold still."

Very carefully indeed, he reached up and pulled the dart out. Cutt made a strange noise. It was something like a deep note played on a bowstring, and something like the distant boom of ice breaking in polar seas.

"We hunted," he repeated, in a satisfied kind of way.

By the time the sun had risen above the trees, it looked down on the *Kingfisher's Nest* inching its way up the portage trail on the massive shoulders of Cutt, Crish, Clubb, Stabb, Strangel, and Smosh, preceded by Smith and Willowspear hacking madly away at the nearer edge of the forest canopy to make them room. Smith had only the kindling hatchet and Willowspear the largest of the carving knives from the galley, so the work was not going as quickly as it might have done.

Nevertheless, before the sun stood at midday they had arrived at the top of the bluff, sweating and triumphant, and by afternoon the *Kingfisher's Nest* was clanking away upriver at last. Her owner, who had made the whole remarkable journey in his bunk, fastened in with sheets like a dead chieftain in a particularly splendid tomb, was sound asleep and hence unconscious of his good fortune.

⤳

But he was sitting up in bed and smoking by the time Smith moored that evening and went below.

"Well done, Smith," he called cheerily. "I must remember to buy you a nice big shiny machete of your very own when this is all over. One for Willowspear, too."

"So you didn't die again, eh?" Smith leaned against the bulkhead. His arms felt as though he had been hammering steel all day. "Great."

"Must be all this damned fresh air," Lord Ermenwyr said, and blew a smoke ring. "Our humble servant Willowspear actually handled meat to prepare me a cup of broth, can you believe it? And he grilled the ribs of whatever-it-was for you. They're in the kitchen."

"Galley," said Smith automatically.

"In the covered blue dish," Willowspear called.

With a grateful heart Smith hurried in and found that Willowspear had indeed inherited his mother's ability to cook. He carried a plate back to the lordling's stateroom.

"How much farther is this monastery?" he inquired, slicing off a portion with his knife. "I went aloft three times today, and I couldn't spot a building anywhere."

"Oh, well, it's not what you or I would think of as a building," said Lord Ermenwyr dismissively. Willowspear looked indignant.

"The brothers live in bowers, open to the air," he said. "They need no more than that, because they own nothing the air can hurt."

"Except for writings," said Lord Ermenwyr.

"They have a library," Willowspear conceded.

"So they do have one building?" Smith inquired through a full mouth.

"No; the library is housed in a deep cave," Willowspear explained. "All the Lady's epistles are archived there."

"So . . . will I have any way of knowing when we're close?"

"Oh, you can't miss, it," said Lord Ermenwyr. "There's

this whacking great rock spire, and the river goes behind it through a gorge. There's even a landing."

"Great," said Smith. "The sooner we can get this over with, the better."

He told them about the dart he had found on Cutt. Lord Ermenwyr scowled.

"Nine Hells. I'd have thought the Steadfast Orphans were all at Hlinjerith for the big race war by now. Well, perhaps the boys got them all."

"We have to go past Hlinjerith on our way back!" said Smith.

"Don't get excited! I'll be downstairs here, well out of sight. If you just sail past, they shouldn't bother you," Lord Ermenwyr said. "Other than shooting at you a little."

"They would do no such thing," said Willowspear severely. "They're surely going there to protect a sacred place and for no other purpose."

"But if you time it right with the, er, tide and all that nautical business, they'll be past before you know it," Lord Ermenwyr assured him.

⌐

Mounting aloft the next day, as a hot wind filled the sails with the scent of forest and plain, no least hint of sea, Smith beheld Rethkast.

It looked like a fist of rock standing in the land, an improbable mountain upthrust alone, towering and strangely streaked with colors. Smith could see no sign of habitation at first, though as he stared he thought he could make out a certain regularity of green along the valley floor below the rock, in long lines. He watched it until a range of hills rose to obscure everything but the rock, and told Willowspear about it when he came down.

"That would be the orchards, and the garden," said Willowspear, looking pleased.

"What do they grow there?" Smith inquired.

"Healing herbs," Willowspear replied. "The Lady sends them seeds and cuttings with Her letters, cultivars of Her own creation, whose purpose it has not yet pleased Her to reveal to us. They have kept this garden for thirty years in Her name, in this open land where the air is mild and warm."

"Thirty years?" Smith was astonished. "We can't grow anything longer than *two* years, before the land goes dead."

"What do you mean, *goes dead*?"

"Well, you know. The first year your cabbages come up fine, then the second year they're not so big, and the next year all this chalky stuff comes up out of the ground, and the cabbages are tiny and yellow," said Smith. "Nothing for it then but to move on. The only place that doesn't happen is in the grainlands around Troon, because the barley grows itself. We don't do anything but harvest it."

"You've never heard of crop rotation?"

"What's crop rotation?"

Willowspear turned and stared at him, saying nothing for a moment. At last he said, "Merciful Mother of All Things, no wonder your people go through the world like locusts!"

"What the hell's crop rotation? Does it have anything to do with irrigation? Because we know how to do that; our aqueducts will take water anywhere," said Smith defensively. "We've made deserts bloom, you know. Just not for more than two years."

"But you can't—" began Willowspear.

He turned and staggered away from the helm, and Smith jumped into place at the wheel. "We know how to steer, too," he snapped.

Willowspear collapsed on a barrel, holding his head in his hands. "All this time, I thought—"

"That you're better than us," said Smith. "I know."

"No! I've been trying to teach your people the Way of the Unwearied Mother. I've been teaching them meditation and prayer. What I should have been teaching them all along was simply *how to garden*," said Willowspear.

Smith shrugged. "I never thought it was as easy as just saying the Green Saint's name over and over again, whatever you told me."

"If you only took the filth you dump into the sea and put it on your fields instead—" Willowspear rose and paced to and fro on the deck in his agitation.

"So I guess interracial orgies aren't the answer, either?"

"You don't—there must be love. There must be tolerance, and faith. But—there must be much more, or none of it will do any good! It's *complicated*."

"Well, nothing is simple, son," Smith told him. "Not one damned thing in this world is simple."

Willowspear did not reply, staring ahead at the spire of Rethkast.

"It's just as well you figured this out now, since you're going to be a father soon," Smith added. "By the way . . . was that sorcery the other night, that cold light in the jar?"

"No," said Willowspear. "It was the powdered bodies of certain insects in a solution of certain salts. Mix them, and the mixture glows. When the powder precipitates out, the glow fades and dies. The Lady's invention." He looked oddly at Smith. "But She must purchase the jars from your people. The Yendri have never learned how to make glass."

⌐

As they drew nearer, yet they were driven back; for now the river narrowed between high hills, and the current had greater force. Yet the *Kingfisher's Nest* put on all her canvas, and with a fair wind and the steam oars going at full speed they made way at last, and moored in a backwater where a landing pier did indeed welcome them.

"So where's this back door?" Smith inquired, staring upward at the sheer rock wall.

"We have to climb up and knock," said Lord Ermenwyr, setting his hat at a rakish angle. "How's this look? Suitably adventurous? An appropriate ensemble for sweeping a lady off her feet?"

"I guess so. How do we get up there?"

"There's stairs, concealed with fiendish cleverness," the lordling replied.

"Here," said Willowspear, pointing, and after Smith had looked for a moment, he spotted them: rough steps cut out of the rock, angled in such a way as to be nearly invisible in the crazy-swirled colors in the strata. They moved up at a steep angle. There were no handholds, nor any rail that Smith could see.

"Boys, you'll wait here," Lord Ermenwyr told his body-guard. They nodded gloomily and stood to attention on the deck.

"What about this threat we're rescuing your sister from?" Smith inquired. "Wouldn't they be useful if we have to fight somebody?"

Lord Ermenwyr checked his reflection in a pocket mirror. "I have to admit, Smith, I may have exaggerated just the tiniest bit about the amount of danger Svnae is in," he said. "It's actually more sort of an awfully embarrassing fix, to be honest."

"I see," said Willowspear, in tones of ice.

"No, you don't, and don't go all peevish on me like that!" said Lord Ermenwyr. "All will be revealed in good time. For now let's just mind our own little businesses and obey our liege lord, shall we?"

He started up the stairs. After looking at each other a moment, Smith and Willowspear sighed and followed him.

They climbed steadily for several minutes, as the stairs zigzagged first left and then right, but Smith was unable to spot anything resembling a doorway or even a cave mouth.

"Can't imagine who carved out all these fiendishly concealed stairs," he grumbled, "unless it was one of us poor benighted Children of the Sun. We're *so* clever with little engineering feats like this."

"Oh, shut up," said Lord Ermenwyr, gasping for breath. He leaned on the wall at a slightly wide place and motioned them past him. "Go on, damn you. But you'll wait at the top until I get there! I get to knock on the door."

"I have had an epiphany, Smith," said Willowspear, as they ascended.

"Really?" Smith panted.

"There is a parable the Lady tells. I will translate it for you. The *trevani* Luvendashyll is traveling through the forest, he comes to a village, he sees a woman lamenting. 'How can I help you?' he asks her, 'What is wrong?' and she says, he thinks she says, 'Oh, kind sir, I need wisdom!'

"He says, 'My child, you must travel a long road to find wisdom, for it is not easy to get. You must struggle, and suffer, and speak to all you meet and study their ways, learn what is in their hearts; and even then you will only have begun to find wisdom,' and the woman says back, 'No, no, that can't be right! Can't you give me wisdom?'

"And Luvendashyll says, 'I have a little wisdom, my child, but it cannot be given so easily. You would have to become my disciple, and give all you owned to those who are less fortunate than you are, and travel with me to the ends of the earth, and hear me disputing with other *trevanion;* and perhaps in twenty years I could give you a little wisdom. Or it may be that the wisdom of other *trevanion* would seem better, and you might leave me and apprentice yourself to them for a score of years, in order that they might give you wisdom.'

"And the woman is angry, she says, 'That's ridiculous! Why should I have to do all that to get a little wisdom?' So Luvendashyll is offended, and he says, 'Impatient woman! You do not know what I had to go through for the wisdom I possess. I studied with my master from my earliest childhood, for his wisdom. I spent many days lying in a dark place listening to the Seven Stories of Jish, repeating them for my master until I knew them by heart, to obtain his wisdom. I fasted and prayed and stood on one leg in the bitter cold of winter, that I might be worthy of his wisdom. I walked on cinders and scored my back with a knotted thong, and yet in the end I was granted a little wisdom only, for my master did not like to part with his great wisdom.'

"And the woman says, 'Look, all I want is wisdom, because the one I have has a hole in it and my acorns keep falling out!' "

"Huh?" said Smith.

"The *trevani* Luvendashyll has misunderstood the woman," Willowspear explained. "It's a funny story in Yendri, because he thinks she has asked him for wisdom, *trev'nanori*, when all along she asked only for a new basket, '*tren atnori'e.*"

"Oh," said Smith.

"And your confusion adds a further dimension to the parable, because you don't speak Yendri in the first place," said Willowspear, taking great strides upward in his enthusiasm. "And for the first time, I see the hidden meaning in it!"

"I never thought it was all that funny," said Lord Ermenwyr sullenly, struggling along behind them. "I mean, so the *trevani* is deaf, so what? Or maybe the woman is missing a few teeth."

"The point is that the woman needed a simple thing," said Willowspear, "but the *trevani* did not comprehend simplicity, and so he wasted her time—" He scrambled up on a wide flat landing, and turned back to pull Smith after him, "wasted her time with advice, when what he ought to have done was simply taken reeds and made her a basket! And I, Smith, will make baskets for your people. Figuratively speaking."

He pulled Lord Ermenwyr up as well, and turned to gesture triumphantly at the shoulder of the mountain they had just reached. "When we go up there, Smith, we will look out upon the Garden of Rethkast, and I will show you your future."

"All right," said Smith. He plodded after Willowspear flat-footed, envying the younger man his energy.

"The door is this way," Lord Ermenwyr shouted after them, pointing to a cave.

"One moment, my lord," Willowspear promised. He scrambled up to the crest. "Now, Smith behold the—"

Smith climbed up beside him and stood, gazing down at the wide valley below the mountain. He frowned. Regular lines of green, stretching to the near horizon . . .

"Those are tents," he pointed out.

"But that was—" began Willowspear, and his eyes widened in horror as he saw the piled mounds of cut trees far below, that which had been the bowers of Rethkast, fast yellowing.

Smith was distracted by a slight sting in his foot. He shifted his weight in annoyance, thinking to kick the wasp away. How had he been stung through his boot? He looked down and saw the tuft of green feathers sticking in his foot, and father down the mountain the Yendri who had shot him, clinging to a precarious handhold. There were others below him, like a line of ants scaling a wall.

He had a rock in his hand before he knew what he was doing, and had hurled it down into the Yendri's glaring face. There was some sort of horrific and spectacular chain reaction then, but he didn't have time to notice it much, because yanking the dart out of his boot took all his concentration. Then Willowspear pulled him away from the edge, and they were staggering back the way they'd come. Lord Ermenwyr was at his elbow suddenly, dragging him into the cave.

There was a dark passage running into the heart of the mountain, but not far, because they came at once to a sealed door. Lord Ermenwyr was pounding on it, yammering curses or prayers. Smith could hear Willowspear weeping behind him.

There was a calm voice in Smith's head saying: *Some of the poison may have stayed in the leather of your boot, and after all you survived a much stronger dose, once before, and there is always the possibility you've built up some immunity. On the other hand . . .*

But he was still conscious. He was still on his feet, though events had begun to take on a certain dreamlike quality. For example: When the door opened at last, he beheld the biggest woman he'd ever seen in his life.

She looked like a slightly disheveled goddess, beautiful in a heroic kind of way, gorgeously robed in purple and scarlet. A bracelet like a golden serpent coiled up one graceful biceps. Smith thought she ought to be standing on a pedestal in a temple courtyard, with a cornucopia of fruit under her arm . . .

"Did you bring him?" she inquired.

An instinct Smith hadn't used in years took over, and he found himself turning and running back the way he'd come, without quite knowing why. At least, he was trying to run. In actuality he got about three steps before collapsing into

Willowspear's arms, and the last thing he saw was the young man's tear-streaked face.

⌇

Smith was walking along a road. It was winter, somewhere high among mountains, and the hoarfrost on the road and the snow on the peaks above him were eerily green as turquoise, because it was early morning and a lot of light was streaking in under the clouds. There were mists rising. There were shifting vapors and fogs.

He was following his father. He could see the figure walking ahead, appearing and reappearing as the mist obscured him. He only glimpsed the wide-brimmed hat, the sweep of cloak; but clearly and without interruption he heard the regular ring of the iron-shod staff on stone.

He tried to call out, to get his father to turn and stop. Somehow, the striding figure never heard him. Smith ran, slipping on the patches of black ice, determined to catch his father, to ask him why he'd never . . . never . . .

He was lost in a cloud. The gloom enveloped him, and all he could see was a sullen red glow—

He was holding a staff. It rang, struck sparks from the rock as he swung it. He could not stop, he could not even slow down, for he was following True Fire though he could not see her, and she would not wait for him.

You bear my name.

I do? No, I don't, it's an alias. How could you be my father? I never knew my father. My aunt always said he might have been a sailor. This is a dream.

You walk in my footsteps.

You don't leave footsteps! You never leave a trace. Not one shred of proof. Damn you anyway for never being there.

You kill like a passing shadow, just as I had to kill.

Never liked it. Never wanted to. Never had a choice, though.

Neither did I.

Things got out of hand.

Things got out of control.

I just wanted a quiet life. Why can't people be good to one another?

Why didn't they learn? I should have made them better.

Whose fault is it, then?

You bear my fault.

Like hell I will.

Try to put it down.

Smith attempted to fling the staff away, because somehow it had become the fault, but it wouldn't leave his hand. Instead it shrank, drew into his arm, became part of him.

I don't want this responsibility.

It's your inheritance. And now, my son . . . you're armed.

He tried to run away, but his feet were frostbitten. The right one, especially. He slipped, skidded forward and crashed into a painful darkness that echoed with voices . . .

∽

"I didn't know you were *really* in danger!" Lord Ermenwyr was saying.

"Neither did I, until I looked out the window and there they were," a woman was saying in a bemused kind of way. She had an alto voice, a red velvet voice. "Things became rather horrible after that; but until then, I was enjoying myself with the puzzle."

"How the Nine Hells did they know you were here?" Lord Ermenwyr demanded, panic in his voice. "How did they know *it* was here?"

The woman's shrug was audible.

"Spies, I suppose."

"Well, what are we going to do?"

"Hold them off as long as we can."

"Hold them off? You, me, and a handful of monks hold off an army?" Lord Ermenwyr's voice rose to a scream. "They're fanatics who'll stop at nothing to see my head on a pike! Yours too!"

"It's not as though we can't defend ourselves. We're demons, remember?" The woman's voice grew bleak. "The Adamant Wall ought to keep them out for another week. And if the poor man dies, they won't even be able to get what they've come for. Is he likely to die, Willowspear?"

"Probably not, my lady." Willowspear was speaking very close at hand, speaking in a voice flat with shock. "He's responding to the antidote."

"That's something, anyway." Lord Ermenwyr seemed to have got up. Smith could hear his pacing footsteps. "As long as we're here, let's have a look at this spell of yours."

"It's a terribly old Portal Lock," said the woman, and she seemed to be rising too, her voice was suddenly coming from a long way up. "That was why I thought of you at once. You were always so much cleverer at that kind of composition."

Their voices were moving away now; with their echoing footsteps. Smith could hear Lord Ermenwyr saying, "Ah, but you were always better at research," and the woman was saying something in a tone of chagrin when the echoes and distance made it impossible to hear more.

Silence, a crackle of fire, breathing; several people breathing. A hesitant male voice; "Brother Willowspear?"

"Who is that?"

"Greenbriar. I made the Black Mountain pilgrimage five years ago. You brought us bedding in the guest bowers."

"I remember." Willowspear's voice still sounded unnatural. "She was teaching Fever Infusions that season."

"Will She come to us, at the end? When we are killed?"

"You must trust Her children's word that we will withstand the siege," Willowspear replied, but he sounded unconvinced himself.

"I don't know how I can face Her," the other man said, with tears in his voice. "We failed Her trust. They came like a grass fire, they wouldn't even talk to us, they just laid waste to everything! Brother Bellflower tried to save the orchard. He stood before the palings and shouted at them. They shot him with darts, then they marched over his body and cut the trees down. Thirty years of work killed in an hour . . ."

"It's an illusion," said another voice, too calmly. "She will bring the garden back. She can do such things. They have no real power over us."

"They are madmen," said a third voice. "You can see it in their eyes."

"One can forgive the Children of the Sun, but these people . . ."

"We must forgive them too."

"It was our fault. How could we keep the secret from Her own daughter?"

"Pray!" Willowspear's voice cracked. "Be silent and pray. She must hear us."

They were silent.

Smith was regaining the feeling in his limbs. Surreptitiously, he experimented with moving his fingers. He squinted between his eyelids, but could make out nothing but a blur of firelight and shadow.

He was moving his left hand outward, a fraction of an inch at a time, groping for anything that might serve as a weapon, when he heard the echoing voices returning.

". . . right about that. I wouldn't reach in there for an all-expenses-paid week in the best Pleasure Club in Salesh."

"This was probably a bad idea," said the woman, sighing.

"Well, I'm sure our poor Smith would prefer you should get hold of it than the Orphans," said Lord Ermenwyr briskly. "We can make much better use of it."

"I only wanted to study it!"

"My most beloved sister, it's Power. You don't study Power. You wield it. I mean, it pays to study it first, but nobody ever stops there."

"I would have," said the woman resentfully. "You really don't understand the virtue of objective research, do you? Even Mother isn't objective."

"Mother especially," said Lord Ermenwyr. His voice drew close to Smith. There was a pause. "Poor old bastard, he's in a bad way, isn't he? I suppose you can't use him if he's unconscious, either? If all you need is his hand—"

Instinct took over again in Smith, and if it had been able to make his body obey, it would have propelled him out of the room with one tigerlike spring. Unfortunately, his legs were in no mood to take orders from anyone, and he merely launched himself off whatever he was lying on before dropping heavily on his face on the floor.

There was a stunned silence before Lord Ermenwyr asked, "What was *that*? Premature rigor mortis?"

Smith felt Willowspear beside him at once, turning him, lifting him back on the cot in a sitting position. They were inside a cavern whose walls were lined with racks of bound codices. There were hundreds of volumes. He saw the light of a fire, and Lord Ermenwyr and the stately lady standing before it, staring at him. There were robed Yendri in the near background, seated in attitudes of meditation, but even they had opened their eyes and were staring at him.

He glared back at them.

"You lied to me," he told Lord Ermenwyr, in a voice thick with effort and rage.

The lordling looked uncomfortable, but he lit his smoking tube with a nonchalant fireball, and said, "No, I didn't. I just wasn't aware I was telling the truth. Here's my sister, see? Svnae, meet Smith. Smith, you are privileged to behold the Ruby Incomparable, Lady Svnae. And she *is* in mortal danger. It was uncanny precognition, gentlemen."

"You lied to us both," said Willowspear quietly. "You brought Smith here for some purpose. My lord, I will not see him harmed."

The lady looked chagrined. She came and knelt beside Smith, and he was acutely aware of her perfume, her purple-and-scarlet draperies, her bosom, which was on a scale with the rest of her and which could only be adequately described in words usually reserved for epic poetry . . .

"It's all right," she said kindly, as though she were speaking to an animal. "Nobody's going to harm you, Child of the Sun. But I need you to perform a service for me."

Smith labored for breath, fighting an urge to nod his acceptance. He believed her without question. For all that she was dressed like the sort of wicked queen who poisons the old king, turns her stepchildren into piglets, and exits with all the palace silver in her chariot drawn by flying dragons, there was something wholesome about Lady Svnae.

"Tell me—" Smith demanded. Lord Ermenwyr flipped up his coattails and squatted down beside his sister, looking like an evil gnome by comparison, perhaps one the wicked queen might keep on the dashboard of her chariot as a bad luck mascot.

"There's something hidden in this rock, Smith—" he began.

"It's the Key of Unmaking, isn't it?" Willowspear stated.

"Yes, actually," replied Lady Svnae. "Good guess! Or did Mother tell you about it?"

"Erm . . . I've been trying to explain this to them a bit at a time," said Lord Ermenwyr. "Giving them hints. Well, Smith, what can I say? The damned thing's worth a lot right now. I want it."

"*I* want it," said his sister firmly.

"But we can't get it. It's sealed in the rock, and only one of your people can reach in there and get it. That's why you're here, Smith."

"You're asking him to betray his people," said Willowspear. "My mother's people. My wife's people."

"Don't be an idiot!" said Lord Ermenwyr sharply. "The thing's not safe here any longer, don't you understand? The Steadfast Orphans are waiting their chance out there and if they get their hands on it, they *will* use it, Smith."

"All I want to do is learn how it works," pleaded Svnae. "If I knew that, I might discover a way to disarm it."

"Well, let's not be too hasty about that—"

"It's not real," said Smith at last.

The lordling sat back on his heels. "You don't think so? Come have a look, then." He stood and made a brusque summoning gesture to the monks. "Bring him."

Greenbriar came forward and, between them, he and Willowspear got Smith to his feet and supported him. They followed the lord and lady down a corridor cut in the rock, lit only by the firelight behind them and a faint flickering red light far ahead.

"You people didn't make this place," said Smith.

"We found it," said Greenbriar wretchedly. "We came to here to make a garden. The earth was warm, there was plenty of water . . . but in the caves we found the piled bones of Children of the Sun. Terrible things happened here, long ago. And in the deepest place, we found the thing.

"We told Her about it. She gave us wise counsel. We buried the bones, we made this place beautiful to give their souls peace. We labored as She bid us do. And then, Her daughter came and asked to see the thing . . . and we thought no harm . . ."

"There wouldn't have been any harm if the Steadfast Orphans hadn't shown up," said Lady Svnae, her voice echoing back to them.

"You really ought to do something about your household security," said Lord Ermenwyr. "I'll interrogate your servants, if you like."

"As though I'd let you anywhere near my chambermaids!"

"Well, how do you think the Orphans knew where it was?"

"They probably sat down and read the Book of Fire, the same way I did. There are perfectly blatant clues in the text, especially if you happen to find one of the copies that was transcribed by Ironbrick of Karkateen. But there are only three copies known to exist . . ."

Smith tuned out their bickering and concentrated on making his legs work. Unbidden he heard a voice years dead: that of the old blind man who used to sit on the quay and recite Scripture, holding out his begging bowl, and Smith had been no more pious than any other child, but the sound of it never failed to make him shiver, all the same . . . *the dead on the plain of Baltu were not mourned, a hundred thousand skulls turned their faces to Heaven, a hundred thousand crows flew away sated, in Kast the flies swarmed, and their children inherited flesh . . .*

. . . on the Anvil of the World, Forged his fell Unmaking Key, Deep in the bones he hid it there, Till Doomsday should dredge it up. Frostfire guards what Witchlight hides . . .

"It isn't real," he muttered to himself.

"Here we are," said Lady Svnae, as though they had come to a particularly interesting shop window.

Smith raised his head and flinched, averted his eyes.

Frostfire. Witchlight. Doomsday . . .

All he had really glimpsed was an impression of a spinning circle, the same eerie color as the snow in his dream, and sparks flying within it as though they were being struck from iron. But the image wouldn't fade behind his eyes. It grew more vivid, and to his horror he felt a solid form heavy against his palm, the weight of the iron staff.

He opened his eyes, stared. It wasn't there, but he could still feel it.

"It's only a little recess in the wall," said Lady Svnae soothingly. "The lights and things are just illusions, you see? All you have to do is reach in your hand and take it."

"He's not an idiot," said Willowspear.

"Uh-oh; temperature's dropping in here," said Lord Ermenwyr. "Come on, Smith." He looked at Smith, followed Smith's stare down his arm, saw the fingers clenched around a bar of air. "*What is it?*"

"I—my arm's moving by itself," said Smith.

"It is?" Lord Ermenwyr went pale. The arm and hand were turning, as though to direct the invisible bar like a weapon . . .

Lady Svnae reached into her bosom and pulled forth what looked like a monocle of purple glass. She peered through it at Smith for a moment.

"He's got a Cintoresk's Corona," she announced in a calm voice, and lunged forward and caught Smith in her arms. The next thing he knew he was being dragged backward up the tunnel at high speed, gazing back at Lord Ermenwyr, who was running along behind, knees up and elbows pumping. It was suddenly much warmer.

They emerged into the firelit cavern again, and Willowspear and Greenbriar came panting after them. The other monks, who had now given up any attempt to meditate, watched them fearfully.

"What happened?" Willowspear asked.

"We all came very close to getting killed," said Lord Ermenwyr, wheezing as he collapsed on the cot.

"Get off of there," said Lady Svnae, shoving him as she set Smith down. She took out the monocle once more and examined him closely through it. "Tell me, Child of the Sun, are you experiencing any unusual symptoms not related to the poison? Perhaps voices in your head?"

"No," said Smith dully. He watched as she raised his left arm cautiously, palpitated along it as far as the hand. "It felt as though I was holding something cold. An iron bar."

"You think he was being possessed?" Lord Ermenwyr asked his sister, looking speculative. "Because of proximity to the Key?"

"I think I need to study the Book of Fire again," said Lady Svnae. "I think I might have missed something crucial."

"Well, this is a fine time to figure it out," said Lord Ermenwyr pettishly, groping for his smoking tube.

"Better now than thirty seconds later, when we all might have been blasted with balefire," she retorted. "Child of the Sun—"

"Smith," he said.

"Interesting choice of an alias. Well, Smith, have you had any strange dreams recently? Any kind of psychic or spiritual conversation with your ancestors?"

Smith was unwilling to talk about his dream, but she looked earnestly into his eyes. Her own were wide, dark and lovely. Unwilling, he found himself saying: "I might have. But it didn't make any sense."

"No, I don't suppose it would," she said, and patted his cheek. "That's all right. You just lie down here and rest, now, Smith. And if you feel the least bit odd, especially in that hand, please tell us. Will you do that, Smith dear?"

"All right," he said, too dizzy to be annoyed by her tone of voice. He sank back on the cot and closed his eyes.

He heard the rustle of her gown as she went somewhere else, and the faint thump and crackle as someone added wood to the fire. He heard Lord Ermenwyr settle down, muttering to himself, and a noise suggestive of a boot flask being uncorked and drunk from . . .

Sound went away, and he was flying over a plain, and he knew so many terrible things.

There below him was the city of Troon. Burning in the air above it was the formula for its destruction: a certain smut introduced into the barley, four ounces of a certain poison poured into its central well, one letter containing a certain phrase sent anonymously to its duke, one brick pried loose from the foundation of a certain house. These things accomplished, Troon would fall. And then . . .

Here was Konen Feyy-in-the-Trees. One water conduit casually vandalized and one firebrand tossed into a certain tree, hung with moss, would begin the sequence of events that would kill the city. And its survivors might flee, but not to Troon, and then . . .

Here was Mount Flame City, seething, pulsing, so overripe with clan war that all it would take would be one precisely worded insult painted on a certain wall, and all four of its ruling houses would lie in ashes. And so would the great central marketplace of Mount Flame, and so would all the little houses who depended on it.

Here was Karkateen: a brick thrown through a window. A suggestion made to a shopkeeper. A rumor spread. A sewer grating removed. These things accomplished, in a certain order and at a certain moment, and Karkateen would be gone, and with it its great library, and with the library all the answers to certain desperate questions that would soon be asked in Troon, in Konen Feyy, in Mount Flame. Deliantiba and Blackrock were already in the throes; they'd need only the slightest push to complete their own work. And Salesh . . .

But wasn't it grand, to have secret knowledge of such terrible things?

His arm hurt.

But wasn't it a finer destiny than he had ever supposed he was intended for, high and lonely though it might be? Being the Chosen Instrument of the Gods? His arm hurt but he was flying high, beside a sharp version of himself that was cool and clever as he had always wanted to be, an elegant stranger made of diamond and chrome, the Killer, sneering down from a great distance at the insects crawling below. Stupid bastards. Wasteful. Quarrelsome. Banal. Ignorant and proud of it. And every year more screaming brats born to swell their numbers, and every year more urban blight on the land to house them all. Better if the whole shithouse went up in flames. Everyone said so. His arm hurt.

"Heavens, what've you done to your arm?" Mrs. Smith was peering at it.

"It really hurts," he told her, obscurely proud. "It's turned into blue steel. Isn't it fine and lonely?"

"You ought to run that under the cold tap, dear," she advised.

"No!" he said. "Because then it'd rust. It's better to burn than to rust. Everybody says so."

She just laughed sadly, shaking her head.

∽

Smith sat up, gasping, drenched with cold sweat, and saw Lord Ermenwyr scrambling to his feet. The monks were hastening out of the chamber. Someone, somewhere, was shouting.

"What's happening?" Smith asked.

"The Steadfast Orphans have called for a parley," said Lord Ermenwyr.

"What are we going to do?"

"Nothing," the lordling replied. "They don't want to talk to us. I think we'd best eavesdrop, though, don't you? Just in case the holy brothers allow themselves to be persuaded, and we have to make a hasty escape?"

"Can we do that?" Smith got to his feet and swayed. The room spun gently for a moment, and he found Willowspear beside him, keeping him upright.

"He should rest," Willowspear told his lord, who shook his head grimly.

"Not alone. He needs someone to keep an eye on him, don't you, Smith? We're not going far. I found a nice little spy hole while you were asleep. This way, if you please."

They set off down another of the winding corridors in the rock. Smith walked without much help, and was mildly surprised that his foot wasn't giving him trouble. He had a feeling that if he took his boot off, he'd never get it back on; but who knew how much longer he'd live, anyway? His arm, however, was still throbbing.

They rounded a bend, and he was temporarily dazzled by what seemed a blaze of illumination at the end of the passage. As they approached, it resolved into wan afternoon light, coming through a barred and partially shuttered opening in the rock. Closer still and he saw that pigeons had nested in here for generations, and the last few feet of the passage were chalky with ancient guano, littered with feathers and bits of old nest.

"Phew." Lord Ermenwyr drew out his smoking tube and lit it. "Nasty, eh?"

He stuck the tube between his teeth, clasped his hands together under his coattails, and stood scowling down through the bars. Smith and Willowspear edged closer, treading with care, and looked down too.

They saw the ranks of green tents, and the assembled Yendri standing in tight formation before them, tall unsmiling figures each in an identical baldric, each one bearing a simple cane tube. A shimmer in the air, a faint haze only, betrayed the presence of the Adamant Wall that kept them from coming closer; now and again a hapless bird or insect struck it, bouncing away stunned or dead. Close to the Wall stood the Yendri leader, cloaked in green sewn with white stars, and he was addressing someone unseen, speaking at great length.

"I can't understand him," said Smith.

"He's speaking Old Yendri," Lord Ermenwyr explained. "Nobody's used it in years. It's an affectation. They speak it to show how pure they are."

"*Pure!*" Willowspear glared down at them. "After what they've done?"

"What's he saying?" Smith asked.

"Oh, about what you'd expect," Lord Ermenwyr replied, puffing smoke. "Hand over the abominations, that we may cleanse the world of them and so bring the Suffering-Deluded-Ensorcelled Daughter so much closer to sanity and blah blah blah. I think he's just warming up to his main demand, though."

Someone else was speaking now: Greenbriar, out of sight directly below them. He sounded angry, accusatory.

"Good for him," Lord Ermenwyr remarked. "He's telling them off properly. Asking the Grand Master how he dares to wear the Star-Cloak. And . . . now he's just said he can't drop the Adamant Wall. And . . . ha! He just said something that doesn't really translate, but the closest equivalent would be, 'Go home and simulate mating with a peach.' "

There was a crunch of twigs. Svnae came up behind them,

bending low and holding the train of her gown up out of the debris. She had slung a bow and a quiver of arrows over one shoulder.

"I'd never have thought he'd use that kind of language," she said in mild surprise, peering over Lord Ermenwyr's shoulder at the scene below. "However would a monk learn about the Seventeenth Shameful Ecstasy of—" She noticed Smith and broke off, blushing.

The cloaked man spoke again, quietly, with implacable calm. Before he had finished, Greenbriar shouted at him in indignation. It was the closest Smith had ever heard to a Yendri being shrill.

"What's going on now?" he asked.

Lord Ermenwyr snorted smoke. "He says it's all our fault," he replied. "That we made the destruction of the garden inevitable by taking refuge here. They are not responsible. And Greenbriar just called him—well, you'd have to be a Yendri to appreciate the full force of the obscenity, but he just called him a Warrior."

"Well, isn't he?" Smith inquired.

"Yes, but ordinarily they hire mercenaries from your people," Lord Ermenwyr explained. "They don't like getting their own hands dirty. This is some kind of elite force, I suppose."

"You know what this reminds me of?" said Svnae in a far-away voice. "Watching the grown-ups through the stair railings when we were supposed to be in bed."

"Staying awake to see whether Daddy'd drink enough to discover the eyeball I'd hidden in the bottom of the decanter," Ermenwyr agreed fondly. Then his smile faded. The man in the cloak was speaking again. He spoke for a long while, and the lordling listened in silence. So did Willowspear and Svnae.

"What is it?" Smith asked at last.

"He's calling on them to put aside their differences and rise against a common enemy," Lord Ermenwyr replied at last, not looking at Smith. "He means your people, Smith. He's talking about Hlinjerith of the Misty Branches now. He says it'll be profaned if they don't act. And he . . . I thought so. He knows the Key of Unmaking is here. He says he'll spare them if they'll deliver up the Key to him. Now we know why he didn't bring mercenaries from your race, Smith."

Greenbriar had been making some kind of reply.

"And *he's* telling him no, of course," Lord Ermenwyr went on. He fell silent as the voices went on down below. He turned to regard Smith with a cold thoughtful stare. Lady Svnae turned too, and though there was a certain pity in her gaze, it too was terribly thoughtful.

"What're they saying now?" Smith stammered.

Willowspear cleared his throat. "Er . . . the Grand Master of the Orphans is saying that the brothers have been deceived. He just told them that all the high-yield cultivars and medicinal herbs they've been growing here have been intended to help the Children of the Sun, not the Yendri. He said Mother betrayed them."

"Why would your mother want to help *us*?" asked Smith.

"She has her reasons," said Lord Ermenwyr. "Now . . . he's saying there have been signs and portents that the Star-Cloaked Man is returning to this world. He will be the . . . hm . . . the Balancer. He will bring harmony. They are confident he will come in wrath to take by her hair the disobedient—" He stopped, aghast.

"What?" Smith asked.

"Just something really nasty about Mother," said Lord Ermenwyr briskly, though he had gone very pale. "And I'll have to kill him. Perhaps not today, though. Sister mine, I have a getaway boat and six big bodyguards watching it for me. Are you positive there aren't any other hidden back doors to this place?"

"We could make one," Svnae replied.

"I've got a remarkable rock-melting spell."

"An explosion might be quicker."

"Just what I was about to say."

"We can't just leave!" said Willowspear. "What about the brothers? What about the Key of Unmaking?"

"The brothers will be fine as long as the Adamant Wall holds, and as for the Key—Smith, old man, I'm sorry, but your race will have to take their chances. I make it a point never to try to pinch anything that belongs to a god, especially when he's paying attention."

"If it's too dangerous for us to take the Key out of there, it will be even more dangerous for the Orphans to try," said Lady Svnae. "Cheer up! Perhaps nothing very bad will happen after all."

"Other than a race war?" Smith demanded.

"Well, er—" Lady Svnae was searching very hard for a response both reassuring and noncommittal when there was a shout from beyond the window.

They all turned to look. The shout had been a summoning. From the back ranks of the Yendri came a very young man, striding confidently to the front. He halted before the Grand Master and made deep obeisance. The man put his hands on the boy's head in a gesture of blessing. Then he turned and addressed Greenbriar.

They listened at the window in silence. Suddenly, Lady Svnae put her hands to her face in horror. Lord Ermenwyr's smoking tube fell out of his mouth.

"That tears it," he said. "Willowspear, Smith, we're going now. I hope the monks have the sense to run."

"Why?" Smith peered out at the boy, who was standing proudly beside the man in the cloak.

"They're going to take out the Adamant Wall," Lord Ermenwyr replied over his shoulder, for he had already grabbed his sister by the arm and was pulling her down the passageway with him. "Come on!"

Willowspear seemed to have taken root where he stood, so Smith caught his arm and began to stagger after the lordling and his sister. "Let's go, son."

Willowspear turned his face away and ran. "Innocent blood," he said. "Willingly offered. The boy will let them behead him, and his blood will break the Wall."

Smith could think of nothing to say in reply. He concentrated on following Lady Svnae, just close enough to avoid stepping on the train of her gown. He congratulated himself on the fact that he was able to run so well, all things considered. Thinking about that, and watching where he put his feet, kept him from dwelling on the fact that his hand was cold as ice and turning blue.

Down and around they went, through long echoing darkness pierced now and again by the light of a distant barred window. The air was a roar of echoes. Something was echoing louder than their footsteps. Something was loud as surf on a lee shore—

The train of Lady Svnae's gown stopped moving.

Smith cannoned into her. She felt like a warm and beautifully upholstered wall. He staggered backward and collided with Willowspear, who cried, "What is it?"

It was a moment before anyone answered him, but the silence was amply filled by the thunder of their beating hearts and the other sound, the louder sound. Smith, who had been a mercenary, knew what it was. He felt a sharper pain in his hand and, looking down, saw that he had pulled a stone from the wall. He hefted it, getting the balance, knowing exactly where it should be fractured to make an edged weapon.

"The battle cry sounds familiar," said Lady Svnae.

"Nine Hells," said Lord Ermenwyr. "It's *Daddy*."

Lady Svnae turned on her heel decisively. "This way," she said, and they followed her up yet another tunnel, one with quite a lot of daylight at the end. It was bright because it opened out on a gallery of stone, lower in the face of the rock than their previous vantage point but still well above the floor of the valley. It had clearly been cut from the rock for persons wishing to enjoy a spectacular view. The view now was indeed spectacular, if not exactly enjoyable.

The Adamant Wall was still in place. The order of the previous vista had been destroyed, the neat green ranks broken up by a chaos of black and silver that was streaming over the hill to the south. An army, liveried and fearsome, had arrived.

It was like no battle Smith had ever seen. More horrible, if possible, because many of the Yendri stood straight and let themselves be cut down by the invading force, but it appeared that they did so to enable their comrades to advance on their targets without interference.

They made for three targets.

One ran with the demon-army in its black plate and silver mail, and he was a white stag of branching antlers, silver-collared. He bounded, feather-light, across the tips of their spears. He dropped like a bolt of lightning on the Yendri. Where he struck his hooves slashed, his antlers raked. Yet the Yendri fought one another to get at him, though they fell bleeding at his feet and were trampled. He dodged the green darts and danced on the bodies of the slain, belling his frenzy, exulting.

One had come alone over the hill to the north, a solitary figure. He wore no armor, he carried no blade. He had only a long staff, but in his long hand at the end of his long arm it cleared a wide space around him as he came, and where the steel-shod end of the staff connected, his opponents fell and did not rise again. Smith could hear the skulls cracking from where he stood; still the Yendri came scrambling over the dead to reach that lone fighter, ignored the armored host that hacked them to pieces as they advanced.

All these died willingly, that they might get close enough to strike a blow, even in vain; but more aimed themselves at the one who stood on the southern hill, overlooking the brief contest.

The man wore black. He watched impassively as the banner guard kept off his enemies. He bore two long blades in a double scabbard on his back, and not till the end, when the Grand Master himself fought close, did he draw steel over his shoulder.

He said one word, and his guards parted to let the man through. The Yendri vaulted forward, pipe to his lips, sending his poisoned dart flying. One blade cut the dart out of the air; its backstroke cut the pipe from his hands. Then he disappeared under a tackle pile of guards, as he screamed at the dark man.

And then it was over, and the field was silent.

Willowspear left the gallery. They heard him being quietly sick in the corridor.

Nobody said anything.

There came a wind off the field. It brought the groans of the wounded, though only the armored fighters; none of the Yendri were left alive to cry for help, save their leader. The survivors were stepping carefully across the devastation. Near the Adamant Wall lay the boy who would have been sacrificed. He had died fighting, his blood spilt to no purpose, his holy destiny unfulfilled. Was his death cleaner?

The man in black was giving orders, in a low voice, and stretchers were being made and his guard were moving out to collect the living. But they kept well away from the white stag, which was still bounding and trampling like a mad thing, tossing the dead on its antlers. It clattered all the way to the Adamant Wall, and collided with it; danced back, snorted its rage, and stamped.

The solitary figure with the staff had been making his way to the Wall also. He came to it and extended his hand cautiously, stopping just short of the surface. Ignoring the stag, he looked up at the gallery.

He had a long plain face, austere and dignified. He looked more like a high priest than a warrior, and his eyes were sad.

"Svnae," he called.

The stag noticed him. It threw its head up in surprise, rearing on its hind legs. They lengthened, the antlers shrank and vanished, its whole body altered; and Lord Eyrdway strode along the perimeter of the Wall.

"What are you doing here?" he demanded.

"Mother sent me," said the other. "What are you doing here?"

"I'm being Daddy's herald."

"I didn't hear you offering terms." The other gestured at the mounded dead.

"I didn't bother. But the fight's over, so you can turn right around and go back home."

"Are you at all concerned with how our sister fares?"

"You'll observe that neither one of them has deigned to notice *me*," Lord Ermenwyr remarked to Smith.

"She's fine," said Lord Eyrdway. He turned, waved at Svnae, turned back and went on, "I know what you're really here for, you know. You won't get it. Not if Daddy wants it."

The plain man looked up at the gallery again. "Svnae, let me through. I must speak with you."

"Who's that?" Smith inquired.

"That's our brother Demaledon. Demaledon is good and kind and wise and brave and clean and reverent," muttered

Lord Ermenwyr. "The only reason he isn't a bloody monk is because he kills people once in a while. But only *bad* people, you may be sure."

"You can damned well speak to me from out there!" Lady Svnae shouted, clenching her fists. "This is none of Mother's business!"

"Yes, Svnae, it is," said Lord Demaledon. "Mother knows why you're here. You should have come to her for counsel first."

"My entire life has been one long session of Mother giving me counsel," Lady Svnae replied sullenly, "and Mother knowing exactly what I'm doing and why, and Mother always being right, and Svnae being wrong."

"Hey, look, isn't that, what's his name, Smith?" said Lord Eyrdway. "The Child of the Sun? Hello, Smith!"

Lord Demaledon looked up and spotted Smith. He murmured something in a horrified tone of voice.

"Thank you for asking, I'm miraculously unharmed!" Lord Ermenwyr screamed.

Lord Eyrdway grinned at him and pulled out the corners of his mouth with two fingers, stretching his grimace a good yard wide before letting it snap back.

"Did you hear a fly buzzing, Demmy? I didn't. But you may as well collect Svnae and her baggage and escort her home, because Daddy is taking over here. He wants the Key of Unmaking."

"Well, he can't have it," Lady Svnae said, looking arch. "Not even Daddy knows everything."

"Stop it, both of you! Svnae, why is the Child of the Sun here?" Lord Demaledon asked.

Lady Svnae flushed deeply and dropped her gaze.

"I had him brought," she admitted. "I, er, didn't have quite all my facts straight at the time, and I didn't realize how dangerous it was. But we stopped—"

"Oh, who cares? Look, Smith, I'm sorry about this, but you have to admit your people have needed thinning out lately," said Lord Eyrdway. "And Daddy has nothing against Children of the Sun personally. But if anyone's going to own an ancient weapon of fabulous destructive power, it ought to be Daddy. So drop the damned Wall!"

"Shut up, you idiot! You don't understand!" cried Lord Demaledon. "Svnae, *when* did you stop?"

"Well—" Lady Svnae bit her lower lip.

"You know, Smith, I think it's time we got the hell out of here," said Lord Ermenwyr *sotto voce*. He glanced over his shoulder at the battlefield, then did a double take. "Uh-oh. Too late."

The man in black was walking to the Adamant Wall, unhurried. He looked up at the gallery. His gaze was blank and mild as a sleepy tiger's. When he spoke, his voice was very deep.

"Daughter, come down," said the Master of the Mountain.

He towered over his sons. Given all that Smith had heard of him over the years, he had expected someone about whom dark rainbows of energy crackled, a walking shadow of dread, faceless. All Smith saw, however, was a very large man with a black beard, who folded his arms as he waited for Lady Svnae's reply.

"Daddy, I really can't let you in here," said Lady Svnae.

He extended one gauntleted hand in a negligent gesture, and the Adamant Wall melted into a curtain of steam that blew away.

"Then you come down to me," he said. "And bring the man Smith."

Moving deliberately, Svnae took her bow and nocked an arrow. Smith gaped at it, for it was not the kind of sporting gear one would expect a lady to use. The arrow was tipped for armor-piercing.

"Daddy, go away," she said, and in an undertone added, "Ermenwyr, get out. Take Smith and get away down the river as fast as you can."

"I can't blow the hole in the damned wall by myself!" hissed her brother.

The Master of the Mountain did not smile, but something glinted in his black eyes

"Child, you are your mother's daughter," he said.

Svnae gritted her teeth. "That was just exactly the wrong thing to say."

She fired. Lord Ermenwyr shouted and grabbed her arm belatedly, but the Master of the Mountain smiled. He put up his hand and caught the arrow an inch from his throat. In his hand it became a black-red rose.

"And you are also *my* daughter," he said, sounding pleased. Svnae reached for another arrow, but found her quiver full of roses. Glaring, she took the bow and hurled it at him as hard as she could.

"Damn you!"

"Stop this nonsense and come down," said the Master of the Mountain. "Your mother is going to have a great deal to say to you about this."

Lord Ermenwyr groaned, and Lady Svnae went pale.

"We'd better do as he says now," she said.

꙳

"Is it painful?"

"Yes, it is," Smith said, gasping. "It hurts a lot."

The Master of the Mountain regarded Smith's arm, which was colder and more blue than it had been. Below the elbow it looked as though it was turning to stone. It was in no way stiff or swollen, however. Shaking his head, the other man dug a flask from a camp chest and offered it to Smith.

"Drink. It may help."

Smith accepted it gratefully. "Thank you, my—er—lord."

"The name's Silverpoint," said the Master of the Mountain. "Most of the time. Though my son calls himself Kingfisher, doesn't he?"

"Lord Ermenwyr?" Smith nodded. Mr. Silverpoint poured himself a drink and sat down in the chair opposite Smith's.

"*Lord* Ermenwyr," said Mr. Silverpoint, with only the faintest trace of irony. He stared at the hanging lamp and sighed, shaking his head. "He's a costly boy. Doctors, tailors' bills, theater tickets. Brothels. Health resorts. And now I understand he's bought a slaveless galley."

"Yes, sir."

"When I was his age, I'd never seen a boat, let alone a city." He looked at Smith, raised an eyebrow like a black saber. "And I owned nothing. Not even myself."

"You were a slave?" Smith asked.

The other man nodded. "Until I killed my masters. I broke my own chains. I owe no miracle man for my salvation.

"But I owe you a debt, Smith. You've made a habit of saving my children. They haven't been as grateful as they should. I'd like to help you."

"I'm not sure you can," said Smith. He drank. What was in the flask was white, and it did dull his pain a little.

Mr. Silverpoint did not reply at once. He sipped his own drink, considering Smith. The lord's pavilion was made of rich stuff, black worked with silver thread, but it was spare and soldierly within. Without, the camp sounds had tapered off; only the creaking of insects now, and the occasional challenge and password from the guard.

"I've been following your career with a certain amount of interest, Smith. Tell me: How long were you an assassin?" Mr. Silverpoint inquired.

"Ten years, I guess," said Smith, a little dazedly. He hadn't expected to be discussing his personal history. "I tried being a soldier. I tried a lot of jobs. But it always came back to killing. It just—happened."

"You were good at it," stated Mr. Silverpoint.

"Yes."

"You never trained with a master-at-arms. You never studied weapons of any kind."

"No, sir. My aunt never had the money for that kind of an education," Smith explained, drinking more of the white stuff.

"But the first time you ever found yourself in danger, you acted without even thinking and—"

"And they were dead," said Smith wonderingly. "Three of them, in an alley. Two throats cut with a broken bottle and the other killed with a five-crown piece, and I'm damned if I remember how. Something about hitting him with it in exactly the right place to make something rupture. I don't know where I learned that trick."

"But you didn't like the work."

"No, sir, I didn't. So I kept trying to quit."

"You were an orphan, weren't you?"

"What? Oh. Yes, sir."

"And Smith is an alias, isn't it? A name you selected purely by chance?"

"Well, it's very common, sir."

"Interesting choice, all the same. What is your real name?"

The question was uttered in a tone of command, not loud but swift as a green dart. And Smith knew perfectly well what folly it was to tell one's true name to a mage, especially one with Mr. Silverpoint's reputation, but he felt the reply rising so easily to his lips! He fought it until he sweated, with those quiet eyes regarding him all the while.

"I'll tell you my first name," he said. "What about that?"

"You *are* strong," said Mr. Silverpoint. "Very well, then."

"My mother died when she had me," Smith said. "She looked up at the door as they were wrapping me in a blanket, and she said there was a shadow there. That was the last thing she ever said. So my aunt named me Carathros. That's how a priest would say, 'The shadow has come.'"

Smith stared into the past. Mr. Silverpoint watched him. At last, "I've heard what Ermenwyr thinks is the truth," said Mr. Silverpoint. "Insofar as he's ever capable of telling the truth. Svnae and Demaledon have told me what they know. Now, you tell me: there is no Key of Unmaking hidden in Rethkast, is there?"

"There is, sir," said Smith. "I saw it. It was in a hole in the rock."

Mr. Silverpoint shook his head.

"That's the keyhole," he said. "My daughter didn't realize the truth until it was too late. Your Book of Fire says that the Key of Unmaking was hidden, but not in the *bones*, not in a place full of bones. Not in the charnel house of Kast. There's an error in the text, you see.

"What it actually says is that the Key was hidden in the *bone*, in the sense of flesh and bone. Descendants. Heredity. A trait passed on in the blood. Something that would lie dormant, until the Father of your people decided to use it."

Smith looked at his arm. It was iron, and ice, and it knew exactly how to put an end to the cities of his people. He had dreamed its dreams. It had always killed for him, all his life, gotten him out of every dark alley and tight corner in which he'd ever found himself, earned him a living with what it knew. But now it knew its purpose.

"*I'm* the Key of Unmaking," he said.

Mr. Silverpoint was watching him.

"A courtesy to the children of other gods," he said.

"When there are too many of you, a slaughterer is born on the Anvil of the World. His destiny is to bring on a cataclysm. What are you going to do now?"

"I don't want this," said Smith, though he knew that what he wanted no longer mattered.

"It seems a shame," Mr. Silverpoint agreed. "But you're stuck with it, aren't you?"

"Can you help me?"

"I don't meddle with gods," said Mr. Silverpoint. "All I can do is witness your decision. Whatever you do, though, you'd better do it soon. That's my advice, if you want any control over what happens at all. The pain will only get worse; until you obey."

"I have to go back in that room, don't I?" said Smith sadly.

Mr. Silverpoint shrugged. Setting his drink down, he rose and selected an axe from a rack of weapons in the corner.

"Let's go for a walk," he said, holding the tent flap open.

They stepped out into the night, and the guards on duty came to attention and saluted. Mr. Silverpoint nodded to them.

"At ease," he said. "This way, Smith."

He walked to the near pavilion that had been set up for Lady Svnae. Taking a torch from its iron socket, he cleared his throat loudly outside the entrance.

"Daddy?"

"Rise and come with us, Svnae," he said. "You're being punished."

She stepped out a moment later, wrapped in a dressing gown. She looked lovely, frightened, young and—next to her father—small. On any other night of the world, Smith would have been profoundly interested in her state of undress.

They stopped at the next pavilion, and Mr. Silverpoint said, "Come out of there, son."

There was no answer. Mr. Silverpoint exhaled rather forcefully and tore open the tent flap, revealing Lord Ermenwyr. The lordling was still fully dressed, sitting bolt upright on the edge of a folding cot. He looked at his father with wide eyes.

"You're being punished, too," said Mr. Silverpoint. "Come along."

He led them away through the night, across the day's field where a banked fire still smoldered, the bones of the slain falling into ashes in its heart. Guards fanned out and walked with them at a discreet distance.

They came to the rock, and Mr. Silverpoint nodded at Svnae, who led them in. The chambers and corridors were deserted; the monks had withdrawn to the camp to tend the wounded. They climbed through the darkness, and their passage echoed like an army on the march.

The pain in Smith's arm grew less with every step. It was still so cold he imagined waves of chill radiating from it, but it felt supple as it ever had. He looked up at the barrel-vault ceiling as they walked along, wondering who among his ancestors had cut these tunnels. *The charnel house of Kast . . .*

What had taken place, here, that the Yendri had found it crowded with the dead? It must have been in Lord Salt's time, so long ago it was nearly fable. What had been the cause of the war? Why had the granaries of Troon been put to the torch? That was never clear in the stories; only the great deeds of the heroes were sung about, how they drove the vanquished before them like wraiths, how they enacted wonders with their swords and war hammers, how they triumphed in the last day of glory before the gods had been sick of them and wiped them out of existence.

And only a handful of people had survived, crouching in fishing-huts at the edge of the land, terrified of something in the interior.

Yet from those wretched ashes they had risen, hadn't they? And built a fine new civilization on top of the old, better than what they'd had before? What other race could do such a thing?

What other race would need to?

It was true that they multiplied until they must build new cities, and it was true that crime and war and famine followed them inexorably . . . and now there were others in the world, other races who might be more worthy to inherit.

His arm felt fine now. Better than fine. Superior to dull flesh and blood. It was the part of him that belonged to the gods, after all.

Smith heard the sound of footsteps behind him, running, and Willowspear caught up with them.

"Where are you going?" he gasped. *"What is he going to do?"*

Mr. Silverpoint's voice floated back to them along the tunnel. "Nothing, boy. I'm only here to observe."

They emerged into the chamber. Mr. Silverpoint set the torch in a socket by the door. "Here we are," he said. "What happens now, Smith?"

Smith blinked at the Keyhole, at the whirling fire before it. He knew that he could raise his cold blue arm and thrust it through that barrier and feel no pain at all. He knew he could grasp the dimly seen objects beyond and draw them out. They were only vials of poisons, and small ingenious devices. Still, once he had them, there would be no stopping him ever again.

He felt History pulling at him, like a tide sucking sand from beneath his feet. All that he had been, all the mundane details of his life, were about to be jettisoned. Once he reached through the fire, he would be purified, perfect, streamlined down to his essential purpose. He would bring a sinful race to its ordained end. It was the will of the gods.

Smith, the old Smith that was about to be cast off like a garment, looked away from the whirling fire.

The others were watching him. Mr. Silverpoint's gaze was blank, enigmatic. Lady Svnae was biting her nether lip, her dark eyes troubled. Lord Ermenwyr stood with arms folded, doing his best to look nonchalant, but he was trembling. And Willowspear was staring from one to the other, and at the bright fire, and horror was slowly dawning in his face.

Why was the boy so upset? Ah, because he had a wife, and a mother, and a child on the way. Personal reasons. The concerns of mundane people, not heroes.

Clear before his eyes came an image of little Burnbright disconsolate on her perch in the kitchen, and of Mrs. Smith singing in her cloud of smoke. Fenallise.

Smith flexed his hand.

"I need to borrow your axe," he said to Mr. Silverpoint. That gentleman nodded solemnly and handed it over.

Smith knelt.

He laid his blue arm out along the rock and struck once, severing his hand and arm just below the elbow.

There was one moment of frozen time in which the arm lay twitching in its pool of black blood, and the severed end reared up like a snake and something looked at him accusingly, with glittering black eyes. It told him he had failed the gods. It told him he was a commonplace and mediocre little man.

Then time unfroze, and there was a lot of shouting. Lady Svnae had torn the sash from her dressing gown and knelt beside him, binding it on the stump of his arm, pulling tight while Willowspear broke the axe handle and thrust it through the tourniquet's knot. There was blood everywhere. Smith was staring full at Lady Svnae's splendid bare bosom, which was no more than a few inches from his face, and only vaguely listening to Lord Ermenwyr, who was on his other side saying, "I'm sorry, Smith, I'm so sorry, you'll be all right, I'll make you a magic hand with jewels on it or something and you'll be better than new! Really! Oh, Smith, please don't die!"

Smith was falling backward.

"You see?" he told no one in particular. "It was just a metaphor."

"I'm impressed," said Mr. Silverpoint, nodding slowly.

Smith lost consciousness.

⌐

He spent the next few days in a pleasant fog. Willowspear never left him, changed the dressings on his arm at hourly intervals and kept him well drugged. Lord Demaledon came often to advise; he and Willowspear had long sonorous conversations full of medical terms Smith didn't understand. Smith didn't mind. He felt buoyant, carefree.

Lady Svnae brought him delicacies she had prepared for him herself, though she was not actually much of a cook, and she kept apologizing to him in the most abject manner. When he asked her what she was apologizing for, she burst into tears. When he tried to console her, he made an awkward job of it, having forgotten that he no longer had two arms to put around anybody. So then he apologized, and she cried harder. Altogether it was not a successful social moment.

Lord Ermenwyr came several times to sit beside his bed and talk to him. He chattered nervously for hours, filling the tent with purple fumes as he smoked, and Smith nodded or shook his head in response but couldn't have got a word in with a shoehorn. Principally the lordling discussed magical prostheses, their care and maintenance, and the advantages of complicated extra features such as corkscrews, paring knives, and concealed flasks.

And there was an afternoon when Smith lay floating free

on a tide of some subtle green elixir that banished all care, and watched through the opened tent-flaps as a drama unfolded, seemingly just for his entertainment. Mr. Silverpoint was seated in a black chair, with a naked blade across his knees. The Yendri war-leader was brought before him in chains.

A lot of talk followed, in words that Smith couldn't understand. Most of the Yendri leader's lines were badly acted, though, he seemed given to melodrama, and Smith would have jeered and thrown nutshells at him but for the fact that he couldn't spot a snack vendor in the audience, and no longer had an arm to throw with anyway.

Then there was a thrilling moment when the action came right into his tent, and everyone was staring at him, and Mr. Silverpoint explained gravely that the Yendri had admitted to conspiring to exterminate the Children of the Sun. As the only member of his race present, what was Smith's judgment? Smith thought about it, while everyone, the Yendri included, watched him.

Finally he said he thought it was a bad idea.

But do you condemn him to death? everyone asked.

Smith knitted his brows and puzzled over the question until he realized that he was free of all that; he'd never kill anybody again. He just lay there laughing, shaking his head *No.*

Then the drama retreated to the stage again, and a lot of other accusations were made. The word *Hlinjerith* was spoken several times, and the Yendri stood tall and said something proudly, and there was a gasp of horror from a lot of people watching. Willowspear, beside Smith, groaned aloud and buried his face in his hands. Smith asked him what was wrong and Willowspear said that the Orphans had done something dreadful. Smith asked what they had done. Willowspear, mastering himself with difficulty, said that they had made certain that Hlinjerith would never be desecrated by the Children of the Sun.

So the Yendri was condemned to die after all. The three lords stepped forward, Eyrdway, Demaledon, and Ermenwyr. Each one presented some argument, and Mr. Silverpoint listened with his head on one side. Then there was a wonderful bit of sleight of hand where he pulled three rods of blue fire from the air and held them out in his fist, and the three brothers each drew one. Lord Demaledon got the one that was longest.

A circle formed, though people were considerate enough to leave a space so Smith could see. The Yendri's chains were struck off. He was given a staff. Lord Demaledon stepped into the circle with his staff, too. Smith became terribly excited and struggled to sit up so he could see better, but by the time Willowspear had arranged the pillows behind him it was nearly over. *Clack*, *whack*, *crash*, two stick-insects fighting, and then *CRACK* and the Yendri was down with his head caved in, and that was all.

Smith was disappointed, until Willowspear injected him with more of the elixir, and he floated away into happiness again . . . the body was dragged offstage, the crowd dispersed, the curtain flaps fell, and he tried to applaud. But that was another thing he couldn't do anymore.

⌒

One morning they told him he was going to be taken back to the boat, and he watched as they bound him into a litter and four of Mr. Silverpoint's soldiers hoisted him between them. Their mail and livery was identical, but otherwise they were monstrous in exuberant variety: scales, fangs, fur, unlikely appendages. Still they carried him gently through the rock, out the new waterside entrance and so to the landing.

And there was the *Kingfisher's Nest,* anchored as safe as though the siege and battle had taken place in another world. Cutt, Crish, and company were lined up ashore like a row of bollard posts, looking proud of themselves insofar as they had expressions. They greeted their master with howls of joy and abased themselves before Mr. Silverpoint when he came down to see them off.

He loomed over Smith.

"My son will take you back to Salesh now," he said.

"Thank you, my lord," said Smith.

Lord Demaledon and Lord Eyrdway loomed too, one on either side of their father.

"I still can't believe what you did," said Lord Eyrdway, a little sulkily. "All that power, and you threw it away! Don't you know what you could have done?"

"He knows, son," said Mr. Silverpoint.

"I've given Willowspear salves for the wound, Smith," said Demaledon. "Don't try to seal it with boiling pitch, whatever your physicians tell you. Yours may be a race worthy to live, but your grasp of medicine is . . . inadequate."

"All right," said Smith vaguely, looking around, blinking in the sunlight. There were others of the demon-host loading chests of something heavy on board the *Kingfisher's Nest*. The Master of the Mountain followed his gaze.

"Gold specie," he explained. "Readily convertible anywhere. It ought to get you through the next few years."

"Oh. You mean . . . the race war and all that?"

"No," said Mr. Silverpoint, scowling briefly. "There will be no race war, now. Not over Hlinjerith of the Misty Branches. Nor will your people be destroyed this time, since you have broken the Key of Unmaking. But you're owed some compensation, after what my children did to you."

"Oh, well . . ." Smith racked his brains for something polite to say. "I guess I would have come here sooner or later anyway. If it was the will of the gods."

Mr. Silverpoint grinned, a flash of white in his black beard.

"Yes, of course, we must respect the will of the gods." He

leaned close and spoke in a low voice. "You be sure to take my son for the most expensive prosthesis on the market, understand? If he wants to buy you one that tells the time and plays "The Virgins of Karkateen," you let him. The little devil can't bear feeling guilty."

⌒

The journey back was dreamlike and very pleasant for Smith, who had nothing to do but sit under a canopy on deck and watch the scenery flow by. Everyone else was either preoccupied—like Willowspear, who was now obliged to man the helm—or quietly miserable, like Lord Ermenwyr and Lady Svnae. Even the portage descent to the Pool of Reth went smoothly.

And it was in that place, as Willowspear navigated the clear green water, that they saw the first of the white butterflies.

"Hey, look, there's your spirits," observed Smith, pointing to the two tall stones. White wings fluttered in a long shaft of sunlight, like poppy petals in the wind. Lady Svnae, who was arranging cushions and a lap robe for Smith, looked up and caught her breath.

"I've never seen butterflies like that," she said.

"That's because they're cabbage moths," said her brother, pacing. He regarded them sourly, shifting his smoking tube from one corner of his mouth to the other.

"It is a good sign," said Willowspear, guiding them into the river.

"They're following us, too," said Smith, and he was right; for as the Pool of Reth fell astern, the butterflies drifted along after them, or settled on the spars and rigging like birds.

"Get away, you little bastards!" Lord Ermenwyr cried.

"Oh, leave them alone. They're pretty," Lady Svnae told him. "What can I bring you, dear Smith? Ortolans braised in white wine? Sugared pepper tarts? Rose comfits? Tea with Grains of Paradise?"

"Tea sounds nice," said Smith. She raised a silver pitcher cunningly wrought with peacocks and adders chased in gold, and with her own fair hands poured the long stream of tea into a cup of eggshell-fine porcelain, costly and rare. Smith watched as she took Grains of Paradise from a tiny golden box with silver tweezers, unable to find a tactful way to tell her he preferred his tea plain.

◡

Some days later, after a supernaturally quick journey, at the Sign of the Three Hammers . . .

Mr. Smallbrass sat at his desk, chewing on the end of his pen as he studied his account books. He wasn't very good at accounts—he was more of an idea man—but he had had to let his accountant go, along with his personal secretary, his chair-bearers, his masseur, and some of his better furniture.

He heard a commotion in the courtyard below his office and peered out a window, wondering if he should bolt his door and pretend he wasn't in. But it wasn't the collections clerk from Redlead and Sons Contractors, nor was it Mr. Screwbite the architect, also unpaid these six weeks. It was a very large man in very well cut clothing, accompanied by equally large liveried servants who took up posts at the entrance to the courtyard.

Mr. Smallbrass watched until he was certain the large man was ascending the staircase that led to his particular office, then he became a blur of frenzied motion. Unpaid bills were swept into a drawer. Threatening letters were stuffed under the carpet. Other items that might tend to detract from the impression of success went into a closet. When the knock on the door sounded, Mr. Smallbrass straightened his tunic, took a deep breath, and waited until the second knock before opening the door.

"I'm sorry," he said to the man who stood without. "My clerk's just stepped out to make an immense bank deposit. Your name, sir?"

"Silverpoint," said the man, in an oddly smooth bass. "Aden Silverpoint. I have a proposition for Mr. Smallbrass."

"Really?" said Mr. Smallbrass. "I am he, sir! Business is brisk at the moment, but I can certainly spare you a moment—or two—" He edged backward into the room, reaching out hastily to shut his accounts book. Mr. Silverpoint followed him, and so did two more of the liveried servants, who carried a chest between them.

"I, er, I'd offer you wine, but we had a board meeting this morning—all our investors, you know—temporarily out of refreshments," chattered Mr. Smallbrass.

"I want to buy Smallbrass Estates," said Mr. Silverpoint.

"Certainly!" shrieked Mr. Smallbrass. "That is to say— lots are selling rapidly, but I think we can accommodate you—in fact, a prime waterfront parcel became available just this morning, poor arms dealer in Deliantiba had to forfeit his deposit, what with the peace treaty and all—yes, I'm sure we—"

"You have no investors," said Mr. Silverpoint. He didn't say it in a particularly threatening manner, but something in his dark eyes caused the hair to stand on the back of Mr. Smallbrass's neck. "You haven't sold one lot, in fact, and you're heavily in debt."

Mr. Smallbrass looked at the window, wondering if he could make it in one leap, then remembered the servants standing guard below. He looked at the servants in the room with him, who had the stolid faces of men who were capable of doing quite unpleasant things in the line of duty and sleeping soundly afterward.

"Are you from the Bloodfires?" he asked in a little deflated voice.

"I might be," said Mr. Silverpoint, with just the suggestion of a purr. He snapped his fingers, and the servants opened the chest. How softly the afternoon light fell on the bars and bars and bars of gold specie ranked within! Mr. Smallbrass gaped at it.

"Unmarked. Enough to cover your debt and pay for your passage out of town," said Mr. Silverpoint. "And you'll transfer the development claim to me, here and now."

Mr. Smallbrass rallied slightly.

"Oh, sir, the claim's worth more than that!" he protested. "All those waterfront lots! Unspoiled paradise!"

Mr. Silverpoint just looked at him. His stare was fathomless as a night full of jungle predators.

"I have inside information that the property has recently undergone devaluation," he stated, quietly, but with a suggestion of reproach.

Mr. Smallbrass winced, thinking of the desperate message he had received from his caretakers the day before. He made his decision.

"Let's just step across the street to the claim office, shall we?" he said. "They've got a notary and bullion scales on the premises. Most convenient."

⁓

The journey continued, in its effortless and silent way, flowing with the current. The *Kingfisher's Nest* had no need of its mechanical oarsmen yet, nor even of its striped sails, drifting through the blue-and-gold weather. But there came a morning when Smith saw the fog wall rising in the north, pink with sunrise.

"Hey, look!" He waved his stump at it. "We'll make Salesh inside of a week. Two weeks at most, if we play it safe and go all the way around the blockade. Do you think you're a father yet?"

Willowspear, who had been watching the fog bleakly, smiled.

"Surely not yet," he said. "I would know."

"Have you settled on a name?"

"If it's a little girl, Fenallise," said Willowspear. "Kalyon, if it's a boy."

Smith nodded slowly. Willowspear looked out at the fog again.

"I miss her so," he said.

Lord Ermenwyr came on deck, saw the fogbank, and groaned. He slumped into a chair next to Smith.

"I need brandy for breakfast," he muttered.

"That had better not be a remark about my cooking," said Lady Svnae sharply, rising from the companionway with a tray. She set it beside Smith and unfolded a napkin for him with a flourish. "I tried something new this morning, anyway, for our dear Smith. Look!" she whisked the cover off his bowl. "It's a sort of Potted Seafood Surprise! There's shrimp relish and fish eggs boiled in *straj*, and that dark stuff is fish paste swirled through."

"Sounds delicious," said Smith gallantly. "Thank you, my lady."

"Can I have brandy in mine?" asked Lord Ermenwyr.

"Stop it!" She whirled on him. "I told you I was sorry about yesterday, and how was I to know you were allergic to clove honey?"

"Remember when I went into anaphylactic shock when I was ten?"

"Oh. Well—" Lady Svnae spotted the fogbank. She blanched. "We're nearly there, aren't we?"

Lord Ermenwyr nodded mournfully. She sank down on the deck beside him. After a moment they clasped hands, staring together into the mist. Willowspear began to sing, quietly.

Smith ate his breakfast. A white butterfly settled on the edge of his bowl. Two more fluttered out of nowhere and landed on the helm, between Willowspear's hands.

⮑

The current drew them on, gently. Within another hour they had entered the gray world.

Smith, watching the bank from where he sat, saw the black twigs bobbing in the reed beds before he noticed the scent. It was harsh, acrid, unforgettable.

"That's clingfire," he said, sniffing the air.

"That's right," said Willowspear, staring straight ahead as he steered.

Smith looked at the white scum high on the tideline and knew what it was, then, and when the first of the black skeletons emerged from the fog, he clenched his one fist. Gradually the fog lifted farther, and he saw the wilderness of mud and ashes that had been Hlinjerith of the Misty Branches.

"Oh, I'm sorry," he cried.

Lord Ermenwyr shrugged.

"It wasn't your people, at least," he said. "It was the Steadfast Orphans. They destroyed it, lest it be profaned."

Lady Svnae bowed her head and wept.

Smith made out the shape of the landing ahead of them. Its red-and-yellow banners were gone; a scattered mound ashore was all that remained of the caretakers' hut.

"Please, can we put in?" he asked. "If there's any chance one of them is still alive, I'd like to get him out."

Willowspear steered to the bank, and brought them up against the pier like a master. At Smith's signal Stabb and Strangel dropped the anchor. Smith got unsteadily to his feet and peered through the drizzle.

"Ai-ai-ai!" he called.

A moment later there was an indistinct response, echoing from someone unseen.

Smith looked hard. Gradually through the fog he made out shapes moving, pale upright figures in the landscape. A wind came off the river, sighing in the rigging and the waving reeds, and the mist opened, and the scene before them became clear.

There were people struggling in the wet churned ashes, turning the earth with spades, raking it level, bringing muddy armfuls of roots or even small trees to be planted. One man stalked from west to east, moving with a smooth and endless rhythm as he drew a fistful from the seed bag he carried, swung his arm wide, scattered seed on the earth like rain, dipped again.

The three standing stones were toppled, lying in a blackened tangle that had been rose briars, but there was a team at work raising one of them with makeshift levers and ropes. And on the bank of the river a woman stood, weaving hurdles from green willow wands.

She was a tall woman robed in white, though her robe was work-stained and muddy, and so were her feet and hands. Rain dripped from the wide brim of her hat. With strong hands she wove the slick palings, effortlessly shaping walls, driving them into the mud with a blow to set them; and where she struck each one it sprouted, gray catkins on the nearer, green leaves already shooting forth on the first she had set. Were the walls flowering, too? No; white butterflies were settling on them here and there.

"It's Mother," said Lord Ermenwyr, in a ghost of a voice.

She raised her head and looked at Smith. He caught his breath.

The woman had clear, clear eyes, and their gaze hit him like a beam of light. She was the most beautiful woman he had ever seen in his life, but somehow that fact went unnoticed by his flesh. She was spare and perfect as a steel engraving, and as ageless. She was simple as water, implacable as the white comber rolling, miraculous as rain in the desert.

᠆

They went ashore and picked their way through the ruins at the pier's base, and the lady walked down to meet them.

Lord Ermenwyr cleared his throat. "Why, Mother, whatever are you doing here?" he inquired cautiously.

"Making a garden," she replied. Her voice was beautiful, too.

Willowspear knelt before her, and she raised him with a hand under his chin, smiling. "Don't worry," she told him, and the phrase seemed to resonate with meaning, silence a hundred unspoken questions. "Now, let me see the hero."

Smith wondered whether he ought to kneel. He had never felt so awkward in his life, obscurely ashamed of his maimed arm and the fact that no one had shaved him in three days.

"G-good morning, ma'am," he said hoarsely. "There were some men who were stationed in—in the ruins over there. They were just watchmen. Were they killed, when the Orphans burned the place down?"

"No, they weren't," she said. "They got into the reeds and hid themselves. Though poor Mr. Bolter was dying of pneumonia when we arrived." She turned and pointed at the stone, just lurching upright in its cradle of rope. Smith squinted at the figures surrounding it, and realized that three of them were Children of the Sun, covered though they were in mud and ashes like all the others there.

"Mr. Bolter!" the lady called. "Mr. Drill! Mr. Copperclad! The ship has come back. Would you like to go home now?"

The three turned abruptly, staring. They exchanged glances and began to walk across the field, but in a slow and reluctant manner. Three-quarters of the way there they stopped.

"Are you from Smallbrass?" demanded the one called Copperclad. "You can tell him, we quit. We haven't been paid. No supply ship ever came, and she"—his voice broke—"she *saved* us. So we're staying to help her!"

"Please, ma'am?" added Bolter.

"Thank you," she said. "I would be grateful for your hard work." They turned and walked rapidly back to the stones.

"Mother, how can you plan a garden here?" cried Lord Ermenwyr. "They're going to build a city on it!"

The lady turned and regarded her son with a look of mild severity. He flinched, and Smith had to admire his composure; he himself would have been on his knees pleading for forgiveness.

"No," she said. "Hlinjerith belongs to me, now. Your father made the necessary arrangements in their claim offices. When the Beloved comes again, he will find his sacred grove and his garden waiting for him."

"Ah. How nice," said Lord Ermenwyr, groping in his pocket for his smoking tube. "Well, I think I'll just go on to Salesh—"

"The city will rise across the river," his mother went on calmly. "You will build it for me, my son."

Lord Ermenwyr froze in the act of lifting the tube to his lips. "What did you say?"

"You will build a city on that bank," said the lady. "Bowers to shelter the pilgrims who will come. Gardens and greens, where classes will be taught. And a great library, and a guesthouse for the Children of the Sun, who are unaccustomed to living out of doors."

"But—but—Mummy, I can't!" Lord Ermenwyr wrung his hands in panic. "I don't know anything about building! And I can't live here, it's so bloody damp and cold I'll start growing toadstools! Why don't you make Demaledon do it?"

"Because you would be better at it," said his mother. "He doesn't go among the Children of the Sun, as you do. You understand their culture, and their money, and their business practices. You will draw up plans, and order shipments of cut stone. You will hire workmen."

"I think I'm starting to run a fever—"

"No, you're not. I won't see your talents wasted, my child. You've been running about the world on your father's business long enough; it's time you started tending to mine."

"But the Children of the Sun wouldn't come here," Lord Ermenwyr protested.

"Yes, they would!" cried Willowspear. "I taught them meditation. I can teach them farming, and medicine."

"Wait. Let's consider this objectively, shall we?" Lord Ermenwyr said, widening his eyes in an attempt to look calm and reasonable. "They're *already* overrunning the world. The only advantage we have over them is our knowledge of medicine, of agriculture, of, er, birth control and so forth. Now, do we really want to give them that knowledge?"

The lady looked at him sadly. "My child, that is a base and cynical thing to say. Especially in front of this man, who has suffered through your fault."

Lord Ermenwyr winced so profoundly, he nearly lost his balance and fell over.

"Smith, I didn't mean it like that! You almost wiped them out yourself, after all. Didn't it seem the right thing to do, for a moment, back in that cave? Wouldn't mass annihilation have solved a lot of problems? What I'm saying is, if the gods themselves thought that was a good idea, who are we to argue?"

"Maybe they're not very nice gods," said Smith. "If they kill their children. Maybe we should argue."

"Perhaps," the lady agreed. "And perhaps the gods were

waiting to see if you'd give in to the temptation to destroy your world in a blaze of glory. It's always so much easier to smash mistakes than to correct them. But if it wasn't a test, then what can one assume but that the gods are foolish and not very powerful after all?"

She reached out and touched his shoulder. Where her hand passed, warmth flowed into him.

"I think that if your race could produce a man willing to make such a sacrifice, it's a sign that they ought to be given another chance," she said. "I intend to see that they have it."

Lord Ermenwyr, who had been trying unsuccessfully to light his smoking tube in the damp air, said sullenly, "I'll build your city for you, then. But if you're expecting the kind of twits who sign up for meditation classes, I warn you now: They're not interested in learning anything *useful*. All they want is a new religion."

"They want it because they know there must be something better than violence and stupidity," she told him sternly. "Their hearts are in the right places. We will make certain their minds follow. And one is coming who will lead them here, in the morning of the new world."

Without warning she turned and looked directly at Lady Svnae, who had been edging gradually back in the direction of the landing.

"Are you so eager to go, daughter?"

Lady Svnae flushed and strode forward, muttering. She towered over her mother, but somehow looked like a gauche adolescent standing before her.

"Well, you didn't have anything to say to me," she said.

"I have a great deal to say to you," the lady replied. "But you must take poor Smith home to his family first. You owe him that; if you hadn't pried into matters that didn't concern you, he might still have both his hands."

"No, that was fated to happen, whatever *I* did," said Lady

Svnae stubbornly. "And the death of a whole people *did* concern me. And I've said I was sorry. What more can I do to
atone?"

The lady smiled at her. "You can use the strength of your
great heart, child. You can help your brother build the city.
The library, especially."

Lady Svnae brightened at that. Her mother surveyed her
scarlet-and-purple silks, her serpent jewelry, her bare arms,
and she sighed.

"But please buy yourself some sensible clothing in Salesh,
before you return."

Lord Ermenwyr sidled over to his sister.

"Cheer up!" he said. "Think of the fun we'll have shopping." He looked sidelong at his mother. "I'm going to
spend an awful lot of your money on this. I ought to have
some compensation for being a good boy."

"You have always been a good boy," his mother said
serenely, "whatever you pretend to yourself."

Lord Ermenwyr gnashed his teeth.

↬

One day's journey out upon the sea, they spied bright-
striped sails on the horizon, traveling steadily though they
hung slack in the motionless air.

"That's another slaveless galley," said Smith, waving
away the butterflies that danced before him. "Maybe we
should hail them for news."

Within an hour they were close enough to distinguish the
clanking oars of the other vessel, louder even than their own,
and in yet another hour they saw the revelers dancing and
waving to them from the other vessel's deck.

"Ai—aiiiii!" shouted a fat man, pushing back the wreath
of roses that had slipped over one eye. "What ship is that?
Where d'you hail from?"

"The *Kingfisher's Nest* out of Salesh, from the Rethestlin!" bawled Smith. "What ship's that?"

"The *Lazy Days* out of Port Blackrock! Have you heard the news, my friend?"

"What news? Is the war over?"

"Duke Skalkin choked on a fish bone!" the man cried gleefully. "His son signed the peace treaty the next day!"

"A little death can be useful now and then," muttered Lord Ermenwyr.

"The blockade's gone?"

"All sailed home!" the man assured them, accepting a cup of wine from a nubile girl. He tilted his head back to drink, then pointed at the *Kingfisher's Nest,* shouting with laughter. "You've got butterflies too!"

"They flew down the river with us," Smith said, turning his head to look up at the ranks of white wings perched all along the yards. He looked back at the *Lazy Days.* "You've got a couple, yourself. Where'd they come from?"

"Nobody knows! They've been floating along in swarms!" The man peered closer. "Say, what the hell kind of crew have you got?"

"We've just come from a costume party," Lord Ermenwyr told him.

"So, we can go straight home along the coast, then?" Smith asked hurriedly.

"It's clear sailing all the way!" The man made an expansive gesture, slopping his wine.

And so it proved to be, over a sea smooth as a mirror, under a sky of pearly cloud. If not for the unbroken line of the coast that paced them, they might have been sailing in the heart of an infinite opal. Warm rain fell now and then, big scattered drops, and the sea steamed. They passed through clouds of white butterflies making their way along over open water, seemingly bound on the same journey.

Many settled on the spars and rigging, despite Lord Ermenwyr's best efforts to bid them begone.

"Oh, what've you got against the poor little things?" said
Lady Svnae crossly, as she spooned poppy-petal jam on a
cracker for Smith.

"They stink of the miraculous," growled her brother,
pacing up the deck with his fists locked together under his
coattails.

⤚

They rounded Cape Gore without incident, and by dawn
of the next day spotted the high mile-castles of Salesh,
with its streets sloping down to the sea and the white
domes of the Glittering Mile bright along the seafront. So
calm the water was, so glassy, that they were obliged to
keep the boiler full the whole way, and never ran up a stitch
of canvas.

But as they rounded the breakwater and came into the
harbor, Smith gave the order to cut power and come in on
the tide alone. Willowspear threw open the stopcock, and
steam escaped with a shriek that echoed off the waterfront.
The thrashing oars shuddered to a halt; but when the echoes
died an unearthly silence fell, and they might have been a
ghost ship gliding in.

"Oh, my," said Lady Svnae, shading her eyes with her
hand.

White butterflies, everywhere, dancing in clouds through
the sky, flickering on the branches of trees like unseasonable
snow. They were thick on the rigging of every ship in the
harbor. They lighted on the heads and arms of the citizens of
Salesh, who were standing about like people in a dream,
watching them. Nobody paid much attention to the *Kingfisher's Nest* or her outlandish crew as they moored and
came ashore.

"This is a portent of something tremendous," said Willowspear, striding up Front Street.

"It's the heat wave this summer," said Lord Ermenwyr, glaring about him at the fluttering wings clouding the sky above the marketplace. "Unusual numbers of the nasty things hatched, that's all. Wait up, damn you!"

"He does have a wife to get back to, you know," Lady Svnae chided him.

"We will carry you, Master," Cutt offered.

"Yes, perhaps that's best," said Lord Ermenwyr, and when Cutt bent obligingly he vaulted up to his shoulder and perched there, sneering at the butterflies that swirled about his head. "On, Cutt!"

"Do you often get butterfly migrations at this time of the year?" Lady Svnae inquired of Smith.

"Never that I remember," he replied breathlessly. "How long has this been going on?" he inquired of a shopkeeper, who stood staring at the white wings clustered upon his hanging sign.

"They came in the night," he replied. "The watchman saw them flying in from the sea. He said it looked like the stars were leaving Heaven and coming here!"

"It's a sign from the gods!" cried a city runner, swinging her brazen trumpet to dislodge butterflies.

" 'Sign from the gods'! Poppycock," said Lord Ermenwyr, and then "Aaargh!" as Cutt bore him through a particularly thick cloud of floating wings.

"At least I don't see any signs of riots," said Smith.

"No," Lord Ermenwyr replied, twisting on Cutt's shoulder to peer up the hill. "I note Greenietown's all hung with mourning over Hlinjerith, however."

"I just hope they know it wasn't us," said Smith.

"Oh, they know who did it," said Lady Svnae grimly. "Mother's people don't have runners, but you'd be amazed how fast news travels through the bowers. It's a good thing you—"

They had turned up the last curve that led to the Grandview, and there the butterflies were thickest of all, drifting and sailing between the buildings, whitening the gardens. At the Grandview itself they beat against every window, patiently walking up the glass, seeking a way in.

"They'd better not be infesting my suite," Lord Ermenwyr said.

"Hush," said his sister. "*Something* unusual is going on. Look!"

They saw Willowspear, far ahead of them now, reach the street door and throw it open. He ran inside without bothering to close the door, and butterflies streamed in after him.

"Come on!" cried Svnae, and, putting her arm around Smith, she half carried him with her, racing up the street. Lord Ermenwyr shouted an order and Cutt, Crish, Clubb, Stabb, Strangel, and Smosh thundered after them, and the white wings parted like cloud as they ran.

The lobby was empty of guests but full of butterflies, drifting gently up the staircase in an unceasing eddy. A man came out of the bar and stared at them. It was Porter Crucible.

"Nine Hells, Boss, what happened to your arm?" he cried.

"It's a long story. What's been going on here?" asked Smith.

"Everything's gone to bloody rack and ruin," Crucible replied gloomily. "Hardly any guests at all. We've had to cancel the seafood specials in the restaurant on account of the fishermen jacked the price up to five crowns a pound. We'd have gone out of business if it wasn't for Nurse Balnshik dancing for the gentlemen in the bar." His gloom rose momentarily. "What an artist! And now our Burnbright's having her kid upstairs. Was that the greenie we heard go running up there?" He looked out at the lobby. "Where'd all these butterflies come from?"

"Beats me," said Smith.

Lord Ermenwyr scrambled down from Cutt. "Stay," he told his bodyguards. Without another word he, Smith, and Lady Svnae mounted the staircase.

They brushed through white clouds as they climbed, and came to the narrow little attic room where Burnbright and Willowspear lived.

There, at last, the air was clear; but only because hundreds of butterflies had settled, opening and shutting their wings, on the bedstead. Burnbright was sitting up in the bed, clutching a bundle to her shoulder as she kissed Willowspear, who was on his knees beside the bed with his arms around her.

There was no other furniture in the room, so Balnshik and Mrs. Smith were seated on the floor, with a bottle of Silverbush between them.

"That kiss has been going on for forty-five seconds now," observed Mrs. Smith. "They'll have to come up for air sooner or later. Oh, my poor Smith!" She struggled to her feet. "Your arm!"

"It's well lost," he replied, kissing her. "I'm going to have a replacement made of silver and gold with emeralds, and it'll do tricks."

"But you told me you'd bring him back safely, you horrid little man!" she said to Lord Ermenwyr. He shrugged and lit up his smoking tube with a fireball. It was immediately seized from his grasp by Lady Svnae, who looked outraged.

"You can't smoke in a room with a new baby!" she admonished.

"So you're an expert on the damned things too?" Lord Ermenwyr raged, his eyes beginning to stand out of his head.

"Master, you mustn't shout," said Balnshik, uncoiling from the floor gracefully and grabbing him. "Welcome to

Salesh, Mistress," she added to Lady Svnae, before bending
Lord Ermenwyr backward in a kiss that silenced him.

Burnbright and Willowspear had broken their embrace at
last. They were huddled together, looking at the tiny red
infant dozing unconcernedly in her lap.

"He doesn't look anything like you," she fretted. "Except
I think he has your mouth. And your nose. And maybe your
eyes, but he hasn't opened them yet. You want me to wake
him up? I'm sorry he's not—you know—like you."

"I'm not sorry," said Willowspear. "Not at all. Hello,
Kalyon!"

"And then again, maybe we won't have to get him registered as a resident Yendri," Burnbright added hopefully.
"That'd be nice, wouldn't it? All the demonstrations and
fighting stopped last week. Just stopped, boom. So maybe
things will be better now anyway."

"Hush, child, you're waking my grandbaby," Mrs. Smith
scolded. Kalyon Willowspear was worming about in his
blankets, drawing his fists up to his chin, grimacing extravagantly. He opened his eyes.

They were remarkable eyes. They were a misty green, like
Hlinjerith in its glory.

"Oh, look!" screamed Burnbright gleefully. Startled, the
baby flung out his little arms, starfish hands opened wide.

Immediately the butterflies rose and descended, hundreds
attempting to settle in his two hands. They spilled through
his fingers. They circled his head. The adults watched in
frozen silence a long moment.

"Oh, gods," said Mrs. Smith huskily, beginning to cry.
"The poor little thing."

"Aren't we all supposed to fall to our knees at this point
and sing a hymn or something?" Lord Ermenwyr inquired
wearily.

"No, no!" said Lady Svnae, tremendously excited. "Don't

you see what all this portentous stuff means? This is obviously what those prophecies were all about! This is the one Mother's restoring Hlinjerith for! This is the Beloved with his imperfections forgiven!" She peered at him. "Though I'm surprised he came back in that color."

"I bloody well know what it means," wept Mrs. Smith. "Better than you do, my girl. He'll never have a moment's rest. The same old story's beginning again."

"No," said Smith. "This is a new story beginning."

He looked down at the stump of his arm, and thought: *Well lost. I'd give the other one too, if that's the price of hope. The shadow has passed from the door.*

Rising Tide Charter Public School Library